River's Reach

River's Reach

Christina Green

ROBERT HALE · LONDON

© Christina Green 2008
First published in Great Britain 2008

ISBN 978-0-7090-8595-9

Robert Hale Limited
Clerkenwell House
Clerkenwell Green
London EC1R 0HT

www.halebooks.com

2 4 6 8 10 9 7 5 3 1

Typeset in 10/13pt Classical Garamond
by Derek Doyle & Associates, Shaw Heath
Printed and bound in Great Britain
by Biddles Limited, King's Lynn

ACKNOWLEDGEMENTS

My thanks to Richard Harris, B. A. Hons., historian, and to authors J. H. Trump and The Ball Clay Heritage Society for information upon which this fictionalized story is based. My thanks also to my writing friends who have been generous with their encouragement.

CHAPTER ONE

Rose made Billy Netherton button up his patched coat. 'Off you go, and don't get into any fights. Just ignore those lads from the village. Keep out of their way.' She smiled resignedly at his pugnacious expression and gave him a gentle slap on the back of his worn-out old trousers.

Billy, eight years old, small, and aggressive because of the other boys' constant taunting and bullying, shrugged away from her, glowering back over his shoulder as he set off for the path across the marshes.

Miss Hodge locked the schoolhouse door behind her and for a moment she and Rose stood watching the small figure cross the green and then go slouching through the overgrown scrub and windblown trees of the marshes.

'Another week done, Rose,' she said at last. 'And you're being such a help, my dear. How I ever managed without my certificated pupil I can't imagine . . .' Her ageing blue eyes were warm and they smiled at each other. Then she put a gloved hand to her dark felt hat and pulled it closer about the wispy white hair. 'This wretched wind. Knocks everything about. We must say a prayer for the fishermen. Ah well, better weather's always just around the corner.'

'Let's hope so, Miss Hodge.' Rose's own hat was skewered on safely, but the wind off the river suddenly surged across the marshes, blustering around their skirts.

'Goodness, let's get home – goodbye, Rose.' Miss Hodge shivered and then headed for the village, bag in one hand, stick in the other. Watching for a moment until she had safely reached the cobbles of Cross Lane, Rose called after her, 'Goodbye, Miss Hodge.' The stick lifted in reply and then she was gone.

Negotiating the path across the marshes was tricky in the best of weathers, with the little streams oozing water and mud and overflowing into hidden puddles, but today, after the night's rain and the wild wind, it was trickier than ever. Rose's boots were soon squelching as the wet grass enclosed them. Her hair twisted out of its bun, blowing in great carroty tendrils across her face and eyes.

But she didn't really care. Born and brought up here at Sandiford she was used to the weather's swift and unexpected turns of speed and force. The river sounded clearly, overtaking the diminishing waters of the canal which started half a mile upstream and ended at the lock, just beyond the railway bridge. Swirling and surging down towards Culmouth and the sea, the river was a force and joy she had known throughout her child-hood at No 2 Canal Cottages. For a second Rose thought she heard voices, but put it down to the gulls flying inland to safer feeding grounds. And that made her remember the boats: she frowned.

Father and Joe were taking the barges up to the estuary this afternoon. They'd have a rough ride. As usual they'd waited for the tide to turn, working from dawn onwards loading the boats with ball clay further up the river at the clay cellar near Abberton and then poling them down river to the sea, using the dirty red sails if the wind was right. Now they would be on their way. She shut off the picture of the heavy barges sway-ing and rolling in the rough waters because worrying did no good. Perhaps a prayer might, like Miss Hodge had suggested. But Rose wasn't one for praying. She decided to think of something else instead.

She had always loved the river, its song and strength usually calming her down when life became too unhappy. Today, though, she had the strangest fancy that, like her, it was a living creature, journeying on, look-ing for something, although not sure what. And she was just the same, her life living through wildness and the surging bits of flotsam that crowded into her brain. What did she want? She didn't know. But the river found its destiny when it flowed into the wide ocean. Would she, one day, do the same?

With her mind full of these fanciful thoughts she walked on as fast as the wind would allow, feeling spray drenching her clothes and face, but now instead of feeling anxiety about Father on the barge, she relived what had happened yesterday at home and the worry went, replaced by the feelings of anger and frustration that grew daily at the back of her mind.

Father, a huge, shaggy bear of a man, had come back from the inn down the river path, reeling a bit as usual. He'd been demanding and harsh with Mother, and snappy with Rose. She was used to it. In particular, her name was always a red rag to his drunken bull.

'Rose Victoria Adams!' His loud voice was slurred and he belched as he lowered his body into the cane chair beside the hearth where Mother stood, stirring the stewpot. 'What a name for a useless carrot-topped bargepole of a girl who won't ever do what 'er's told! We be ordinary folk, not gentry, us don't want uppity names like Rose Victoria!' His raucous laugh filled the small room, echoing off the stone limewashed walls. Then he glared. 'Here, maid, bring us a mug o' cider. Can't expect a man to eat his vittles afore he's warmed his belly, can you?'

'Thought your belly was warm enough already . . .' The words were out without thought, and she bit her tongue. Would she never learn? Why feed his wretched anger?

Handing over the mug, keeping her eyes down, Rose expected a swipe of his great calloused hand, or the fumbling loosening of his belt, but the drink was unexpectedly on her side. Already he was away on his favourite subject. 'Rose Victoria! What a name for a flibbertigibbert of a maid like you!'

He slurped his cider, and suddenly Alice turned from the fire, looking directly at him. Rose saw her rheumaticky hand gripping the metal spoon fiercely as if it were a weapon. 'That's enough, Jack,' she said in her quiet voice, brown eyes sparking at him. 'The maid's got a good name because I wanted it and you were too drunk to argue about it. I wanted my maid to grow up as beautiful as a rose and as dignified and clever as the Queen, God bless 'er. Those pictures of her golden jubilee last year were beautiful – always upright, and so proud. . . .'

Just for a moment Jack's sozzled face cleared. He stared at Alice, who stared back and they both looked distraught. The moment hung in the air, silent, full of memories, full of unrevealed likes and dislikes, of things said and left unsaid – of secrets, even – charging the cold, comfortless cottage with an atmosphere of fearful power that had nowhere to go.

Rose shivered. There was deep love and unhappy hatred here; she felt it, growing together in a knot that she could see no way of undoing. But then the silence ended with discomfort and longing filling her.

Alice turned again, bent painfully forward, stirred the stewpot hanging over the flames in the hearth, then hitched the pot off the hook and limped across to the table with it. 'Ah well, let's thank the good Lord for those fish you caught yesterday. Sit up now, Jack, and have yer tea.'

He'd slept off his drunkenness while Rose and her mother cleared the pots, then they stoked the fire and slipped out of the cottage, walking back up the river path and across the marshes towards the village. Alice took Rose's arm because her knee was painful, walking over the uneven ground.

'Just look,' she said softly. Looking across the marshes she lifted her head and sounded almost wistful as she said slowly, 'there's the old House. Going to ruin, they says, but Susan next door told me the agent's lookin' for a new tenant – mebbe he or she'll do up the place . . .'

Following her gaze, Rose saw the outline of Sandiford House against the sky, a gaunt, dark house that, as children, she and her friends used to say was haunted. But that hadn't stopped them scrumping apples in its orchards.

She watched her mother looking up at the wide grey sky, turning away and smiling as if she were young again. 'Forget the bad times, maid, your dad don't mean to badger you so much. 'Tis only your name. Rose Victoria.' For a second Rose thought she meant to go on, but instead her lips tightened. Then her arm pressed against Rose's side, and the thought came: *thank goodness for Mother – and forget Father*. It seemed sensible, but not easy.

As if Alice had read her mind she added quietly, hardly loud enough to hear, 'Jest dream something nice instead, maid – and mebbe one day it'll come true.' Then she paused, pain contorting her pale face. 'Let's go back now, I've had enough.' And slowly they walked back together, hearing the river's song deepen as the wind rose, to find Jack gone and the wind-blasted fire dead.

The pattern of our lives, Rose thought sombrely now; could she ever dare hope it might change? Not for Mother – or Father, come to that – but perhaps for her? If she dreamed, as Mother said, would all those longings and needings come her way? Why should they? She was twenty already, and nothing had changed since her birth. They still lived in one of the poor cottages along the river bank and Father still poled the clay barges up to the estuary. The cottage was no more than a hovel with a well-trodden earthen floor, a leaking thatched roof and an outside privy. Money was always short, comforts lacking. But then she lifted her head, even though the gusts of wind, as she approached the river, were increasing and almost throwing her backwards – at least she had a situation. She was now a certificated teacher at the village school having studied there as a pupil teacher for the last five years. Miss Hodge had become her friend as well as mentor, and she had an education behind her. Yet her life was narrow and restricted. Almost suffocating. Then an urgency came, surging through her, followed by an optimistic thought that anything could happen – she only had to wait for it.

But wait no longer – it was happening. A gaggle of rough boys was rushing towards her, shrill enraged voices rising against the noise of the water and the wind. 'Canal rat!' screamed Charlie Wheeler, while Teddy Moore piped up, 'Clay ball! Rubbish scraps! Water rat! Jest you wait, Billy Netherton – we'll throw you in the river and watch you drown . . .'

Rose sucked in a deep, furious breath. *Here we go again*, she thought. *Cullington village boys against us canal folk*, a sorry ongoing conflict which each side seemed to enjoy and took every chance to continue. Grabbing her hat and yanking it more firmly on to her head, she marched forward, intent on once again helping young Billy escape from his tormentors.

For a few minutes they did battle through the mud and the wind as she tried to get Billy away, at the same time shouting to the village lads to stop their wickedness. Then the tide's rising waves started spilling over the path and the boys slid and fell on the muddy, wet surface. She grabbed hold of Billy's sleeve, only to feel it rip between her fingers. He went down and Charlie aimed a kick, but she pulled him out of the way just in time.

Rage grew then and she flew at Charlie, forgetting she was a school-teacher with standards of good manners and education. 'You great bully! I'll teach you to kick someone so much smaller . . .'

Her hand flew out and she aimed at his red, grinning face, but then a deep voice sounded from behind, the boys stood unexpectedly still and, turning, Rose retreated down the path, dragging along a howling Billy, to face Will Sharcombe.

'Stop that, Charlie Wheeler, or 'ee'll feel my fist!' A massive hand reached out, grabbed Charlie by his collar, another seized Teddy, and Will shook both boys as if they were rats, and then let them go, watching them slipping and sliding and turning tail down the muddy path without look-ing back.

He rubbed his hands together, rammed them into his pockets, looked at Rose and grinned. 'Thought I might see 'ee if I come home this way. What's this little pup been up to, then? Stand up, Billy Netherton – be a man.'

But poor Billy was still moaning and rubbing the places where Charlie's boots had landed. Rose said quickly, 'it wasn't his fault, Will – those two ruffians just set on him, and it's not the first time. I can't do anything with them in school, and out here they're a pair of real bullies.'

Will's smile faded. He shoved his cap further down on his head, pursed his lips as if considering the truth of what she'd just said, and then nodded – reluctantly, she thought. 'Rosie, you can't be responsible fer the whole world, you know. This young boy must learn to stand up fer himself. Tell you what,' the wide grin was there again, 'come to the next fair, Billy boy, and I'll teach 'ee to box. Get you inside that booth and show you how to get even with anyone who jumps on you. What d'you say, lad?'

But Billy was off, running like a scared rabbit, looking back over the shoulder of his sodden jacket to make sure that big Will Sharcombe didn't reach out again and haul him back.

Rose laughed with Will as the lad disappeared, then she looked at Will appreciatively while he just stood there, looking back at her.

Large and heavy, his boxing hobby showed in the powerful shoulders and arms beneath his wet and clay-stained corduroy jacket. She'd seen him fight once, at the annual fair in the village, amazed at how such a huge man could be so light on his feet as he danced around his opponent, finally flooring him with one enormous uppercut.

There was definitely much about Will Sharcombe that she found attractive, even his broken nose not spoiling the sheer good nature that shone through his easy smile and air of friendliness to the world in general.

She said lightly, 'Why come home this way, Will? Takes you much longer, surely, coming over the marshes, instead of going through the village?'

'You know why. In the hope of seeing 'ee, Rosie.' His voice was deep and deliberate, each word well thought about.

She was moved by his faithfulness, but knew at the same time that she must be truthful and stop him hoping too much. 'Will, I know we've been friends for a long time . . .' Pausing, she found herself running out of excuses.

'All our schooldays.' He nodded. 'An' after that – childhood sweeet-hearts, we was.' He was watching her, dark eyes steady and uncompro-mising.

She fidgeted with her wet coat and squelched her boots about in the mud. 'I know. But now – well . . .'

Suddenly he was a step nearer, his arm heavy around her shoulder, his strength turning her, pointing her along the path towards home, moving her along, almost lifting her across the wide pools of the incoming river water as they approached the cottages. 'I wants to marry you one day, Rosie – you know that. I've asked you, oh, how many times before? Till then why can't we be sweethearts again? Going out together – making plans for the future. . . ?'

He came to a stop and Rose was powerless to free herself. Instead she found she was looking into his determined face, smelling the damp earthiness of the clay he dug out as his livelihood, seeing in his expression something so powerful that for a moment she almost feared him.

'Say you'm still my sweetheart, Rosie.' There was pleading as well as hope in the low words. 'I miss you, every day – want to see you, be with you.' A twinkle gleamed in his eyes and his mouth lifted into a big soft smile. 'If we were still sweethearts, Rosie, you wouldn't have to worry about working no more.'

Swallowing the lump that had come into her throat, Rose wished desperately that she didn't have to hurt him. But he had to understand. They had moved apart. 'Will – thank you, thank you very much, you've done me a great honour. But I'm afraid I can't ever marry you.'

They looked into each other's eyes in a silence broken only by the wind and the slap of the river beside them. Then Will took his arm from her shoulder and reached for her hand. He rubbed it between his own calloused and clay-stained fingers and Rose felt strength and a warmth so seductive that for a moment she wavered in her determination. Could she marry him, after all? Settle in a small cramped cottage, make friends with the new neighbours, cook his meals, wash his filthy, sodden work clothes, do the marketing and cleaning that such a life entailed? Make love with him? Have his babies? No. She had moved on, while Will stayed behind in his world of childhood memories.

'Well,' he said quietly, his thumb stroking her cold, wet hand. 'In my mind we're still sweethearts. I shan't ever stop thinking that.'

It was a fearsome thought, that Will would be thinking about her, on and on and on . . . So unfair. Guilt stabbed, and rapidly Rose pushed it away. 'But I don't want you to, Will! I want you to find another girl, someone who's more – more . . .' She sighed. Trying to justify her cruelty was very hard. After a pause she whispered sadly, 'I don't know. More homely, I suppose is what I'm trying to say. Someone who won't argue with you, want her own way.' And then her own needs took over and the words rushed out more freely. 'Will, I still love you in a way – a friendly way – but I've got to – got to . . .' she ended hopelessly, 'somehow find another sort of life.'

Her voice died away and he let her hand slip. His eyes seemed to retreat in his head and the familiar grin vanished. Rose's heart pounded when she saw how grim and hurt he looked, and she knew it was all her fault.

But he was a strong man. 'Well, Rose, all I know is that I still want you to be my sweetheart. I shan't stop thinkin' that.'

'Oh please, Will, no . . .'

By now they'd reached the Adams's cottage and stopped just short of it. He nodded, half-turned and then looked back at her. His voice was cool, almost cold, and she sensed his deep hurt. 'I'll be waiting for 'ee, Rosie.' Another nod and then he walked away, his large, heavy figure sloshing through mud and water and fast disappearing as he went past the cottage, down the path towards the inn and then back to his home in the village.

Rose's voice echoed in her head as she, too, went home, opening the cottage door and smelling Father's tobacco, the sourness of clay and cider fumes. Her mother sat by the fire, her welcoming smile adding to the agony that Rose felt inside her.

But whatever she'd done, whatever she'd said, she clung to the truth of it. She needed to find a new life. Perhaps, like Will, she just had to wait.

Jack Adams came home very late that night, slamming the door on the wild weather and bringing with him the noisome smells of wet clay, salt water and cider fumes, the wind rocking the oil lamp on the table and setting the shadows dancing. Alice eyed him warily, and Rose went to the fire where his tea was keeping hot on an enamel plate over the cauldron of simmering water.

'Take yer wet clothes off, Jack, or you'll catch yer death. Here,' Alice hobbled across the room, holding out her hand to take his coat, but he pushed her aside, moving clumsily, just making it to the chair by the hearth and collapsing into it.

'Never mind all that, jest bring me me tea. I'm starved – an' you, Rose Victoria,' a huge thunderclap of a chesty laugh filled the room, 'get me some cider. Don't jest stand there, maid, not too proud to do a hand's turn fer yer old dad, are you? Got to look after me, you know – I'm the one bringing home the wages. Yes . . .' His voice thickened, slowed. Clearly it was an effort to talk. 'Money – you an' me's gotta talk 'bout that, Rose Victoria Adams . . .'

The words slipped away and his eyes closed, but he opened them enough to see the mug she filled and brought to him. He took a huge mouthful, slurping loudly, and let cider drip down his wet coat on to the rag rug at his feet.

'Well, where's me tea?' A moment later he was looking at Alice and trying to sit up as best he could, grabbing the plate from her without a word of thanks, and then tucking in like a starved animal.

Alice went back to her chair and looked at Rose. She beckoned her close, made her bend down to hear the whispered words. 'Don't 'ee stay up, love, I'll see to him. He'll be asleep afore he's finished, I dessay, an' I don't want all that food wasted on the floor.'

Rose hesitated, hating the idea of leaving her mother to cope with his drunkenness. But in that moment, as if instinctively knowing what Alice had said, he lifted his head from his plate, and glared over at them both. 'Go on, then, go to bed an' termorrow you an' me'll have a talk – I've got the hope of a good situation for 'ee, Rose Victoria.' Another dip of the spoon into his mouth, and another gurgle of throaty laughter.

Rose couldn't leave it there. She shook her head at Alice and sat down on her usual stool beside the table. 'Why not tell me now?' she asked quietly. 'You might have forgotten in the morning.'

Jack raised his head, eyes narrowed, fleshy mouth pursing and a big stained hand lifting to wipe away the scraps of food surrounding it. 'Meanin' what?' he growled, and Rose heard Alice whisper, 'Oh, Rose, don't rile him . . .'

If she'd had any sense she would have followed that advice, but tonight she was already upset after that business with Will Sharcombe. So why not hear what Father had to offer? School would finish for the summer very soon and that would be the end of her wages. Father was right, of course he was. Money was short and those few pounds had been a great help. Without them she knew they'd be back to counting every penny, her poor mother scrimping and tightening where ever she could. Life would be even harder for her.

So, calming her irritation, she fixed what she hoped was a patient smile on her face and sat there, trying not to condemn her father's lack of manners, watching as he ate every scrap on the plate, finishing off the gravy with a last crust of bread, then letting the plate slip to the floor while he leaned back in the chair, bleary eyes closing again.

She refused to let him get away with it. 'Father,' she said, louder.

'Please tell me what you were talking about just now – what offer is this?'

His pouched eyes opened grudgingly. 'God's name, go to bed, maid, let a man have his sleep after all I've been through today. Rough water an' that wind, barges drifting towards the shore, enough to fling a body overboard, took all me strength to keep us afloat, me and Joe.'

Time to try and calm him, persuade him, thought Rose carefully. Her smile increased. 'You're a brave man, Father. And you and Joe work so hard. I know what the river's like when the wind's up. But you'll sleep even better if you've told me what all this is about. Get it out of your mind, see?' She caught his eye, saw a hint of interest, and added quickly, 'and even better if I agree to it.'

By the humming fireside Alice shook her head, fidgeting with her knitting. 'Rose, Rose, don't go on so.'

'Come along, Father.' Rose put on her best schoolmistress manner, and unexpectedly he reacted.

Slowly his eyes opened wide and he made a conscious effort to sit up, producing a belch followed by a harsh cough. But it put sleep out of his mind. He looked very straight at Rose and nodded his head. 'You'm a determined maid, I'll say that fer 'ee.' He bent to the floor, reached out for the cider mug and took a slurp, then sat back and balanced the mug in his lap. 'Well, we was loadin' the barge this morning when Mr Sanders comes up. He'm the clay manager, as you do know. "Ah, Adams," says he, "that girl of yours, she who teaches up at the school, won't be working soon, eh, what with summer nearly here? Needs a position, no doubt. So tell her to come and see me Monday morning in my office and I'll offer her one. Domesticated, is she? Biddable?" '

He stopped, suddenly shaking with ear-clanging mirth. 'Biddable! If I hadn't had a shovel in me hand I'd have fallen down laughing. Oh ho, I thinks, you don't know our Rose Victoria, do 'ee, Mr Sanders? Didn't say so, of course. No, I jest thanked him and says as how you'll be there on Monday. Nine sharp. So you be there, maid, dress neat and talk polite like an' he'll take 'ee on, I dessay. An' then we'll have more money coming in.' He grinned at Rose, showing stumps of stained teeth, and she stared back. 'Can't say I'm a bad feyther now, can 'ee, maid?'

Again Alice whispered across the room but Rose was unable to take in what she said. Emotions flared and inside she fumed. How dare he? Ordering her life, treating her like something he could turn this way or that, to suit his own needs.

He had no thought for what she might want, or deserve. Rose felt almost suffocated with frustration. Was that the sort of life he thought she wanted? To be subservient to Mr Sanders's sour-faced wife who, everybody knew, wanted to be a grand lady, which she wasn't, being the youngest daughter of a local farmer. Rumour said she treated her servants badly and changed them regularly. This, of course, was the reason for Mr Sanders's suggestion. Cook? wondered Rose with horror. Housemaid? More like a kitchen skivvy, she thought furiously.

'No, I shan't go.' Her clipped words seemed to echo round the tiny room. She heard Alice's breath suddenly sucked in, saw her father's eyes open wide and become hot with rage. He propped himself up in his chair, drew in his legs beneath it and somehow managed to stand up, swaying as he did so. 'You'll do as yer told!' he shouted. 'I've had enough of yer grand ideas and hoity-toity ways. Want to do better, do you? Well, you'm jest a bargeman's daughter, an' don't fergit it. You'll see Mr Sanders on Monday an' thank him fer his kindness and you'll bloody well take what-ever he offers. Or else . . .'

He glowered at Rose, and she stood up to face him, feeling an almost tangible clash of wills as their eyes met. She understood the truth of what he said, but he didn't understand . . . he never did. He never would. Inside her something strong and determined braced her body, gave courage to her racing thoughts.

Slowly and deliberately, she said, 'Or else what, Father? A beating? Or turn me out of the house, perhaps? Well, don't bother, because this has made me see what I've got to do – I'm going. I won't stay here and be bullied. I'm a woman, not a small child to be browbeaten like this. How can I stay, after you shouting and threatening me? You got away with it when I was small, but now I've had enough. By Monday morning, Father, I'll be on my way, and you can tell Mr Sanders what you like.' She stepped past him, went to the staircase and then turned, glaring back at his astounded, open-mouthed face. 'Maybe he'll understand why I've gone – everyone round here knows what you're like.'

She raced up the narrow, creaking stairs, too enraged to even consider what Jack might say or do next. Or even how her mother would cope with the situation. As she undressed and slid into her cold truckle bed beneath the eaves, Rose heard the wind still roaring and through it came the ageless, never ceasing song of the river. As she lay there, thoughts turning over and over, it came to her that she and the river were as one, both on a restless, uneasy journey, and who knew where it might take them?

Just as she was drifting into sleep, a great roar from downstairs jerked her wide awake again. Listening anxiously, she was aware of silence, and then heavy snores came trumpeting up the stairs, and realized that her father's hard day's work, coupled with cider and her own rebellion, had pushed him beyond the barrier of consciousness. Through the snores she heard her mother's smothered sobs and realized, too late, the pain she was causing.

Then she heard Alice come up, sensed her standing outside the door, listening desperately to Father downstairs and perhaps wondering whether to come in here and talk things over. But then the big bed beyond the thin partition creaked and she knew her mother had decided sleep was the best remedy.

But Rose's sleep eluded her. The cottage was still, cold and empty. No warmth, no understanding, no love. She lay there, arms hugging her body, thinking back over what had just happened.

Thoughts circled and then returned. Tomorrow she would leave home. She would find a new life for herself. But doubts began to creep in. All very well to rebel – but where was she to go? And, if she left, how would her poor mother manage?

At last sleep came, restless and full of disturbing dreams, but when Rose awoke in the morning the wind had quietened, the river sang a calmer song, a frail beam of sunlight filtered through the curtains, and suddenly she knew what she must do.

CHAPTER TWO

Jack Adams had gone, plodding up the path towards the lock and the clay cellars, after a silent breakfast, with Alice not looking at him and Rose watching both parents to try and discover how they were reacting to her threat to leave home.

Breakfast dishes were washed and put away before Alice said at last, 'You didn't mean it, love, did you? Not to leave us?'

Rose didn't reply at once. She saw her mother's lined, anxious face, watched her limping about the cottage and wondered yet again at the words she'd shouted so furiously last night. At the time she had meant all she said; well, now she had changed her mind. But the problem of Jack's harsh treatment and lack of understanding remained.

'I don't know,' she said at last. 'Last night it seemed like I just had to go. Father's always on at me. He won't let me live my own life – and I have to. Mother, you understand, don't you, that I've got to, somehow, find my own way?'

'Yes, love, I do.'

For a second or two Rose thought she saw memories in Alice's sad eyes. Perhaps she was wrong, for Alice added quickly, 'But not to go away? I mean, where to? And what'll you do?'

A knock sounded at the door and Rose opened it. Jessie Smith stood there, a small, dumpy girl with frizzy dark hair and saucy black eyes. Her smile was like a sunbeam. 'Ma says can you lend us a cup o' flour? She'm out of it cos Mrs Bankes is ill and can't do her marketing in Abberton this week.'

Alice tutted before turning to the cupboard and opening the half-sack of flour. She was tired of the Smiths always wanting to have a cup of this or that. But she handed it over with her usual good humour. 'Tell your ma she can have this small bag. I can spare it. But what's wrong with May Bankes, then?'

Jessie took the flour, and propped herself against the door, looked around her with unconcealed interest, and grinned. 'Dunno. But she can't take the boat out. Reckon we'll have to walk to Abberton instead of her rowin' up an' down this week.'

Rose said quickly, 'But surely someone else can do the trip?' May Bankes's weekly journey to Abberton market took her up the river, which flowed past the land-locked canal and the basin beyond, fulfilling her orders as best she could, and delivering on the way back later in the day. 'Hasn't she got someone to take her place, Jessie?'

'Dunno. Don't think so.' Already the girl was on her way home, shouting back over her shoulder.

Alice pursed her lips. 'That young madam'll come to a bad end, all I've heard about her goings-on. Down there in the inn o' nights an' only jest fifteen – why, dancin' on the table, so Susan Upcott told me . . .'

Rose laughed. 'Don't believe all Susan says, Mother. She's such a gossip, we all know that. But . . .' She turned, looked at Alice and said firmly, 'I'll go and see May. I could do her river trip if she can't manage—'

'What, row all the way up to Abberton? Too far, and too dangerous, love, with these high tides . . .'

But Rose was pulling a shawl about her shoulders, already out of the door and walking rapidly down towards the inn and the cottage next to it where May Bankes lived.

May sat by the fire, coughing and trying to keep warm. 'I got a real ol' cold. Goes on me chest, always. Weak as a baby I am. You'm a good maid to offer, Rose. I wouldn't let just anyone take over my trade, but I can trust you. Manage the boat, can you? Got good strong hands, my lover?'

'I can manage, Mary. I've rowed all my life. So tell me what I've got to do and I'll get straight on with it. It's a fine morning, no wind, I'll be up in Abberton inside of an hour. Got your orders ready, have you?'

If she hoped for a written list, she was unlucky. May had a good memory, but couldn't write. So Rose repeated the orders and the names several times, and then trusted to her own memory. 'Upcotts want flour and any vegetables I can find – and candles. Smiths want vegetables, faggots and cup hooks. Pritchards want vegetables, flour, sugar and tea.' She laughed. 'And while I'm there, I'll get myself a shopping list and a pencil! What about you, May? Anything I can get for you?'

'Candles an' baccy, love, and a bottle of gin.' May grinned, handed over a well-worn purse, and put another few sticks on the fire. 'I'll pay 'ee when 'ee comes back. Good luck then – an' if the wind gets up don't let the boat ground . . .'

It seemed a long, hard row up the river, and Rose found it more strenuous than she'd imagined to reach the quay at Abberton. But the midstream current took her with it and by the time she had moored and tied up the dinghy she was proud of herself. Hard work but worth doing. Here she was with a job that would put some extra shillings into Alice's purse, and at the same time develop her growing sense of independence. Rubbing sore shoulders, she took May's large rush basket and headed for the market.

Noise, smells and crowds of people enveloped her. Ordinary towns-folk doing their shopping and a handful of well-dressed strangers, probably spending holidays in Torquay and coming here to see how country folk lived. She wasn't used to being in a town and found the marketing very wearisome, what with haggling over the goods and being jostled by the other shoppers. The basket took both hands to carry back to the quay and by the time she got it into the boat and sat down ready to cast off she knew this was a job which would either defeat or develop her, both physically and mentally. Sucking in a huge breath, she got ready for the journey back.

Casting off, she was instantly caught up by the strength of the river, with the current pushing the boat along, and she could think only of firm wrists and the sense of direction that would keep the bow steady. Then gradually she realized that the tide had started to ebb and she was thankful for the drift of the water taking the dinghy along with it. The steady discipline of rowing, of bending her back and concentrating on the moment became almost a pleasure, and as she grew nearer to the journey's end she realized that her mind was for once free of the usual dissatisfied thoughts. Indeed, as she rested on the oars for a moment, enjoying the sun gilding the restless waters and shining into her eyes, she could almost say she was content. Never mind what the future held – this was pleasure and exhilaration.

When she reached Sandiford dock she saw a group of children playing. They stopped to watch her. 'Give me a hand,' she called, and at once Billy Netherton ran down the bank.

'You bin up the river, miss?'

Rose saw keen interest on his small face. 'Yes. May Bankes is ill. So I've got all the orders.'

'You goin' again, miss?"

Rose stepped on to the bank, gave the rope to Billy, watching the way he handled it as if he'd done the job all his short life, then leaned back and pulled the laden basket towards her. 'I expect so, Billy.'

'Can I come too, miss? I'll help. I likes boats. Me dad takes me out sometimes . . .'

Seeing him neatly coil the rope she recognized an expertise that might well be helpful if she was to carry on with May's marketing. 'All right, Billy – but ask your ma if she agrees. Say I'll look after you.'

He nodded fervently before rushing towards his home, coming back just as Rose was sorting out the orders with May and putting things into piles by the door of the cottage, ready for collection. 'Ma says yes, miss! Are you going termorrer?'

Rose thought quickly. Was she going to carry on doing this difficult, and even dangerous job? May was no better and Billy's knowledge of boats could well prove a blessing. Also, he could carry some of the orders. So, 'Yes, Billy. I will. You'll need a coat in case the weather blows. And Billy . . .'

His peaky face was alert. 'What, miss?'

'I can't pay you anything.'

'Don't care, miss. Jest like being in the boat.'

The agreement worked well over the next few weeks. Mrs Netherton said she was thankful to have that young varmint out of the way, always fighting he was, and May slept easier because she knew her trade was still going on, while Rose found herself growing stronger and the rowing easier. She walked home in the afternoons tired but satisfied, the purse in her skirt richer by a few shillings, which she gave to Alice, saying quietly, 'get something nice, Mother – just for a change.'

Now Jack Adams looked at her with a new respect and muttered that he'd told Mr Sanders his maid had already got a situation. Rose, amused, wondered what everybody thought of it. But Jack even stopped making a mockery of her name, so she understood that a certain respect was acknowledged. She told herself that of course, this was only a job for the time being – until May recovered and school started again – but even so, it was better than working in a smelly hot kitchen, or fuelling Mrs Sanders's ambition to become gentrified. At least here she had the river and countryside to herself.

As the journeys continued Alice rubbed Rose's aching shoulders and back with a soothing ointment of wintergreen. 'And I've got a good old-fashioned receipt for some cream for your hands, love,' she said, busily stirring a concoction over the fire.

Rose looked at her hands, red and showing a few callouses. Stretching them out she winced. 'I suppose I'll get used to those rough old oars.' She smiled. 'What've you got in that pot, Mother? Smells good.'

Alice showed her the coated spoon. 'A salve, love. Very old, it is. Comfrey root, almonds crushed in oil, an egg, and a spoonful or two of Mr Bartlett's honey. Why, you'll have a lady's hands once you start rubbing this in!'

'Sounds wonderful. Where did you ever hear of it?'

Alice put the spoon back into the steaming pot and didn't look up as she said quietly, 'someone I knew told me.' Then, very quickly, she added, 'Can't remember who it was, but I know it works. Now, love, put that little jar on the table and I'll pour the salve into it.'

Watching the hot, creamy liquid settling in the jar, Rose wondered at her mother's words; wondered, too, how she came by what was obviously such a knowledgeable receipt, but then the moment passed, and her mind drifted on to everyday events.

May Bankes was slowly recovering, but wasn't yet strong enough to make the daily journeys herself. Meanwhile Billy was a help, and even Jessie Smith had offered to come and assist with the shopping. Rose knew Jessie was a problem to her family, having run away from the situation she had as a kitchen skivvy. Here in Sandiford the girl had nothing to do and tended to hang around the men as they loaded their boats, which usually ended in bawdy remarks and loud mirth and even more shouts from her irate parents. If Jessie helped with the marketing, maybe things would improve.

Rose put a dab of the hand cream on her rough skin, and rubbed gently. It felt good. If she was returning to school at the end of the summer, then she must somehow get her hands looking presentable again. The village children were quick to notice things like that, and she wanted no more rude questions or remarks. Billy's life had become quieter of late, the Cullington boys finding some other unfortunate victim for their bullying, and the familiar hostility between village and Sandiford dwellers seemed to have settled down. She hoped fervently that it would stay that way.

Laurence Vane looked around the dank, gloomy room with its folds of peeling faded wallpaper and wondered what he was doing here.

'Ideal for your studio, Mr Vane,' Eric Sims, the Sandiford estate agent said, standing a little too close, hopeful eyes wide and fingers pulling at his straggling beard. 'North light, you see – and plenty of space for all your canvases and paints.'

Deliberately, Vane stepped away. 'And also dirty and neglected. I can't say I share your enthusiasm for this old house, Mr Sims. Yes, I know it's Georgian—'

'Even older, we think, Mr Vane . . .'

Laurence ignored him. 'And it has some good features, but I don't think I care for it enough to sign your contract.' Turning, he moved to the bleary window at the far side of the room, where the light was strongest. 'Perhaps I'll try a different location,' he mused. 'Torquay might have something better to offer.'

Eric Sims's smile vanished, and he braced himself, so that his shiny suit shifted on his bony body. 'But, Mr Vane, you did say you wanted a country house – somewhere with good views and where you wouldn't be overlooked by neighbours. So surely, Sandiford House is a most satisfactory choice?'

No answer, so he gabbled on. 'And, of course, the house can be repaired and cleaned and – and—'

'I'll think about it.' Laurence was bored with the agent's persistence. 'I'll let you know.' Moving rapidly across the room, ignoring Sims's hopeful gaze, he looked back at the window, saw a shaft of faint sunlight filtering through the blotchy stains, and found himself grudgingly caught by what he saw outside.

Views. Yes, by God – and what views. A wild grey-brown river rushing by, close to the green wilderness of scrub and trees that stretched from the house's boundary wall. And, on the far bank of the river, a bosomy landscape rising and falling into the distance, patched with small fields and stands of dark woodland. As the sun shafted through the racing clouds, so the land lightened and took on a new dimension. Excitement triggered as colours raced through his mind.

As if he realized his prospective client's new interest, Eric Sims came a sly pace nearer. 'Yes, Mr Vane, there's the river, and the sea at Culmouth, and of course we've got the wilderness of the moor only a short drive away . . . such views! And a landscape painter like you could surely—'

'I'm a portrait painter.' The words came out without any thought, and Laurence swung around, staring at the agent with a grim expression as the past suddenly resonated, ugly and shaming. He narrowed his eyes, remembering.

During the past weeks of tumult in London he had been reluctantly forced to acknowledge that his sister Elizabeth's word was now law. No longer was he master of his own fate, it seemed. Turning away now from the seductive landscape, he felt dull and uninspired. He didn't want to be here. But she was right, London was a hotbed of gossip and recrimination, while down here in Devon no one knew him. It was a quiet backwater, and certainly the views were spectacular.

And it was quite true what Elizabeth had said only last week. 'We must get away from London, Laurence – my nerves won't stand this any longer. I know it will soon die down – just a seven-day wonder like every other shocker – but I think you should concentrate on something new – forget your indecent portraits, and try landscapes, why not? We'll rent a house somewhere in the country, and start a new life.'

He'd promised Elizabeth she should inspect anything he found on his reluctant journey west. And no doubt she would be very cross if Sandiford House, a first choice on her list, was merely ticked off as hopeless before she'd seen it. He frowned. 'Give me a day or two, Sims – I'll let you know.'

Leaving the house he paused before telling the waiting cabby to take him back to his hotel in Abberton. Again, he looked towards the river. Head tilted, he listened; in the distance it was a subtle voice speaking of waves and surges and grinding pebbles on tidal beaches. And beyond it, those greens and golds and warm ochre browns contrasting with the shadowy green patches of trees.

He took in a huge breath. Perhaps it might work – the house could be made habitable, and yes, there was work waiting for him here.

Then he turned away, face set, unsettled mind persuasively taking him back to his studio in London. To the happy clutter of canvases, rough bits of furniture, hangings, flames in the fireplace, a bottle or two of brandy and a warm, human, smiling, enticing body posing on the dais.

The waiting cabby lifted the reins and tilted his hat. 'Back to yer hotel, sir?'

About to say yes, Laurence suddenly stopped, something making him turn back and look at the distant hills once more. He could hear birds, cattle lowing, and the strange, subtle song of water flowing. Perhaps he should just go and look at the river. . . .

As he walked over the rough, uneven marshland, avoiding the worst half-concealed ponds and drifts of muddy water, he reminded himself yet again that London was not the most appropriate place for him. Not at the moment. So perhaps he should stay here and make the best of it. Not that it would be easy, but – the colours, the views, the river . . .

When the boat came into view he had to narrow his eyes to see it properly for the sun reflecting on the rippling water almost concealed it. But then, as the rower's hands moved, so the boat went forward, and Laurence was able to see properly. The rower was a woman. Her straight back moved in a quiet rhythm which captivated him – easy and elegant. The wind touched a few stray strands of red-gold hair from beneath the dark hat, and altogether the picture of woman, boat and gilded water became an excitement touching his heart.

Momentarily the London studio flashed through his thoughts. The model's body posed on the chair, firelight glow on the concealing drift of rich, dark-red satin falling over her half-naked body. Oh, to be back there, the painting going well and a glass in his hand! Now his heart hammered and certainty came in a hot rush. For God's sake, he had to paint living models, not static landscapes.

He watched, entranced, as the boat steadily moved on. A boy and a girl sat in the bow, talking and laughing, and for a second he heard the rower replying – a few soft words, not audible save for the hollow, gentle sound relayed by the wind. A sound and a picture he understood were both instantly engrained in his mind.

That night, at the hotel in Abberton, he wrote a letter to Elizabeth.

'I've found an old house, standing alone and in countryside, which I've decided will suit us well. I suggest you come down and inspect it. Meanwhile, to save time, will you write to Eric Sims, who is the agent for the Sandiford estate, tell him I've decided to rent the house and instruct him to put certain repairs in hand immediately. And also send funds for the local builder to start work.'

Before signing the letter Laurence sat back, drank his wine and thought deeply. If Elizabeth was to fall in with his plans, he must throw her a sop which should do away with any possible arguments.

Picking up the pen again, he smiled wryly as he wrote the half-lie, 'Such views, dear sister! I can hardly wait to start painting again.'

Jessie Smith was in her element at the market. From stall to stall she searched out the colourful bits and pieces attracting her. Brass earring hoops, couldn't afford them, but wouldn't they look good with her dark curly hair? And that silvery bracelet – touching it she knew just how it would feel on her wrist.

The stallholder watched, growled, 'Keep your hands to yourself, young woman. I need to see your money before you can try on . . .'

Pulling a face, Jessie went on to the next stall, catching the eye of the young man selling fish. 'What a stink!' She grinned at him. 'When did you catch this, last year?'

His tanned face lit up and he turned to take a good look at her. A pretty girl was more fun than the usual old customers. 'Mind your tongue, maid! Caught 'em yesterday evening. Fresh as daisies, they are. Want one for your tea, then?'

'On'y if you gives it me . . .' Jessie knew how to flirt. It was second nature along with her wicked smile and pouting lips. And it usually worked – today it certainly did.

'Half a chance an' I'll give you something else, better'n a dead ol' sprat, maid. Where you come from, then?' He was a few years older than her, tired of working on his pa's fish stall, keen to get back to the river and the sea and the adventurous life of youth. He wanted excitement. Girls came and went. This new one might be a bit of fun.

'Sandiford,' she told him, sidling nearer and twisting around so that her skirt twirled, showing a shapely calf that even old cracked boots couldn't hide. 'What're you called?'

'John. John Mott. Who're you?'

'Jessie. Just Jessie. Ever come to Sandiford, do 'ee? I helps in the inn some nights. Washing glasses, you know . . .'

'Ah. Then mebbe I'll see you there, Jessie.'

Their smiles met, understood and lingered.

Until Rose called from the next stall. 'Jessie – have you bought the candles? Come on, I want to get back before the tide turns.'

A last glance, a silent agreement, and the girl ran, looking back over her shoulder and giving him a final smile. If Rose had known, she would have been worried, and with due cause.

Walter Wheeler from the grocery shop met Rose in Cross Lane as she walked towards Miss Hodge's cottage. He'd been waiting for this meeting, watching out for Rose's customary weekly visit. Today he'd left Ben, his assistant, looking after the shop, and was working up an enjoyable rage as he strode towards the approaching figure.

He stopped a couple of paces from her and said loudly, 'Rose Adams, I want to talk to you.' Clearing his throat, he pursed his lips and stood with legs apart, thumbs in waistcoat pocket, staring belligerently at her as he sorted out the words that had been running around his brain ever since yesterday.

Rose halted. She and Mr Wheeler had never got on. He was definitely village while she was canal. His son Charlie took immense pleasure in continuing his father's attitude; beating up Billy Netherton was only one way of showing it, and Charlie was constantly working out new ideas of making those canal rats realize how miserable and worthless they were. She had no trust in the entire family.

Moving her basket to her left arm, Rose clasped both hands in front of her. That this was to be an unpleasant interview she had no doubt. But she would give this angry, rude and very intolerant man something in return, showing him that even canal rats were polite and courageous. 'Good afternoon, Mr Wheeler. So what do you want to say?'

He frowned, not expecting this insolent response. 'That Jessie Smith, that girl you take up to the Market every day, know the sort of things she gets up to?'

Rose was wary. Yes, she knew some of Jessie's tricks. 'I know she's a lively, intelligent girl who's finding it difficult to settle down into a situation, Mr Wheeler.'

He snorted, sniffed, fished out his large white handkerchief and blew his nose. 'Huh!'

Rose gathered her breath, smiled and waited.

'Lively, intelligent? You're joking of course. More of a guttersnipe with no manners and, worse, no morals, I'd say. So what do you think about that?'

'That you should be speaking to her mother, Mr Wheeler, and not to me. I'm not responsible for Jessie's behaviour, if that's what you're complaining about.'

His rough voice rose. 'I'm complaining about her light fingers, that's what! Come into my shop yesterday, just when we're trying to tidy up and close down, and when I go to put the box of ribbon bunches away, they're gone.' He sniffed in a huge breath and glowered at Rose. 'A thief, that's what she is. And if she does any more of it I'll be fetching in the constable. So you can tell her that, see? And let her know that I'll be watching next time she comes flouncing into my shop, all grand airs and no money!'

Rose remained silent, watching while his tight red face slowly relaxed into its more usual folds and sags, waiting until she could reason with him. 'Mr Wheeler,' she said quietly, 'I'm sorry to hear that Jessie's been thieving. I know she has some bad habits, but please – please, give her another chance. Talk to her mother, if you must—'

He cut in, satisfaction souring his expression. 'What good'll that do? Mrs Smith still owes me for last month's groceries and I can't see her paying until that useless layabout man of hers gets another job. Like father, like daughter, I say. No,' suddenly his voice dropped and he took a step nearer Rose. 'No, maid, what I want you to do is take her in hand. You're the schoolmistress, you can give her rules and see that she obeys them. She takes no notice of her family, but maybe she'll take it from you.' And then the old familiar expression returned, together with his raised voice. 'Canal people! Always trouble! Us villagers have a lot to put up with your useless ways. Can't pay your bills, drunk half the time, ready for a fight any day—'

Rose drew away, her hands forming tight fists. Somehow she controlled her voice. 'Thank you, Mr Wheeler. I don't want to hear any more. And while we're on the subject of rules and behaviour, I'd be grateful if you would control your bullying son. Charlie is forever picking on the smaller children at Sandiford. One day someone's going to get really hurt – and we'll all know who the troublemaker is.'

They stared at each other. Rose's cheeks grew red but she managed a brief smile as she said curtly, 'Good-day, Mr Wheeler.' Stepping out, she was met by his immediate move towards her. She paused. 'You're in my way. Kindly let me pass.'

There were another few seconds of eyes meeting eyes, then Walter Wheeler was the first to look away, blustering as he did so. 'Just you wait, young lady. Talking like that 'bout my son won't do you no good. Wait till your ma wants a few things on tick – oh, I know how your dad spends all his wages at the inn – and then we'll see who's got the last word.'

But Rose was on her way, not looking back, heading for Miss Hodge's cottage and feeling the furious gaze that followed her. Upon reaching Myrtle Cottage she closed the gate behind her and knocked at the door. Thank goodness for someone who saw both sides of every question, she thought angrily, who was intelligent and compassionate enough to understand that girls from unsettled homes frequently found it hard to settle down in life. Miss Hodge would give her tea and advice, and soon that unpleasant encounter with Walter Wheeler would become just a memory. But it had definitely left her with an overheated reaction and a renewed longing to stop this ancient feud between village and canal.

When Miss Hodge opened the door and welcomed her in, Rose was slowly able to calm down and look at everything more sensibly. She realized that Miss Hodge's health was more important than a few harsh words and evil thoughts, and as they sat by the fire with the teapot filling thin china cups and Rose nibbling at homemade gingerbread, Miss Hodge's lively conversation acted like a charm. So much so, that, after the usual inquisition about health and everyday matters, Rose was able to broach the subject of Jessie without feeling too incensed.

'Jessie Smith's been taking things from Wheeler's shop,' she said. 'What should I do, do you think?'

Miss Hodge sipped her tea, replaced the cup on its flowery saucer and looked across the laden table. 'Find her a situation,' she said, smiling a little. 'The girl is obviously too much for her poor mother and that sick, unemployable father. I think you're doing what you can, Rose, letting her help with May Bankes's trade, but of course she needs to settle somewhere. A pity she's too old to come back to school – I always hoped to make something of her, but the wildness was there, even when she was smaller.'

Rose thought. 'She's helping in the inn in the evenings,' she said at last. 'And Susan Upcott said she's behaving badly.' She met Miss Hodge's understanding eyes and smiled. 'Dancing on the table, can you imagine it?'

'Yes,' said Miss Hodge mildly. 'I can. Jessie was always nimble and quick.' She paused, then continued, 'I believe, as you know, that girls, just as much as boys, need to be educated and so helped to find a situation that will support them throughout their lives.'

Rose saw the brilliant eyes grow even brighter. 'You, Rose, are a prime example of that happening. You were sensible enough to realize that study would enable you to gain a position – a teacher certification. You grasped the opportunity.'

'Yes, but Miss Hodge, only because you gave me the chance. You said study, and—'

'And so you did, child.' But if you hadn't already had that longing for independence and knowledge in yourself, you wouldn't have bothered.'

They looked at each other, and Rose nodded. 'Yes. You're right.'

Miss Hodge sat back in her chair, straightened her shoulders and said quietly, 'And I think that Jessie Smith has the same feeling inside her. She wants more than this place and a domestic situation can give her.'

Rose thought before saying anything. She finished the tea in her cup and replaced it on the table. 'Yes. I understand what you're telling me, Miss Hodge. And I'm sure you're right. But the thing is, how do we help Jessie?'

'By doing exactly what you're already doing, Rose. Giving her a chance of work, even if it's only rowing up to market every day with you, and trying to make her understand that thieving will get her into trouble.' Miss Hodge drew in a breath and sighed it slowly out. Her voice sounded tired, but amused, as she added, 'And if all else fails, then perhaps we can help her to marry a good man who'll give her lots of babies and keep her occupied that way. Perhaps marriage would tame her and give her something new to think about. A family might do that.'

'She was flirting with the fish boy in the market this morning,' Rose said, laughing a little. 'Maybe something will come of it . . . though I can't see her as a fishwife dealing with that smell and all those scales.'

They talked then of other things, and it was only as Rose prepared to leave, once she'd put the tea things in the scullery and made sure that the coal scuttle was filled for the evening, that Miss Hodge got to her feet, swaying a little as she clutched at the chair behind her, and followed Rose to the door.

'I have something to tell you, my dear.'

Rose heard an uncertain note in the mellow voice and turned quickly. 'Yes? What is it, Miss Hodge?'

For a moment the old lady just looked at her and Rose saw an expression of regret shadow the amazingly bright blue eyes.

'Dr Ingles thinks I have run myself down at school this last term. My heart, you see – well, it's old age of course, but I'm inclined to agree with him. I do find term-time rather wearisome . . . even with your help, dear Rose.'

Rose's hands on the empty basket tightened. She had a presentiment of ill news about to come, both for her and Miss Hodge. 'Tell me,' she whispered.

'I shan't be coming back to school in the autumn, Rose. I'm retiring. And a new teacher will take over. It's all arranged. But of course, I hope and trust that you will continue there . . . the poor man will need all the help he can get at first, a new school, new children and so on—'

'Man?'

Miss Hodge reached for the doorway and pulled herself up straight. Her smile was reassuring and affectionate, as she said quietly, 'Yes, a Mr Devlin – Thomas Paget Devlin, such a good name – moving here from Exeter. He's a widower. I do hope you'll get on with him, Rose.'

CHAPTER THREE

Sandiford House was in the throes of repair and rehabilitation. Builders, carpenters, painters and numerous cleaners from the village walked there every day and got to work.

Eric Sims was proud of his achievement. 'Yes, Mr Crowther, the lease runs from the end of this month when Mr Vane and Mrs Mount take possession. Yes, sir, everything is signed, the builders and the other workers are there and already the old place is looking quite rejuvenated. No, sir, I know you don't wish to visit – you never did – but if I might say so, Sandiford House is now back in the present after all those sad years in the past.'

Smiling, he watched Mr Crowther, senior partner of the law firm dealing with the Sandiford Estate Trust, nod sagely and then leave the room. There used to be tales about the old house – but that was years ago. No need to remember them now.

At the house, the chatter was ceaseless and imaginative.

'Who did you say was comin'? An artist? What, paintings and suchlike, you mean?' Nancy Briggs continued scrubbing the kitchen floor even as she looked over her shoulder at the woman who was cleaning the windows.

'That's right.' Daisy Pellew spat on her cloth and rubbed extra hard at a greasy spot that refused to budge. 'With his sister, I heard. Widow, she is – got all the money so he has to do what he'm told.'

Both women paused in their exertions to exchange glances and squawk with laughter.

Nancy bent again to the scrubbing. 'Ah well, we shall see . . .'

For once, villagers and canal folk shared the same thought. *We shall see. . . .*

And what they saw at the end of the month was a large wagonette slowly swaying down the narrow, winding lane towards Sandiford House, followed by an elegant horse-drawn carriage in which two indistinct people could be seen. A youngish man and an older woman.

Tongues wagged, heads turned to scrutinize as best they could, and then both conveyances disappeared through the iron gateway and on into the tree-lined grounds of the house and supposition was all that remained.

Elizabeth Mount said little as Laurence conducted her up stone steps and through the thick oak front door of the house. He had been here for a few days already, staying at the hotel in Abberton and visiting regularly to oversee the renovations. As far as he was concerned, it was clean, dry and habitable. But whether Elizabeth would agree with that he was uncertain.

Persuasively, he said, 'Look at this wonderful marble-floored hall. Welcoming, isn't it? Establishes the age of the place at once.'

She paused, allowed her little Cavalier King Charles dog, Henrietta, to jump out of her arms, then looked down at the black-and-white stones. Drawing her mantle closer about her, she said grudgingly, 'Yes, very elegant. But cold. And there's no fireplace.'

'Ah, but come into the drawing-room – you'll soon get warm in here.' He went through the open door and walked over to the huge granite inglenook where the grate was already laid with kindling and logs ready to be fired. 'If you look up the chimney you'll see the sky.'

'Thank you,' said Elizabeth with a tight smile. 'I'll take your word for it. I fear that'll mean draughts.' She called the dog, picked her up and stroked the small, warm head. 'We don't want to catch colds, do we, Henny?'

Testily Laurence moved towards the window. 'At least you can't say anything about the views, Elizabeth. Just come and look.'

Together they took in the garden, with its newly dug beds and trimmed shrubs beneath old, heavily foliaged trees. And then on to the river, which today, in early summer, was gliding along like a passive grey-brown snake between green banks, intent only on enjoying the sun which gilded its ripples. Laurence's eyes stayed on the water for a long moment, but no boat appeared. He looked up and beyond, enjoying the rich greens and golds of fields growing kitchen produce and corn, and touched his sister's arm.

'What do you think, Elizabeth? Made a good choice, haven't we?

Plenty of landscapes to paint, a garden where one can sit in the sun without being overseen and the countryside all around us.' He looked directly at her and smiled.

She had always been a good sister, and this removal from town must be quite a challenge to her social life. He could afford to give in to any of her whims or to orders she cared to give.

'Yes, Laurence, it's certainly quiet and beautiful. And,' she paused, touched his face with a loving hand, and lowered her voice, 'And you'll be able to forget all that unpleasantness in town, all that gossip. Why, here there's hardly a soul to be seen!'

Then she turned and walked towards the door, saying over her shoulder, 'And now I'd like to see the rest of the rooms. And didn't you say you had engaged some servants? A cup of tea would very welcome.'

Laurence followed her out of the room, calling to the man unloading their bags at the door to take them upstairs. Then he went into the kitchen where Mrs Briggs waited with the kettle already boiling.

'Tea, if you please, Mrs Briggs. My sister will be down again very soon. We'll have it in the drawing-room.' He smiled at her, then followed Elizabeth upstairs.

Nancy Briggs took in a big breath, pursed her lips, tidied the cups already laid on the tray, and warmed the teapot. This was a big moment. What would the lady be like? she wondered. Couldn't be as charming as that nice Mr Vane – so what news would she have to relay to the village on her first Sunday afternoon off?

Elizabeth sipped her tea, took a small bite of a scone lavishly spread with cream and jam, gave a small piece to drooling Henny at her feet, and looked at Laurence sitting opposite her by the hearth.

'Very rich,' she said, sternly. 'If this Devonshire cream is going to be served with everything I can see you losing your fine figure, dear brother.'

His eyes twinkled. 'And you, dear sister?'

'No, no. I never overeat. I'm not at all self-indulgent.' But her face relaxed into an expression of pleasure as she took another bite.

'So what do you think of the house, Elizabeth? Now that you've had a good look around, and time to consider?' He was slightly worried. If she really disliked the place she would be quite capable of moving again.

In the pause that followed he looked at her very carefully. She had removed her mantle, and her tailor-made dark-blue dress fitted very closely around her body, with a high collar and tight sleeves. Pleated draping around the front of the skirt conferred the elegant touch necessary in today's fashions. Elizabeth's hats had always amused him, but this one was different from countless others which were mostly large and decorated with birds' feathers; this was small with a seaside air about it and perched neatly on her upswept greying hair. She was dressed for London and the social life that had, until now, made up her world. How would she react to Devonshire and the remote countryside?

He drank his tea, accepting that he didn't really care about Elizabeth's world even though she had always made a point of caring for him. She was five years older, with a marked resemblance to their London banker father who had made many investments and provided well for both of them on his death. Alas, Laurence thought, looking at the scones greedily, he'd got through Father's inheritance far too quickly. Thank goodness that Elizabeth had appointed herself his protector as the money disappeared and the bills came in. Indeed, thank goodness she still was.

When her husband Frank died of bronchitis that cold winter two years ago, she had come into even more money. And had still paid Laurence's overdue bills, the rent for his studio, all the expenses that a painter who was trying to establish a name for himself without much success demanded. His own meagre earnings when a portrait sold had disappeared far too quickly; Laurence, deciding that temptation must be given in to, took his third cream-and-jam scone, shooed Henny away from his side, and told himself that good models had expensive tastes, paint and brushes were costly, and a man in search of fame had to dress well and frequent the usual society high spots.

By the time he'd licked the last spot of cream from his fingers and passed his cup for another refill of tea, Elizabeth was speaking again and he listened intently.

'I think the house has distinct possibilities, Laurence,' she said at last, wiping fingers on a linen napkin. 'It's old but has a certain quaint charm. I like the garden – Henny will be safe there. But I'm not at all sure that I want to keep those portraits that line the staircase – perhaps we could store them, or maybe the estate would like to house them – and I shall send to London for some of my own furniture. Some of this junk,' a sniff and a moue of distaste, 'is really quite terrible. But, yes, I think we could well settle here for a while and be happy, dear boy. And . . .' leaning forward she gave him her most loving and understanding smile, 'and of course, the views are magnificent. You'll be painting again in a day or two, I'm quite sure.'

They smiled at each other and Laurence nodded. Yes, she was right. He would most certainly be painting very soon. But not those pastoral views. Tomorrow he would start the search for the woman in the boat. Then a dark cloud entered his delightful heaven: when Elizabeth realized that his passion for red-haired models still existed, what would she say? Or do?

May Bankes was slowly recovering. 'This sun, that's what does it. Warms me up so's I can get on me feet agen. Now.' Standing up unsteadily and balancing herself with a hand on the mantel, she smiled at Rose who had called, as usual, for the day's vegetable and fruit orders. 'Now, maid, we've gotta think about my benefit. Soon be here.'

Rose nodded, smiling. May Bankes's annual benefit was a rough, rowdy party held in the field just behind the inn. All her customers and friends attended and the day was a celebration of May's sterling help in keeping trade routes open all the year round. The river journey couldn't have been much fun in the winter, thought Rose now, with the experience of five or six weeks' rowing in all weathers behind her. The old woman deserved to be fêted for her hard work.

'It's all arranged,' she said. 'I heard Susan Upcott talking about it, May. Seems this year will be better than ever – you being ill has made everybody realize how important you are. So look out for all sorts of excitement!'

May grinned back at her. 'But you'll be part of it too, this year, maid – what should I've done without you, eh? You and that boy Billy – oh, an' I s'pose that flighty maid, Jessie, too. Still going with you, is she?'

Rose's smile died uneasily. 'No,' she said at last. 'Jessie said she'd found another job helping Will Sharcombe's dad with the hay harvest. I haven't seen her all this week.' Resolutely she looked for more positive thoughts. 'Perhaps it's for the best – she needs to settle into a regular situation.' Then, briefly, she wondered if Will had much to do with Jessie, as she ran riot in his dad's hayfield.

May's sniff said everything that she thought about Jessie Smith. 'Nought'll come of it that's good,' she said darkly, and then waddled to the table where Rose's shopping list lay. 'Manage on yer own, can you, then, maid? Or is the boy leaving, too?'

'He isn't coming today,' Rose said, picking up her list and bending down to reach the basket on the floor. 'Had to go and see relatives in Exeter. His mother wouldn't take no for an answer. But he'll be back tomorrow – can't keep him away from boats for long.'

'Hm.' May frowned. 'Well, mind you watch out for that old sandy beach up river by the railway bridge. Water runs fast there; time an' agen I've grounded the boat there and it's a devil to get off if you'm by yerself.'

'I'll be careful.' Rose was at the door, her mind on the task ahead. Yes, she would watch out for the many dangers but she was experienced by now; and didn't foresee any trouble.

The day was hot and she felt the sun burning the uncovered parts of her body. Even the straw boater she wore – an indulgence from a market stall when her old felt hat seemed too hot and heavy for the summer weather – didn't quite shade her face. The boat danced and swayed on the fast-flowing water and she felt in tune with the spirit of gaiety it offered.

Life had become no more than a daily routine of rowing, shopping and more rowing during these last weeks, but she had found a freedom which had eluded her when teaching in the school. And having Billy and Jessie with her, listening to their sometimes rude and often semi-illiterate chatter, she'd learned a lot about other people's lives. Billy longed to go to sea, but his father said no, too dangerous, and Billy was becoming uncharacteristically rebellious. And as for Jessie, well; for a second Rose leaned on her oars and let the boat drift – she was as wild as ever. There had been some talk of the fish boy and evenings spent with him. And then suddenly it was all about Will Sharcombe and helping with the hay.

Rose shook her head, decided Jessie must make her own life, and began rowing again. Not far to Abberton now and then the long journey back, with the boat heavily loaded and no one to give her a hand. She'd done it before, she could do it now. And it was good to be alone. She felt strong and content, more able now to visualize her future. Go back to school in the autumn and see what happened next. Then she recalled that Miss Hodge was retiring and a new man taking over, but that was still weeks ahead.

Her thoughts were busy as she began the journey home, day-dreams and warmth creating a world far from reality, when suddenly the boat slipped sideways as a great surge of water hit it. Strengthening her hold on the oars she looked behind her and saw just how far off course she was. And the railway bridge close by meant she was near to the sandy beach that May had warned her about. Too near. . . .

There was a slow, softly menacing scrunch, a bump that tipped her sideways and the boat grounded. It fell on its side, water slapping around it. Rose leaned forward to prevent the goods slipping over the tilted side. One oar fell from her hand, and she almost fell overboard as she hurriedly grabbed it and pulled it to safety before the water swirled it out of reach. She was angry, furious with herself for not being more aware of May's warning words. But anger wouldn't get her very far. How on earth could she, alone, get the boat back into the right position to be rowed out of danger?

'Hold on, let me help you.'

Rose looked up, met dark eyes full of energy and interest, and breathed a sigh of relief. The darkly bearded man was big, and young enough to have the strength to right the boat and set her afloat again.

'Thank you. If you could get hold of this . . .' She bent round and threw him the mooring rope. Would he know how to handle it? Watching, she saw long, slender fingers catching it, hauling it to a handy alder tree growing out of the bank and fastening it so that the boat, while still beached and lying at an awkward angle, was under steady control again.

She let the breath out of her tense body and allowed the oars to balance on the gunwales as she smiled at her rescuer. 'Thank goodness you came along! I was stuck fast.'

The well-dressed man came to the side of the boat and looked at her, eyes narrowed against the sun, and his heavily moustached mouth lifting in an answering smile. 'Thank goodness I did. Do you always go out on the river on your own?'

Then, not waiting for a reply, he added quickly, 'I've seen you before – you had a boy and a girl with you then.'

Rose was slightly disconcerted. She certainly hadn't seen him – was he a tourist? Someone who walked the river paths watching birds and enjoying the trees and surging water? 'I row up to the market every day,' she said, wondering really what concern of his this was, but for some reason intrigued by his good looks and educated voice.

'Strange work for a girl.' He was watching her with obvious interest.

'I enjoy it. And there's not much work around here for anyone, let alone a girl,' she answered sharply. 'And now, if you could help me a bit more, I need to get the boat back into the current.' Then she said, more carefully, and with a hint of a smile, 'Please untie the rope, if you will.'

He did so, coiling it and leaning forward to replace it in the bow of the boat. 'What next?'

'Just give me a good push off, please . . . Mr— Mr. . . ?' She must know his name, thank him for his timely help. The despairing thoughts of what she would have done without him still stayed in her mind.

'Laurence Vane. I live at Sandiford House.' The words came out from gritted teeth as he took the weight of the boat against his body and pushed. Rose watched, at the same time pushing at the shore with one oar. Could they do it between them? And would the vegetables and other goods stay safely where they were? Suppose she lost the lot of them. No, don't even think of it . . . She gripped the oars more tightly.

'Nearly there,' said Laurence Vane in a hard-pressed voice. 'One more push.'

Rose's head suddenly spun. So this was the new tenant, the handsome man Jessie had gabbled about, the Mr Vane all the canal women were discussing and trying to get glimpses of. An artist, they knew, for he'd been seen setting up his easel, painting the scenes along the river. The gossips said he lived with his sister, who was a widow with money; here they'd grinned and nodded eloquently. And a few villagers, like Nancy Briggs and Daisy Pellew actually worked for this Mrs Mount.

Feeling the boat float once more, with the current carrying her back to the usual channel, all the tantalizing facts vanished as Rose smiled and shouted over her shoulder, 'Thank you, Mr Vane. I'm really grateful for your help.'

He answered with a yell of surprise, and glancing back, she saw him struggling to reach the path, his waterlogged, well-polished boots held fast by the treacherous wet sand of the little beach. And his clothes – oh dear, they were wet through.

Rose couldn't help it. She laughed, and waved a departing hand. Poor man, he'd have a long wet walk back to Sandiford House when he eventually escaped from the water, she thought.

May was in high spirits when at last Rose tied up the boat at the Sandiford mooring and heaved the heavy baskets into the cottage.

'Where you've been, then? Thought you'd have got back sooner than this . . . an' there's a message for you, maid. Mr Wheeler's young Charlie come round with this note from Miss Hodge, ses to give it to you when you comes back.' May fumbled in her apron pocket and pulled out a crumpled envelope, passing it to Rose before unpacking the bottle of gin from beneath the vegetables and fruit. She took it to the table, where her mug was already waiting, and had a good slurp. Then she sat down again, eyeing Rose keenly all the while.

'Well? What's the news, then? Everything all right on the journey? Market doing well? See, maid, now I'm back on me legs I'll be doing the trip meself from now on. Oh, I'm grateful to you, don't think I'm not. But I must get back to work, or there'll be no nice benefit for me next month, will there?' And her wheezy laugher ran around the airless little room.

Rose stowed the envelope in her pocket. May was obviously agog to know what it contained, but gossip spread too quickly amongst the neighbours, and often without too much truth, so the message must wait until she was on her own. She finished unpacking the baskets and gladly found a chair. Deciding against telling May of the grounding of the boat she just said, 'So I'll be out of a job, will I? Have to find something else to take me on till school starts again, then.'

May poured another tipple. 'You'll find summat,' she said shortly. 'Good clever maid like you. Now – let's settle up. Here's what I owes you.' She passed over a handful of coins and watched as Rose got to her feet again.

'If you need help again, just give me a call. I've enjoyed doing the trips.' Rose gave the old woman a last smile and then left the cottage.

She walked slowly down the path, fingering the envelope in her pocket and waiting till she was away from any possible watchers before sitting down on the grassy bank and reading Miss Hodge's letter.

It was short and to the point.

My dear Rose
I should like you to come and take tea with me on Wednesday after-
noon at 4.30. I shall have a visitor whom I want you to meet.
Yours sincerely,

Louise Hodge.

Rose put the letter back in her pocket and stared at the river flowing past. A visitor. Well, it would be interesting to meet whoever it turned out to be. She knew Miss Hodge had several schoolteacher friends who occasionally called on her. Perhaps this was one of them.

She got up and dawdled home, smiling to herself as the formal invitation ran around her mind. How nice to read proper English, to imagine Miss Hodge's old-fashioned, clipped voice, and to know that she was invited *to take tea* ... the expression made her smile grow and she started thinking about what she would wear. Not this dirty old skirt and faded blouse with the ripped sleeve where a splinter on the oar had torn it. A teatime visit required something cleaner and smarter. But she hadn't got any smart clothes, apart from the new straw boater, which had been second hand at the market stall and wasn't really new. Perhaps she could brighten it up with some flowers around the brim. She supposed, resignedly, that she would have to make do with the dark skirt she wore at the school in term-time, and ask Mother if she could hurry up and finish the new blouse she was making.

Her thoughts were still busy when she got home and found Alice sitting by the window, hands busy stitching the material Rose had bought a few weeks ago when Mrs Hannaford's material stall had offered a discount on each yard bought that day. She'd felt guilty at snapping up this lovely cotton floral print, but now it seemed the answer to the problem of what to wear at the tea party.

Alice smiled. She laid down the thin material and stretched out her knobbly fingers with a grimace of discomfort. 'So here you are! And I've got the kettle singing. Everything all right, maid?'

Rose bent and kissed her mother. No need to say anything about the boat grounding; she knew Alice had enough worries over her father's job on the barges without adding to them.

'Yes,' she said, putting May's payment on the table and pushing it across to her mother. 'Everything's all right, except that I shan't be doing the trip any more as May's so much better she's going herself.'

Alice paused before answering. Then she looked down at her sewing again. 'I'm glad,' she said quietly. 'Rowing that ol' boat's not a job for a girl like you, love. You should be doing something better, something more, well, suitable.'

Rose pondered the word. Surely anything was suitable for a canal girl? 'What do you mean, Mother, suitable?' She watched Alice's face suddenly twist as if a sharp memory had struck her. But quickly the placid expression returned.

'I don't know what I mean, love. Just a silly word, of course. Now – make the tea, will you? and then I'll get you to try on this blouse.' She held out the half-finished garment and Rose understood that the subject was closed.

'Got the sleeves stitched in,' Alice went on, smiling again, 'but it's the neck I need to look at.'

The blouse, Rose thought gladly, was just what she needed to wear tomorrow. Alice was a clever seamstress, and had made the sleeves just that bit too long so that they almost hid her red, rough hands. And the high-standing collar was decorated with a ribbon of heavy ivory lace. Rose fingered it. 'Where ever did you find this, Mother?'

Quickly Alice looked down as if searching for a lost pin. 'Found it in me box of treasures, love. Got it somewhere, oh, years ago.'

And then, when Rose dressed up in the finished costume, the dark skirt and the new blouse, her waist tightly cinched by one of Jack's leather belts cut to fit, and the straw boater pinned securely on to her tied-back hair, Alice sighed, nodded her head, and said quietly, in an unsteady voice, 'Rose Victoria, you look a real lady. That's what you look, love.'

CHAPTER FOUR

That evening Jack Adams came home in a rage. 'Them boys, messin' about in the boats – told that Billy Netherton if I found him up to his tricks again I'd tan the bottom off of 'im'

Rose had said nothing, just waited for the anger to subside. Then, when Jack had eventually taken off his coat and changed wet leggings for dry corduroys, she sat beside him at the table, watching as he ate his tea. She kept her voice steady and quiet, saying, 'Billy thinks of nothing but boats, Father, and his dad won't listen to him. He wants to join the Merchant Navy when he's older, and he's trying to learn all he can until then. Could you . . .' She stopped, seeing him turn towards her, chewing and frowning at the same time. No, of course he couldn't – wouldn't. Foolish to even try and ask.

Jack swallowed loudly, banged his fork down on his plate and glared at her. 'One of your lame dogs, is he, that li'l brat? Like that giddy maid Jessie Smith, always carrying on? Taking them under your wing, are you? Full of good works, Rose Victoria? Not content with school teachin', tryin' to make a name for yourself, then? Adams not good enough for 'ee?'

She caught her breath, held it tightly, and refused to take the bait. Jack loved a fight and he usually won because his voice was louder than hers; he had plenty of things to argue about and he enjoyed raising issues that he knew she cared about. Slowly Rose let out her held breath and managed to smile at him.

'Adams is my born name and I'm proud of it,' she said calmly. 'But I don't see why I shouldn't try and help people – specially children – if I can.'

'Huh!' He pushed away his empty plate, grated the chair back from the table and fumbled for his pipe.

Rose saw a small – the tiniest – possibility of talking plainly to him as he relaxed, twisting tobacco from his pouch into the clay pipe and then reaching for a taper from the fire. 'Father,' she said carefully, 'Billy is a sensible boy. If you took him on he could help you in loading the barges from the cellars. That's all he wants – someone to take an interest in him and offer a few suggestions.'

She stopped. Jack puffed, sat back in his chair, stretched legs out to the warmth of the hearth and looked at her. 'Huh,' he growled again, but his voice was quieter, his expression less aggressive. 'He'd want paying, of course. Haven't got the money to do that. Things are hard enough with you not working . . .' For a moment his dark eyes gleamed and Rose knew he was delighted to have won a point.

She tried again. 'No, he wouldn't. Billy would work just for the love of it. And you could talk to his dad, perhaps, tell him that the boy's good at the job.'

Jack sat in a cloud of smoke and looked at her. He sniffed. 'What about schoolin' then?'

'There's another month before school starts again. He could be useful for those few weeks.'

Another sniff, a fumble in a pocket for a handkerchief, a blow of the nose and again the familiar cough echoing around the room.

'You'm a determined maid, I'll say that fer 'ee.' Jack wiped his mouth, put back the handkerchief and stared at her.

Alice cleared the empty plates from the table and Rose took them to the shelf by the door, returning to the fire to carry hot water and pour it into the waiting basin. As she washed the dishes she could hardly believe what had happened. Father hadn't refused, hadn't even succumbed to the usual rage. Was there was a chance that he might help Billy? But Jack said no more.

Next morning they were up at first light as Jack and Joe had to catch the tide. Leaving the cottage, Jack looked back over his shoulder. 'If I finds that boy's been tinkering with my boat again I'll – I'll . . . well, never mind,' he growled. But Rose saw the hint of a smile playing around his whiskery mouth, and smiled back.

'Thank you, Father,' she said and saw him nod before striding up the path towards the clay cellar.

The day was busy. Rose undertook errands for Alice and two of her neighbours, carrying buckets of water home from the well by the railway bridge, and listening to Mrs Smith complaining about Jessie and her tricks. 'Comes home covered in messy ol' chaff, gobbles her tea and then off again won't say where – how Will Sharcombe bothers with her I jest don't know. Proper li'l madam her is.'

'But it's good that she's working, Mrs Smith.' Rose was about to add that Jessie had been a real help with the marketing, but another string of complaints stopped her.

'She'll come to no good end, I knows it. Told her agen and agen I have, but goes in one ear and out the other.'

Rose was glad to escape, going home and helping Alice prepare vegetables and fish for Jack's tea. When everything was ready and the fire stoked, Alice sat down and looked across the room to where Rose was cleaning the mould that collected on the insides of the rotting window frames.

'Leave that, maid. Don't give your hands more to do than you need. They'm looking softer now, that ol' cream I made I dessay. And you'll be getting ready to go and see Miss Hodge, soon. Don't be late, whatever you do.'

At just after half past three Rose left the cottage, kissing her mother and thanking her again for making the new blouse. 'I feel quite smart.' She laughed. 'Wait till I've got a flower or two for my hat – then, like you said, I really will look like a lady! Goodbye, Mother.'

'Goodbye, love.' Alice's voice was warm and her eyes shone.

Rose went out on to the sunlit river-bank with a feeling that all was going well with her world. Until she met Charlie Wheeler mooching along the path, catapult at the ready, eyes searching the hedges and water-side for victims.

'Well, Charlie – nothing better to do than kill things?' Her words were sharp and the boy bridled immediately.

'Nothing wrong with that,' he said surlily, frowning at her and drawing back the elastic on the catapult. He took aim at a sparrow that was hopping down the path, but then let the catapult drop as Rose pulled his arm away. 'Hey! Leave I alone . . . I'll tell me dad and he'll have you chucked out of school.'

'Oh yes? Well, you can tell your dad something else, too, Charlie. That if I catch you hunting down the path once more I'll get Will Sharcombe to deal with you. Just watch your step, my lad, you hear me?'

Charlie edged away. He glared and had the last word. 'Will Sharcombe's got better things to do than bother 'bout a few birds.' His adolescent voice crackled with laughter. 'He'm got a new one of his own.

Ask him what he an' Jessie Smith gets up to an' mebbe you'll get a surprise, Miss High'n Mighty Adams!'

He disappeared beneath the railway bridge, leaving Rose trying to deal with the images that arose as a result of what he'd just said. Will and Jessie? Surely not. Will wouldn't play around with a child like that – would he? Will loved her. Or so he'd said.

Leaving the path, she turned up through the marshes, for once hardly seeing the lush grass and thickly leaved hazel bushes, the willow trees and alders that lined the streams running through the scrub. The fragrance of summer, the busy butterflies and the birdsong passed her by, and all she could think of was Will.

So it was with a strong effort to regain control of her thoughts that she left the marshes behind, crossed the village square and then went on towards Cross Lane. At the gate of Myrtle Cottage she paused, determined now to be the perfect listener for whatever Miss Hodge wished to say. The cottage door was ajar, but she knocked and then waited, straightening her hat, realizing she'd forgotten to find a few flowers to put around the brim. Well, Miss Hodge's visitor would have to make do with a plain hat, she thought, and then smiled as the old lady opened the door wide, saying, 'Good afternoon, Rose. How charming you look. Yes, child, come in – come in.'

Rose followed Miss Hodge into the front room, finding it sunlit and full of flowers. A vase of dark-red roses sat on the windowsill, scenting the air, and a tall arrangement of delphiniums and green Irish Bells graced the bureau beside the far wall. The room was cherished and lovely and she was glad to be here. For a second she thought of her home on the river-bank, and felt a twist of her stomach. But then she stopped, looking straight into the eyes of the tall man who stood by the fireplace with a small girl at his side. She hadn't expected Miss Hodge's visitor to be a man.

Miss Hodge stood at her side, smiling and saying in her crisp, elderly voice, 'Rose, this is Mr Thomas Devlin and his daughter, Lucy. Mr Devlin, allow me to introduce Rose Adams, my associate at school. She is a certificated teacher, and extremely good with the children. I think you'll find her most helpful when you take over next term.'

Rose felt hot colour patching her cheeks. The new schoolteacher. The man with whom she must work. And he was looking at her with something close to what she felt sure was antipathy in his cool silvery-grey eyes, while the little girl clung to his hand and whispered something that he bent to hear and which Rose at once feared was about her and not at all complimentary.

He held out his hand and Rose took it. Dry, strong, a little rough, as if he was also a working man. She looked into the searching, not very friendly eyes and wondered what to say. But he spoke first. 'How do you do, Miss Adams?' His quiet voice was low and steady and Rose guessed he kept his emotions well under control. There was a hint of a northern accent which made her even more confused. What sort of man was he? And what was he thinking about her?

Words came suddenly to her then – foolish ones perhaps – but they were out before she could stop them. 'I hope you won't object to a woman in your school, Mr Devlin. I'm qualified – as Miss Hodge has just said – and I'm keen to do the best for all the village children.'

She saw his eyes narrow, heard a suspicion of stiffness in the quiet voice. 'We must wait and see, Miss Adams. I've always worked with male colleagues before so this will be a new experience for me.'

Rose was even more confused. Had she sensed a hint of wry humour in those words? She looked at him intently, but his clean-shaven, slightly saturnine face beneath the thatch of thick fair hair was expressionless. They regarded each other uncomfortably until Miss Hodge broke the silence. 'Tea, I think, don't you? Rose, if you'll help carry in the cups I'll bring the cakes. And Lucy,' turning to the little girl, still clinging to her father's hand, 'would you like to sit in that small chair over there? It belonged to my mother when she was a little girl like you.'

Thank goodness for Miss Hodge's awareness, thought Rose as she took off her hat, laid it on a handy chair and followed her hostess out of the room. But Lucy's piping voice was just audible. 'Is she going to teach me, Papa? Will she be very strict?' And then his firm reply. 'Of course not, Lucy. I shall be in charge, and I won't let anyone be strict with you, my love.'

In the kitchen Rose put cups and plates on a tray while Miss Hodge made the tea. So he'll be in charge, she thought, feeling her irritation rise. And very much in charge, too, by the sound of it.

They had tea in the warm room, with the sunlight sending bright shafts through the print curtains. Polite conversation flowed with Lucy watching Rose all the time. Lucy had hair the colour of pale apricots and matching eyelashes over big blue eyes. She sat still, hands busy with first bread-and-butter and Miss Hodge's homemade raspberry jam, and then dealing with gingerbread and sponge cake.

Strange for a small girl of some seven years to be so still, thought Rose. Until Lucy, finishing her tea, got clumsily to her feet and asked to be allowed to wander round the room. 'May I look at your curiosity cabinet, Miss Hodge?'

'Of course you may, Lucy. Just be careful with the more breakable things.'

Miss Hodge caught Rose's eye and smiled warningly, then Rose, looking at the child limping to the cabinet and reaching to pick up a small china dog, understood. Lucy was crippled, her left leg ending in a pathetic little foot that stuck out at the wrong angle.

Something inside Rose turned over and she realized guiltily how intolerant she was; how impatient to make quick judgements. Naturally Mr Devlin would make sure that his small daughter was treated well. He would do anything to ensure her happiness and well-being. Then she recalled what Miss Hodge had told her, weeks ago, that he was a widower, and once again wished her first impression of him had not been so quickly prejudiced.

Now he was looking at her across the small table, watching her face and saying very quietly, 'Yes, Lucy was born crippled, Miss Adams. And she has no mother. So perhaps you understand what she means to me – and how much care and time I have to give her.'

She met his deepset grey eyes and nodded, aware that he must notice her suddenly flushed face but intent only on repairing any damage she had done earlier. 'Yes, Mr Devlin. I do understand. And I shall see that she comes to no harm when I have her in my class at school.'

'Thank you.' He put his plate on the table and looked at Lucy, who was busy with a small ivory figurine.

Miss Hodge offered second cups of tea and conversation resumed. But Rose knew something unexpected had happened. She had made a mistake and then apologized. Would he perhaps now seem a little warmer and more inclined to smile? Apparently not. When Miss Hodge asked him about lodgings, she saw his mouth twist slightly as he replied, 'We're staying with Mrs Benthall in Church Street for the time being. I hope to find something better before long.' He hesitated, then continued, 'Perhaps with a different landlady who has a warm enough heart and free time with which to look after Lucy on the occasions when I have to be absent. Meetings, you know – duties I can't avoid.'

'If I can be of any help, Mr Devlin, I shall be only too glad to look after Lucy. I enjoy being with children.' Rose wondered if she had been too quick, too gushing in her response. After all, she'd only met the child half an hour ago.

'Thank you. But I imagine you have plenty to do – even though it's still holiday time.' He glanced at Miss Hodge before turning back towards Rose and she fancied he had a more relaxed look about him. 'I hear that you're busy helping out a neighbour with her shopping trips. I wouldn't want to interfere with that.'

'No, I'm not doing that any more. May Bankes is much better.' She smiled. 'Of course, she would be better now, with her benefit due next week.'

'Benefit? What is that, exactly?' Interest lit up his eyes.

'All May's customers give money to hold a celebration for her. She's done their shopping, you see, all the year round, so this is a party when we can thank her for it. It's held in the field behind the inn at the end of the river path. There are swimming and rowing races, all sorts of things happening. It's a lovely day.' Rose's voice warmed as she recalled the jollity of past benefits.

'I'd like to be there. Do you think it would be possible for me to come? With Lucy?' His words were quick and Rose thought his face lightened, showing a hint of unexpected emotion.

She looked quickly at Miss Hodge, who nodded and then turned to talk to Lucy and explain some of the small objects she was looking at in the cabinet.

'Of course, Mr Devlin. I think everybody would be glad to welcome you.'

'And it would certainly introduce me to the village. Yes, thank you, Miss Adams, we'd definitely like to accompany you there. Next week, you said? Exactly when?'

He drew out a pocketbook and a pencil and entered the date. Rose thought he looked and acted like every other schoolmaster she'd encountered, and wondered how the village would react. A man with strict attitudes, who idolized his crippled daughter, and yet was interested enough in village business to want to join in the local customs. She thought him a complex character and then felt uneasiness grow; how would he act towards her when they were at school together?

Tea ended, again Miss Hodge deftly turned the conversation to May Bankes's coming benefit. By the time Rose got to her feet, ready to leave, she saw Lucy's face shining with excitement. 'Papa, shall we swim? And row boats, like Miss Adams said? But I can't swim . . .' Suddenly her voice fell and all the joy left her face.

Thomas Devlin bent down and put his arm around her shoulder. 'My love, the river is very dangerous so I'm glad you can't swim, but perhaps I'll take you out in a boat and there will be lots of other amusements that you can enjoy. Don't fret, Lucy, we'll have a good time.'

His words were gentle and intended only for the child's ears, but Rose heard and felt a great warmth swell inside her. Clearly, Mr Devlin was a devoted father; the idea pierced her memories, and abruptly she recalled Jack rowing her into the middle of the stream, then insisting that she jump. 'On'y one way to learn to swim, maid, and that's to do it for real.' And yes, she had learned, although with bursting lungs and frozen legs and hands. She'd made the river bank and he had praised her and that had been a good time, one of the few when Jack had made much of her.

Turning away, Rose picked up her gloves. Mr Devlin was a different sort of father from the one she knew. She looked at him, wrapping Lucy's shawl around her shoulders before he reached for his hat. How different he was, in every way, from Laurence Vane. She hid her wry smile by turning aside.

Then she realized that Miss Hodge was looking at her. 'Rose? I asked if you would care to take this cake home to your mother? I shall never eat it on my own.'

'I'm sure she'll enjoy it, Miss Hodge. And thank you for inviting me to tea. I'm glad to meet Mr Devlin and Lucy.' Her voice sounded almost childish to her ears and she thought how naïve she must appear to this sophisticated and experienced schoolmaster, a man who would soon be her superior.

But he smiled politely at her as they all walked out of Miss Hodge's front door. 'Glad to have met you, Miss Adams.'

She needed a last chance to show him that she wasn't just a village girl who'd worked her way up the school, so she nodded, and said calmly, 'Perhaps I could call on you before the term starts, Mr Devlin, so that we can discuss the curriculum?' But of course that was the worst thing she could have suggested.

His face tightened. 'I don't think that's necessary, Miss Adams. I have my curriculum already formed. But by all means prepare your own – for the smaller children. I'll be glad to look it over in due course.' He nodded, buttoned his greeny-brown tweed jacket, bowed before putting on his hat, then took Lucy's hand and gave Rose a last, dismissive smile. 'Good day, Miss Adams.'

Rose swallowed the lump suddenly forming in her throat and turned in the opposite direction. She would not look back, wouldn't give him a chance of thinking she was impressed by his authoritative manner. As she walked quickly away towards the marshes, her mind spun angrily. When school started again she would show him just what an excellent teacher she was, and how well the children fared under her rule. They needed none of the canes or punishments which he was probably used to inflicting. And all that love for Lucy! Could she believe it, when the rest of him was so stiff and unfeeling?

Walking back through the green grasses and gently swaying trees, she allowed the beauties of nature to pacify her wild thoughts and she calmed down. Indeed, she even smiled, recalling certain small points about Thomas Devlin that amused her. He wasn't quite the fashion plate he at first appeared. She'd noticed the worn collar of his tweed jacket, the threadbare cuff of his white shirt. Even the tie at his neck needed ironing, she thought, delighted to have found so much to complain about. And as for all that blond hair – surely it needed a good cut? It hung down over his pale eyes, giving him the appearance of a shy pony – shy? she asked herself and then laughed aloud. No, whatever Thomas Devlin might turn out to be, he was perhaps self-contained but definitely not shy. More a controlled man who assessed everybody and everything before passing judgement. Indeed, a bit of mystery, one way and the other.

And then, suddenly, all thoughts of the new master fled because something more pleasurable and exciting took her thoughts. She was very near to Sandiford House now, already approaching its iron gate and the long gravel drive leading up to the front porch.

Something stopped her as she reached the gate, and she stood, looking as far as she could into the garden that hid behind the thick hedges. There was the pool that she and Will had paddled in when trespassing as children. They had made camps in the laurel bushes and eaten the apples from the trees in the orchard beyond the garden. It had been a wilderness then, growing far worse over the years, but now? She shook her head, sucking in her breath; the Sandiford estate must have paid many men to work long hours to make it this handsome.

She loitered, wishing she could smell the roses entwining through trellis and arbours, let her bare feet swish through the grass, sit there in the sun, or under the shade of the huge old magnolia tree. Then she thought of Mr Vane, who lived here with his sister. Mr Vane who had got his elegant shoes and clothes wet through, helping her to push out the grounded boat. She laughed, but only for a moment, for she heard voices and the yapping of a dog, coming from the house into the garden.

Just for a mad second or two she toyed with the idea of going in and asking to see Mr Vane – of thanking him for rescuing her, or apologizing for the wetness of his clothes. It would be good to see him again, that handsome, courteous man who had looked at her in such a warm way, who had remarked on having seen her before, rowing up the river.

But then she remembered the bag of cake she carried and wondered wryly how she would appear to the rich sister, coming to call in this unasked fashion, and with a handout from Miss Hodge in one hand. No, of course she mustn't do any such thing.

Sensibly, she went on her way, but the idea remained in her mind and she knew that she would very much like to see Laurence Vane again. And then, suddenly, as if brought to reality by her imagining, there he was – a figure in the distance carrying painting equipment. As he neared, she saw easel, palette and a bag no doubt filled with paints and brushes. A laugh bubbled up inside her and she quickened her pace until they were within hailing distance. Then she raised her hand and called, 'Hallo, Mr Vane.'

He paused, put down the things he carried and waited until she reached him. Then he held out his hand, smiling, and saying, 'What a pleasant surprise. Miss Rose Adams on a lovely summer day – what could be nicer? And just what I need to cheer me up.'

Standing quite still, she looked at him. Yes, a handsome man, even if slightly – what was the word – Bohemian? with his collar-long hair, beard, moustache and thick sideburns that hid the angle of his jaw. Her smile grew. 'And why do you need to be cheered up, Mr Vane? Isn't all right with your world?'

His mouth twisted into an ironic grin and he nodded. 'You may well think it is, Miss Adams, but, alas, the painting doesn't go well. I stand on the river-bank for hours on end, looking at the view and daubing my canvas, but what I paint doesn't really excite me. Now, if it were a different sort of view . . .' His smile grew and he raised an eyebrow. His voice grew softer, more intimate and Rose waited, half-shocked, half-excited.

'Miss Adams, please say if I'm being insolent, or rude, or even patronizing – but I must tell you that I have a longing to paint you. Would you consider posing for me? Oh, not out here, of course, I mean in my studio at home. At Sandiford House. My sister is always there, also the servants, and I would be so very pleased if you agreed to do so.'

Rose was dumbfounded and said nothing. Pose for a painting? Images

flew into her mind. Naked models, drink and possible unwanted intima-
cies. And then, as if he read her mind, Laurence Vane stepped nearer and
took her hand in his.

He lowered his voice and she thought she heard a tinge of humour
colour it. 'Whatever you're thinking, Rose,' he said quietly, 'just isn't
what I have in mind. Let me tell you this: modelling for an artist is an
everyday job in London – where I come from – and since I've been down
here I've felt the need for someone to come and inspire my painting. And
now, when I look at you, I feel I've found that someone.'

He looked into her doubtful eyes, and added very softly, chuckling
slightly, 'You owe me a favour, you know. Those wet clothes and ruined
boots – do you remember? Well, they deserve a little thank you, don't
you agree? So please say yes, Rose Adams.'

A huge wave of longing – painful, exhilarating, thrilling – swept
through her. Yes! She wanted so badly to go into that old house, to meet
the rich widow, see her clothes, hear her cultured voice, learn about the
moneyed lifestyle Mrs Mount shared with Laurence. Rose caught her
breath; already she was thinking of him as Laurence, no longer Mr Vane.
Thoughts charged through her mind. *It's what I want! The new life I'm
looking for – yes, yes!*

But then, as fast as they came, the honeyed images changed. She was
back inside her own poverty-stricken home. She looked at Mother's lined
face and saw the pain etched on it. Father was back, eating his tea, cursing about the fish bones, smelling of drink. . . .

For a seemingly everlasting moment she looked into Laurence's
amused and hopeful eyes and saw there the reflection of a red-haired
daughter of a rough bargee, a girl with no right to dream so wickedly, so
extravagantly. A girl who had, above all, a duty to her family.

Taking a deep breath she stepped away from Laurence and said, with
only a hint of a tremble in her voice, 'Oh no! Thank you, Mr Vane, but
I couldn't possibly do such a thing.' Then, picking up her skirt to avoid
the long grass, she walked around him, towards the river, and Canal
Cottages where she belonged.

CHAPTER FIVE

Jack Adams came lurching home late that night and slept with his head on the kitchen table, snores trumpeting up the stairs and into Rose's wakeful ears. She heard her mother restlessly moving on the big bed next door and thought perhaps she should go to her. But she knew Alice was used to Jack's drinking bouts, and she disliked the idea of a possible confrontation if he should wake up while they were together, talking about him.

She slept at last, but felt weary when she awoke. Her first thoughts were of Sandiford House and Laurence Vane, but then she heard Alice going downstairs and the fire being kindled for breakfast. Low voices rumbled but there seemed no disturbance between her parents. Quickly she dressed and went down to join them, longing to tell them about the suggestion that she should model for Laurence, but fearing that her father would pounce, making the whole idea dirty and ridiculous. And no doubt her mother would also have doubts. Girls like Rose Victoria Adams were only fit for domestic service, it seemed.

Rose's mouth turned down as she helped Alice cut chunks of bread and stir thin porridge. Jack washed in the bowl by the door, throwing glances over his shoulder, making Rose feel as if her very presence irritated him. When he sat down at the table he stared at her turned-away face. 'Well? What you doing next? Another job, is it? Someone told me as 'ow you fancy the chap up at Sandiford House. Saw you with him, apparently. So what's that all about, eh?'

Rose tensed, half-turned and looked into his eyes. 'Yes,' she said curtly, 'I was talking to Mr Vane. He helped me last week when I had trouble with the boat. That's all.' She couldn't help adding, 'Who said they'd seen me, then?'

Jack laughed and crammed bread into his mouth. He munched noisily before saying, 'Wouldn't you like to know, eh? Guilty conscience, is it, then, Rose Victoria?'

Alice, pouring tea into thick mugs on the table, shot a dark glance at him. 'Jack, don't go on so. You'm making something out of nothing. Now, eat up or Joe'll be here an you'll miss the tide.'

Muttering something, he finished his bread, slurped porridge out of his bowl, at the same time putting on his jacket and reaching for his cap hanging on the door. 'Women,' he growled. 'I dunno . . .'

The door creaked open and they heard him shouting to Joe as they went up the path towards Abberton and the clay cellars.

Alice looked at Rose as she sat down to have her own breakfast. 'What was that he said? You and that Mr Vane?'

Rose was silent, thoughts running around in confusion. Should she tell Mother, who would quickly put paid to any local rumours? Or keep quiet and let it die away? Her mouth pursed. But rumours never died away here in the canal community. They just grew bigger and nastier.

Looking across at her mother she saw uneasiness tightening the pale face, and knew she must tell the truth, come what may. She and Alice had never had any secrets – until now. It would be a relief to tell her about Laurence's suggestion.

'Mr Vane was coming back from painting when I met him yesterday, Mother,' she said, pushing her mug across for a refill from the big brown teapot. 'He asked me if I would agree to let him paint me. To become . . .' She paused, the word still slightly unacceptable in her mind, '. . . a model, he said. To go to Sandiford House and sit for him.'

She wasn't ready for Alice's response. 'Oh, my dear soul, no!' Suddenly the mug dropped from her hand and tea spread all over the table. 'You can't do that, Rose, not go to the house.'

'Why not?' Rose fetched a cloth and wiped the pool of spilt tea, looking at her mother as she did so.

Alice's face was flushed and her mouth trembled. She stood up, moving the teapot to allow Rose to wipe beneath it. 'Because, because – it wouldn't be seemly, that's why. Not you up there, and a painter – why, who knows what he'd get up to? Painters are . . . well . . .' Abruptly she sat down again, but her eyes were locked on Rose's face.

Rose crossed the room, dropped the wet cloth in the bowl Jack had used and returned to her chair. 'Painters are just men, Mother,' she said drily. 'And his sister, Mrs Mount, is there. And the servants. He wouldn't get up to anything – he'd just paint a portrait of me. So what's wrong with that?'

Alice shook her head. Rose thought her mother looked smaller than ever, huddled in the cane chair, staring into the fire. She half-wished she'd never told her about Laurence. But then the old rebellious thoughts returned; she only had one life – did she have to give in to other people's wishes? And why couldn't Alice understand the wonderful chance it was, to step into a different sort of life? To meet cultured people? To earn some honest money for a job well done?

'I'm going anyway,' she said sharply, and met Alice's agonized eyes. 'I'm sorry, Mother, if you don't like the idea, but I see nothing wrong in it. I'm going to call and tell Mr Vane I'll model for him just as soon as I've washed these dishes.'

She stood up, collected plates and mugs, then looked at Alice with new eyes. Now she saw hurt, worry and unnecessary fears. Gently, she went to her mother, put her arms around her and kissed her cheek. 'Please try and understand,' she whispered. 'It's such a chance for me – I need to do it, Mother.'

They stayed in their embrace until Alice slowly sat up, slipping out of Rose's arms. 'Yes, I see,' she said and managed a small, painful smile. 'I'm sorry I was so quick to try and stop you.' She found a rag and wiped wet cheeks. 'You must do what you want, Rose. But be careful, my love – be very careful. I mean, you don't know nothing about this man.'

Rose felt relief and renewed excitement. 'I know one thing, Mother; he's a gentleman,' she said brightly. 'A big, heavy one, and he dresses elegantly. And he's got a lovely voice. And he's friendly – so you've got nothing to worry about. I'll make sure he brings my portrait and shows you when it's finished! You'll be proud of me then.'

Alice nodded. 'I'm always proud of you, maid.' Her voice was hardly audible, but they looked at each other lovingly until Rose said briskly, 'I'll do the dishes, Mother, and then I'm going up to Sandiford House.'

But it was mid-morning before she got away from the chores and walked slowly up the grassy river path, enjoying the fresh breeze blowing down from the moor and the shushing song of the river flowing so peacefully at her side. Her thoughts strayed to the future. If Laurence Vane wanted her as a model, she would be earning regular money again. Mother, in spite of her naïve fears – Rose laughed to herself – would be glad of the extra, and Father could no longer make spiteful comments on her lack of employment. And school would start in another four weeks . . . here, her smile died and she began to quicken her pace. Thinking about Thomas Devlin and her position working with him was something that just didn't fit in with this beautiful and hopeful day.

The marshes were green and lush, the trees in full-leafed splendour. A heron fished sedately at the end of one of the bigger pools, and Rose thought she saw the flash of a kingfisher's brilliance speeding away down the stream which flowed through the marshes and on into the village. She paused, hearing a dog barking and a voice shouting, then walked on. Villagers often walked on the marshes with their dogs.

But this dog sounded as though it was in trouble. She turned off the path, heading for the house. And there she saw him – Charlie Wheeler at the open iron gate, shouting and taunting a small dog that raced around his feet, yelping as his long stick flicked over its back.

Rose's anger knew no bounds. She was at the gate in three quick strides, her hands snatching at Charlie's jacket and pulling him back. 'Stop it! Drop that stick and leave the dog alone. Charlie, do you hear me? *Stop it* this minute . . .'

The boy shrugged away from her, turned and grinned into her angry face. 'I'm just talking to dear little Henrietta.' He gave another wave of the stick, reaching out with it and making the dog leap backwards. 'Henny, Henny, what a stoopid little dog you are . . . bet you wouldn't know a rabbit if you saw one! I'll bring my collie Fly tomorrow – he'll teach you a thing or two.' Again the stick rose and fell, catching the little dog in the ribs, making it howl with pain.

Rose heard a flurry of feet, a voice calling out in anguish, but was too busy wrenching Charlie's arm away from the dog to pay much attention. 'I'll be seeing your father about this, you wicked boy . . .'

Charlie laughed but turned away, running suddenly as the voice in the garden grew nearer and louder. Rose picked up the frightened dog, and made sure the gate was closed behind her before walking up the drive towards the house. She'd only got halfway when a large woman appeared around a bend, marching along and calling, 'Henny, Henny! Where are you, my darling?'

Suddenly they were face to face and Rose stood still, clutching the dog, knowing this must be Mrs Mount, Laurence's sister. How on earth should she introduce herself? 'Good morning,' she began, but said no more as the woman thrust out her arms to take the dog into her embrace, burying her face in its fur, and covering the soft little head with kisses as she murmured endearments.

Rose was touched. Forgetting the awkwardness of the meeting she said gently, 'I don't think the dog is badly hurt – just frightened and so she made a lot of noise.'

The woman looked up and said unsteadily, 'Thank goodness you were here. It was that hateful boy, he's been here before, taunting the poor little darling.' Slowly her voice steadied, and she smiled at Rose. 'I'm Elizabeth Mount – the new tenant here; who are you?'

'Rose Victoria Adams.' She saw Elizabeth's florid face register ignorance and added quickly, 'I'm a schoolteacher. I work here, in the village. It's holiday time at the moment – yes, I'm glad I was . . .' she paused, then added the word 'passing' with a quick stab of guilt at the lie, before continuing, 'I shall tell Charlie's father of his shocking behaviour and make sure he comes and apologizes to you.'

She watched Elizabeth Mount shift the panting little dog from one arm to the other. Then she held out her right hand, shaking Rose's and beaming at her. 'I'm delighted to meet you, Miss Adams. You must come in, my brother will be glad to have some company.' She began walking towards the house and Rose had no option but to accompany her, listening to the cultured, rather high voice saying, 'We've only been here a few weeks so our social life is very quiet.'

Rose felt herself being assessed before Elizabeth Mount smiled at her 'Yes, do come in – I expect you'd care for a cup of coffee after all your exertions with that horrid boy.' She led the way into the house through the open french window on the terrace. 'Do sit down – I'll tell my brother we have company.' She put the dog down who at once raced back into the garden and disappeared, and indicated a large Chesterfield covered with cushions. She went to the wall beside the fire, rang a bell, and then disappeared into the passage in search of her brother. Her voice drifted back to Rose. 'Coffee in the drawing-room, Pellew, please.'

Rose stood in the middle of the spacious high-ceilinged, wood-panelled drawing-room and held her breath as she looked around her. Had she been picked up by some magic genie and unexpectedly dropped into a cave of delights? The sun gleamed through the windows, shining on dark, polished furniture and lighting up the china and silver ornaments placed all round the room. On the walls were portraits of men and women in unfamiliar clothing. Their hard eyes stared down at her, following as she moved her head looking from one delight to the next.

She thought her heart might overflow, so great was her pleasure. There was something about this room that captivated her, brought strange feelings and images. Like a dream encompassing her, suddenly it was full of memories, and quick visions of those who had spent their lives here. She shook her head, *stop imagining – come back to reality*. Such a warm room where every chintz-covered chair looked inviting, where life was elegant and not wanting for a single thing. She caught her breath: *imagine living here . . .*'

Footsteps approached, and a man's voice sounded. 'I've told you before, Elizabeth, Henny shouldn't be allowed so much freedom. She gets excited and then she barks all the time, and quite honestly I find it very distracting. No wonder the wretched boy teased her . . .'

Laurence Vane followed his sister into the drawing-room and came to a quick stop. 'Why, Miss Adams! What a pleasant surprise.' He stood in front of her, holding out his hand. Taking it, she felt her heartbeat surge, wondered what was happening to her. She had no idea what to say. There was amusement in his eyes, concealed mirth in the conventional words of greeting and his hand pressed hers for a moment longer than she expected.

She stepped away, turning to Elizabeth Mount, trying to explain. 'Your brother did me a good turn the other day . . .' when again she met his eyes and saw the wicked gleam in them, 'I had a slight accident on the river. My boat grounded, and he kindly helped me right it again. I'm afraid he got very wet.'

Laurence was leading her to a chair by the open window. She sat down, looking at Elizabeth Mount to see what reaction her words had caused. But he stood in the way, laughing as he made the excuse of plumping up the cushion at her back. 'Yes, indeed, I did get wet. My boots won't ever be the same again, I fear. Ah, here's coffee. How do you like it, Miss Adams? Dark, or with cream? And sugar?'

Rose's pride swelled. He was making fun of her – how dare he. Of course he guessed that she'd never drunk coffee in her life. But she was educated. She knew about coffee beans and the paraphernalia of the drinking of the brew. So she sat up very straight, smiled into his amused face and said calmly, 'Thank you, Mr Vane. I prefer mine without cream, and no sugar.' Desperately, she prayed that she would like the taste and not show her ignorance.

If he was surprised, he didn't show it, instead going to the table where the maid had put the tray carrying a silver coffee pot, milk jug, sugar bowl and three fine china cups and saucers. He began to pour. 'Sit down, Elizabeth, you've had a nasty shock and you look a little pale. Perhaps a tot of brandy in your coffee would do you good.'

His sister shook her head, but Rose saw Laurence take a silver flask from his pocket, unscrew it and add a drop, not only to his sister's cup, but a larger amount to his own. He raised an eyebrow at Rose, holding out the flask, and chuckling when very quickly she said 'No, thank you.'

'Nectar of the gods,' he remarked, bringing their cups to them. At Rose's side he lingered, eyes amused, and saying quietly, 'A drop of spirits is very good for the nerves, you know . . .'

Rose stirred her coffee and returned his glance, her annoyance aroused. 'Thank you, Mr Vane, I'm quite aware of the properties of brandy, even if I don't require them at this particular moment.'

He cocked an eyebrow, as if acknowledging her sarcasm, nodded and carried his cup to a chair opposite hers. There, he sat and crossed his legs, watching her as she sipped the coffee.

It was difficult for her to drink without showing how much she disliked the strong, bitter taste. Why had she refused the cream? It might have made the stuff palatable. As she put down the cup she met Laurence's wry gaze and smiled, determined to pass off the awkward moment. 'And are you painting today, Mr Vane?'

Elizabeth Mount cut in at once. 'Yes, he'll be off to the river-bank soon, I daresay. Such wonderful views all around here, Miss Adams . . .' She paused, looked at Rose over the rim of her cup. 'And do you live locally? In the village, perhaps?'

Rose's confidence faltered, but she met the curious gaze evenly. 'Not in the village, Mrs Mount, but down by the river. Actually' – she raised her head an inch higher – 'in one of the cottages just beyond the canal. My father is a lighterman – he takes clay from the pits down to the estuary at Culmouth in his barge.'

There was a silence, registering intense shock. Elizabeth Mount pointedly averted her eyes. She dusted one sleeve of her dark dress and then looked across the room at her brother. Her voice was stiff. 'Perhaps you will accompany Miss Adams when she returns home, Laurence. It sounds as if she has a dangerous journey – down there by the water.'

Her tone told Rose exactly what she was thinking: *a poor girl who has no right to be here in my house.* Rose's spirits flared. How dare this red-faced fat woman look down upon her? 'Thank you, Mrs Mount, but I'm perfectly safe – I've lived here all my life, and I know every inch of the path.' She turned her head sharply, meeting Laurence's eyes, and seeing a gleam of admiration in them. 'And of the marshes. Indeed, I've known this house since I was old enough to come and scrump apples from the orchard in the autumn.'

Again silence, but this time full of expectation and surprise. Elizabeth Mount looked at her with a different expression on her florid face. 'Really? So you know this house?'

'I've never been inside before,' Rose said, 'but I'm used to seeing it here. It was empty for a long time after Miss Edwina Grey died.'

She saw interest mounting in Elizabeth's eyes despite obvious disapproval. 'Miss Grey? Why, I believe her bedroom is still untouched – there was no time to do all the repairs. It will have to be seen to before long. So Edwina Grey was the last person to live here?'

'Yes. She was the daughter of Harold Grey, who owned many of the clay pits in the district. After her death the house was left to decay.' Rose offered a placating smile. 'That is, until you came, Mrs Mount – and of course, as I can see, the house is beautifully restored now.'

'Yes.' Elizabeth Mount turned her head, met her brother's watchful eyes. 'What a strange tale, Laurence, is it not? To think that Miss Adams has been able to tell us so much . . .' She looked back at Rose and now her smile seemed warmer and more genuine. 'You must call again, Miss Adams. And perhaps you might remember a few more details about the house to tell us.'

Rose took this as her cue to leave. She rose and was about to thank her hostess when Henny's shrill barking at once made Elizabeth Mount turn and rapidly walk through the french windows on to the terrace, her voice wailing back to them. 'If that vile boy has come back, I shall get the gardener to deal with him.'

As she disappeared, Laurence came to Rose's side. 'Just the chance I need, Miss Adams. Come along, I'll show you my studio and then you can tell me if you have changed your mind about modelling for me.' He slipped a hand beneath her elbow, and she felt herself being guided towards the staircase in the middle of the hall.

Unsure whether to refuse to go with him, but extremely interested in the idea of seeing his work in the studio, Rose allowed herself to be taken up the stairs, her hands resting on the elegant mahogany banisters, along long shadowy passages and then up another flight of stairs, uncarpeted this time and with rough handrails, until Laurence opened a door and she stepped into a large, airy and sun-filled room at the top of the house. Laurence closed the door behind them, then gestured to the wide, uncurtained windows. 'Look, Rose! You can see a different world from up here. This was servants' bedrooms long ago, I understand, but I've made it into my studio. The light is wonderful.'

So she was Rose, no longer Miss Adams. Elation made her suddenly sure of herself and the idea of working in this warm, spacious room. Following him to the window, she stared out. The marshes gleamed beside the dancing river. She heard birds calling, saw them in the garden below, flying around the blue cedar tree at the end of the double borders. Elizabeth Mount could just be seen, cuddling Henny and no doubt telling the attentive gardener beside her the sorry tale of the boy teasing her beloved pet.

Rose felt Laurence come close. He had a certain presence about him; that of a gentleman with cultured tastes and opinions, and a definite charm. She savoured the word *presence*, often read about but never before experienced. She felt something dangerous, too – was it a sense of wildness, of nonconformity? Smelling brandy and cigar fumes, suddenly she longed to turn her head and smile at him. But she did not do so, her upbringing was too strongly implanted. She was only here as his servant.

Nodding, she said quietly, 'Yes, the view is beautiful. And this room is . . . interesting.'

Turning, she looked all round her. Wide floorboards were bare and polished, with a couple of Turkish rugs in the centre of the room where an empty easel stood. Canvases with their paintings turned away lined the pale, empty walls. There was an unfamiliar smell – she guessed it was turpentine and perhaps size. An armchair covered in plum-coloured brocade with matching cushions stood at the other end of the room, beneath a window facing away from the marshes. Then her eyes rested on a scuffed wooden dais facing the easel and she slowly exhaled the held breath in her body.

This was where she would pose. A bentwood chair stood on the dais and she imagined how she would sit on it, her face turned towards Laurence at the easel, the all-important light falling on her features. She would have to sit very still. How long did a sitting last? What clothes would she wear? As if the question had its answer within the room, she turned her head, looking around for – what?

She realized now that Laurence had been watching, no doubt perceiving her naïve thoughts. He went towards a wardrobe at the far end of the room, opened it and took out a dark dress, carrying it over his arm and coming to her side.

'I want you in this colour,' he said, the words tumbling out. 'That hair, and this dress – when can you come, Rose? I long to start work . . '

She saw passion in his eyes and felt a quick stab of apprehension. 'I haven't agreed to do it yet, Mr Vane.'

'Please – Laurence.' He held the dress up, his hands touching her shoulders. 'Of course you'll come. You want to – I know you do. I can see it in your face – you like the idea of being here.'

Uncertainly, Rose smoothed her hands over the soft silk, feeling its quality and sensuousness, looked into the colour which seemed to change in the gleaming sunlight; dark blue one moment, darkest sea-green the next. Yes, it would show up her red hair. She felt something of his impatience, his excitement – indeed, his passion – and said quickly, 'All right, I'll be your model.'

He smiled into her eyes as if she'd given him a joyous gift. 'Thank you, Rose. *Thank you.* You won't regret it. I'll pay you what I paid my girls in London. Come tomorrow, will you? As soon as you can – first thing in the morning, when the light's strong . . .'

Rose strove for self-control, and achieved it. 'Thank you, Laurence,' she said calmly. 'I'll be here at ten o'clock.' Suddenly the day was drab and ordinary again, and the recent past filled her mind. Her smile died. 'I hope your sister won't object to my coming?'

His face tightened and he frowned, taking the dress back to the wardrobe. 'My painting is nothing to do with Elizabeth. Come in the back way and straight up the servants' stairs. She need never know you're here if you're careful about it.'

Rose paused. Secrets, with a hint of a slightly inappropriate relationship? For a second her mind darkened. Then she went to the door, looked back over her shoulder and met his following gaze. 'I wouldn't dream of doing that,' she said crisply. 'I feel no shame in being your model, so I shall come to the front door. And perhaps you'll be there to greet me, and explain to Mrs Mount?'

Just for a moment she thought he was angry. His face was rigid, his eyes narrowed, but then his whole expression softened, and he came to her side, laughing, as he said, 'I'll be there, Rose. We'll face Elizabeth and her old-fashioned ways together, shall we? Come, I'll take you home. A walk by the river will do me good and as I come back I'll gather my thoughts about how I shall pose you tomorrow.'

Together they went down the stairs and out into the garden, where the sun warmed Rose's suddenly cold body, and encouraged her to think positively. Had she taken a fateful step into the new life that she had always felt was waiting – could it be here?

CHAPTER SIX

'We'll face Elizabeth and her old fashioned attitudes together . . .'

Laurence's parting words yesterday were echoing around Rose's mind and reinforcing her natural optimism and courage as she opened the gate of Sandiford House and walked up the drive, a smile on her lips and head held high. *Together* – what a warm, pleasant word that was. All her life she'd felt herself to be alone – perhaps because of being the only child in the family. But it had been deeper than that: a sense of strange knowledge insisting that in some way she was different from her playmates living in the other cottages along the river-bank.

I wonder . . . thought Rose, but got no further, as crunching footsteps approaching her on the gravel drive brought her back to the present reality.

'Good morning, Rose.' Laurence halted, smiling broadly and holding out his hand to take hers.

Instantly she felt protected – cherished, almost: something so unfamiliar that her returning smile was as broad as his. 'Good morning, Laurence.'

Strength and a feeling of companionship travelled through their momentarily clasped hands, and then she slid hers away. 'How good of you to come and meet me.' Then, for a second, anxiety stabbed; would he tell her if Elizabeth had disapproved of her becoming his model?

But he had read her thoughts, understood the expression on her face. 'Elizabeth and I discussed my need of a model, Rose, and we – quite amicably in the end . . .' here he paused and winked before finishing, 'came to a civilized agreement. You are to be referred to as Miss Adams, the schoolmistress, who is working with me in my studio on a project which will help to educate the children when school starts again.'

Rose was silent. Of all things she had not imagined this, but slowly she began to smile at the ridiculous fantasy of it. And then she knew she must enforce certain conditions.

'That sounds a good idea, Laurence,' she said crisply, 'but I want your assurance that you really will do something for the children, as well as paint me.'

He half-turned, looked at her, smile vanishing. 'Oh come now, Rose, it was just a subterfuge to get you into the house without losing your reputation – you know that, surely?'

'I understand, but I cannot come unless you promise to keep your word to your sister.' She stopped, staring into his eyes, willing herself to keep calm, to keep strong, to do the right thing.

He frowned, twisted his mouth and then with relief she saw the smile appear again. 'What a strange girl you are, Rose.' His voice was low. 'Very well, I'll agree to your terms. How would it be if I painted a picture of the marshes and then brought it to the school so that your pupils could tell me what animals and birds I've put in it?'

Rose clasped her hands. 'That would be wonderful – just what they need as an object lesson, which is how we teach them to observe things. Thank you, Laurence.' They approached the front door, which was half-open, and she added, 'And thank you, too, for persuading Mrs Mount to accept my respectable situation in your house.'

On the steps he put a hand on her arm and turned her to face him. His chuckle grew into a loud, appreciative laugh, and he said, 'Rose, Rose, you're a girl in a million. A respectable situation, indeed! I've never heard modelling called that before but I can see how wrong I've been. You'll bring the job into the realms of the aristocracy, I'm sure!'

Not sure how to answer this, Rose just said quietly, 'I can only promise to do my best, Laurence.'

'Of course.' He was guiding her through the door and up the stairs. 'A woman with intelligence and wit as well as beauty – you're exactly what I need, Rose. And I can't wait to get to work – come along.'

They went up the stairs, along silent corridors and up the bare, creaking staircase leading to the attic and the big, light-filled studio. In the doorway Rose stopped, eyes at once going to the dais and the chair on which lay the dress Laurence had shown her yesterday. Today she saw a Japanese screen in a corner of the room, and immediately turned to him. 'You expect me to undress behind that?'

'Of course. It's what all models do.'

His grin made her stiffen. 'But I'm not just one of all your other models, Laurence. I'm respectable Miss Adams – have you forgotten already?' She smiled, trying to make her complaint humorous, and was reassured to see him smiling even more.

'What do you want, then?' Was he laughing at her?

She didn't care; the imagined intimacy of going behind the screen, knowing he was just a few feet away, was unthinkable. Her cheeks flushed. She had no intention of this being anything other than a business proposition, even though he was so friendly; especially as he was so attractive. 'Some proper privacy,' she said, head in the air. 'A room, perhaps?'

He considered. 'There's nothing else on this floor . . . Oh, very well – go down the stairs and there are a couple of unoccupied rooms in that corridor.'

He turned away and she saw him gathering up brushes and finding a paint-covered smock as she picked up the dress and left the room.

Down the stairs the corridor lay in shifting sunlight. She stopped outside the first closed door and tried the handle. The door opened slowly and reluctantly, with a creak. The room was musty and dim, the curtains pulled across the windows. For a moment she hesitated, then shut the door behind her and looked for a dust-free space, knowing that she had done the right thing in insisting on having this privacy.

Blouse, skirt and belt neatly folded and placed on a chair beside the bed, Rose laid her hat on top of the pile, lifted the dress and slipped it over her head. It eased itself over her camisole and petticoat as if it had been made for her, the whisper of silk making her shiver as she enjoyed the sensuous feel. Tiny buttons fastened tightly at wrist and neck and she was ready. Enjoyment touched her as she quickly left the room, closing the door, climbing the stairs again, and entering the studio's brilliant light.

Laurence, at his easel, clad in the old smock, looked across the room and stared at her. She thought he was seeing his imagined woman in a boat – not Miss Adams, at all, and then, abruptly, she realized they were sharing dreams – his of the next portrait, and she of a lifestyle she had never known.

Strangely, she felt at ease as she approached the chair on the dais and sat down. She wondered, as he lifted his eyes from his palette and looked at her, whether, with his perception and sensitivity, he could possibly know how she felt. Would he be aware that in this dress, this room, on this dais in this old house, she had suddenly become a different, new woman? A smile lifted her lips, and she hoped he did.

Rose's life had changed. Now she spent her days organizing her time between modelling for Laurence, helping Alice and her near neighbours with the chores of fetching water, walking to the farm for milk, hanging out washing and keeping an eye on the small children as they played at the river's edge. But the chores were soon forgotten as soon as she crossed the marshes and knocked on the door of Sandiford House.

Daisy Pellew, the housemaid who had brought coffee into the drawing-room on her initial visit, had gossiped around the village, and Rose realized that by now everybody knew she was accepted by Mrs Mount and Laurence – even though she was modelling for him – and was therefore someone to watch. But she no longer cared. If the village folk – and their enemies in the canal cottages – all wanted to make fun of her, what of it? She was earning good money now and quite enjoying it, which was something she had been worried about.

At first Laurence had been peremptory with his instructions. 'Sit straighter, will you? I want to get the line of your shoulders . . . no, no, don't twist like that! For goodness sake, Rose . . .'

She had been in two minds then whether to get up and leave, hearing the impatience and irritation in his quick words, but then knew she would be foolish to do so and so always regret the opportunity of sampling a better life. So she sat there, meekly accepting his orders, and, within the first week, discovering that she enjoyed the business of sitting, watching his brush moving, making a picture she couldn't see, meeting his eyes as they looked at her across the room and, most of all, thinking about the pleasure and strangeness of being here, in Sandiford House.

She walked home over the marshes at the end of each day feeling quite content, and wondering how long it would be before Laurence allowed her to view the portrait.

'Not yet, Rose, I'll tell you when I'm ready.' He was charming and friendly again, no longer having to keep changing her poses. She imagined the portrait would be merely of a girl in a blue-green dress sitting upright on a hard chair. It would be exciting to see the finished picture. She smiled to herself, and then:

'Rose! Rose!'

Jessie Smith emerged from behind a full-leafed hawthorn tree, swinging her hat by its ribbon and holding a wilting bunch of sky-blue vetch and white moon-daisies. Her hair blew in the mild breeze and her smile was radiant 'Rose, I was coming to see you. Your mam told me you was up at the house. Rose, do you think . . .'

'Wait a minute, Jessie. You're talking so fast I can't make out what you're saying!' Rose stopped and looked into vivid hazel eyes dancing with excitement. 'Now, why do you want to see me?'

For a second Jessie paused, seeming to be considering her words, which Rose found very uncharacteristic. Then she said, more sedately, 'Shall we sit down for a minute? The grass is dry – here's a nice little patch . . .' She went down on her knees, brushing away leaves before looking up at Rose and smiling invitingly. 'Come on, sit down.'

'Well, how are you, Jessie? Still haymaking with Will Sharcombe? That's the last thing I heard . . .' Rose sat beside her, thinking how refreshing it was to sit among lush grass with flowers wafting fragrance all around and the river's quiet song filling the background. She watched Jessie's expression. Was that a blush? Was Will the reason for it?

But Jessie tossed her head. 'That's finished. Haymaking's over. No, I'm looking for a settled situation, and that's why I'm here, Rose. You see . . .' She picked out a couple of daisies from her bunch and began threading one through the stem of the other, adding a floating bit of vetch to weave into a chain.

Rose watched, wondering. So Jessie had decided to grow up, had she? 'Go on, then, tell me.' She smiled approvingly, knowing she would try and help the girl if she could.

'You're up at the big house now. You know the gentry. Everybody says as you do. Rose.' Jessie turned and looked intently into Rose's widening eyes. 'I wants a job in the kitchen there, Rose. You could get me in, couldn't you? Tell 'em how good I am, quiet and a good character an' all that. . . . Rose, will you do that? Oh, please, Rose.'

What was she to say? If Jessie really wanted to go into service of course she must be encouraged. But – working for Mrs Mount? Could she truthfully recommend Jessie as having a good character? And, supposing the girl was taken on, how would Daisy Pellew and the other villagers employed up there treat her?

Rose thought hard, watching Jessie's adroit fingers working on the flower rope, finally linking the top to the bottom so that it became a real chain. Then she blinked as the girl leaned towards her, put the flowery necklace around her neck and said softly, 'There, you looks lovely, Rose. And you'll help me, I knows you will.'

Jessie's pleading smile was too much for Rose. She fingered the flowers, returned the smile and said, with only a touch of wryness, 'All right, Jessie, but you've got to promise that you'll behave. No arguments, no running off like you did before.' She paused then added sternly, 'and no more visits to the inn and dancing on the table – oh yes, I know all about that.'

For a moment the girl said nothing, just looked at the grass around her. Then she lifted her head, met Rose's eyes, and said quietly and with what sounded like a convincing sincerity, 'I promise. I wants a good situation, see. I needs to settle down.' She bent her head and smiled.

Rose was curious. She waited, but Jessie said no more. So she got to her feet, dusted off her skirt, and took the girl's hand, pulling her up. 'Very well, Jessie. I'll certainly recommend you to Mrs Mount and ask her if she'll consider taking you on in some capacity. I don't suppose it'll be more than a skivvy.'

Jessie's smile glowed. 'I don't mind what I do. When will you ask her? Tomorrow? No, it's May Bankes's benefit, isn't it? On Monday, then? Oh, Rose, I can't hardly wait!'

'I'm afraid you must. I shan't be at the house again until then. Yes, I'll mention you and see what Mrs Mount says.'

Skipping along at her side, the girl smiled, looking as if she'd been given a present, Rose thought. 'I'll come and see you on Monday afternoon when you comes back from the big house, then. Thank you, Rose,' and Jessie was off running quickly back towards the river, heading for Abberton, leaving Rose wondering and feeling definitely uneasy. She didn't like the idea that Jessie and, presumably, everyone else knew her daily movements. And the fact that the girl wasn't going home, but running towards the town also worried her. The clay cellars were on the way to Abberton – was she going to tell Will Sharcombe the good news that Rose would help to get her into the old house? And how would Will feel about that?

Rose walked home soberly, arriving back at the cottage unsmiling and deep in thought. So deep that when Alice said, 'My word, you looks pretty, love. Someone give you flowers, then?' she looked up in surprise before fingering the necklace and then smiling.

'Yes. Jessie Smith.' She stopped. Something told her not to relate what the girl wanted, and what she had promised to do. Sandiford House wasn't a place her mother liked to talk about, though goodness knew why not.

Alice spread the ironing blanket on the table and reached for the cloth to cover it. She glanced at Rose and there was a shine of excitement in her eyes as she said, 'You'll never guess! Young Charlie Wheeler come this morning with a message for you. Looked all spruced up, never seen the boy so clean and tidy. An' he spoke up well, too, no more of that ol' rudeness.'

'What did he want?' Rose cut into Alice's chatter, watching as she spat on the flat iron heating up on the range, wiped it with a rag, then spread a white shirt on the table and began to smooth out the creases.

'He says that the new schoolmaster, Mr Devlin, is it? wants to see you at five this afternoon. In the schoolroom. Oh, now look at this stain on Jack's best shirt – an' I thought I'd got it off. Oh my, he'll be cross, wanting to wear it tomorrow at the benefit—'

'Five? It's nearly that now – almost teatime.' Rose's impatience flowered. 'Why does he want to see me? And sending Charlie along here? Who does he think he is, this Mr Devlin?' She sat down, watching the iron working on the creased shirt, her irritation growing at the thought of such a peremptory message. If Mr Devlin needed her advice or help, then surely he could have come himself? Not send that young rogue, Charlie. Her thoughts circled. And how could Charlie have been neat and tidy and not as rude as usual? And what did he have to do with the new schoolmaster?

Then it came to her annoyingly that the only way to answer all these questions was to comply with the order. She pursed her lips, took off the floral necklace and stuck it in a jug, put on her hat again and said to Alice, 'Looks like I've got to go, then, Mother. I won't be long. He can't just order people about like this.' She went to the door, then turned back. 'And leave that old ironing. You look much too hot, and Father'll be back for his tea in a minute – let me finish the shirt when I come home.'

Alice nodded, but the excited look was still there in her eyes. 'All right, love. But don't get cross with him – I mean, he'm the one in charge of the school an' you don't want to lose your good situation there, do 'ee?'

Rose left the cottage without replying. Her mother was right, of course, but the surge of anger she felt at the mere idea of having to obey Mr Devlin's every order grew as she strode rapidly up the footpath towards the village, rehearsing words her head and feeling proud of herself as she did so. This Mr Devlin must realize that she wasn't just a humble and ignorant pupil teacher, but a highly respectable young woman who was quite well educated, and also accepted by the local gentry. Clearly, thought Rose, smiling to herself now and enjoying the strong feelings inside her, he had a lot to learn.

Approaching the school, she heard noise inside it. Hammering? Voices loud enough to be heard over the din? Whatever was Mr Devlin doing?

The door was ajar and she entered, stopping at once and staring around. A group of boys was gathered at the far end of the room, with two men standing beside them, all of them looking at piles of timber lying on the floor, beside which lay the long chenille curtains which usually divided the schoolroom in two. What a mess, she thought – *and Miss Hodge and I made quite sure it was tidy when we left at the end of last term.* Why had the curtains been taken down? And what on earth was happening? The vicar, Mr Toogood, full-bearded and whiskery, was there, and beside him was Mr Wheeler, red-faced as usual and bending his head as he talked very loudly and impatiently, frequently pointing down at the pile of wood and then looking at the boys as if challenging them. Words floated across to her.

'Make sure you keep a good straight length with that saw and follow through – haven't I explained that already? You, Charlie, my boy, show the others what I mean . . .'

Rose could hardly believe it, but Charlie Wheeler, neatly dressed and with his hair cut, smiled proudly as he picked up a saw and began work on a piece of timber stretched over the sawbench standing by the far wall.

She couldn't imagine what it all meant. Over by the fireplace she saw Lucy sitting in a hard chair, eyes wide and unsmiling, looking as if she hated being there and would run off if only she had the ability to do so. At once Rose went across, sorry for the child, and hoping to put a smile on the small, pale face.

'Hallo, Lucy – what a noise, isn't it? And all that sawdust . . .' She stopped as someone approached.

'So here you are, Miss Adams,' said Mr Devlin, looking at her sternly as if he considered her late for school. 'I could do with some help. Perhaps you would clear that cupboard and put the contents on the table so that I can sort them out. Yes, that one.'

He stood at her side, pointing to the cupboard where the slates and chalks were kept. Rose stared. He was in his shirtsleeves, threadbare cuffs turned up, his waistcoat covered with dust and tiny chippings of wood. He met her eyes, blinked and then, surprisingly, smiled at her. 'Sorry, Miss Adams. I don't mean to be curt. But there's so much to do, and those lads need a lot of direction, though I'm sure they're doing their best.' He nodded towards the wood-sawing party, his mop of blond hair falling over his eyes. He brushed it back impatiently. 'So if you could deal with this, I'll go along and see what they're up to.'

'But what's happening? Why turn the cupboard out? I tidied it before school ended. It can't possibly need turning out again. And what's all that woodwork about? I don't understand.' Rose's voice rose over the surrounding noise and she watched Thomas Devlin's slate-grey eyes narrow. Clearly he thought she was speaking out of turn, but she didn't care. She kept looking at him, waiting for an answer.

He took a deep breath, sighed it out, then rocked back on his heels, obviously finding it highly disruptive to have someone question him. 'Miss Adams,' his voice was clipped, 'this is now my school and I'm making some much needed alterations. You needn't worry; Mr Toogood and the other trustees of the board all approve of what I'm trying to do. So, if you'll just get on with that cupboard, I'd be obliged.' He turned, looking down at Lucy. 'And you, love, must just sit there for a bit longer. Perhaps Miss Adams can find you a book or something to look at.' He swung away, marching across the room and, thought Rose indignantly, instantly forgetting all about her and his poor little daughter.

By now her opinion of Thomas Devlin had sunk even lower but, grudgingly, she recognized the need to do as he instructed. If she was to keep her situation here, and carry out the plans she had for helping the children, she must hold on to her temper and do as he asked. She walked towards the cupboard, still fuming, but she quickly found a book and took it to Lucy.

'Here you are, it's full of pictures – I'm sure you'll enjoy looking at this, Lucy.' She paused. The child was so still, so pale. 'Are you warm enough? Pull your shawl around your shoulders a bit more.'

Lucy looked at her and managed a weak smile. 'Thank you. I'll just do as Papa said, sit here and wait.'

Rose returned to the cupboard, thoughts raging inside her. The child was either a dimwit or else completely controlled by that madman. As she piled up the slates, carrying them across to the table Thomas Devlin had indicated, she reasoned that Lucy, being crippled, was at the mercy of her father's every whim. And, of course, the child was too small, too young, to feel any rebellion towards his strict regime. Well, Rose thought firmly, if she comes to my class she'll soon learn to speak up for herself.

The continuing work with saw and hammer was raising dust and noisy vibrations now. She watched Charlie and his friends manhandling large sheets of boarding and measuring them against the height of the surrounding walls. A tall bit of rough timber had already been inserted into a dug-out patch of floor, and now the boarding was being attached to it. The curtains remained in a heap on the filthy floor, and Rose began to understand. The schoolroom was about to be divided in a much more permanent way than thin curtains could ever effect.

She sucked in a huge breath, decided enough was enough, and, putting the last box of chalks on the crowded table, walked across the room to where Mr Devlin was showing Charlie and the other boys how to ensure that their hammered nails went in straight and true.

She interrupted him without caring. 'Lucy is cold, Mr Devlin. And I don't imagine all this dust will do her any good. I've cleared the cupboard as you asked, so have I your permission now to take her home? I'll ask Mrs Benthall to make her a hot drink and see that she's looked after until you return.'

Her voice was clear and firm and at once he turned and looked at her. She saw surprise on his saturnine face, and then an expression of frustration. He stood up very straight and she thought, *so still – he's like a tree in winter – bare limbs, waiting for some warmth to help him develop into summer foliage. And so full of energy.*

The ridiculous image brought an unexpected smile to her face, but it went instantly, as he said in a cold, sharp voice, 'Thank you, Miss Adams, for your advice, which I'm sure is well-meant but my daughter will stay where she is until I'm able to take her home myself.'

Rose felt her cheeks colour, but said quietly, 'Very well, Mr Devlin. Just as you wish. And now, have you any other orders for me to perform? If not, perhaps I, at least, may be allowed to go home?'

She sensed his hostility at her tone and enjoyed silently returning it, anger rapidly kindling inside her. And, when he said dismissively, 'nothing else today, Miss Adams, thank you. But I'd be obliged if you could be here at the same time tomorrow. There's still plenty to do in the other side of the room,' she was delighted to have a ready answer.

'Not tomorrow, I'm afraid, Mr Devlin. I think you've forgotten that we shall all be going to May Bankes's benefit.'

She watched his face slide from frustration to grudging acceptance and then back again to irritation. 'Thank you for reminding me. I'd forgotten. Of course, I understand – but perhaps on Monday afternoon you could come again?'

Rose held his gaze and said levelly, feeling she could afford some politeness now that the situation was clear between them, 'If you need me, then I'll come. But before I go, please will you explain what you are intending to do here?'

He raised his shoulders, stretching them and again pushing back the flopping hair, grey eyes lightening with sudden enthusiasm as he said, 'Divide the classroom, of course. Boys need to be taught apart from girls. The partition we're making will help dampen the noise and make learning easier for them.'

Surprise and instant resentment made her voice sharp. 'And the girls? What about improving their conditions, too?'

He smiled and suddenly his face grew warm, his expression light-hearted – almost patronizing, she thought furiously. 'Come now, Miss Adams, we all know that girls don't need the instructions that boys do – after all, most of them will either go into service or get married. Education would be wasted in either case.' He glanced down at the boarding as it was being put in place. 'Now, please excuse me, I really must get on with this.'

Rose left the schoolhouse in a highly inflamed mood. Such egotism. Such high-handedness. She wished with all her heart that Mr Devlin would disappear and take all his uncalled-for and old-fashioned ideas with him.

CHAPTER SEVEN

A thrush's song drifted into Rose's bedroom along with the first flush of dawn and as she awoke to the new day with a mixture of uneasy thoughts and emotions, the liquid notes – sweet, sweet, sweet – soothing and comforting, at once brought her a new sense of contentment.

Yes, the school business was annoying, and she found Thomas Devlin difficult to understand, let alone like, but her life was developing in an unimaginable way. Modelling for Laurence and her acceptance in Sandiford House had done so much for her confidence and her determination to make the most of this new life.

Meeting Mrs Mount, a usual daily encounter now, had been awkward at times; at first there had been just a stiff, 'good day, Miss Adams,' and no more than a quick, disapproving glance as the large woman swept by, but yesterday there had been the hint of a smile, a pause in the hallway, and the greeting had sounded warmer.

'A lovely day, Miss Adams. I hope the school paintings are going well?'

Rose had seized the opportunity to enlarge on the small pictures of animals and household items that Laurence was doing in between painting her portrait. 'Yes, thank you, Mrs Mount. The children are often given things to look at which they must then describe. Object lessons, we call them.'

'Really? What sort of things would they be?' Elizabeth's eyes suddenly showed interest.

'Whatever the teacher can find. Sometimes it's an old shoe,' Rose dared a slight chuckle, and was rewarded by the raising of an eyebrow and an encouraging nod, 'perhaps a kettle, or a box of slate chalk. They don't often see pictures, so these will be very exciting for them.'

'Indeed. I look forward to seeing them, too – and perhaps hearing more about your pupils.' Elizabeth Mount smiled a little more broadly, and then added, with what sounded to Rose like a note of triumph, 'Mr Toogood, the vicar, has suggested I might become a trustee of the school – of course, I haven't decided yet, but it's a possibility. He seems to think I could be very helpful.'

Your money could, most certainly, Rose thought at once, but returned the smile, saying enthusiastically, 'I hope you will accept the post, Mrs Mount – our school needs people who are interested in the improvement of the children's education.'

'Yes. So I imagine. Which reminds me, Mr Wheeler called last week, bringing his son Charles with him. The boy apologized for intimidating Henny,' a loving hand caressed the small dog, 'and promised never to be so wicked again. I accepted his apology, but I fear poor little Henny ran away the moment she saw the boy!'

Rose had joined in the laughter. Then she had watched Elizabeth Mount proceed on her way into the garden before herself climbing the stairs to the attic studio.

Now she dressed quickly, knowing the day of May Bankes's benefit was to be a busy one. So much to do and only a morning in which to get it all done, for the festivities would begin the moment the ancient, traditional horn sounded the noon hour.

Downstairs she found Alice already cutting sandwiches and baking scones. The fire was burning well and the small cottage was hot and full of fragrance.

'Mother, let's have a cup of tea before we finish off the picnic.' Rose steered Alice away from the table and into her cane chair. 'I'll help you – we'll feel a bit stronger once we've had a bite to eat.' She pulled the kettle off the hob and filled the teapot, letting it brew for a few minutes before pouring out a cupful and handing it to her mother.

They sat, eating lumps of bread spread with rosemary lard and drinking their tea until Alice said, 'I do hope your dad will be home in good time. I've got his clean clothes all ready – and he'll need to shave, so we must make sure the kettle's on the boil.' She got up, looking fussed and red-cheeked, thought Rose with a stab of concern.

'Don't worry, Mother. We'll join in the fun when we're ready, and not before. Now – what're we putting in these sandwiches?'

'I've made a mix of mackerel and butter with a touch of gooseberry preserve – young Jessie brought the fish in yesterday morning – got them from that fish boy of hers, I dessay.' Alice spread the mixture on to the slices of bread and Rose began cutting open the still warm scones, ready for their final decoration of clotted cream and home-made raspberry jam.

As she worked she watched her mother. Alice's rheumatic hands were fumbling with the sandwiches, her small face twitching with pain as she forced the knotted fingers to do their work, and Rose was suddenly furious with fate for sending all these problems to her small, patient and uncomplaining mother. To live in a damp, cold cottage alongside the rough and dangerous river was one thing, but to have to cope with pain and disability was another and no one should have to endure it.

One day, she thought determinedly, putting the scones into a laundry basket and covering them with a clean piece of linen cloth, *one day Mother will sit in a comfortable chair with people waiting on her for a change, and no more cares and pain. Yes, she will. I will make it happen. Somehow. . . .*

Anger, coupled with firm resolution, made her thump the table as she worked and Alice looked up with a smile. 'Don't 'ee frown like that, maid. This is gonna be a good day for all of us. Oh, and look, here's your dad back already.'

Jack came into the cottage, filling the doorway and blocking the sunlight from the room. 'Boats're moored,' he said, nodding over his shoulder in the direction of the basin at the head of the canal. 'Now I wants me breakfast. Move over, Rose Victoria, give yer dad a bit of room. Jest remember he's been up all night bringing those old boats back from the harbour. My word, offloading that last lot took me an' Joe a time with the tide bringing in rough waves and all. An' young Billy was a help.' He gave Rose a quick glance and she smiled. 'Well, I'm back now – deserve a bit of some'at good to eat ad drink, don't I, maid?'

'Yes, Father.' She understood he was weary, soaked with seawater, and hungry because last night's meal was eaten twelve hours ago with only a bottle of cold tea and some lumps of stale bread to keep hunger away during the night. Abruptly, she felt a sense of pity for him; something she had never experienced before. But now it came to her that he was a man beyond middle age who worked long hours in dangerous waters where anything disastrous could – and often did – happen. Like her mother, he deserved better of life. So what could she do to ease things along?

But it was Alice who had the answer. 'See, here's a duck egg, Jack. Susan Upcott's eldest girl brought me a couple yesterday and I've saved this one for 'ee. Like it fried, I dessay? And that scrap of salt bacon left over from last week. . . .'

Soon the pan was sizzling, Jack had prised his wet boots off along with his salt-stained jacket and hat, and sat humped in his chair just by the table. He closed his eyes, put his head back on the hard wood and Rose saw exhaustion sweep over his weather-beaten face. Life was so indifferent to people's problems, she reflected bitterly, her dismay increasing and there often seemed little one could do to improve things. *But I can – and I will. I'll get away from here and make a difference to both of them – somehow.*

For a long moment her thoughts circled and she only became aware of her parents talking as Jack scraped the last bit of bread around his empty plate and looked at Alice over the table. 'Done well, ol' gal. Thank 'ee.' Then he put his head back again, closed his eyes and appeared to drift off into noisy sleep.

Alice put a finger to her mouth as she took dirty dishes to the bowl by the door. 'A good nap an' he'll be good as new. And then we must get ready to go.' She looked over her shoulder and smiled. 'Go and get yourself primped up – must look nice for the benefit, you know. All your little pupils'll expect to see their Miss Adams lookin' her best. No, I'll manage this and wait fer yer dad to get dressed afore we joins you up in the field.'

No hope of changing her mind, thought Rose, smiling, and suddenly realizing exactly how much love there was concealed under the everyday bickering and often, on Jack's part, cruel words and actions. Love, such a strange, unpredictable emotion. She climbed the narrow stairs to get her hat and shawl, and wondered if she would ever know it herself.

Noon, and Matt Hook, the oldest inhabitant of Canal Cottages, carried his ancient hunting-horn out into the sunshine, commanded silence from the watchers gathering around him, and blew a long, wavering blast. A second of silence, and then the shouts and cheers rang out. 'Here we go! Off to the field now . . . come on, c'mom. . . .'

Rose, carrying the basket full of sandwiches and scones, followed the throng as they walked into the field bordering the marshes. The sun was overhead, banishing the threat of grey clouds sweeping up from the distant moor, a tantalizing scent of cooking meat filled the air, the river sang a gloriously full song as the tide surged up to Abberton and everybody knew it was holiday time.

May Bankes, in her best straw bonnet trimmed with blue cornflowers, was picked up by two men who linked hands to carry her bandy chair from her cottage along the footpath and into the field where a huge tent had been erected. The cottagers crowded around her, children shouting and running ahead, pet dogs at their heels. Rose smiled as she saw all the excitement and bubbling over happiness, and when she'd watched May eventually collapsing into the chair that was waiting for her outside the tent and not far from the fire where the traditional ox was roasting, she pushed her way to the long trestle-table under the shelter of elm trees where all the donations of food were piled high, adding her own offering to the plates and dishes already on display.

Such a day, thought Rose, retreating from the noise and hubbub of children clamouring for goes at the Aunt Sally stall, or the shooting gallery set up behind the tent. She would pause here, close to the entrance gate, and wait for Mother and Father to arrive. Meanwhile, she looked around her, picking out her pupils among the crowds still arriving. Billy, young Charlie and his accomplice, Ted, in a gang of rowdy boys, teasing the accompanying band of giggling young girls, all dressed in muslin summer frocks. Seeing Charlie made her wonder whether Thomas Devlin really would come – and then the thought fled as she enjoyed the gaiety and jokiness around her.

She saw Alice and Jack deep in the scrum of villagers and canal folk, Alice in her Sunday-best lavender dress, hat trimmed with nodding purple cherries, her hand on his arm, and Jack looking quite neat for a change. His whiskers and beard had been trimmed, his shirt was shining in the sunshine, and the shabby old jacket looked better than usual. Rose thought how handsome he was, except for that hard expression, and felt a stab in her heart. Her mother and father, yet she had always felt so different from them. She waved, making her way towards them.

'What a crowd,' Alice said, smiling, but needing to hang on to Jack's arm for support. 'An' May looks real pleased with it all – we had a good old talk just now.'

Jack looked at Rose and nodded his head. 'Look after yer mum, Rose Victoria – I'm off fer a drink.' He released Alice's arm and disappeared into the tent.

Alice smiled, though her eyes were sad. 'Jest like a man. Now, you go on, maid, and see all yer friends. I wants a word with Susan Upcott – see, she's brought the new baby with her.'

Together they slowly walked across the field until Alice found a chair beside the Upcott family with all six children present, including the newest one, bound round his mother's body in a shawl. 'Sit down, Alice, sit down,' said Susan with gleaming eyes. 'Have 'ee heard about. . . ?'

Rose smiled. There was always something for Susan to gossip about, but her mother would be happy here for a while. She turned away, heading for the river, to watch the races. Already the sun was shifting across the sky, lengthening the shadows and the afternoon fun would soon start. Someone from the village was setting up the greasy pole and handing out pillows from his barrow. A woman was releasing a white duck from a basket, prior to taking bets on how long it would outwit the crowds chasing it around the marshes.

Laurence had been determined to come to the benefit and join in whatever jollity there was, but he hadn't envisaged that Elizabeth would also come. He was halfway across the hall when her autocratic voice made him stop and look round. 'Laurence – where are you going?'

Hiding a frown, he said, 'I'm looking for inspiration for my painting. There's a local fair not far away. I shall be back for luncheon.' He continued on his way to the front door.

But Elizabeth's voice was firm and elder-sisterly. 'Don't be in such a hurry. Wait for me, please, I should very much like to join you.' She came to his side, smiling. 'If I'm to become involved in village affairs I must start finding out about the locals. Wait for me to get ready, Laurence.'

As he wondered crossly how to persuade her to change her mind, she looked doubtfully at his panama hat and Malacca cane. 'Aren't you dressed rather too well for such a peasant affair?'

Laurence scowled. 'Nonsense. This is what I always wear in the summer. And they're not all peasants, you know. Think of our little schoolteacher. Well, if you're coming, Elizabeth, for goodness' sake hurry up. Go and get a hat or what ever you need.' He looked at her, accepted his duty to escort her, and grinned wryly. 'You'll have to walk a bit – and, remember, there aren't any well-swept London pavements in the country.' An afterthought hit him as she moved towards the stairs. 'And leave that wretched dog behind – she'll probably be eaten alive by the farm dogs if she comes.'

Elizabeth didn't reply, but swept away, reappearing five minutes later with a silk-fringed parasol, a reticule, gloves and a large straw hat decorated with gleaming pink feathers.

By this time Laurence had discovered that the increasing noise of voices came from the field bordering the marshes, not far down the lane leading to the village. He offered his arm to Elizabeth as they left the garden. 'What did you do with Henny?'

'I told Mrs Briggs to keep her in the kitchen until I returned.' Elizabeth looked askance at the rough path towards which she was being led. 'Are you sure this is the way? It only leads to a field—'

'Where the cows have been grazing. Pick up your skirts, dear sister – you don't know what you might be treading on.' Laurence's grin brought a faint smile and a cluck of alarm from his companion. They walked on, at last entering the noisy, crowded field and standing still for a moment to get their bearings.

'Ah! A tent – no less than a temple of Bacchus, I expect.' Laurence began walking towards it, until a firm hand pulled at his arm. 'Now, Laurence, don't start drinking so early in the day.'

He pulled away snappishly. 'For heaven's sake, Elizabeth . . .' And then he stopped, seeing Rose threading her way towards them. His frown vanished and he took off his hat, greeting her with a wide smile as she came nearer.

Elizabeth nodded. 'Ah, Miss Adams. How nice to see a face one recognizes amid all these . . .' but Laurence nudged her fiercely and she bit off the patronizing words.

Laurence asked, 'Tell us what to look at first, will you, Rose? You mentioned races and so on – what, in this field?'

Rose laughed. 'On the river, of course! But not until we've had May's celebratory meal.' She smiled at Elizabeth. 'Good afternoon, Mrs Mount. I'm glad to see you here. Why don't you come into the shade beneath the trees by the hedge? They're putting some chairs out there . . . do mind where you tread, won't you? It's easy to trip over in this dry grass.'

Carefully they walked up the field, out of the immediate noise of the crowds already trying their luck at the shooting gallery set up behind the tent, and throwing wooden balls at the Aunt Sally stall not far away. Elizabeth sat down with a heavy gasp. 'I'm just not used to walking in this hot weather,' she complained, but Laurence wasn't listening.

Sitting next to Rose, he was soon chatting away about fetching food from the tent, although his mind was entirely engaged in memorizing her face, her hair, her stance. Her beauty.

'Are we to have some of that roasted animal down there?' he asked lightly, but his thoughts murmured – *pale skin with a touch of cream; straight, elegant neck with never a fold and not one tiny slender bone out of place. And then that hair. . . .* His fingers began to itch, longing to remove the pins that held in place the loose, tidy bun at the nape of her neck.

Rose looked at the ox carcass, by now turning dark brown and smelling rich and strong. 'Of course, Laurence, if you're feeling hungry.' She gave him a mischievous smile. 'Tuppence a slice. Can you afford to treat your sister and me?'

'I'd be delighted to treat you to whatever you like,' he said, quietly enough to avoid Elizabeth overhearing. 'And when all the junketing's over, we'll go into the tent and have a drink to your portrait. Will you come with me, Rose?'

Giving him a straight look, she shook her head. 'Women don't go into inns or tents, Laurence, unless they want to lose their reputations. And I have no mind to lose mine, so I thank you, but must say no.'

They looked at each other for a long few seconds, during which Elizabeth sighed and manipulated her parasol to shield herself from the burning sun. Then Rose said lightly, 'But there's lots to do before the drinking starts. Let's think about the races, shall we? Will you take a turn on the river, Laurence? Can you row?' She paused and her eyes shone. 'How about having a race with me? We can borrow two boats and the men will take bets on us.'

He pretended to consider. 'A race? Where to?'

'Across the river. From the quay by the inn at the bottom of this field, to the inn over on the other side – the Anchor. And then back again.' She was laughing, watching the expression on his face and guessing that somehow he would find a reason to escape from her saucy invitation.

Brushing pollen from his sleeve, he glanced at Elizabeth, who showed signs of extreme boredom. 'I think I must be excused,' he said, smiling as he stood up. 'I'm sure all you really want, Rose, is to get my clothes wet again, so I'll stay safely on firm ground. And now, how about helping me persuade Elizabeth to have a go at the coconut stall?'

And, despite Elizabeth's prompt refusal to do any such thing, some-how they got her up and walking towards the stall where Billy and some of his young friends were chattering. Their shrill voices grew louder. 'Give us a penny, mister, an' if I gets the nut us'll share it . . .'

Onlookers grinned and turned away, but Laurence delved into his pocket, produced four pennies and distributed them to the wide-eyed youngsters. 'Now,' he said sternly, pointing his cane at them, 'let's see what you're made of. And remember, you've just promised me a piece of your nut.'

The boys swallowed hard, took it in turn to throw the balls without any success, then turned, stared at Laurence, who held out a demanding hand, and instantly took to their heels, pushing their way through the laughing onlookers.

Rose shook her head, laughing. 'Those boys! I'm afraid they have few manners, Laurence, but this is their great day, and perhaps we shouldn't be too cross with them.'

He turned, leaving his sister still staring at the running boys in the distance. 'You're too soft by half, Rose. Lads like that need a firm hand.'

'Which they'll get when the new master takes over the school next term.' Her voice was suddenly sharp and Laurence stared, abruptly aware that here was a new Rose, no longer the soft-voiced seemingly amenable girl who had been sitting long hours on that hard chair up in the studio. The thought stirred him. Beauty and a complex personality was something he cherished in a woman. For a second he recalled a certain girl in London, a model, a little like Rose with that heart-stopping same bronze-gold red hair, and then he banished his thoughts. All in the past. This was a new chance.

The meal began with gusto and obvious appreciation. May Bankes's health was drunk, in ale by the men and in tea or cider by the women. 'Good ol' May – three cheers fer the maid. Hip, hip . . .' Hats came off, smiles wreathed every face, and May herself was a bit tearful as she smiled at her grateful customers before dipping back into the mug of gin a well-wisher had treated her to.

Laurence fetched laden plates of puddings and cakes for Rose and Elizabeth and himself; and they sat beneath the same shady elms, watching the rest of the world go by in their noisy groups, waving mugs of small ale and munching great slices of the dripping, roasted ox on thick lumps of bread. A fragrance of food, people and cider fumes from the tent filled the air, and Elizabeth was soon complaining again.

'My head aches so much, I really cannot stay here any longer. Laurence, I wish to return home.'

He sighed, put down his half-empty plate on the grass, glancing longingly at the tent and then looked at his poor, overheated sister. 'Very well, Elizabeth. Can you walk?'

Rose saw how distressed Elizabeth was and cut in at once. 'Just sit here for a moment longer, Mrs Mount, while I see if I can find someone with a gig to take you home. No, Laurence, stay with your sister . . .' She left them and quickly headed for Farmer Sharcombe, sitting outside the tent, gossiping with neighbours.

When she politely explained the situation and asked for a lift home for Mrs Mount, Farmer Sharcombe drank up his cider and agreed to take the lady at once. Like his son, he was ready to do anything for Rosie Adams.

'You'll come with me, of course, Laurence?' Elizabeth, pale beneath her usual florid colour and clearly wilting, bestowed a stiff smile on her willing driver and then looked back at her brother with a frown. 'You can't possibly want to stay here any longer, I mean, all this noise, and the heat, and . . .' She said no more, merely pursed her lips and pulled the parasol closer over her head as if to hide from the noisome fumes surrounding her.

Laurence glanced at Rose, grinned, raised an eyebrow and said reluctantly, 'Of course I'll accompany you, Elizabeth. Is there room for us both?'

The gig swayed and the pony fidgeted as he climbed in behind her, but then it moved carefully through the crowds, out of the field and up the lane towards Sandiford House. Rose watched them go. She wondered very much what they had thought of this peasant celebration and knew, with a wry smile, that no doubt Laurence would tell her exactly what his views were on Monday, when she went to the studio again.

CHAPTER EIGHT

Alone, Rose left the field, wandering along the river path towards the inn. Here, beside her and the cottages was the river, part of all their lives, cool, dangerously still, apart from the wake ripples of passing boats. Oh yes, she thought instinctively, it really is alive today. Swallows dipping and hawking over it, those boys down there flicking each other with water. Does it know that we shall soon be playing risky games on it? Taking chances as we row and swim? Are the weeds on its sandy bottom already to float up, grasping bare legs and bodies and sucking them down again?

Suddenly she was glad enough to hear a voice call her name.

'Rosie!' Will Sharcombe was making his way towards her, his eyes smiling and his suntanned face full of pleasure. 'I bin lookin' fer 'ee.'

'Hallo, Will.' Thoughts of the gossip about him and Jessie Smith flashed through her mind, but she banished them. *For goodness' sake, this is a celebration today, a time when we're all set to enjoy ourselves. Why make trouble?*

So she put a hand on his arm, returned his smile and said, 'I'm just going down to the inn. The races will start soon, and it'll be cooler down there under the trees. This heat's getting worse.'

Will glanced at the sky. 'Storm's comin',' he said, pulling her hand through his bent arm. 'Rain afore night's out, I reckon. And I'm real glad to see you, Rosie – heard that you were working for those new folks up at the big house – that right?'

'Yes, Will. But only till school starts again. Then I shall go back to teaching.' Some inner sense told her not to mention Laurence Vance. 'So tell me how the hay harvest went.'

He was off then and she listened for mention of Jessie, but not a word did he say about anything except the hay, one horse going lame, the ricks not being thatched right, and how the cost of everything soars. Same old farming talk, she thought wryly, and then, suddenly the river's song filled her mind, and she stopped abruptly and shivered, staring into the grey-green waters. Something warned her, but she didn't know what it was.

Will frowned 'What's wrong, Rosie?'

Shaking her head, she forced a smile. 'Nothing. Someone stepping over my grave, maybe.'

He pulled her into the shade of an elder tree, put an arm around her shoulders and said, very quietly, 'No one'll do that any more if you'll make it real, us bein' sweethearts again, Rose.'

She struggled to free herself, stepping away and into the comforting sunlight again. 'No, no – let me be, Will . . .'

His powerful body was only a step behind her, and she quickened her pace, knowing instinctively that she must get away. And then there were yells and shouts on the path behind them, filling the air with alarm. Something small and furry dashed past her legs, a panting, yelping dog followed by a chasing gang of boys wielding sticks and shouting threats. Charlie Wheeler's voice was the most insistent – 'Henny! C'm yere, Henny, you li'l beggar, see what I got fer 'ee . . .'

Rose flung out an arm to stop them but was roughly pushed aside into the brambles at the side of the path as they followed the terrified animal towards the quay and the space around the inn. 'Stop it,' she shouted after them, 'Charlie, stop it . . .'

Will's face was thunderous. He pushed past her. 'Stay here, Rose, I'll get them kids an' teach 'em a thing or two.'

She stood still, watching the unpleasant scene and holding her breath. Elizabeth's little dog must have escaped from the house. *Poor Elizabeth, when she discovers – oh, don't let those boys hurt Henny.*

Her heart thumped as she saw the panting animal stop at the river-bank, look behind at the following whooping boys, and then leap into a moored boat, taking refuge under the seat. Two terrified eyes stared out as Charlie skidded to a stop on the bank, clearly furious at being cheated of his prey. Even as the onlookers shouted and several men ran forward to stop him, he untied the mooring rope and pushed the boat out on to the water.

It rocked, quickly slipping into the eddies of the retreating current, and began moving downstream. An exclamation of shock rose from the gathering crowd, with shouted threats from the cottagers against the villagers for letting their children play such tricks. Will reached Charlie, grabbed him and delivered several loud slaps to the lad's cringing body, but no one did anything to save poor Henny. Now the shouts were louder and more fearsome, and Rose was afraid violence might break out.

Then, suddenly, out of the crowd, a small figure erupted who paused at the water's edge, kicked off her boots and dived into the river, swimming strongly out to the now fast-moving boat. 'I'll get him . . .' Her voice wafted out across the water.

Rose gasped. Jessie Smith, sporting her brass earrings and a red ribbon in her curly hair, reached the boat, grabbed the mooring rope and turned. She came swimming back to the bank, towing the boat after her. As she neared the shore, hands reached out to pull her to safety. The mooring rope was secured to its post, someone took Henny out from her hiding-place, and a cheer went up as Jessie stood up, dripping but grinning, her dress clinging tightly around her body as she ran quickly towards the open door of the inn.

It had all happened so quickly and was over just as fast, that Rose could hardly believe what had happened. She watched Jessie, surrounded by anxious friends, disappear inside the open door and then saw Will picking up the terrified dog, tucking it under his jacket, while with the other hand he held on to Charlie's arm and marched him up the path towards the village, leaving behind him a small knot of still belligerent locals. Rose heard the raised voices and prayed that the incident wouldn't degenerate into roughness. But now the uncouth growls of anger were dying away as calmer voices overtook them.

'That Charlie Wheeler . . .'

'Jessie swimming out, like that – brave maid . . .'

A raucous laugh, and then: 'What'll the big house have to say, d'ye think?'

Rose wondered, too. She could well imagine poor Elizabeth's frantic worry when, on her return, she had found Henny absent. The kitchen staff would get a good telling-off, she thought, and what would Laurence do about it? Had he come looking, or was he back again in his studio, not caring about Henny?

Now that the excitement was over the men crowding around the moored boats began organizing the next event of the afternoon: the swimming and rowing races. Afternoon sun filtered through the trees, and Rose was content to sit down on a grassy bank where she could watch. Briefly she wondered where her mother might be, but guessed that Alice was probably enjoying being with her gossiping neighbours, and free from the usual domestic tasks. Jack, she knew, would be in the drinks tent and, she guessed wryly, half-sozzled with cider by now.

For half an hour, Rose thought, she could stay here without anyone making demands on her until it was time to take Alice home.

She watched Billy and a couple of other lads who were the first competitors in the swimming races. Skinny and stripped to the waist, they plunged into the water and raced out to where Billy's Uncle Bert had rowed his boat halfway across the river and was waiting to pick them up. A betting-book had been opened and encouraging shouts accompanied the boys as they swam. Billy and George were neck and neck, but Billy was pushed under by a final stroke from George's flailing arms and failed to win the race. Back on the shore they clambered out of the boat and, shivering, were given their clothes and told to run about until they were dry. The winner, Rose saw, was given a small token of appreciation, while the punters shared out the winnings by disappearing into the inn, all smiles.

The sun relaxed her, the river sang a less menacing song, and a feeling of lazy enjoyment filled Rose as she stayed on her sheltered bank. The strange sense of impending danger she'd felt earlier had gone now and she was deeply relieved. Tidal water was always dangerous, but now all was calm.

People watched as the rowing races began, but something made her look up towards the field and away from the competing boats. She gave no more than a glance, but what she saw brought her to her feet with a feeling of expectancy. Thomas Devlin was walking straight towards her; she waited, wondering what he wanted.

'Good afternoon, Miss Adams. Your mother said I might find you here.' He stopped at her side, tall, slimly muscular, neatly dressed in the same green-tweed jacket and dark trousers, his hat in his hand and an expression on his lean-angled, clean-shaven face that instantly ignited her earlier feelings about him. He looked like a man on a mission; what did he want her to do this time? And yet, unexpected and unwanted, something made her conscious of his undoubted charisma; the look of him, clean and spare, his voice, low with a touch of north-country flat vowels, fell on her ears with a pleasant resonance, and, she conceded wryly to herself, his air of quiet authority.

She collected her thoughts. 'You saw my mother?'

'I did. Lucy and I accompanied Miss Hodge to the field, and Miss Hodge introduced me to your mother. She kindly promised to look after

Lucy while I came to find you.' He was looking at her doubtfully, she thought, as if he were wondering what to say next.

'And now you have found me, Mr Devlin. . . ?' She met his gaze challengingly. Was he about to give her further orders? Did he want her to look after Lucy, as she had offered to do?

Suddenly the well-formed mouth lifted in a brief twist of a smile. 'I'm delighted to see you. And please don't look at me as if I'm the villain of the piece.' His grey eyes had a glint of humour in them that took the edge off the unexpected words.

Rose felt her colour rise. 'I don't know what you mean! I'm simply surprised that you should take the trouble to come and see me—'

'Why shouldn't I? We're going to work together, so surely it's time we became better acquainted.' His gaze was direct, she wondered if she was mistaken in seeing, again, that hint of amusement, and her confusion grew. Then he crooked his arm, clearly suggesting they should walk back up the path, away from the inn and the shouting cheering people watching the races.

Momentarily speechless, Rose bowed her head, trying to find a non-committal topic of conversation. Eventually she asked, as they headed towards the field, 'Is Lucy enjoying herself?'

'She's had a turn at the coconut-shy, and also at the Aunt Sally.' Thomas met Rose's eyes. 'It's difficult for her to join in all the games,' he said quietly, 'but I promised her I'd find you to ask what other things she could try.'

'Yes.' Rose blinked. So he was making an effort to be friendly.

Smiling to herself, she felt slightly more hopeful about the future. Perhaps, after all, they would work together better than she'd feared at their first meeting. 'I expect she'd enjoy skittling for the piglet,' she said lightly. 'She only has to stand up for that, and you could be beside her, supporting her . . .'

'Excellent idea. I knew you'd help us, Miss Adams.' Again, that hint of a smile. She couldn't help it, the words seemed to utter themselves as she said: 'Please call me Rose.' Then she was fearful in case he thought she was being too forward. But he didn't. The smile grew. *Goodness, not just a smile, almost a grin!* 'Thank you, Rose, I will. And you must call me Thomas.'

'But not in school—'

'No, not there, of course not. We must establish our professional identities and teach respect to the children.' Again the words were stiff, but his eyes softened and she nodded, wondering at the all-important adherence to duty.

They turned off the path into the field and once again a hum of voices surrounded them. Thomas looked ahead. 'Miss Hodge and your mother are sitting over there, yes, and Lucy is with them.' Looking at her, he added quietly, 'Miss Hodge was very tired. She's not well, I'm afraid, and I think I should offer to take her home. Will you care for Lucy while I do so? Unless, of course, you have other plans . . .'

Rose felt the warmth of his arm against hers and at once edged away, though she had no idea why. Then she saw the anxious expression that suddenly darkened his brilliant eyes, and found herself touched by a strange and unfamiliar emotion. She hadn't known that fathers cared so deeply for daughters, her own experience being exactly the opposite. But Thomas Devlin did and she knew at once that she would willingly do what she could to help him.

'Of course I'll look after Lucy, Thomas, if she's happy to stay with me.'

'Lucy will do whatever I ask, Rose. She's a good child and understands that I can't always be with her.' Again: duty.

Rose put the thought at the back of her mind as they continued walking up the field. By now Alice had seen them, was waving and pointing them out to the little girl sitting by her side.

'Papa!' Lucy was on her feet, trying not to lose her balance, trying hard to run towards them. Miss Hodge put out a hand, but it was too late. The child fell and lay on the grass, her small face suddenly miserable, her fingers reaching out for help. 'Oh! Oh!'

Thomas was there in three long strides, his arms scooping her up, clutching her to his body, his face hidden in her blonde ringlets. Rose followed and stood watching, unhappy and feeling useless. Until suddenly Thomas turned to her, his eyes dark and his mouth taut. 'Rose, can you get a drink of water? She'll be all right in a minute – these falls happen so often.' Tenderly he seated the child on the empty chair and crouched down beside her. Rose heard his gentle, soothing words as she passed on her way to the tent to find a drink. 'All right, my love. I'm here with you. I'll look after you.'

When she came back with a cup of water, Lucy was smiling again and asking questions about skittling for the piglet. 'What happens if I win the pig, Papa? Can I take it home?'

Thomas was standing now, smiling down at her. He glanced at Rose and they shared a wry glance. 'I don't think Mrs Benthall would welcome a pet pig, Lucy – but perhaps we could find someone who would give it a good home and let you visit it.'

Rose offered the cup. While the child sipped from it she said, 'You've got to win it first, Lucy. But before we watch the skittling, would you like to come and see the boys gurneying?'

'Gurneying? Whatever's that?'

Rose chuckled. 'Making horrid faces! Take my hand and we'll go and watch. I'll make sure you don't trip over again.'

She was very aware of Thomas watching as she and Lucy slowly began the short walk over the grass towards the rowdy crowd that was gathering where the competition was to take place. Lucy turned. 'Are you coming, too, Papa?'

Rose saw indecision on his face and said mischievously, 'Do come, Thomas. Why, you might even enter the competition!'

Clearly it was a challenge and, of course, she smiled to herself, he couldn't resist. 'Very well, I'll come. And if I'm to enter, I hope the prize is worth having. Not another pig, is it, Rose?'

'More likely a pot of cider! But you'll find it hard to outdo these ugly boys.'

In the middle of the circle of grinning entrants, old Matt stood holding up a worn leather carthorse collar. 'Come on,' he shouted. 'Make yer faces and see who done the worst. Who's first?'

How Lucy laughed when she saw the first boy go up behind the saddle and then pull a terrible face, using the collar as a photograph frame. The laughs and jeer and cheers grew even louder as one by one the competitors gave of their best. Finally, Rose couldn't resist pushing Thomas forward. 'Your turn,' she said lightly, wondering whether, like Laurence, he would somehow escape from almost certain public humiliation.

But he didn't even try to escape. With a wink at Lucy he took his place behind the collar and then pulled the most horrible face imaginable. How could he do it? thought Rose, shocked. With wide, rolling eyes, mouth pushed out, teeth bared, his expression was wild enough to scare the bravest soul. And he let out a fearsome growl as he pushed himself into the centre of the collar. Lucy gasped, and Rose held her breath, full of sudden admiration. Who would ever have thought stiff-laced Mr Devlin could do such a thing?

'He'm the winner!' shouted Matt. 'H'm worse nor any o' you lads . . .'

Thomas withdrew, arranged his face into its normal features and came back to Lucy's side. He was laughing unrestrainedly. 'Didn't know I had such talent, did you? And what's my prize, then?'

The small stone pot was handed over, and he turned to the circle of onlookers, offering it to them. 'I think you all deserve this more than me,' he said with a grin. 'Have a drink on me, and try harder next year.'

A cheer greeted this unexpected gesture, and as Rose and Lucy walked away, someone shouted out, 'If you'm as good a teacher as you be at gurneying, my boys'll be there when school starts again.'

Thomas turned, saluted the speaker and called back, 'I'll be looking out for them.' Then he followed Rose and Lucy as they walked back towards the tent, where Alice was still sitting.

Rose was amazed. How could she ever have guessed that Thomas Devlin, so straight-faced and brusque when it suited him, had such a ridiculous sense of humour? But she said nothing when eventually they stood beside Alice and Lucy asked was Papa coming to watch the pig now?

Thomas bent down to her, took her hands and said gently, 'No, my love. I'm taking Miss Hodge home, and then I'll be back. Miss Adams will look after you. And make sure you skittle well.' He waved and Rose saw the little girl's expression lighten, felt the small hand warm and trustful in her own, and felt an unusual sense of pleasure in being able to help a disabled child towards enjoyment. And a revealing flash through her mind told her quite certainly that this was the aim towards which somehow she must plan her future.

Of course, Lucy didn't win the piglet, but clearly she loved every moment of watching the local boys hurling their wooden balls down the haybale-lined space towards the caged pig at the far end. 'He's won – that boy with the patched coat – look, Miss Adams, he's won!'

Rose watched the youngster, one of Susan Upcott's large family, grin bashfully as he was awarded the prize of the snorting, wriggling piglet and carry it off, wrapped in his jacket. Rose fielded Lucy's questions about where the pig would live and guessed that its life would be short, its timely meat providing meals that would nourish the big family for a week or so.

Then Alice joined them. 'Would you like to come home with us, Lucy? We'll make a pot of tea, and there's a few scones left over, I dessay. And your papa knows where to find you, so he'll come when he can.'

The field was still crowded as they made their slow way back towards the river path. Alice leant on Rose's left hand side, while Lucy held her other hand, chattering all the while. 'What's this flower, Miss Adams?' And then, suddenly stopping, 'Do you hear that bird? I can't see it . . .'

And into Rose's busy mind came suggestions for lessons that she would include in her class when school began again at the end of the summer. The children must be taught to learn about the world they lived in. Life was far more than being poor and cold and hungry; it also held small wonderful pleasures that would mitigate poverty and discomfort. As they walked into the cottage she wondered what Thomas Devlin might think of such irrational plans, but felt strong enough not to care. Time would see what might happen.

He found them a short time later, knocking at the open door of the cottage while they were sitting around the table, Alice telling Lucy about the time she was a small girl, and Rose listening and learning.

She jumped to her feet. 'Come in, Thomas – we've had ours, but there's some tea left in the pot – will you have a cup?'

His eyes immediately centred on Lucy, but he gave Rose a quick glance. 'No thank you. Miss Hodge insisted I had one. And how kind of you, Mrs Adams.' He bowed towards Alice and gave her the full blast of his smile. How warm and full of charm he could be when he bothered. 'You've been so good, looking after Lucy. And I'm sure she's had a lovely time . . .'

'I have, Papa. Oh, I have!' The little girl limped towards him and Rose saw how he instinctively put out his hand to steady her before drawing her close. 'Can I come again?'

Now Thomas looked properly at Rose, saw the slight nod of her head, and smiled as she said, 'I hope you will come and see us at any time, Lucy. And don't forget that I shall have you in my class at school in a few weeks' time. Will you look forward to that?'

Lucy glanced up at her father as if to ask consent and then said quietly, 'Yes, Miss Adams. I will. Thank you.'

Thomas bowed again to Alice and then turned to Rose. 'Thank you. You've been wonderful – such a great help, and I know Lucy has enjoyed being with you.'

Rose stood, watching him take the little girl's hand, and wondered at the problems in his life; a disabled child, a lonely existence without a wife, and all the time knowing that one day Lucy would be on her own.

She nodded at his words, smiling, and then stood outside the door in the late-afternoon sunlight, following them with her eyes as they walked away, down the path and past the inn, towards the village and their less than comfortable home there.

Left full of strange impressions and ideas, she kept thinking of Thomas's comic faces, his strict schoolmasterly standards, and that gentle, warm love for his child. A complex man, she thought, and wondered then how he would greet her when she again went to the schoolhouse on Monday. Had they formed a new friendly understanding today, or would it be back to Mr Devlin and Miss Adams?

As she stood at the water's edge she became aware of the slow drift of late afternoon into early evening, brilliant colours painting the western sky into a backdrop of glowing beauty. Laurence had broadened her knowledge of many things as they talked while he painted, and now she saw flame-charged clouds drifting into umber shadows and then into pale orange streaks before rolling towards the indigo-tinted distance which in turn became pearl-grey touched with the remnants of dying fire. Looking down she saw the whole palette reflected in the slow movement of the river and thought humbly of the often unperceived magnificence of nature. So absorbed, Rose never heard the approaching footsteps until two bodies slipped into her personal world of vision.

'G'night, Rose.' Jessie Smith whispered the words as if no one must know she was there, or that the man at her side encircled her waist with his arm.

Rose started. 'Oh! Goodnight, Jessie.' The incident with Henny flashed through her mind. 'How brave you were . . .'

The girl paused and Rose saw two pairs of eyes glinting at her through the falling twilight. Jessie giggled. 'Tell the lady at the big house as it were me who rescued her li'l dog, won't you, Rose? Then she'll be glad to give me a position,' She gave a quick glance at the man beside her, a nod of the head, and they moved away. Their shapes drifted into the enclosing shadows and Rose's thoughts expanded. So Jessie was walking out with the fish boy from Abberton, which explained her change of attitude and her need of security. A sense of satisfaction came into her mind then as she took one last look at the fading sky, the moving water, and realized, as if it were a welcome and surprising epiphany, that she was becoming the growing centre of a small world of friends and kin, all depending on her for their wellbeing.

And then, as if to remind her that there were still problems to be faced, she heard the first low growl of thunder rolling up from the distant moor.

Here was the storm Will had predicted. With raindrops starting to hiss on the river, she turned and went back to the cottage, where Alice's taut face and anxious eyes greeted her.

'Yer dad's still not come home. He'll be in a praper state and not fit to catch the tide tomorrow. What'll we do, love?'

CHAPTER NINE

Rose stared at her mother. An uneasy feeling ran through her as she realized the implication of Alice's words, and then anger kindled. *It was all his fault.* Staying up in the tent, spending the week's wages on cider, drinking as though there was no tomorrow.

But tomorrow was coming, and if Jack was still too drunk in the morning to catch the tide, even more tomorrows would be threatening them. Losing a tide with the result that the barges did not make their journey down the river to the estuary meant that the clay-pit owner would lose his profits. And his anger would surely descend on the one lighterman responsible: *Jack Adams.*

Rose's fury grew. 'How dare he! He's a drunkard, always thinking of himself and never anyone else! Why can't he think of us for once?' Then, seeing Alice's face droop and tears begin to gather, she put her arms around the frail, shaking body, wishing she could wipe out the hasty words. 'I'm sorry, Mother, but it's too bad of him.' She tried to think what to do next.

By now the storm was nearer. A flash of lightning seared the uncurtained window and Alice moved quickly, reaching for a cloth, draping it over the frame to keep the night out. 'He'll be soaked, coming home in this – Rose, what'll we do?'

'I'll go and find him.' It was the obvious answer and at once she went to the hook on the door where the old boat cloak hung, the one weatherproof garment they shared when venturing out in heavy downpours.

'No, not in this rain you can't – and it's comin' down so hard the river'll flood soon – an' the path'll be under water, and if he falls . . .' Alice's voice rose into an explosion of shrill fear, and again Rose put her arms around her.

'Sit down, Mother, you'll do no good imagining things. Father and I'll be all right. I expect he's halfway here already. I'll just go to the marshes end and see if he's coming.'

'Take the lantern.' Alice lit a stub of candle and fixed it in the storm lantern. She passed it to Rose, who was already wrapped in the thick cloak, and then went to the cupboard beside the fire. 'Put this over your head, love.'

Rose folded the thin shawl around her hair, tying it under her chin. She smiled, hoping she looked less anxious than she felt. 'Make some tea, Mother, we shall need warming up when we get back. And stop worrying.' A last smile, then, opening the door she stepped out into the sheeting, stinging rain.

Jack Adams lurched down the path across the marshes. He didn't care about storms, not when he was nicely filled with cider, and certainly not here on land, boots safely squelching across ground that didn't hold the dangers of treacherous water. He pulled his cap down and turned up the collar of his jacket. What a day! Plenty to drink, good company to laugh with, and all that food there, ready for a plateful when you wanted it. 'Well done, May Bankes,' he said loudly and then laughed at the way the wind and rain took the words and threw them all around the dark sky. Nearly home now. Sniffing, he scowled. Alice looking sour and worried cos he were so late, those creaky stairs to climb – well, he'd manage them somehow, wasn't the first time he'd got a bit drunk, was it? And tomorrow? Time enough to think of that when it came. Coughing, he floundered on.

Through the thunderclaps and the whistling wind thoughts came and went. That maid, Rose Victoria – oh God, he thought, having to pause as his foot slipped into a runnel of water – she'll be all uppity and going on about me coming back so late. That maid needs a good man to wed an' bed her and put paid to all her fancy ideas about life. Rose Victoria married? He laughed with abandon and spat. The maid wed – *and o' course, I'll take her up the aisle. Well, that'll be a praper day, won't it?* Flowers and costly new dresses, Alice in tears, and a gathering of old drinking mates. And then the girl would be gone, and settled. A weight off his mind. Always on at him. Always wanting more'n he could give . . . never been happy about her.

Jack stopped as the wind caught his coat and pushed him off balance. One foot in the boggy water, the other trapped under a broken branch spread across the track, startled, he fell. Mud oozed about him, filled his boots, soaked his trousers, rain crept down his neck, his cap was off, and suddenly he could see nothing. Rain, thunder overhead, crashes and bangs, and his mind had had enough. Weighted with drink, stupid with fumes and buffeted by the forces of nature, face down in the grassy marsh, he lost consciousness.

Rose was wet through. The old cloak did its best but it couldn't stop the steady soaking of the lashing rain. The lantern flickered and nearly died, but somehow it kept going. She reached the end of the flooded river path, thankful that she knew the track, so avoiding the waves lapping down its length. No sign of Father. Again, her mind delivered furious epithets as she thought of him, drunk and hopeless, trying to find his way home. *Selfish. Impossible to live with. How could Mother ever have loved him?*

She reached the end of the path heading towards the village and looked into the dark distance, feeling, with every minute, more and more apprehensive about what she might find. Surely someone would have seen how drunk Jack was? Offered to bring him home? No, of course not – he only had fair-weather friends. No one cared enough for him to put themselves out and whose fault was that?

Stumbling on she began to give up hope. Had he fallen? Could still be in the tent, even? And then her foot tripped over something and she stopped, startled, lowering the lantern and looking down at the ground.

Was it a dead sheep? They grazed the marshes and maybe a thoughtless farmer had left one here to drown in the flooding waters. Bending, she forced her eyes to make sense of what lay beneath her. Something large. Wet. Snoring . . She gasped. *Father!*

And suddenly, stronger than anger, came concern and strength. She must get him up, get him home, get him warm and dry . . . her father, he needed her now in a way she'd never imagined. And then an extra burst of knowledge – for Mother's sake, she must take Father home.

'Father? Wake up. It's me, Rose. I'll help you.'

How she did it she never recalled but an inner force was suddenly there. Her wet hands pulled at his head, wiping the mud and the water from his face. Kneeling beside him, she slapped his cheeks, saying over and over, 'Wake up, Father. We've got to go home . . .'

Lightning sizzled the sky and in that flash Jack came to. Staring upwards, he saw his daughter's pale face outlined against the darkness, felt her hands on his drenched body, and the lust for life generated an impulse of new strength, enough to make him sit up, force energy into his shaking legs and, with her help, stand straight.

'Rose,' he muttered, spitting the mud from his lips, 'Rose, maid, get me home . . .'

Together, slowly and with every other step lost in water or mud, clinging together, they made progress, leaving the marshes behind and turning down the river-swept path. 'Hold on to me, Father. Mind where you put your feet . . .' The lantern gave no light now and only Rose's knowledge of the way ahead brought them safely to the cottage. The door was ajar, and Alice stood just inside, her face pale and her voice trembling.

'Jack! Oh, my lover – is that you? Oh, Rose, is he safe?'

Rose pushed her father through the doorway and followed him inside. And in that moment, when she was at last able to drop her fearful anxiety, she heard the note in her mother's voice and learned one more lesson.

Love, she thought. *Will I ever find it?*

In the morning she left the newly washed marshes waiting for the levels to dry out beneath a glowing sun and walked down through the village towards Sandiford House. The night had been disturbed with Jack struggling up the stairs and then collapsing, snoring, at the top. Alice had brought pillows and blankets and laid beside him on the hard landing boards. Rose, in her bedroom, heard sobs and soft loving words interspersed among her father's crude noises. And had wondered, again and again, at the extraordinary compassion which is part of love.

In the village she paused by Walter Wheeler's shop door and looked inside. 'I hope Charlie has apologized for his behaviour yesterday, Mr Wheeler? He could easily have killed Mrs Mount's little dog.'

Walter came to the door and stared aggressively at her. 'What's it to do with you then, Rose Adams? We've dealt with the boy, me and Mr Devlin.' He paused and she read enjoyment in his sneering smile as he went on, 'And let me tell you, that Mr Devlin, he's got more sense than you'll ever have about teaching children. Why, he's got Charlie joining the school woodworking class, and the boy'll work hard, or else I'll know why. Get a good job in carpentry, he will, that way – better than all the nonsense reading and writing stuff he gets from the likes of you.' He stood there, heavy and stolid and Rose at once stepped away.

'I'm glad to hear he's been given something to work at. And I hope the woodwork course – and Mr Devlin's influence – will encourage him to stop being such a bully around the village. It'll be a change for him to learn to do something useful.'

'Why, you bitch . . .' Walter took a step forward, colour filling his fleshy face, fists forming as they leaped out of his pockets.

'Good day, Mr Wheeler.' Rose went on her way, mouth tight, but resolute.

She was met at the door by red-faced Nancy Briggs, hair mussed beneath her cap and apron all askew. 'Madam's in bed, Rose – can't get over the dog being nearly killed. All my fault, she said, too – but there, I on'y opened the back door to fetch some parsley and the little beggar was off.'

Rose removed her hat and smiled encouragingly. 'Never mind, Nancy. He's safe enough now. Do you think Mrs Mount would like to see me? Shall I take up her morning chocolate?'

'Keep away, if I was you,' said Nancy darkly. ' 'Er's full of grumbles. No, I'll take the drink, she can't tell me off any more'n she has done. And Mr Vane's in the attic. Take his chocolate, if you likes.' She turned towards the kitchen, her face pulled up into a grimace. 'Not much help from him about the dog – heard it were missing and then went into the library and drank hisself silly.'

Rose took a deep breath. Why was everyone being so unpleasant? In half a mind to leave again, she paused and then a door was flung open upstairs, and Laurence's voice called down the staircase, loud and impatient. 'Rose? Is that you? You're late – hurry up, I want to get on.'

Smiling wryly at Nancy, she collected two cups of chocolate on a tray and went upstairs.

The studio was quiet but not as peaceful as she'd expected. An atmosphere prevailed. After a brief 'good-morning' which Laurence didn't bother to acknowledge, she went downstairs into the musty bedroom and changed into the green dress. Upstairs again, she sat on the hard chair while Laurence ranted on about Elizabeth having hysterics over the wretched dog.

'Would that it had disappeared down the river and done with it, forever yapping and being a nuisance, wretched creature – and now I have a headache that won't go, and how on earth am I supposed to paint anything while this damned sunshine comes and goes?'

She said nothing, but sat there, sipping her chocolate, eyes closed, trying to concentrate on the bright day and the distant voice of the river, still flooding as it flowed down to the estuary, and the embracing ocean.

Only half-listening to Laurence, she thought about how Alice had somehow got Jack to his feet this morning, helped him downstairs, poured water for him to wash, gave him breakfast and then walked with him up the river path towards the canal, her arm holding his, to make sure he reached the clay quay safely. The image in her mind was strong. Alice, limping, had come home looking wan and tired, but refusing to blame Jack for anything.

'That's a man's life, maid. They do like to drink an' we gotta put up with it.' And she'd turned away from Rose, pulling up her sleeves, ready to work through the day and prepare for his return late in the evening.

I'll never put up with it; when I wed a man we shall share our life together, thought Rose as she put the empty chocolate cup on the floor at her feet and focused on Laurence. He was still frowning and cursing, but mixing his paints and starting to look across the room at her.

She saw his eyes relaxing, his mouth softening, and his hands taking on a life of their own as he concentrated on painting. After a little while he stopped, lifted his head and smiled at her. 'Is it you being here, Rose, or the fact that my headache's stopped at last? But it's coming along . . . yes, I think so.'

Rose watched him, looking at her, then back at his canvas. He smiled again, put down his brush, wiped his hands on his smock and came around the easel towards her. 'You're a miracle girl. You've made me feel quite well again. Rose.'

At her side he put an arm on her shoulder, looking down into her upraised eyes. 'Rose, I want a favour, please. Say yes, will you?'

She laughed. 'Not until I know what it is, Laurence! I'm not that silly, even if I can work the odd miracle. What do you want?'

He didn't answer at once. She felt his hand moving from her shoulder to the side of her neck. Warm, sensitive fingers began stroking her and then slowly went round to the back of her head. 'Your hair, Rose . . .' He was looking into her wide, alarmed eyes, letting his fingers toy with the pins holding the coil at the nape of her neck. His voice lowered into a murmur, gentle and pleading but vibrant with urgency. 'I want to see it flowing. I've imagined it, like a stream of red-gold fire, but that's not enough. I need to know what it really looks like – to put the magic into the portrait.'

She shrank back against the chair, unsure of what was happening, and at once he began pleading. 'Don't you understand? It's part of the portrait, Rose, so let me see it – please?'

She was afraid yet entranced, her heart pounding. Will Sharcombe had kissed her many times, but the nearness of Laurence, the demand in his voice, was something new and she had no idea of how to respond. Did he expect her to say casually, 'yes, of course I'll let my hair down, Laurence, if you want me to'? Perhaps, but deep inside she felt that it was more like some sort of strange and dangerous ritual he was conducting. Dangerous, but – yes, exciting.

Slowly she nodded. Although common sense told her to be careful, her need to find out what this was leading to was overwhelming. Shaking her head, she brushed aside his hand and took out the hairpins, feeling her hair at once flow down her back. Looking up at Laurence, she saw his pupils dilate. He stepped back, eyes not moving from the weight of hair streaming over her body, and then he came near again and from the look of delight and urgency on his face she knew he meant to kiss her.

Suddenly all the dreams vanished. She'd thought, once or twice at night, slyly, even shamefully, that perhaps Laurence was growing fond of her He was certainly opening a new world, full of educated voices, lovely clothes, and comforts that she and Alice and Jack couldn't even guess at. It was tempting to think that that might be happening – but Laurence's eyes were growing hot and impatient. She smelled his musky smell, the scent of tobacco on his breath, and then, still clinging to him, the fumes of all he'd drunk last night and, like a shaft of red-hot pain, her mother's words ran around her mind: *that's what men are like, they gotta drink. . . .*

No, never! It wasn't part of her dream. Nothing to do with her vision of a new life. A man, when she found one, must be more disciplined than Laurence.

With one quick movement she was out of the chair, running to the door. She opened it and left without looking at him, words flying back over her shoulder: 'No, Laurence – no!'

His voice followed her down the stairs. 'Rose! For God's sake – come back. Please . . .' Curses followed, and the door was angrily slammed.

In the bedroom she flung off the green dress, knotted back her hair and pulled on her own clothes while her mind ran in circles of confusion. She had made a decision yet was already uncertain about it. But all that mattered, surely, was to get on with life, discovering what lay ahead.

She hadn't bargained for the next move, for, after leaving the bedroom she met Nancy at the foot of the stairs. 'There you are, Rose – I means Miss Adams. Madam says she wants to see you. Now.'

Rose paused. Temptation slammed into her mind. The open air called, with the wind from the moors, the song of the river and the freedom from people that lay beyond this house. But curiosity wouldn't be denied. What did Mrs Mount want? Only one way to find out.

'Very well, Nancy. I'll go at once. Thank you.' Outside the front bedroom door she stopped again. Working so closely with Laurence over the recent weeks, speaking often to Mrs Mount, she knew she had lost most of her country accent. She smiled ironically. *I sound almost gentrified these days.* As she knocked at the door, she smiled with something like her usual good humour, despite the shadows at the back of her mind that still lingered up in the attic with Laurence.

The voice bidding her enter was weak and as Rose closed the door behind her she saw a surprisingly pale Elizabeth Mount propped up in bed, surrounded by vast white pillows and shawls, with Henny clasped in her arms. 'Rose, thank goodness you're here. I need some help.'

At the bedside Rose looked anxiously at the lined face, no longer full of determination and hauteur, but rather weary and worn. 'What can I do for you, Mrs Mount?'

Elizabeth shifted slightly, and at once Rose replaced a slipped pillow. 'Thank you, you're a good girl. You have more decency and manners than that reprobate of a brother of mine.' Large eyes regarded Rose with a hint of the return of the familiar strong personality. 'Did he look for Henny when she was stolen? Did he say anything soothing, or helpful? No. Not one little thing. Do you know what he did, Rose?'

Elizabeth's voice was slow, her manner dramatic. She drew herself up straighter and fixed Rose with a terrible look. Her voice lowered. 'He got drunk. Went to the library as if he had no duty to me, his only sister – his sister who cares for him, pays his bills, who helped him in London when . . .' The words were bitten off and Elizabeth's mouth tightened like a gin trap.

Rose sought for consolation. 'I'm so sorry, Mrs Mount. But I believe some men fly to the bottle when things go wrong. Perhaps you could forgive him?'

Elizabeth shook her head and tears filled her eyes, as she said slowly, 'I have forgiven him enough all through our lives together. This is the last straw. I feel I cannot spend the rest of my days worrying about Laurence, his temper and his drinking.'

Rose drew in a deep breath and put out a hand, reaching for the chair by the bedside. Elizabeth nodded. 'Yes, sit down, my dear. This has probably shocked you as much as it has me. But I assure you that once I've regained my strength, I shall do all I can to help other poor men like Laurence recover from the pit of drunkenness which they all seem to fall into.'

She paused, the big eyes widened even more and a smile of triumph began to spread over Elizabeth's pale cheeks. 'I think I have found a solution to this problem. I talked to Mr Toogood, the vicar, yesterday afternoon, and he told me of a local movement to set up an institution which will offer succour to all such hardened drinkers.' She peered at Rose. 'What do you think of that?'

Rose thought hard. She knew of certain ladies around the area who dabbled in this sort of good works – trying to keep working men from their comforting mugs of cider after long, hard days. She had even laughed at their efforts. But now, with Jack's drunkenness still in her mind, and the memory of Laurence's spirit-laden breath about her, she experienced a change of heart.

'It sounds a very good idea, Mrs Mount. Particularly if you can find people who will help you do it. But I feel you must improve your health before you think of starting the work.'

Elizabeth's cheeks were more colourful. She patted Henny comfortingly before putting the dog at the end of the bed, and then sitting up straighter, pulling her pillows around her. 'Exactly, my dear Rose. Yes, you've said precisely what I was thinking – that I must build up my strength before embarking on this crusade. And to do that I want your help.'

Her determined smile made Rose uneasy and she clasped her hands together, knowing that Mrs Mount could be a demanding woman when she wanted, but the next words caught her completely unawares.

'I want you to recommend someone who can take over the running of the household for a few weeks, until I am properly recovered and able to resume my usual duties. I'm sure you know of someone suitable in the village?'

Rose sat in silence, staring at Elizabeth and wondering if she dared suggest the idea that had instantly flown into her mind. *I could do it. I've learned enough about running a home from Mother, and anyway, Nancy Briggs is here to do all the hard work. I would only have to supervise . . . and I should be here, in this wonderful old house . . .*

Her answer was out before she knew it. 'Mrs Mount, would you allow me to take over this position for you? I'm sure I could manage it.'

The older woman frowned, conflicting thoughts evident on her face as she pulled her bedjacket more closely around her body.

Rose saw and understood: uncertainty, worry as to how people might react; and, of course, what would Laurence think? But then, very slowly, Elizabeth came to a decision and firmly smiled. 'What a splendid idea! Yes, of course, Rose, you'd be most suitable. You're educated, well-mannered, and you have a good idea of the way we live – I mean, during the last few weeks you've been in and out of the house so often.'

They looked at each other and Rose's thoughts expanded. She would be running Sandiford House while Laurence mooched upstairs with his painting, while Elizabeth regained her strength and began the great crusade against the devil drink. But what about the school? What about Thomas Devlin needing her help with the alterations? And – Rose's smile died – what about Alice and Jack, what would they think of their only child suddenly becoming a lady, earning far more money, Rose guessed, than they had ever dreamed about?

How could she fit all these extraordinary and conflicting things into her life But even as the problems grew, she knew she would accept the post. She felt a rise of excitement, of self-confidence and growing satisfaction, that shouted loudly into the humming world of her busy mind – *you can do it. It's what you've always wanted – a different life. Well, it's here now, waiting for you. Take this opportunity and don't even think that anything might go wrong.*

Getting up, she patted Henny and tidied the coverlet about Elizabeth. Already she felt in charge, and it was a wonderful feeling.

CHAPTER TEN

A new life, indeed. Rose had never felt under such pressure, never known how the days could flash past, leaving her with a humming mind that kept recalling things left undone. And yet she enjoyed it.

Even Thomas Devlin's outraged face when she confronted him on the first afternoon of her new position at Sandiford House, hadn't really disturbed her. She had hurried to the school directly luncheon had been finished. Elizabeth's tray was delivered to her bedroom, and Laurence gave orders that he preferred to eat alone in the library, so Rose had finished up with her solitary plate at one side of the long table in the empty dining-room with Nancy Briggs hovering in the doorway, watching her. But there, she had expected it. And on the way to the schoolhouse she'd met Jessie Smith and had to tell her that she must wait another few days before presenting herself for possible employment. Rose breathed in very deeply as she resolutely walked through the village.

Inside the schoolhouse Thomas Devlin had stood extremely still, poised, she thought, as if to leap suddenly into action. The screwdriver in his hand fidgeted as he said sharply, 'What do you mean, a position at Sandiford House? You're a schoolteacher, we start the new term in two weeks.' His frown had been severe, the northern accent more marked. 'You can't intend to let me down, can you?'

'Of course not.' Irritated, Rose felt herself to be on shifting sand. She had expected disbelief, even perhaps a hint of amusement, but not this plain and unpleasant confrontation. Already she had had to explain to Alice and Jack that she was merely obliging Mrs Mount for a couple of weeks, hardly leaving home for good, but now it seemed that this tight-lipped man with unblinking grey eyes was thinking the worst.

Anger came then. Let him think what he liked! It was her life, her decision, nothing to do with him. 'I shall be here when the new term starts,

Mr Devlin – you can rely on that. And I am free in the afternoons for an hour or so,' until Elizabeth rang her bell and demanded tea, cakes and a minutely detailed account of all that had been done in the house since she last saw her new companion, 'and of course I will prepare my lessons, and do all I can to help you in any way you need.'

'Hm.' His answer was not exactly a snort, but it was hardly the understanding she hoped for. He turned way without another word, applying himself to a recalcitrant screw and treating it with forceful concentration before straightening up again and looking over his shoulder. He seemed surprised to see her still there, and said dismissively, 'All right, Rose. If that's what you've decided . . .'

He turned away, clearly already in another world, and headed for the group of boys busily planing down some timbers at the far end of the room. 'Charlie,' he called, and three heads looked towards him obediently.

'Yes, sir?'

Rose's jaw dropped. Since when had Charlie Wheeler been so responsive to schoolteachers? But there, she told herself grudgingly, Thomas Devlin had something about him that even the village boys were obviously learning to respect. Leaving him in close conversation with Charlie, she marched off to the lower end of the room to show him just how vital her position here was – to tidy up, sort out the slates, sharpen the slate pencils, get the reading books into order. She had to admit to herself reluctantly that she was finding out unexpected things about the new schoolmaster.

For instance, he stood very still, as if he were a tree rooted deep in the earth. She liked that demonstration of strength. And then, beneath that stillness she was very aware of something raging: thoughts, energy, passion, perhaps. She remembered how he adored Lucy. That puzzled her. A quiet man, politely spoken – usually, but not quite so charming today – with good manners and a neat appearance. She half-smiled, recalling the slightly frayed sleeve cuffs, and wondered if he did his mending himself.

Her mind moved on as she smoothed out folded pages and wiped sticky finger-marks from ancient reading books. If only his hair was cut more elegantly he might be quite handsome. That great blond swathe falling across his eyes, such a contrast with the thick dark, curling-behind-the-ears style that Laurence Vane preferred. She caught herself up quickly. *Ridiculous, such foolish and unnecessary thoughts. Get on with the work.*

Laurence kept up a pretence of continuing to paint, but the attic was empty and lonely. No Rose there to cheer him on with her friendly talk, to excite him at the moments when the painting began to take on real life. He was drinking regularly now, the flask in his pocket was refilled each morning; every evening was spent in the library reading – or pretending to – with a fresh bottle at hand. He daydreamed most of the time; dreams about past life in London, of the girls up there, the smooth, creamy bodies, the fiery-red flowing hair, the delight of male companionship in clubs and friend's homes. Would to God he could leave this benighted place and go back. But money was the problem – that and his damaged reputation. Would people remember? Would they still blame him for that ridiculous scandal?

He poured another drink and told himself to wait just a bit longer. Wait until the portrait was finished and then he would take it to London and unveil his latest work. Closing his eyes, he smiled, hearing the plaudits. *Spectacular. The return of a master. Pre-Raphaelite artistry at its best.* And then there would be commissions – but here the dreams collapsed, for Rose, his muse, was no longer able to spend hours sitting for him. She was in the kitchen, ordering the meals and telling the servants what to do, and visiting Elizabeth, who still languished in bed and kept even tighter fingers on her purse.

The truth hit him painfully. The annoying girl, sweet Rose that she was, now had no time for him, and his wayward talent was nothing without her. He nodded, the glass slipped out of his hand, and he lay back in the chair, slipping into drunken dreams and reveries, wondering how he could persuade Rose to return to the studio, and the unfinished portrait. On the next day it all started again.

Then one day Will Sharcombe came to the back door and told the maid he wanted to know if Mrs Mount's dog was all right now.

Daisy Pellew grinned at him. 'Oh, the little beggar's yapping an' running round as usual. So what do 'ee want, Will? No good looking for Rose nowadays, 'ers our new mistress, too busy to talk to the likes o' you, boy.'

He leaned against the doorframe. 'That's what I heard. The lady in bed and Rose running the house. And what about *him*, then?'

'Mr Vane?' Daisy wiped her nose on her sleeve and grinned even more widely. 'He's a real case. Drinkin' hard, he is. And tell you what, that ol' painting he done of Rose is hidden under a sheet. Had to go up there and clean yesterday, and yes, the sheet was all pinned down. I couldn't get a peep. So what do you reckon he's painted, then? Rose in her nothings, I guess.' Daisy shrieked with glee. 'That's painters for you, that's what they do say!'

Will stood upright and glowered at her. 'You sure?' His jaw jutted and his eyes narrowed. 'My Lord, if I thought that I'd, well, I'd—'

Daisy took a step backwards, her voice placating. 'Now then, Will, boy, you don't want to get worked up – no need. I mean, I on'y said—'

'I wants to see him.' Will was halfway into the kitchen, his face full of passion. 'Go on, tell him someone wants a word. I'll wait here.'

Daisy fled. She found Laurence sitting bleary-eyed, staring into space. 'What do you want?' His voice was thick, his expression unwelcoming.

Swallowing loudly, Daisy said shakily, 'There's someone to see you, sir. Will Sharcombe. He's askin' 'bout the little dog.'

Laurence grimaced, slowly got up and walked towards her. 'Tell him to go away.' He pushed past her, out of the library and down the passage. Daisy hovered behind him uncertainly, aware that Will was already in a state, and what would he say if she took that brief message back? She tried again. 'He wants to see you, sir, wants it bad.'

Laurence swung round. 'All right, all right. I'll see him. Tell him to come to the terrace. I'll be there. Five minutes, tell him, that's all.' He walked through the cool, marble-floored hall and into the drawing-room with its open French windows. Out on the terrace he scented the river and felt refreshed. It even began to dawn on him that he was doing himself no good, drinking and moping. If only Rose were here. . . . A large shabby man came round the corner of the house and headed straight for him. Clearly a peasant. Laurence stood still, waiting. What on earth could the fellow want? Work? Well, there was none here.

'Mr Vane, you'm painting Rose Adams.'

Laurence stared into passionate eyes set in a strong, weather-beaten face and felt the first stirrings of unease. His voice grew sharp and he frowned. 'Well, what of it? That's my affair, not yours.'

'It's mine, too. She an' me were sweethearts once, so I don't want no bad paintings of her round the place, see.' The voice was thick, and Laurence sensed a certain aggression.

The quietness of the garden, the surrounding empty marshes, and the nearness of this large, unpleasant person brought Laurence's unease into active hostility. He lifted his head and looked the man up and down. 'My painting is famous all over the country. I don't know what you're talking about. And as for Rose being your sweetheart, well, you'd better think again. She could have anyone – not just someone like you.'

Will Sharcombe moved fast. In two strides he was facing Laurence, too near for comfort. Very quietly he said, 'If I thought you'd painted her without clothes on, then I'd break your neck. So tell me it isn't like that.'

Laurence scowled at his adversary. 'Get back to the midden where you belong – I've got nothing to say to you.'

'Jest tell me that Rose kept her clothes on an' there weren't no funny business.' Will's face was red, his eyes staring; he was clearly a man pushed beyond his limit.

'For God's sake,' blustered Laurence, 'how I paint and what my models wear is nothing to do with you – you wouldn't even understand if I told you. I'm telling you nothing, you wretched bit of country muck! Get out of here, or, by God, I'll call the constable to deal with you.'

Will Sharcombe stood quite still, his narrowed eyes full of animosity. 'All right,' he said, his voice very quiet, very low and resonant. 'But if that picture's bad, then I'll be back. I ain't finished wi' you yet, not by a long chalk. Jest remember that, Mr Vane.' He turned lightly, so quickly that Laurence blinked. Suddenly the terrace was empty and he was alone. He found a cane chair beneath the sunshade, and flopped heavily into it, considering what had just happened. The afternoon beamed, warm and gracious about him, birds sang and insects buzzed, but he knew nothing of it.

That stinking haybag had upset him, set his dreams flying, got his memories stirring. Dear God, he needed a drink. In one move he was inside the house and into the library. The bottle was empty. Raging, he rushed off to the cellar to find a new one. He didn't hear Rose returning, and by the time he was back in the library she had gone upstairs to have tea with Elizabeth.

'Well,' said Elizabeth, in a stronger voice than usual, sipping her tea, one hand caressing the snoozing Henny. 'Tell me exactly what you've been doing today, Rose. Of course, I'm sure everything is in hand, but – I mean, lying here is very frustrating when I know there's so much to do. And the servants . . .'

Rose took the offered opportunity. 'Mrs Mount, you really don't have to worry. Nancy Briggs and Daisy are working hard and it's a pleasure to see that they carry out all their duties so well. But I do wonder – after all, this is a big house, and there's so much cleaning to be done, perhaps an extra pair of hands in the kitchen might be a good idea. What do you think?'

Elizabeth munched a large slice of Victoria sandwich, oozing with strawberry jam. She looked at Rose, finished her cake, drank more of her tea, then said slowly, 'do you know of anyone suitable?'

'I do. A girl from a cottage not far from my own home. Jessie Smith – she's getting on for sixteen, I think, and very keen to settle into domestic service.' Rose refilled the empty cup and hoped for the best. No need to go into Jessie's history of youthful wildness. Surely all that was past. Jessie was a grown woman now, with a man at her side, and planning for the future. 'May I bring her along for you to interview?'

Elizabeth considered as she replaced her empty plate on the tray and then said with a frown, 'I really can't spare the time. Mr Toogood is bringing Mrs Weston to see me tomorrow morning. I'm very much better now and we are to discuss the creation of a lighterman's shelter in the harbour in Culmouth. I believe Mrs Weston is of the same mind as I am about the evil of drink and so I must give her my undivided attention. Really, these domestic issues are so irritating . . .' Then she produced the firm, dominant smile which Rose was already accepting meant that someone had to do something, and without argument. 'So perhaps you could see the young person, Rose? You obviously know her – and if you think she could assist in the kitchen, well, I've no objection.' The smile vanished. 'She'll receive the usual pay for a skivvy, of course.'

'Yes, Mrs Mount.'

And so, in due course, Jessie appeared at the back door, dressed soberly in a cut-down faded print dress belonging to her mother, and clutching a large white apron. She pushed all her springy black hair into the accompanying cap, looked demure and said, 'Yes, Mrs Briggs. No, Mrs Briggs,' in a voice that Rose could hardly recognize. Leaving the new girl scraping vegetables in the scullery, Rose went upstairs to oversee the pile of clean linen being loaded into the airing cupboard, and kept her fingers crossed. *Well done, Jessie. Just keep it up – please.*

At home Alice was increasingly nervy. Rose watched the gnarled fingers slipping off plates and cups and wondered why. Of course, the rheumatics were always bad hot weather but Alice seemed unhappy, with no pleasantries to chat about now. At last Rose felt she must ask what was wrong.

Alice put a cloth over the rising bread dough, pushed the bowl towards the fire, and sat down heavily. She looked across the table at Rose who was peeling potatoes, and said slowly, 'nothing, maid, nothing. Jest – well, I dunno . . .'

Rose watched her mother bow her head, rubbing her floury hands in her lap. 'What don't you know, Mother? Go on, tell me what's worrying you – surely I can help?'

A sigh. A wipe of swimming eyes. Then a long, direct look that made Rose's stomach knot. 'Mother, please, tell me.'

The clock ticked away the seconds until at last Alice sighed again, arranged a weak smile on her face, and said hesitantly, 'it's the house, maid. You going up to the house. I don't like it, you see.'

'But why not? I'm only doing it for another week – school starts then and I shall be teaching all day. Mrs Mount knows it's only a temporary position. Mother, what on earth do you mean? What's the matter with me being at the house?'

Alice paused, thoughts flying across her face. There came a hint of pain, and then something that Rose instantly recognized as a ploy to change the subject. Forcing her smile to broaden, Alice raised her voice to a more cheerful tone. 'Nothing, love, 'cept that your dad don't like you going there. Don't ask me why – he jest don't. Well, you know what men are like – heard some stories 'bout ghosts or suchlike, maybe.'

'What ghosts, Mother? I've never heard anyone say that the house is haunted.'

'No, no,' insisted Alice, shaking her head. 'It's jest a silly tale. Oh, over twenty years ago now, I reckon. Well, better get on with his dinner or he'll be shouting if it isn't ready when he comes in.' She was up on her feet again, busy with the fish young Billy had brought in. A smile appeared. 'Now, poke up the fire, Rose and let's get the fish on to cook.'

The mackerel was delicious; even Jack enjoyed the fresh taste of the sea. 'That young Billy,' he said, with his mouth full, 'always round the boats, he is. By the time he's ready to join the Navy he'll know it all – or so he thinks!'

Rose said, 'He's a good boy. I wish all the other lads knuckled down to work like he does.' And then she started telling them about the alterations Thomas Devlin was making in the old schoolroom and how Charlie Wheeler appeared to have improved both his manners and his behaviour.

Jack only half-listened, chomping his way through his meal and then reaching for his baccy, but Alice nodded and Rose was thankful to see that her mother's warm smile had returned. Perhaps it had only been stupid ghost stories, after all, she thought.

Rose mentioned the ghost to Nancy Briggs when she was giving out stores the next morning, in an attempt to make things easier between them. Nancy sniffed, put the butter and sugar on the kitchen table and held out her hands for the halfsack of flour Rose was lifting.

Her stiff face relaxed slightly.'No, it's not rubbish. That locked bedroom where the ol' lady slept, that's where it is. I haven't seen it, but I heard it – oh yes, terrible creaking when you try the door. I don't go up that corridor if I can help it. And as fer Daisy, well, don't talk to her or she'll go off into the hysterics. Stoopid maid. Now, don't fergit I needs more jam, Miss Adams. Mrs Mount wants tarts as well as cakes fer her tea party tomorrow.'

Rose locked the cupboard door and turned. 'What ol' lady, Mrs Briggs?'

'That Edwina Grey, the one who lived here with her family and then disappeared.' Nancy inspected the provisions on the table, nodded and looked at Rose again. ' 'Er were never seen again,' she said solemnly, 'an' that's why the house were deserted and left to go into ruins. Until Mrs Mount come and now it's lookin' real handsome. Mind you, belongs to the Sandiford estate trust, and mebbe someone owns that. I don't know how these things work.'

'Nor do I. How interesting.' Rose said no more, but left the kitchen. Her curiosity was aroused. In her childhood the house had been known to be empty and falling to pieces. But the work done to it before Laurence and his sister moved in had made it into a warm, comfortable home. Except for that one room on the upper floor, which was locked and apparently never entered.

She stood in the middle of the hall and thought hard. Laurence was away, driving to Abberton, and wouldn't be home for luncheon, saying he had business to do there. Elizabeth had been invited to Mrs Weston's house in Culmouth and had gone off in a flurry of excitement and new resolution, Henny clasped in her arms, and a spectacularly decorated bat on her head.

I'm alone. I have nothing to do until I go to the schoolroom this after-noon. What shall I do?

The house had always interested her; she had a sort of fascination to do with the people who once lived in it. She knew none of them, of course, but the portraits on the walls, with their staring eyes and old-fashioned clothes, made her aware of those past lives. Now she went slowly through the hall, trying to imagine how shoes and boots would have sounded, walking across those marble slabs. How carriages would have waited outside the front door, horses impatiently pawing the gravel of the circular drive. Servants came and went in her mind; parlour-maids, kitchen-maids – a butler? She'd read about the great houses and their hierarchy of domestic staff. Here it was just Nancy Briggs, Daisy Pellew – when she could be bothered to come – and herself. And now Jessie, in the scullery, working on the vegetables and scrubbing floors.

What changes this old house had seen. And suddenly the word echoed through her mind like a trumpet blast – it was the changes she wanted so badly to learn about. What had Edwina Grey been like? Young, attractive, full of life, happy? A resonance began to flow through her as she moved towards the stairs, looking into each painted face as she went up and she wondered whether Laurence's portrait of her – 'the local schoolmistress' – would ever hang here, too. A sad feeling struck her that he might never finish it and she knew that would be her fault. But her life didn't have to include Laurence, surely? She frowned and let her thoughts move forward.

She knew that the closed bedroom doors upstairs had stories behind them. As she passed them she visualized masters, mistresses, young ladies and stalwart lads, all energetically living in these rooms. Now only two of them were occupied – by Elizabeth and Laurence.

Rose stopped abruptly on the landing as a strange yet exciting thought struck her. Perhaps the house was only sleeping, not dead. If she stood quite still and listened, she could almost hear its damped-down energy vibrating somewhere, longing to fill the empty rooms and corridors with new life. Was she being ridiculous in imagining all this? And what did it have to do with her, anyway?

She went on down the long corridor leading to the back of the house, finding her way to the locked bedroom that had once belonged to Edwina Grey, wondering as she went, where the key might be hidden. There must be a key. When she reached the door she still had no idea of its hiding-place. The door was firmly locked, resisting her efforts to force it open.

Then an idea came. She'd once read a story about a thief who made skeleton keys. And who, if no key fitted, used what ever he could find to manoeuvre the lock. Well, she would do the same. She took a hairpin

115

from the coil of hair at her neck and tried fitting it into the lock. After a couple of useless tries, amazingly it worked. The lock clicked open and she stepped back, curious but startled and full of guilt at the same time. Should she go in? Excitement told her it was far too late to step back now.

The door opened unwillingly, hinges grating and creaking – the ghost, of course, she thought, smiling – needing firm pressure from her hand. Then she had a sudden unbidden thought that she was wrong to do this. Maybe Edwina Grey needed to keep her secrets. But the lure of the past persuaded her to enter.

The room was silent: of course, no one had used it for so long; twenty years since the ghost story started, Mother had said. But where the other parts of Sandiford House had become welcoming to the new tenants, this one room had remained concealed. Elizabeth had not bothered to open it up.

Rose walked slowly into the middle of the dark-red-carpeted floor and looked all around her. Definitely a lady's bedroom. A large oak tester bed stood against the wall on her right with faded brocade curtains, once perhaps pale gold, now dreary beige, enclosing it. She smelt mould, a faint hint of perfume mingling with stuffy, unwashed clothes and felt an urgent need to open a window; to let fresh, healthier air into this melting pot of memories and belongings.

The window, like the door, resisted her efforts and she could only rub her handkerchief against the stained, bleary panes of glass. She looked down on the garden below, and saw the river beyond, a shining ribbon of untouched serenity flowing peacefully this morning and seeming to offer none of its usual menace. Instinctively she felt that the menace was here, instead, in the room in which she stood, shivering – why so cold on a hot, late-summer day? But she wouldn't be forced into flight. There was more, so much more, that she needed to know and a strange certainty told her that it was all here, in this disturbing room.

With a fast-beating heart, Rose turned, almost ran towards the door. She closed it behind her, then found that resetting a lock with a hairpin was not as easy as picking it. She gave up the attempt and went downstairs, out into the garden, thankful to feel the sun warming her. As her panic subsided, she acknowledged that whatever she had felt in that lonely room upstairs had taken root; and that, although today she had fled from it, one day – quite soon – she must go up there again and face whatever it was the past wanted her to know.

CHAPTER ELEVEN

Thomas Devlin stood at the open schoolhouse door as she approached.

'What a beautiful day, Rose.' His smile, she thought, lit up his normally rather angular face. His voice was quiet but had a ring to it and as he stood back to allow her to enter, she smelled the faintest scent of soap.

Yes, he was clearly a man with a clean body – and she felt, a mind to match. New ideas and fresh-smelling clothes, even if well-worn, went well together. Then she kept her face hidden because it was amusing to think that Thomas Devlin used carbolic soap, until, unbidden, her thoughts abruptly ran back to Alice and the awful lye mixture the cottagers always used as they scrubbed and rubbed at their washing. Suddenly she wished that she could give Alice some of the comforts she so truly deserved.

Turning, she looked into Thomas Devlin's deepset and arresting slatey eyes and saw a hesitant request in them. She waited, took off her hat and put it on a chair.

'Rose. . . .'

'Yes, Thomas?'

'I wonder if you would do me a kind favour.' He stood at her side and she was aware of his height and his stillness.

'If I can.' She was enjoying the conversation – why, she wondered?

'It's Lucy. She needs company and I'm forever here, working on the alterations. Mrs Benthall is very good, but she's not exactly – I mean . . .' The hint of a smile stretched his straight lips.

'I know what you mean.' The brief moment of amusement pleased her as they grinned at each other. 'Of course I'll do whatever I can to help out.' Inspiration came suddenly. 'Perhaps Lucy might like to come back to Sandiford House for tea today?' A vision of Elizabeth's surprised face, came and went. Surely, a helpmate, even if only temporary, was entitled to have visitors?

Thomas blinked and then nodded. 'That would be wonderfuL She often asks about you. Would you. . . ?' He paused and Rose smiled back, eager to help.

'I'll collect her when I've finished here. And I'll bring her back to Mrs Benthall after tea.' She changed the subject briskly. 'Now, what would you like me to do today?'

He didn't reply at once. Instead he looked at her. Rose felt colour warming her cheeks – again, why? And then it dawned – this was the way Will Sharcombe looked at her – with warmth, with affection, even with a certain idea in his mind. She was used to Laurence's long stares, but this was quite different. Returning it, she began to understand that Thomas just looked because he wasn't really used to talking to women, that probably he kept away from them because he still missed his late wife. And that he was definitely as astounded at this exchange of unexpected curiosity as she was.

At last he said, low and quiet, 'I don't think there's anything at all, Rose. You've made it all clean and ready for next week. Don't let me keep you any longer.'

She said nothing because this little moment of companionship was as enjoyable as it was surprising. Maybe Thomas Devlin wasn't quite as superior and distant as she had at first thought him. Her smile grew as her thoughts expanded. Amusement grew. He was a man – didn't that explain everything?

'I see you've finished the partition,' she said helpfully.

'Yes, it's done.' He was still looking at her and she realized that for that short moment of mutual exploration he had been a long way from the business of school and work. She watched him thinking things out, and then saw the old Thomas Devlin returning, heard it in his clipped voice. 'The boys worked well. I've told them to have time off. Let me show you.'

He walked her around the partitioned rooms. His room was large, containing the fireplace and had more furniture than hers, which was small and crowded, with the harmonium taking up a lot of space. Rose made no complaint. It was enough that they were talking together, discussing the new term which would start next Monday. Enough that he had asked her to look after Lucy for a while.

When the inspection was finished she complimented him on the work.

Dutifully she said that of course the partition would definitely improve the concentration of both classes. She picked up her hat, smiled a last time, and said, 'I'll go and collect Lucy now, Thomas. And bring her home again after tea.'

He stood in the doorway, his grey eyes silvery in the afternoon sunshine. 'Thank you, Rose. I'm very grateful.'

'Not at all. Goodbye, Thomas.' She walked away, heading for Church Street, and feeling him watching her all the way. She was still smiling as she knocked on the door of Number Ten.

They walked back through the village hand in hand, Rose taking the little girl's weight as she limped along. After a short silence, Lucy said in her quiet, thoughtful voice, 'Can we go into the grassy place again, Miss Adams? Like we did before?'

Rose was charmed. 'Better than that, Lucy – today we'll go into a lovely garden, and sit down under a big sunshade while we have our tea. I think you'll like that.'

The child's upturned face beamed and her lagging steps grew easier. 'I will! But I wish Papa was here too.'

Rose found herself echoing the thought. She was surprised, but intrigued enough to want to know more about Thomas Devlin.

Elizabeth Mount frowned across the bamboo table, laden with tea cups and plates of cakes, at her brother, lounging inelegantly in a bamboo chair, feet apart, coat creased as it hung at his side. 'Really, Laurence, you look like a beggar. And I can smell drink from here . . .' She sniffed, grimaced and looked away into the garden to ease her distress.

It wasn't easy having a brother who had such totally different ideas and values from her own. In London he'd worked all day in his studio, so she'd only seen him in the evenings when he was tired and not inclined to tease her, as he so often did now. Here, he seemed to find so many irritations – the dog and new ideas being only a few of them. She recalled his volatile temper and wondered if he'd even been irritated by Rose, who so seldom went to the studio now. Heaving a great sigh, she allowed her thoughts to wander on.

She had hoped so much that, coming here, into the backwoods of Devonshire, where no one would pay either of them any attention, that perhaps he would settle down, paint landscapes, even eventually recapture the growing reputation for which he had been acclaimed as a reviver of the Pre-Raphaelite Brotherhood style of painting. He had been doing so well, until that unfortunate scandal over the model turned everything upside down.

But this wouldn't do. One must be disciplined and think positive thoughts. She relaxed her tense shoulders, poured out second cups of tea and made herself meet his amused, idle stare, knowing that the familiar ridicule lurked in those gleaming eyes.

'So tell me about your crusade, Elizabeth.' He lit a cigar without asking her permission, and she winced as the smoke hit the back of her throat.

Her colour rose, as did her voice. 'You may laugh, Laurence, but Mrs Weston and I are creating a rest house where the poor bargemen – lightermen they're often called – may go for a break in their hard lives. They can boil a kettle, make a cup of tea, even have some sort of little meal.'

Laurence's laugh boomed out. 'Just what they all want, no doubt! Tea and warnings about the devil they really prefer.'

Elizabeth pursed her lips. 'You may find it funny, dear brother, but believe me, the odd cup of tea when you're thinking of spirits would be far better for you.'

In the distance the gate opened and footsteps approached on the gravel. She turned and looked around. Who would be coming to call? As Rose and a child appeared from behind the sheltering bushes, her curiosity waned. Her new appointment as trustee of the national school in the village meant she must get used to talking to children. Here was a splendid opportunity.

'Rose! I'm pleased to see you.' Rose was always so helpful in reducing the effects of Laurence's outrageousness. And the little girl, with hair the shade of a ripe apricot, was neatly dressed, but limping. Elizabeth smiled graciously. 'And who have you brought with you? Come and sit down, both of you.'

Rose's awareness, as she felt the charge of feeling between brother and sister, told her that she had walked into a maelstrom of emotions. Elizabeth must be extremely anxious about her brother. Not just that, but now Laurence was looking at her, plainly seeking to hold her gaze. What did he want? And – yes – what did she want in return?

She was thankful when he got up, pulled the bench seat nearer and gestured Rose to his vacated chair. He smiled at the little girl who stared at him with great wide eyes. 'Hallo,' he said warmly, 'my name's Laurence – what's yours?'

'Lucy Devlin.' She whispered the two words as she slipped on to the bench and looked at Rose for reassurance.

'The same as Lucy Locket?'

'No. I saw you the other day by the river . . .' Lucy's whisper brought a smile to his face.

So Laurence was intent on making friends. Rose was grateful. She smiled at him. 'Lucy is Mr Devlin's daughter. He asked if I could look after her for the afternoon as he's extremely busy. And so, Mrs Mount,' she smiled hopefully at Elizabeth, 'I thought you wouldn't object to my bringing her to tea. We're going for a walk later on.'

'Where to?' Laurence asked lazily, offering Lucy a plate of jam tarts.

Elizabeth interrupted. 'Laurence, really – the child needs to sit up to the table and eat properly. I'll ring for Mrs Briggs to bring some more cups.' She turned to Lucy and gave her an approving smile. 'How do you do, Lucy? I am Mrs Mount and this is my home. I'm pleased to welcome you here.'

Lucy looked confused, but remembered her manners, bowed her head and then stared at her feet.

Poor child, thought Rose, putting an arm around the thin shoulders. Then she smiled at Laurence as Elizabeth rang her handbell, bringing Nancy Briggs puffing out to take the orders. 'Perhaps after we've had tea you might like to show Lucy some of the object lesson paintings you've done for the school, Laurence?'

He looked at her appreciatively. The sun that drifted through the canopy of tall shrubs around them gleamed fiery-gold on her knotted hair beneath the straw hat. 'Take it off,' he said quietly, leaning forward and touching the hat. 'I want to see your hair in all its glory. I've missed it, Rose.'

Her smile died, she glanced at Elizabeth in embarrassment, received a tight frown in reply, but she did as he asked, and saw how instantly his expression changed. Warmth filled his face and she remembered how, the first moment they met, she had been charmed by his friendly expression. 'And I've missed that hard chair, too. Perhaps . . .'

But Elizabeth was looking at them both, clearly shocked. Rose saw distress beneath the taut expression and wondered just how much love there was for the reprobate brother. Enough to mend their differences and put their lack of understanding on a safer, warmer footing? She hoped so, and determined to do all she could to help.

'Mrs Mount,' she said warmly, 'it's good of you to allow me to bring

Lucy here. Would it be all right if we went up to the studio and looked at Laurence's paintings which he's done for the school?' At the back of her mind a small voice urged *don't go up there alone with him; tell Elizabeth what's going on otherwise she'll start suspecting things and life will be even more difficult.*

'What a good idea, Rose. Why, I might even accompany you myself.' The rather highpitched voice sounded easier and Elizabeth's high colour began to fade. Until Laurence said wickedly, 'I don't think you'll manage all those stairs, you know – just ask Lucy to tell you all about things when we come down again.'

Catching the furious glance that Elizabeth slanted at him, Rose resented his adding to his sister's natural distress at his behaviour. She realized now that she had arrived at an inopportune moment, when Elizabeth was probably trying to make her brother reform. Again, *men,* Rose thought darkly; *never behaving as you expect them to.*

She turned to Lucy, now fidgeting on the hard seat, and said quietly, 'In a moment you'll have a nice cup of tea and perhaps one of those jam tarts.'

Elizabeth pushed the plate across the table. 'Certainly you may have one, Lucy.' She paused, allowed the smile to broaden, watching small fingers selecting a tart. 'And what do you do all day while your papa is so busy, child?'

'Mrs Benthall looks after me.' The voice was low, Lucy's eyes remained on her plate.

Elizabeth turned to Rose, their eyes met in an instant of understanding as Rose mouthed silently, *Lucy has no mother. Poor child.*

When tea was over, after Henny had been introduced to Lucy and made much of, and Nancy Briggs had cleared away the plates and cups, Laurence rose and held out his hand. 'Come on, Lucy Locket. Let's go and look at my pictures.'

She got up without hesitation and put her hand in his. Rose saw the innocent and trusting smile and felt a warm glow inside her. Who knows? Perhaps Laurence and Elizabeth might find themselves reunited with this mutual pleasure in Thomas Devlin's daughter.

Laurence looked over his shoulder. 'Coming, Rose?' His eyes were amused, his smile relaxed and she could do nothing but say, 'Yes, of course. Excuse us, please, Mrs Mount?'

Elizabeth nodded, picked up Henny and seated the dog on her lap. Her face seemed easier than it had been all the afternoon as she watched the three of them leave the terrace, Lucy's hand in Laurence's, her awkward leg helped by the slowness of his steps. She wondered whether perhaps a change had occurred in his mind – if being with the child might even help him to confront his personal demons.

Sighing, she looked down at Henny, already settling down for a nap. 'We'll just have to see, won't we, Henny?' she murmured; thinking hopefully that somehow the day seemed a little brighter.

The studio's windows were closed and a smell of size, paint, cigar smoke and brandy fumes filled the room. Rose stopped in the doorway. 'Laurence! For heaven's sake open the windows! This smell—

'Don't fuss, Rose. Just a good working fragrance.' But he did as she asked and grinned at her over his shoulder.

Lucy stood in the middle of the room, staring around her until Rose led her to the pile of canvases standing against the far wall. She picked up the first, turned it over and held it out for the child to see. 'What's this, Lucy?'

Lucy's eyes widened and slowly an expression of delight filled her small, pale face. 'A boat.'

'Indeed it is.' Laurence was beside them. He looked at Rose. 'You were right about your object lessons, weren't you? I foresee a great future for me as the new educationalist painting expert. I shall bring all these down to the school and make sure the local press is there to report on my undoubtedly talented work.'

Rose laughed. She was more at ease with him now. This was the old Laurence, enjoying her company and making no demands on her. She said, 'I'm not sure about the expert bit, Laurence, but certainly these pictures will help both Mr Devlin and me once school starts next week.'

'Mr Devlin. Hm. . . .' He was busy sorting out more of the canvases, showing them to Lucy, nodding as she told him the name of each subject, but looking at Rose as he did so. 'So tell me about this paragon. Clever, is he?' His eyes grew darker. 'Handsome? Attractive? But married, obviously . . .'

Rose shook her head and frowned, glancing down at Lucy. 'Widowed,' she breathed quietly and was shocked to hear Laurence's great laugh echoing through the room.

'Which makes him even more attractive, of course. Don't tell me you're going to fall for a schoolmaster?' The patronizing tone incensed her at once.

'Don't be ridiculous!' She took Lucy's hand. 'Come along,' she said, leading her back towards the door. 'We'll leave Mr Vane and go for a walk. Say goodbye and—'

'I'm coming with you,' said Laurence at once, grinning down at Lucy and taking her other hand. 'Come on, Miss Locket – I want to know how many flowers you can find out there in the grass.'

If he felt any of Rose's disturbance he made nothing of it, helping Lucy down the stairs, chatting as he did so, and then allowing her to choose which stick he should take from the jardiniere in the hall. Only then, as they moved towards the open front door, did he glance at Rose and laugh.

'Dear Rose,' he said easily, offering her his free hand. 'Don't let anything mar this very happy afternoon. After all, it's not often you find me in such a good mood – and even Elizabeth was smiling again – so why not make the best of it?'

She avoided his hand and looked very directly into his intense gaze. 'All right, Laurence, if that's what you want.' And then some inward thought made her add, 'But please don't let anything spoil it. Lucy's happiness is important to me.'

His voice was low, for her ears only, as they stepped out down the gravel path towards the garden gate. 'Trust me, Rose. Just – trust me. That's all I ask.'

The sun shone, the river crooned a muted song, and it seemed to Rose that suddenly the whole world was smiling, at one with them. She and Laurence, hand in hand with Lucy, walked slowly along the path threading through the marshes. Wind-drifting grasses blew across their bodies and butterflies like brilliant jewels fluttered from moon daisy to purple thistlehead.

Laurence told Lucy that he was going to paint a sheep. What colours should he use? And should it have horns? Rose listened, and saw Lucy's shyness disappear. She wondered at this turnabout – at the quick change from his recent boorishness to solicitude for the crippled little girl, and found her opinion of him was also changing. Perhaps she had been silly in fleeing from the studio when he stood over her that day, bending down, stroking her hair, looking into her eyes; perhaps after all he had meant nothing more than an artistic companionship. Why had she run? Should she apologize, ask to be invited back to the studio so that the portrait could be finished? Would it improve the atmosphere between brother and sister?

By the time they had reached the river path and stood gazing at the river quietly flowing past, she knew what she must do.

In the quietness, while Lucy watched a dragonfly with transparent shining wings patrolling its territory, she glanced at Laurence, saw him watching her, and said, 'I'm sorry I upset you that morning. Could we . . .' She paused, seeing how his dark eyes instantly widened and the full lips beneath the moustache lifted. 'Perhaps we could start again, Laurence?'

At once his free hand reached out, gripped hers. 'Thank you,' he said, very quietly, very intently. 'Thank you, Rose. I need you if I'm to finish the portrait. When can you come? This evening? Tomorrow?'

Rose heard the quick emotion and was deeply moved. Somehow she must find time to return to the studio, to help Laurence to recover what was clearly the motivation in his life and allow him to finish the portrait. Time, she thought, perplexed; *how can I fit all this into my busy life? But I must. For Laurence's sake, I must.*

They walked back across the marshes, with Lucy now chattering freely, her pale eyes smiling first at Rose and then up at Laurence. 'Can I come again?' she asked and it was Laurence who nodded his head. 'Of course. Whenever you like, Miss Locket.' Rose heard the shared laughter – the child's high giggle and his deep chuckle, and thought what a happy meeting this was proving to be.

Lucy's keen eyes saw the distant figure first. 'Who's that?' she asked, nodding towards the end of the footpath. Rose said slowly, 'Why, it looks like Will Sharcombe.'

Laurence stared. 'Who's Will Sharcombe?'

Surprised by the harsh note in his voice, Rose said quickly, 'A friend of mine. He's a clay worker. He doesn't usually come home this way. I wonder . . .'

She got no further. Laurence halted, continuing to stare at the figure ahead of them who waited, half-concealed beneath a thickly leafed willow tres, and said, frowning, 'He's up to no good. What does he want, loitering around here? I'll have a word with the constable. We don't want the likes of him near the house.'

Rose was astounded. 'There's no harm in Will, Laurence.'

His laugh was loud and ugly. 'I'm not so sure! I know his type – hanging about, looking for a chance to break in, more than likely.'

Rose saw Lucy's eyes anxiously flitting first from her, then to Laurence, and at once realized that the child had heard more than she should. 'Come along, Lucy, it's time to take you home now,' she said brightly, turning and shaking her head at Laurence as she did so.

'That man . . .' The little girl sounded distressed and Rose drew her close. 'Nothing to worry about. Look, he's gone now – and we must hurry or your father will be home before us and wonder where you are. Say goodbye to Mr Vane, Lucy.'

Laurence bent over the child's outstretched hand, took it, kissed it and smiled at her as he touched her cheek. Rose saw that he had recovered from his anger and was thankful. She didn't know why the sight of Will Sharcombe should have been so disturbing, but her new knowledge told her that the artistic personality often had odd fads and ideas. She smiled at Laurence, held out her own hand and said quietly, 'Thank you for coming out with us. And, yes, I will come back and sit for you. Just give me a little time, Laurence.'

'You promise?' There was a look on his face that melted her.

'I do. Perhaps after school tomorrow afternoon. Just for an hour.'

To her surprise he kept hold of her hand, swept off his hat, then drew her towards him and quickly kissed her brow. 'Dearest Rose. I shall be waiting.' His smile, as he bowed to both of them, was good to see; then he stood at the end of the path, watching as together Rose and Lucy walked towards Church Street.

Lucy chattered on about dragonflies, Mr Vane's pictures, the big house, Mrs Mount's beautiful dress and those lovely jam tarts, but Rose's mind was engaged elsewhere. She accepted that she had turned a difficult corner, around which there would be no going back – indeed, her life was going forward. Laurence needed her, and already she had a very soft spot in her heart for him. He was lonely, so surely it was the very least she could do for him and his kind sister – to help him finish the portrait. For who knew, perhaps it would help return him to the lost life of artistic creativity that he must miss so much down here in Devon.

After school on Monday she would sit for him, up in that smelly studio, with the roof creaking slightly as the brilliant sun outside slowly heated it. She would don the green dress, smile at Laurence, and allow him to unpin her hair. And this time there would be no quick and foolish flight. Laurence meant her no harm – indeed, she was beginning to think that he had warm thoughts about her. As, indeed, she suddenly realized, she had about him.

CHAPTER TWELVE

Monday morning saw a misty rain sweeping across the river and over the marshes as Rose, with several children from the other cottages, walked to school, first calling at the Netherton home to make sure that Billy would not miss the first day of term.

Mrs Netherton grabbed Billy's arm as he wriggled and scowled. 'You go along with Miss Adams, boy, or your dad'll tan you when he comes home.'

'But I gotta help with the boats. Mr Adams'll say I'm skiving if I'm not there.' Billy's suntanned face had filled out, and his thin body looked much stronger these days, Rose saw with pleasure.

She smiled, pushing him in front of her along the path. 'No, he won't, Billy. He knows school starts today. So come on – you've got a new master and he'll be doing interesting things, I'm sure.'

Billy reluctantly dragged himself along, but soon he was part of the small gang of children coming from the other cottages. They were laughing, chattering, fighting as they spread out over the marshes, but Rose took no notice of the noise and mêlée. They would be shut up for hours today and this expression of energy was necessary if the schoolroom was to be quiet and focused.

At the other end of the footpath came the village children, with Charlie Wheeler leading his group of friends. Canal Cottagers and villagers met, stopped, shouted insults and formed a few eager fists, but as soon as the bell rang outside the schoolhouse entrance, everything quietened down. Inside the door boys went to one side and girls to the other, to hang up their jackets and caps in separate lobbies, straightening their untidy cord trousers and calico pinafores before filing into the main schoolroom.

Rose followed, quickly putting her list of suggested lessons on Thomas's desk. She breathed in the familiar tang of dust and old books and suddenly missed Miss Hodge more than she thought possible. Would Thomas Devlin fill her place with the same understanding and tolerance, she wondered? Thank goodness, at least, that so far no violence was marring the day. She hoped that Thomas understood the age-old conflict between village and canal dwellers, and wondered just what he would do about it when the inevitable fights broke out in the playground.

Inside the crowded room, which was still smelling of the wood stain on the new partition, his crisp voice took her by surprise. 'Good morning, children. I am Mr Devlin, your new master. I hope we shall all work together very happily. Now go to your desks and sit down while I call the register.'

Standing close to his desk, exchanging a smile with Lucy who was sitting at the end of one of the long forms, Rose listened to the voices responding to his list. She saw Charlie Wheeler dart a wicked look at his neighbour, and caught his whisper: 'Devlin? Devil, more like!' A surge of giggles swept over the room until Thomas's head lifted. He looked around the class and at once there was silence. No more interruptions broke the quietness.

Where was the cane? wondered Rose, looking around. Miss Hodge had kept it on her desk in full view, even though she rarely used it. Now it hung on the new partition, next to a map of the world, almost like a decoration, she thought, and felt her lips twitching at Thomas's unexpected wry sense of humour.

He completed the register, closed the book, sat back and looked around the class. Rose noticed how his controlled expression and steady gaze moving from face to face, had an instant effect on the watchful children. Billy had stopped scowling and even Charlie looked interested. Lucy, of course, kept her eyes on her father with an expression of infinite faith and happiness. This discipline was amazing, thought Rose, and she felt her hopes rising; perhaps this term, under a new master, would give more to the children than old-fashioned Miss Hodge had ever done.

Thomas's voice was quiet, each word clear. 'I expect you all to work, to behave properly, to show respect for Miss Adams and myself, and to be nice to each other. That's all I have to say. Except that I don't approve of corporal punishment, but if I have to unhook that cane,' he pointed, 'then I shall do so.' A smile flitted briefly over his face. 'I quite like it hanging there as a decoration, so don't make me take it down, please.'

Silence, while Rose accepted that this was the first time he had acknowledged her presence. She felt curiously stirred up, agreeing with much of what he had said, and yet there was no mention of her new ideas which she had put on his desk just now. Surely he had looked at them? And, if not, would lessons be just the same – Bible readings, memorizing of the collects for the week, occasional object lessons when the children could give vent to their imagination, before copying out long-worded and dull passages from ancient books?

She was on the point of asking him, when the door opened and the trustees entered. The Reverend Toogood, tall and thin as a scarecrow, his black cassock and overcoat flapping as he strode across the floor, was followed closely by Mr Wheeler, wearing what Rose guessed was probably his best dark coat and grey trousers and carrying his heavy bowler hat. Beside these two dark figures, Mrs Mount arrived like a breath of spring, wearing a pale dress beneath a floaty mantle, and a decorated hat which, Rose guessed, the little girls would giggle at and talk about during many playtimes to come.

Smiling, Thomas went to meet them, and Rose wondered what he really thought of this motley crew of gentrified superiors. She admired his relaxed manner as he gestured to the children to stand up, boots grating on the floorboards, benches scraping back, coughs and snuffles ceasing. Rose watched the small anxious faces concentrating on this panel of gentry who, they feared, might ask them impossible questions.

But Mr Toogood was in a hurry. 'Mr Devlin, I can only spare five minutes. My curate is unwell and I have to deputize for him at a funeral. Perhaps I could just say a few words before I leave?'

The few words were ones Rose had heard at the start of every new term. Quotations from the Bible, warnings of the consequences of rough behaviour and lack of respect, and then a blessing. 'Lord, we pray you to let your sun shine upon these poor children and enlighten their young minds.' Then, with a flurry of his black overcoat and a tapping of his stick, Mr Toogood strode out of the school, leaving the remaining members of the board somewhat at a loss.

Thomas asked his guests to be seated, pulling out chairs and making sure that Mrs Mount, in particular, was comfortable. Then he faced the children. 'Our trustees have given up their time to visit us this morning and in return I think we should all do our best to welcome them. So shall we say good morning, Mrs Mount, and Mr Wheeler? With me, then . . .'

Slowly the shrill voices echoed the names. Faces began to relax and smile, and when Thomas turned to Mr Wheeler, asking him for advice about the term ahead, the children stood silently attentive.

Only Rose felt uneasy. She knew Walter Wheeler and his unkind and intolerant thoughts and hoped fervently that he wouldn't upset this new and hopeful atmosphere that Thomas had, so far, created. She was right to be anxious.

'You gotta work, that's what I have to say.' His voice was rough and loud. 'No sloping off, no keeping away from school for holidays and heydays – oh yes, I know all about having to take breakfast to your fathers when they'm working on the clay or the barges at the quay. And just because there's a fair or a flower festival in the village, you don't stay away from school. And if you do . . .' The word was drawn out, followed by a long pause, while he frowned at each distressed face staring at him. 'If you do, I'm quite sure Mr Devlin will know how to deal with you when you comes back again. There's a good saying I'm going to repeat, like I have many times before – spare the rod and spoil the child. And you all knows what that means.'

Silence. Mr Wheeler smiled with satisfaction, looked at Thomas and nodded. 'That's so, Headmaster, isn't it?'

For a moment Rose caught her breath. How would Thomas answer? She looked at his tall, spare body, and thought how assured he looked, in control of what might be an awkward situation. When he replied, his voice was pleasant and quiet, as if she thought, highly entertained, he and Mr Wheeler were merely passing the time of day.

'We've already discussed this, Mr Wheeler,' he said easily. 'The children understand that there are rules to be obeyed, just as there are lessons to be learned if they are to be educated and grow into young people who can find positions and earn their livings. They also realize that times change, and with a change of schoolmaster they will probably learn new things that will give them enough interest to want to keep attending school. I hope so, anyway.'

Rose saw Walter Wheeler's face flood with colour. But even as his mouth opened to argue, Thomas was already smiling at Elizabeth Mount, and saying, 'Is there anything you would care to offer the children, Mrs Mount?'

Elizabeth, to her credit, was quick to reply and so avoid the impending clash of wills. 'Nothing, Mr Devlin, except that I shall always be pleased to come and hear the children read, and to see their work. I hope they have a healthy and happy term, and of course I shall be helping to organize a Christmas party for them – so they can look forward to that.'

The children shuffled, stared at each other, exchanging sideways grins while Thomas nodded and smiled. 'Thank you, Mrs Mount. That sounds delightful.'

But Rose found it hard to conceal the annoyance rising up inside her. Really, what a pantomime this was! What did the trustees think they were doing? Was this the way to help educate the new generation? With strict sermons, dreams of parties and threats of the cane? Was that all they could do? She was thankful when, with excuses and much clattering of chairs, they stood up and bade goodbye to the gawping children.

Thomas escorted his board of trustees to the door, shut it once they had gone, and then returned to his desk. Briefly he glanced at Rose, said, 'Please take your class next door now,' and then picked up a reading book. Rose only had time to register that it was a new book, not the ancient Bible which usually began the day, before she, too, was up and taking her younger children into the room beyond the partition.

But her mind was overflowing. She was hurt at his short, almost peremptory order. And another thing – she must talk to him about the trustees and their ridiculous input. This was no way to start a new term, with a new master already obviously planning his own way of teaching, and a reforming assistant schoolmistress with definite ideas of the better way to educate children and make them useful citizens of today's world.

She would corner him the moment the 12.30 bell rang. Impossible to keep all these complaints stifled inside her for much longer. But now she had her class to organize, to settle and start teaching. The irritation quickly died; she felt that this was her job in life, and she was eager to begin.

Lucy was her prime concern, so the little girl was seated quite close to her own desk facing the ranked benches and desktops in front of her. Eventually the scuffling feet stood firm, the twelve girls and five boys stood, looking expectant, until Rose, smiling warmly, said, 'Sit down, children. Today we shall start our new term with some arithmetic, then we'll look at a new reading book, and after playtime we shall talk about what we all did during the summer holidays.'

At once she felt the buzz of surprise going around the class. She smiled to herself. What they had expected was the usual Bible reading, then the recitation of quotations given by Miss Hodge at the end of last term as a holiday task, followed by some writing in copybooks. Well, she would soon see what they thought of the new curriculum. Her spirits rose as she added to herself *and Thomas will soon understand too.* She could hear his voice through the partition and decided to raise her own voice so that he would be aware of what was going on next door. Childish, perhaps, but then her shoulders tensed. He needed to understand that she was an experienced and, if she could believe what Miss Hodge had said about her, talented teacher and that her new ideas would take much of the old dull routine out of the class work.

She looked at the children. They all showed signs of poverty and lack of care. Patched, even ragged clothes. Pale faces and thin bodies. Emotion raced through her. She was sure she could help them. A great warmth filled her as she took a deep breath, before dipping into the bag she had filled from Alice's meagre pile of vegetables. 'Now, let's start with this apple,' she said. 'And this carrot. One and one makes. . . ?'

At first there was little response, but as she added more and more items to the pile of fruit and vegetables on her desk, holding them up and talking about them, so the voices gained confidence and the answers came quickly.

Rose was delighted. And particularly as she saw that Lucy was coming out of her shyness and taking part in the lesson. When she rang the bell for playtime, telling Lucy to keep with one of the older girls, she was ready to talk to Thomas and tell him how well her class had received at least one of her new ideas.

They met at the door into the playground as they ushered out their groups of children. They looked at each other just inside the door. Rose smiled. 'Have we time to talk, Thomas? I want to tell you—'

He cut in sharply. 'And I want to tell you, Rose, that I've read your list of suggestions and, in the first place, I cannot agree with your idea of teaching arithmetic. I heard no chanting of times tables, which is vital if the children are to learn how to count. What are you thinking of?' His expression was clearly exasperated and she flinched.

But then, incensed, she said quickly, 'Of giving my class a new interest in lessons, of course. All that old chanting and repetition of words is only learning without thinking, without using their minds properly. Thomas, I do ask you to consider – at least let me try my ways for a few weeks and then we can see what results I get.'

She watched his lean face tighten, felt the hurt of his disapproval as well as a swelling sense of annoyance, as she realized that she had no way of making him change his mind. Annoyance swelled into anger and without thought, she added hotly, 'Don't you realize that times are changing? We shall soon be in a new century. Surely new ideas are justified?'

Beneath frowning brows his eyes were dark and cold. 'Rose, this is ridiculous. You're here to work under me and take my orders. You can't just do what you like.'

'But I shall, Thomas!' Now she was well into her stride, feeling proud of saying all that she felt. 'I may be only a certificated teacher, and a woman at that, but believe me, my mind is just as intelligent as yours. And I'm determined to prove it, never mind what you think and say.'

His face was tense and hers was flushed. They stared at each other in hostile silence while outside the children shouted and whooped and then, above the concerted noise, one voice rose in a piercing wail. Rose turned her head. 'That's Billy.'

She pushed past Thomas and ran into the playground. Sure enough, two boys were forming up close to the wooden picket fence. Charlie and Billy, fists up, were dodging around, arms flailing. Billy had a bloody nose and Charlie was grinning triumphantly. Around them other boys gathered, watching and cheering their favourite.

Rose was horrified. Using all her force, she ran straight into the arms that hit out and felt one of them strike her shoulder. But nothing stopped her determination.

'Charlie, stop it immediately! Billy, go and wash your face. Fighting is absolutely forbidden, as you both know. I shall ask Mr Devlin to—'

A firm voice cut in. 'Wheeler, stand still. Netherton, you too.' Thomas was beside her, calm and authoritative and both boys instantly did as they were told, Charlie with a surprised expression on his face, and Billy snivelling loudly as he held his jacket sleeve to his nose.

Rose felt the wind taken out of her sails, but knew instinctively that a man's presence would have more effect on the boys than her own. She stood aside, her hand pressing her shoulder, wondering what Thomas would do next.

'This sort of incompetent fighting is absurd and useless,' he said, almost casually. 'But if you wish to learn to box, both of you, then I will arrange for someone to come and give you instruction. Of course, your parents must give their permission first. Tell me if that's what you want. Wheeler?'

Charlie swallowed, mumbled something and went red. He moved from one large foot to the other and avoided Thomas's gaze.

'Well? I'm waiting, Wheeler.'

Rose began to feel grudging admiration for this approach to playground violence. She watched with growing interest as Charlie eventually looked up, and said hesitantly, 'Er – yes – I'd like to know how to do it proper like.'

Thomas waited. 'Sir.'

'Sir.'

Thomas nodded. 'Very well. I'll speak to your father. And you, Netherton – what've you got to say?' There was the slightest lift to his lip. *Why, he's almost smiling,* thought Rose in amazement.

Billy gulped and shifted around on his skinny legs. His jacket sleeve was stained red and his nose still dripped. He looked first at Rose, who nodded encouragingly, and then back at Thomas. 'Dunno,' he muttered, and raised the other sleeve to his wet nose.

Silence. Until he added: 'Sir.'

'Think about it, Netherton.' Thomas's tone was kinder. He looked at the small boy and a brief smile flowered. 'You can't go through life not being able to fend for yourself can you?'

'N – no, sir.'

Thomas regarded him thoughtfully, then added, 'This has happened before, I suppose?'

Billy stared at his hobnailed boots. 'Yes, sir.'

'Then it's definitely time you learned to stand up and fight back. Bullies like Wheeler need to be stopped, Netherton, don't you agree?'

Billy ceased wiping his nose and looked up in surprise. 'Yes, sir. Yes . . .'

'So you'd like me to speak to your parents and get their approval for you to have boxing lessons?'

The boy's mouth dropped open, but Rose saw a gleam of interest in his eyes. 'With Will Sharcombe, like?'

Quickly Thomas glanced at Rose, and she nodded. 'He's a good boxer.'

'Very well,' said Thomas. 'I'll see what I can do. And now, both of you, into the washroom and clean yourselves up.'

They moved away, but stopped as Thomas added, 'And just remember, I'll have no more of this fighting, and if there is I shall take my cane down from the partition and use it.' He paused and Rose saw his eyes intent on both boys. His voice was firm, but quiet. 'And if that happens you'll both get a damned good thrashing which you won't forget for a long time. Understand?'

Charlie's eyes widened, Billy looked terrified, then they both nodded, muttered 'yes, sir,' before rapidly disappearing in the direction of the washroom beside the earth closets at the end of the schoolhouse building.

Rose watched them, impressed with Thomas's handling of a nasty situation, and amazed at the authority in his quiet voice. She hadn't expected such dominance and began to understand the task ahead of her; trying to make Thomas Devlin agree with her new ideas was going to be far more difficult than she had first thought.

Suddenly, she became aware of the pain in her bruised shoulder, instinctively putting her hand on the sore place.

At once Thomas turned, looking at her with concern. 'What is it? Are you hurt, Rose?' His eyes narrowed. 'If either of those wretched lads hit you I'll . . .'

Rose was suddenly unsure of what she felt about him. Gone was the stern tightness of his expression, and his arresting grey eyes were concerned. She masked her confusion with a laugh. 'What will you do, Thomas? I think you've scared them enough already. Please don't worry about me, it was only a passing blow. Just a bruise, I think. It'll be better soon.'

'Come inside.' His arm was around her shoulder and she felt the strength and warmth of his body close to hers. Something happened in her mind then, echoed by a strange feeling inside her body. She wanted to go on disliking him, but how could she, when this extraordinary excitement was surging through her?

Thomas led her into her classroom and pulled out a chair. 'Sit down, Rose, and let me rub your shoulder.'

'No, really . . .' This was all too much. She wished he would disappear, that the children would return for the next lesson, even that Miss Hodge was here again. But the facts were against her. Everything had changed, and now she must change, too. Where was the strong woman who wanted a new life? Right here, she accepted wryly, sitting on a hard chair with Thomas standing over her, his hands already gently rubbing her painful shoulder.

She swallowed, felt a new warmth running down her arm. 'Th – thank you.'

Shaking his head, he smiled, as if amused at her embarrassment and continued the soft, soothing movement with strong fingers.

And then, abruptly, surprising her with its intensity, a new thought surged around Rose's bewildered mind. She was actually pleased that he was bringing a new atmosphere into the school. Now she wondered whether, even though he disapproved of her ideas, perhaps he might one day consider them. Perhaps, after all, there was far more to Thomas

Devlin than she had imagined. And was it possible that he might have more understanding of her problems than she could guess? Certainly he had magic in his hands and an attraction that was most disturbing. She smiled back at him and began to relax.

'It's better already. Thank you.'

When he stepped away and stood watching her, she felt bereft, foolishly wishing his hands were still at work on her shoulder. But life must go on. She rose, pushed the chair back to its usual position, collected her thoughts and said quietly, 'I'll see if Lucy is all right – I asked one of the bigger girls to look after her.'

Thomas was motionless, still looking at her. Then he moved away, heading for his own classroom. 'We're late for the bell, Rose,' he said, over his shoulder. 'Get them in at once, please.'

His voice was once again crisp and businesslike and Rose felt ridiculously foolish. What had she been thinking? The old irritation rose like a glowing torch. Thomas Devlin was egotistical and patronizing. She was quite sure that he would never agree to any of her ideas.

It was an enormous relief to gather the children again, to go through the rest of the day, listening to them haltingly telling of what they'd done in the holidays, and then, after some copywriting, thankfully ringing the 4.30 bell and seeing them all into jackets and hats and setting off home. She heard, safely distant from the school, Charlie Wheeler and his friends chanting 'Old Devil, Old Devil!' and shook her head. That boy was a problem.

Once the schoolhouse was tidied and safely shut up she, too, went out. She saw Thomas and Lucy walking towards Church Street, while she went the opposite way, heading for the marshes and Sandiford House.

And slowly the anger and frustration died, one thought alone filling her mind. Laurence would be waiting for her. They would have tea with Elizabeth, share an interesting and educated conversation. Elizabeth would be sympathetic about the first day of term, and Laurence, watchful and teasing, would be full of compliments meant to make her feel better.

Rose smiled gratefully as she knocked at the front door.

CHAPTER THIRTEEN

The door opened wide and Rose stared in surprise. Nancy Briggs glared at her. 'Oh! It's you, Rose, Miss Adams, I should say. Well, mebbe you can do something to sort it all out! It's beyond me, what with Daisy going off and then that little slut Jessie sayin' as how she must go shopping and get her new apron if she's gonna be a housemaid now – and then Madam ordering the gig, and what with trying to find someone to clear the stables – the horse'll be here termorrow, so Madam says – and now .. ' Nancy sniffed, and her leathery face crumbled as tears began to trickle down her cheeks.

Rose put an arm around the heaving shoulders. 'Nancy, come into the kitchen. Let's have a cup of tea, and you can tell me exactly what all this is about. Come on.'

The kitchen was warm, scented with the day's baking, and Nancy allowed herself to be seated in her usual chair while Rose made the tea. Tears still flowed, and Rose had the impression that all this upset was mostly because Nancy hadn't been consulted, had been left alone in a situation which was more than she could cope with.

'So what happened to Daisy? Why did she go off?' asked Rose, watching the older woman's control slowly returning.

' 'Er and that Jessie was always on at each other. An' then Jessie said some'at wicked 'bout Daisy's man and that were it. Off she goes. Well,' Nancy took a big gulp of tea. 'I tells madam, who says that it's a nuisance, but all we have to do is find a new scullery-maid and Jessie can be the housemaid. Well.' The old hostility was coming back. 'You can imagine – Jessie, to be a housemaid? I laughed, but she were all acock an' said she was goin' straight out to buy a nice new apron and a cap with streamers – an' would you believe it, she goes to see madam and ask for money to buy them!'

Rose stirred her tea, amused rather than worried. 'And did madam –
Mrs Mount – give her some?'

'Yes!' Nancy's voice was high and aggrieved. 'An' she's not back yet,
and I've got no one to do my veg for dinner.'

'I'll help, Nancy. But I must go and tell Mrs Mount what's happening.'
Rose finished her tea and pushed her chair under the table. 'And Jessie
will be back soon, surely, so she can help you too.'

'Huh!' But Nancy's contempt overcame the self-pity, and as Rose left
the kitchen she was already up and reaching for the ingredients for
dinner.

The house was quiet, but Henny heard Rose's footsteps approaching
the drawing-room and barked. Elizabeth's voice was gentle. 'Hush, now,
my pet.' Then, as Rose knocked on the door and entered, she looked
across the room and smiled warmly.

'Ah, Rose! Thank goodness you're here. Laurence said you would be
coming – well, before you start work on the painting, I want to talk to
you.' Henny was settled on her lap, and Elizabeth's smile dissolved into
irritation. 'Servants! Really, they're more trouble than they're worth.'
Then her colour grew even more florid with embarrassment. 'Oh, my
dear, I didn't mean you – believe me, Rose, I never think of you as
anything but a – well, a . . '

The pause was uncomfortable, and Rose tried to conceal the quick
annoyance those unthinking words had caused. Why was Elizabeth trying
to make excuses? Of course she was just a servant: a schoolmistress, an
artist's model and, if Jessie didn't come back soon, a scullery-maid as
well. The last thought produced a wry smile.

'It's all right, Mrs Mount. I know what you mean.' An awkward pause
and then 'Mrs Briggs has told me about Daisy and Jessie. And the gig and
the horse.'

Elizabeth returned the smile. 'All these things happening at once. But
you see, I do need a carriage of sorts to get me to Culmouth every day. I
mean, the shelter is coming along well, but Mrs Weston and I need to be
there constantly to oversee things. And she suggested the man who is selling me the gig and providing the horse, so that was easily arranged. But
then, well, I merely asked Mrs Briggs if she could find someone to clear
out the stables and she almost shouted at me.' Abruptly her voice grew
high and angry. 'Such goings on! In London servants were only too glad
to have a place.'

A heavy, breathing pause. And then she added, almost humbly, looking at Rose with beseeching eyes. 'My dear Rose, forgive me for all this, but I really feel at my wit's end. I need someone to take the burden of the house off my shoulders. Could you – would you – consider coming back here, as my helpmate, perhaps, to see to all the things I no longer have time for?'

Another pause, then quick persuasive words. 'We have plenty of bedrooms – and surely it would be easier for you, going to school every day and not having that awful walk across those wet and dangerous marshes. And, of course, we would come to some satisfactory agreement about your wages.'

Rose was shocked into confused silence. Schoolmistress, companion, model, daughter . . . how could she cope with such an overwhelming life? But inside her something urgent and exciting moved her to say slowly, 'I'll have to think about it, Mrs Mount. Thank you for asking me. Perhaps tomorrow I'll be able to answer you.'

Now it was easier to smile at each other and Elizabeth nodded, dropping a kiss on Henny's sleeping head.

Rose blinked, her thoughts running almost too fast. 'I expect I can find someone who'll be glad of a few days' work to clear the stables for you. And Jessie should be back by now, helping Mrs Briggs in the kitchen. So, if you don't mind, Mrs Mount, I must go up to the studio. Laur – Mr Vane – will be waiting for me.'

She withdrew quickly, closing the door and not looking back at Elizabeth's rather querulous expression. Breathing deeply, she stopped in the hall, thankful for the coolness of the marble tiles and the refreshing space of the wide staircase. All day she had been shut up in the stuffy schoolhouse with children around her and she hadn't expected to walk into this confused situation here at Sandiford House. Certainly she had enough on her mind without having to solve all the extra problems which had suddenly arrived.

Elizabeth's voice echoed in her mind. *Servants! More trouble than they're worth!* and her anger blossomed again. Who were these gentrified people, with no understanding of poverty and unemployment? None of them had ever done any hard work in their lives. Rose went up the stairs, resentful images flashing through her mind. What would Laurence do, for instance, if he had to dig ball clay and then load thirty tons of it on to a dangerously swaying, drifting flat-bottomed boat like her father did? Or supposing he had been born to a decent but poor family, as she imagined Thomas Devlin had, and had then climbed the ladder until he could teach some forty rebellious, snivelling children in a rural school to reach a certain standard of education, which might – or might not – allow one or two of them to earn a living wage?

And now, did she really want to live here, to leave her family and become part of this well-to-do community as Mrs Mount's helper – albeit as a servant, still?

Passing the portraits with their staring eyes and hard faces, all of them gentry with no experience of squalid rural living, she had a sudden clear image of Thomas Devlin, and unexpectedly she was able to smile, to push away her hot and shocking thoughts as she wondered just how he might deal with the situation she was now facing. On reaching the top of the first flight she paused again and looked down the corridor at the luxurious comfort that surrounded her; and then with a flash of intuition, she knew that in her place Thomas would be standing tall and still, calmly assessing what to do next. And, suddenly appreciating his strength, she felt some of it re-energizing her, so that she was then able to go on, to climb the narrow creaking, uncarpeted stairs and knock on the studio door.

'I'm here, Laurence.'

'Rose! My golden girl! Life hasn't been the same without you – come in, come in.'

When at last she got home Alice was at the door looking out for her. 'Where've you been, Rose? I know you said as you were goin' to the big house for a while, but it's late now and getting dark. Maid, you should a' come home before this.'

Rose took off her hat and jacket and sank into her father's chair, feeling weak with tiredness. School, then Elizabeth with her disturbing ideas, the offer of a new situation, and then Laurence talking, talking, when all she wanted was to sit and have some peace. And now this complaining welcome.

Emotion overcame daughterly thoughtfulness. 'Mother, I'm sorry if you worried. There was no need. I told you I would be late home. And now I'm here, so please don't go on at me.' Her voice was sharp.

Alice opened her eyes very wide and her thin face paled. 'I'm not going on.'

'Well, it sounded as if you were.' Rose leaned forward impetuously. 'I have two demanding jobs, Mother, don't you understand? School is the most important one, and I get quite tired teaching those poor ignorant children, and then, when I got to Sandiford House, Mrs Mount wanted to tell me all her problems, and then Laurence . . .' Rose stopped, seeing the shock on her mother's face. 'Well,' she said dismissively, 'Mr Vane talks a lot and expects me to pose in tiring positions. So I'm really tired. Please just let me be.'

Alice turned away back to the hearth, where a couple of iron pots steamed and hummed. She said nothing, but her expression was enough to make Rose realize how unkind she was being. And then, abruptly, the difference between the two houses filled her weary mind and she looked around with a new awareness. She saw the bare, cold floor, the shabby and stained walls where dampness streamed in the winter; a table, two chairs and a stool; and the hearth, where a fire was always burning, though fuel was hard and expensive to get, crowded with rusty black pots and a kettle, slowly cooking the one decent meal of the day. And, oh, the smell. Wet clay, onions and cabbage, people, and, when Father was here, cider and baccy.

And then she saw Sandiford House again, with its warmth, gaslight, expensive furniture and fittings and space. All that privilege there, and here only the basics. And suddenly, as though a shaft was digging deep into her, she knew she could stay here no longer. If she was to live the life that was slowly opening up for her, she must go and make the most of it.

'Mother . . .'

'Yes, maid?' Alice's voice was flat, her face expressionless and unhappy.

Rose's shoulders sagged. Why did personal fulfilment always come at other people's expense? She sucked in a deep breath. 'Mother, I know you won't like this, but I'm going to live at Sandiford House.'

'To live at. . . ?'

Rose looked away from the unbelieving, pain-filled gaze. 'Mrs Mount has offered me a position as helper, to help oversee her household while she's so busy with her lighterman's shelter. When I see her tomorrow I shall accept the post.'

Alice's hands crumpled and the big pot she had just pulled off the flames tipped sideways. Liquid ran, spitting, down the side of the hot hearth, but she took no notice. She was staring at Rose, her mouth working, eyes beseeching. 'No, you can't do that – not live at the big house – oh, my dear soul, Rose, what are you thinkin' of?'

Rose got up, found a cloth and began wiping the spilt mess. She didn't look at Alice, but said doggedly, 'I'm thinking of what's best for my life. And yours, Mother.' She met the question on Alice's face. 'It'll be easier for me, living there – not so far to go to school, and extra wages, and, Mother, I shall be able to give you money to help out here. Can't you see? It's all for the best.' Even as she spoke, the words rammed guilt into her churning mind. Best for her, yes, but loneliness and more worry for Mother.

Alice sank down into the cane chair by the hearth, hands wringing in her lap, her eyes holding Rose's. 'It doesn't matter 'bout the money. We can manage, we always have. No, maid, it's you I'm thinking of, in that big house . . .'

Rose reached for the stool and looked at her mother. Again, the old business about the house – what did it all mean? Why couldn't Alice tell her what was so obviously worrying her? 'Mother,' she said slowly, leaning forward and touching the clasped hands, 'what is it about Sandiford House that disturbs you so much? Can't you tell me?'

There was silence for a stretching moment and Rose saw emotions and memories flitting over the pale, distraught face. And then they heard Jack outside. He flung open the door, came in, bringing dampness and worka-day smells with him, and their moment of possible communication was broken.

He said nothing, just glared at them both as he dragged off his jacket, flung his cap at the hook on the door and lurched over to his chair. 'Well, nothin' to say, eh? Not a daughterly greeting, or a kind word? An' me wore out from all that blasted polin' downriver and back.' He looked at Rose, gave her a sneering grin, and said, in a false hoity-toity voice, 'Rose Victoria, if it's not too much to ask, get me a mug o'cider.' He watched her go to the cupboard before meeting Alice's eyes across the room. 'An' I'm starving – so get that tea on the table, eh, lover?'

The meal was eaten in silence. Rose and Alice avoided each other's eyes and then, while Jack belched and stretched out in his chair, Rose swallowed the dryness in her mouth and looked at him. 'Father,' she said, 'I have something to tell you.'

Fumbling for his pipe he turned. 'What's that, then?'

Rose paused, then found courage to say steadily, 'I have a new position and I'm going to live at Sandiford House.'

She expected anger, or at least, some coarse guesses at what the position would be, but to her amazement, Jack said nothing. Pipe still unfilled, he looked over the table at Alice and frowned. Rose watched, wondering. Alice merely shook her head and turned away to push the kettle further over the flames.

Jack filled his pipe, pushing the baccy down with his clay-stained thumb, lit it and then sat there puffmg, looking down at his boots. He said nothing and Rose found the atmosphere grow heavy and disturbing.

At last she said sharply, 'Well? I thought you'd be pleased I shall be earning extra money and it'll all come to you and Mother. I can live on my school earnings.'

Suddenly he stared round at her, his eyes narrowed, mouth lifted in an ugly sneer. 'An' what that painter chap gives 'ee, no doubt?'

Rose let the distasteful words die away before answering. She must keep her temper. It was going to be bad enough actually leaving home, but it must be done as amicably as possible. 'I get very little for posing for Mr Vane, Father, and I have already given that to Mother. Now I shall be able to give her more.'

'Huh.' A growl, a cough, then a bellyful of smoke discharged around the room. 'When you goin', then?' No anger, nor expected roaring and ranting. Just these few words.

She seized the opportunity. 'Tomorrow. Mrs Mount needs me as soon as possible.'

Again Jack looked at Alice. Watching, Rose saw an exchange of something she didn't understand. Then Jack nodded, put down his pipe, bent and unlaced his boots, and she realized the matter was over and done with. All that was left was the ordeal of leaving Alice tomorrow.

She needed air and space and freedom. She got up and smiled briefly at Alice. 'I'll be back soon, Mother. I just have to go and do an errand. I'll wash the dishes when I get back.'

She wrapped a shawl around her shoulders and was outside before either of them said anything more. An errand, she thought, confused; just an excuse, of course, but no, she must go and ask Ben Smith if he would consider clearing the stables at the big house. Just up the path, along the river. . . .

'Yes.' He grinned, coughing his way through the word and leaning weakly against the door jamb. 'Middling, but I'll be glad of the work. Eight o'clock at Sandiford House tomorrow morning? I'll be there, and thanks, Rose . . . you'm a good maid to put in a word for me, like you did fer our Jessie.'

The soft, warm evening was seductive and Rose lingered on the path, finding welcome peace, glad to feel the breeze lift her skirts and touch her hair. The sun was setting and already early autumn colours showed on trees and bushes along the path. There were blackberries and sloes, purple and rich, on the bushes beside her. Over the river the bare brown fields were dreaming now in newly harvested idleness, resting until spring again urged them into fresh growth. Colours soothed her, leaves touched with gold, stems and trunks shadowy and dark, the lush grass at her feet sweeping her ankles.

She leaned against the side of the railway bridge, watching the water racing past, gleaming with a metallic sheen in the dying light. Gulls streamed down seawards, their raucous cries slowly dying away leaving a silence that calmed her. Then – was it a shadow? Something was moving, slow and deliberate, among the shallows just a few feet away. She leaned forward. A heron fished there, blue-grey, tall, handsome, unaware of her presence, at one with the moving water and the attraction of food.

For a long moment she watched. Then she became aware of somebody else also watching it: a tall, dark-clad figure standing among the alder trees close by the bridge. Her solitude broken, Rose took a step forward and at once the bird was alerted. Head on one side, it saw her, uttered a loud croak and then, with heavy wings, flew away, the music of its flight filling her ears as she looked again at the figure among the trees and saw Thomas Devlin, watching the bird's departure.

He looked up, saw her, but said nothing. Was he annoyed at being disturbed? She recognized that too familiar tense expression, the straight mouth. Unsure of what to say, she waited, and then managed: 'I didn't know who it was there in the dark . . .'

'I hope I haven't startled you, Rose?' His voice was crisp and he walked slowly towards her.

She drew her shawl closer around her shoulders, wondering if the sudden chill was the evening air or Thomas's obvious wish to be left alone. 'No. I was just watching the heron.'

He nodded, but said nothing.

The pause was awkward, so she said quickly, not quite sure of what she was saying, or why, 'I love this time of the evening. The colours, the shadows, the river.' Then, as she watched, berating herself for even bothering to try and talk to him, she saw his face relax. The wide shoulders went down and one hand went into his jacket pocket. The straight mouth stretched and the beginnings of a wry smile shone out at her.

Almost like a revelation, information came in a flood. There were two Thomases – and this was the one she liked the most. Why couldn't he always be like this? Was it because of losing his wife that he so easily became solitary and unfriendly? Was it – her smile died – because he found the assistant schoolmistress difficult to deal with? That jolted her out of introspection and into immediate speech. Perhaps if she complimented him on his own achievements, he would think more kindly of hers.

'Thomas, you were wonderful with Charlie Wheeler and young Billy today. Such an excellent idea to get Will Sharcombe to teach them to box.'

He was at her side, both of them standing on the path with the river rippling alongside them. Small splashy waves occasionally burst over the bank, and at one point Rose moved back quickly, smiling. 'Mind your feet!'

'Yes,' was all he said. Still he looked at her.

Rose searched blindly for inspiration. How to get him to talk to her? In desperation, she asked brightly, 'And where is Lucy?'

His face darkened. 'She has the beginnings of a cough and cold. I didn't want to bring her out into the night air. Luckily, Mrs Benthall's cousin is staying and offered to look after her for a short while.'

'So you came out by yourself to get some peace.' A strange and urgent need made her try and prise replies out of him.

'Yes.' He hesitated. 'I felt the need to be alone for a while. And as a boy I always found the river a source of interest – and quietness.'

'Did you?' Fascinated, she wanted to know more. 'Where did you live, Thomas? Not here in Devon? I mean, your voice – you sound . . .' This was terrible, she was as good as saying that he had a strange accent.

But the smile broke free. He put his head back and laughed, and at once she felt less alarmed, not so annoyed and frustrated. Intrigued.

'My family lived in the North.' His voice warmed. 'My father worked in a brickyard and my mother was a seamstress in a big house. I was left alone most of the time after school – so thank goodness for the river. I fished and explored – and collected bits of wood.' His mesmerizing eyes were silvery in the half-light and Rose felt herself drawn to what he was telling her.

'Wood?' Firewood, like she and Alice picked up bits of driftwood?

He nodded and the smile grew less strained. 'Odd shapes, different sizes, various woods. I enjoy carving them into – well, other things.'

She was entranced. Her original black-and-white sketch of Thomas Devlin was rapidly beginning to fill with colourful knowledge. So he wasn't as stiff and unbending as he had seemed at first. There was definitely more to this man than she had imagined. She nodded. 'The wood-carving class – oh, I see!'

'Yes. It seemed a good idea to pass on what little knowledge I have. Those boys . . .' suddenly his voice was fuller, words coming more quickly and Rose saw what she recognized as passion in the bright eyes, 'they deserve a decent education. I want them all to find good situations when they leave school.'

Rose had been about to agree and then give voice to some of her own – very different – plans, but she bit back the words. This wasn't the moment. They were just getting to know each other. Let it rest here. 'And you – back to you, Thomas?'

One eyebrow rose and he shifted, standing less stiffly. 'What next? My scholastic achievements? My ambitions? Are you really interested, Rose?' There was humour in the words and her spirits rose.

'Yes, I am. You know about me and I want to know—'

'What makes me tick? Why I can be friendly and then shut away. I'm sorry, I know I'm difficult. Perhaps I'll improve with age.' The smile was pleasant but suddenly not very real.

Rose hated herself for prying. What must he think of her? 'I'm sure you will. We all do. Well . . .' She stepped away, then half-turned, looking back at the cottages further down the path.

'I'll see you home. It's dark now, you might trip on these brambles and roots.'

'Please don't bother. I know the way so well.'

They looked at each other for what, to Rose, seemed a never-ending moment. Then he nodded. His voice reverted to the quiet, impersonal tone. 'Very well. I'll see you in the morning, then. Goodnight, Rose.'

There was nothing for it but to accept her dismissal. She pulled the shawl even tighter and said, 'Goodnight, Thomas.' And then, because he waited, not moving until she did, she walked away, knowing that he watched, and wondering what his real thoughts were – the ones she had no possible way of knowing.

Alice was brisk and straight-faced as Rose gathered her few bits and pieces: the well-worn woollen dress, the winter hat, hairbrush, underwear and summer shoes, her prized certificate of qualification. She put them all into an old fish-basket and stepped outside into the morning sun. She turned, met her mother's eyes and caught her breath. This was awful, worse than she'd imagined.

But Alice was in control today. 'Hope the new situation doesn't tire you too much, maid. Rest when you can.'

'Yes, of course.' Rose put down the bag and raised her arms. 'And Mother, I'm sorry about this – please try and understand . . .'

Alice was small, bony and trembling in her embrace, but her smile, as she looked at Rose was fixed. 'I know, I know. We'll miss you terrible. But you'll come and see us?'

'Of course.' Rose suddenly wanted to weep. What was she doing? Did she have to hurt her mother so? But yes, she did. Life was calling her and if she didn't want to end up living for ever in this hovel of a cottage, with no prospects other than teaching for the rest of her life, she must take the opportunity offered. She kissed Alice's cheek and held her tight.

'Don't forget us, maid – don't do that, will 'ee?'

'Never, Mother – of course I won't. How could I? This is my home, after all.' Quickly, to stop the tears flowing, she dropped her arms, picked up the bulging fibre bag and took the first difficult step away.

'Goodbye, then, lover. . .'

It was an overwhelming moment, leaving, knowing how Alice, despite her bravery, was feeling: betrayed, deserted, alone.

Rose paused at the bend in the path, looked back and waved, saw Alice nod and then go into the house. Only then did she wipe her eyes, straighten her back, and direct her thoughts – as well as herself – into the future that waited at Sandiford House.

CHAPTER FOURTEEN

The morning was sultry, the humid air making her too hot, her bag too heavy, as she walked along the river path towards the marshes, the day stretching ahead, full of too many unknown factors. How would Laurence welcome the idea of her living at Sandiford House, of taking his sister's place in supervising the servants? Of being there, after school and at weekends, to model for him? Did she really want to be so readily available?

Could she manage this new life? What about Thomas Devlin and his plain reluctance to accept the new ideas she had for teaching her class? Yes, last evening he had seemed friendly, if still aloof at some moments, but she knew very well that in school that brief friendliness would disappear. Well, what did it matter how he behaved? Apart from the fact that he was her superior and must, therefore, give her certain orders, her world revolved around many other more important people and events. She dismissed him without further thought.

But Mother and Father – what about them? Alice had shown steely courage when they parted just now, and strangely Jack had made no fuss about her leaving. Rose shook her head as she left the river behind and walked quickly along the footpath through the green, overgrown, marshes. No good worrying. The money she would earn from this new position would go straight home; she hoped that Alice would buy useful things – perhaps a paraffin stove to cook on, which would be more practical than always having the fire burning. And even a few comforts about the cottage – new curtains, some paint to wash the stained walls. . . .

She reached the gate of Sandiford House and paused there, putting her bag down and finding in her skirt pocket the note she had written early this morning. She hoped Mrs Mount would be glad to receive her acceptance of the situation. Presumably she would then order a bedroom to be prepared for her? Rose shook her head again as thoughts revolved in endless circles, Mrs Mount had clearly wanted her to take over her duties as quickly as possible. And if no bedroom had been made available yet, then she would sleep downstairs on the chesterfield until one was ready. Pushing away all uneasy eventualities, she willed herself to think positively.

Stop worrying. Take things one at a time. It's a big decision, but I know it's the right one. I'm on my way. . . .

A knock at the front door to deliver the note and leave her bag in the house, perhaps wonder at Jessie's beaming smile and new print dress. *Hallo, Rose – that old cow Daisy going off means I'm house parlour-maid, now – like my new uniform, do you?* Then, quickly, she could leave and head for school.

Already the children were trailing up the path, chattering, having small fights and bigger arguments, but were suddenly quiet when they saw her. 'Mornin', miss.'

Smiling, she let them pass, then followed behind and watched them form little groups in the playground, the girls to giggle and talk, the boys rushing around yelling and punching. She felt almost parental about them: they must be helped, somehow, to learn to behave, to have respect for themselves and their friends. And now, there was just time to go into the classroom and prepare lessons before Thomas rang the bell.

The room was stuffy and she climbed up on a chair to open the high window. Why couldn't windows be lower? *Because they might distract the students too much.* She could almost hear the trustees pontificating, and laughed aloud. If she had her way, these awful old commands would go out of the door, and Thomas Devlin could argue as much as he liked. Her class would benefit from what she planned to do and that was all that mattered.

At the door, looking out into the playground, she felt a rush of warm care. These children – small, undernourished and badly dressed as they all were, deserved better than the National Board gave them. Her head lifted and she smiled fiercely. She, Rose Victoria Adams, would make sure they received all the teaching, love and help that she could possibly offer.

Lessons must educate, of course, but also they must enhance self-confidence and self-knowledge. As she gazed over the children's heads, across the wooden fence, and into the green vista of trees, bushes and the tall grasses of the marshes, watching leaves fluttering to the ground, hearing seabirds wheeling over the river, suddenly she had a wonderful vision. These children from the cottages and those from the village must learn to care for their roots. She would teach them about the land on which they lived. The marshes, the river, the clay-pits – why not take them around, teaching them, showing them, helping them to rise above the poverty and stultified ideas of their parents? Her mind held visions of enlightenment.

That's just what I'll do. I certainly will. Take them around the village, along the riverside, show them the clay-pits, teach them the point of learning and give them some self respect – tell them they can do better than just stay here fighting other children and not caring about the rest of the world. . . .

Then the bell rang and she was thrown back into reality as the children streamed indoors, already quietening and responding to the customary discipline.

Once her class had settled, boys on one side of the small room, girls crowded along the back desks, and she noted that Lucy, although still sniffing, seemed better, and wondered briefly how difficult Thomas must find it, caring for a motherless child, she decided to provide a sop to his exacting demands.

'Children, we're going to recite our times tables. And then, if you're quiet and good, I have a surprise for you. Now, twice two are. . . ?' The chanting, she was sure, would at once allay any suspicions Thomas had, but what he would think of the next step she was planning, she didn't care about. Rose smiled. It was only the children that mattered.

As soon as all the tables had been chanted, questions posed and answers given, some wrong, just a few correct, Rose left her desk and looked around the desks that filled the room. 'Now,' she said in a quiet voice, 'if you are very good and promise to behave, we're going to do something we've never done before. Do you promise – but only whisper, please . . '

The sibilant *yeses* renewed her determination. 'Very well. File out into the lobby, girls first, and collect your jackets and hats. And not a word, or we'll have to stay indoors after all.'

It delighted her to watch the grinning, wide-eyed children doing as she asked, even hobnailed boots were hardly making a sound on the floorboards. Then, dressed for the outdoors, she led them into the playground and out through the gate, closing it after them.

'Where we goin', miss?'

'What'll us do?'

Even Lucy, limping along beside her, had a question: 'Shall we see a butterfly, Miss Adams?'

Rose smiled, 'Keep your eyes open, Lucy, and you'll see all sorts of things.'

She waited until the were out of sight of the school, on the footpath heading towards the marshes, then she gathered them around her. 'We're going to collect things to make a nature table,' she said. 'You must look everywhere and see what you can find. Berries, leaves, wild flowers, grasses, even. Anything that is interesting and will decorate our new nature table.'

'Feathers?' asked one small lad, bending to pick up the single remnant of a fox's breakfast.

'Yes,' Rose said. 'And that looks as if it has been a pigeon. Now, children, see what you can find and bring everything back to me.'

The half-hour she had allowed passed all too quickly, but with encouraging results. Small hands offered hooky burdock seed-heads, the last flowers of orangey-yellow eggs-and-bacon, even some oak apples and hazelnuts which had to be climbed for, and a dead butterfly found on the path.

'We must go back to school now and make the table,' she told the children and was encouraged by their continuing interest in the marshes. As they walked through the bending grasses and the dead stalks of gold-green dropwort, she saw a new alertness on their faces, a fresh brightness in their eyes and was pleased to note that Lucy had made friends with Stella, who offered her hand when the going was hard. 'Next time we come out we'll talk about why the marshes are always wet, and we'll learn about the birds who come here, and why. But now, into an orderly file, please, and straight back to school.'

But her pleasure soon faded, for the moment the school gate clicked open she saw Thomas Devlin coming to the door, regarding her with a straight face and a hard mouth. He said nothing in front of the children, who hung up their coats and caps and then returned to the classroom. But when Rose followed them, he stepped to her side.

'We'll talk about this later, Miss Adams. Kindly give your class some objects to study and then write about. I don't want to hear any conversation or discussion. Just teach the girls the domestic things that they'll need as women, needlework, for instance, and set the boys to copy-writing. And I insist that they are obedient and disciplined, if you please.'

'I—'

Her quick response was met with a frown as he moved away. 'Later,' he said, the northern accent flat and emphatic, his voice like a whip. Rose went into the room, feeling dispirited and angry at the same time. He didn't understand. He was old-fashioned and autocratic. The older children, both girls and boys, in his class would never learn any pride in their surroundings or themselves, the way he taught. But, yes, she would talk to him later, and the offerings on the nature table would be proof of her rebellion against traditional methods of teaching. Later. . . .

It was worse than she had feared.

As the children streamed out of school at half past four Thomas strode into her room, disregarding the fact that she had her coat over her arm and her hat already pinned on. 'Rose, I'll only keep you five minutes, but I have to talk to you. Sit down, if you please.'

So *he* was going to talk to *her*. And would she be allowed to reply?

Rose breathed deeply, pulled out a chair and sat. She kept her back very straight, her eyes focused on the portrait of Queen Victoria hanging on the wall at the side of the room. He started pacing in front of her, hands behind his back, voice quiet but authoritative.

'We have to work together,' he began, and then suddenly halted, turning, looking down at her with stormy eyes. 'What you did – taking the children out of school, without my permission, on whatever errand you deemed necessary, was quite wrong. But I will accept your apology and must insist that it never happens again.'

Rose stood up. She would not be dominated in such a vile masculine fashion. She had a part to play, too, in this argument, which she knew promised to be longer and more volatile than he was expecting. Words rushed into her mind: she would have her say.

'Really, Thomas, you're being old-fashioned and unbending,' she said crisply, fixing him with a hard stare. 'You haven't even asked me why I took the children out – as if you aren't interested. But I'm going to tell you—'

'Don't.' He clipped off her words and turned towards the door, halting short of it and looking back at her. 'Neither you nor I have the time to spare, Rose, so let us just accept that this was a lamentable occurrence which won't happen again. If you apologize I'll overlook it this once. Now I have to go home, and I imagine you also have commitments. So let us—'

'I insist, Thomas.' She raised her voice, heard the snap in it and was glad. 'Come over here and look at what the children have done as a result of that half-hour outside. Yes, you must – please . . .'

She watched the indecision on his chiselled face and feared he would refuse. But at last he sighed and walked back towards her, saying, 'Very well.'

The nature table was a torn, rectangular cardboard box resurrected from the bottom of the cupboard and now filled with the children's findings. Bits of ragged bark, red-tinged autumn leaves, the pigeon's feather, oak apples, a few nuts and a bunch of yellow ragwort and fescue grasses, all native to the country district in which they lived. Things they could name and appreciate. Rose felt proud of this small achievement and watched him, almost daring him to denigrate their efforts. Firmly she added, 'And Lucy found this beautiful jay's feather – she was so pleased . . .'

Thomas looked, frowned, looked again and then turned his head towards her. His lips twitched. 'Rose,' he said, sighed, and then lifted his shoulders as if in despair. 'What can I say? It's a new idea, of course, this interest in botany as we find it out of doors and not just in books, but I simply cannot allow you to make decisions like this on your own. After all, you're supposed to be under my supervision. Why didn't you ask me about it first?'

'Because I knew you'd say no. And because I don't see why, as a certificated teacher, I can't be allowed to arrange my own lessons for my children.' She dared even further. 'Times are changing, Thomas, and I want schooling to change with them.'

They looked at each other in silence. Rose dug her hands into her skirt pockets and felt her heart pounding. This was an important moment and she was suddenly realizing just how vital it was to her that she should go beyond the boundaries of traditional education. Words rushed out. 'Thomas, don't you see, I want them to become proud of the place they live in, were born in – I want them to have some self-respect so that they're not always fighting and behaving so wildly.'

The grey eyes were cold and steely bright. 'And I want them educated in the proper style, with facts, so that they can become workers who earn reasonable wages.' His voice was as passionate as her own. 'Believe me, Rose, my way is best.'

She swallowed the dryness in her mouth, exhaled the held breath, and turned away. He mustn't see the tears of frustration that were threatening to flow. She pushed the chair back into place, walked to the door and stood there, waiting for his dismissal.

153

It came. 'I'm sorry, Rose, but I have to give the orders here and you must accept that if you are to continue teaching. I don't want to have to recommend your dismissal to the board. So now let us go home and allow our thoughts some time in which calm down.' Although the words were authoritative his voice was lower, more gentle. Glancing quickly at him, she saw that the silvery eyes were concerned, no longer flaming with annoyance.

'Very well. Goodnight, Thomas.' Her voice choked, she went through the doorway and heard him locking both classroom doors behind him and then the entrance door, as he followed. Not looking back, raging with frustration and fury at his masculine domination, she marched down the path towards Sandiford House, trying, without much success, to put school and wretched Thomas Devlin out of her thoughts.

A few paces on she stopped, turned, and listened. Laughter echoing back from the distant figure heading for the village? Nonsense. Rose walked on. No reason for Thomas Devlin to be laughing. She could only have imagined it.

Jessie opened the front door and at once Rose was in another world. 'Look at me, Rose! Lovely white cap with streamers and this nice apron. What a bit of luck that old misery Daisy leavin''—'

'Good afternoon, Jessie. Yes, you do look grand.' Entering, Rose put away from her the instant worries about manners and consistent hard work, wondering if saucy Jessie had taken on a role that might well prove too much for her. But then she saw the beaming smile flash out as the new maid took her coat and hung it up.

'Your hat, too, Miss Adams? See, Rose, I'm learning how to know my place and speak proper!'

The worry vanished before it had time to develop and Rose smiled back as she walked across the hall towards the drawing-room. 'Is Mrs Mount in, Jessie? And am I too late for a cup of tea?'

'Madam's upstairs, dressing to go out, but I'll get you a cup, Rose. I means Miss Adams. Know about the new gig, do you? And the coachman? Mr Bean, he's called – going to live over the stables. And, do you know . . .' and Jessie was obviously ready to give a good old tell of all that had happened today.

Pleasantly, but firmly, Rose said, 'Yes, it's all very exciting. But I really would like that cup, please, Jessie,' which finished the chatter and saw the girl disappear in the direction of the kitchen.

The drawing-room was empty, but as soon as she stepped inside Rose was aware of the atmosphere she had felt before: of people still sitting there, standing by the French doors, looking out into the sunlit garden. Were they waiting? That was what it felt like. She shook her head to get rid of the foolish idea. Really, she must get a grip on herself if she was to succeed in this new position she had taken on.

Steps could be heard on the staircase, then Mrs Mount's voice telling Henny to 'go and find your basket, my pet – I'll be home later on,' then Mrs Mount came into the room.

'Ah, Rose!' The plummy voice was cool but pleasant. 'I was so pleased to get your note of acceptance this morning. And of course we've found a bedroom for you. Not a very big one, but perhaps it will do until Jessie can turn out one of the others. Now, I have to go and visit Mrs Weston for an hour or so. Can you make yourself known to the servants, and perhaps see that Mrs Briggs has an appetizing dinner ready for my return?'

Elizabeth was dressed in a fitted dark-blue stuff frock with slightly ballooning sleeves that fell tightly to the wrist. She sported a felt hat with a large brim, discreetly ornamented this time, with just a cockade of greens and golds. Her gloves, Rose saw, were the finest kid and her leather shoes shone, decorated with mother-of-pearl buckles. Over one arm hung her reticule and over the other the dark woollen mantle that would keep the evening chill from her on the journey home.

Rose was overawed. Elizabeth was a prime example of gentry: bosomy, solid and self-confident, and dressed in expensive clothes. Her voice told of years of experience of giving orders and expecting them to be carried out without any demur. This, thought Rose, with a tingle of nervousness running down her spine, was going to be a more difficult situation than she had thought possible. What was she doing here? This was not her life – so how could she possibly pretend it was?

Words had left her and soon she was certain she would say or do something which would reveal her working-class roots. A girl from Canal Cottages. A schoolteacher, an artist's model – she heard scraps of half-hidden laughter, saw faces smiling behind her back, dreaded the words that would condemn her for being so jumped up. Perhaps, after all, she should go home.

But Elizabeth was standing there, looking at her, clearly demanding a reply, and eventually saying, quietly and with clear concern, 'Is anything wrong, Rose? I do hope you're not having second thoughts about being my helpmate?' She paused, then said, 'I'm feeling so much better and able to get on with my voluntary work now that I know you'll be here, looking after things for me.'

They looked at each other for a moment, and then Rose saw a warm smile spread across the florid face, read friendliness in the expectant eyes and could only smile back, gathering her courage and making her voice positive.

'I'm sorry, Mrs Mount. No, of course I'm not having second thoughts. I'm grateful to you for offering the position. It's just that, well, things were a little difficult at school today, and—'

'Not Mr Devlin being difficult, surely?? Such a nice man, I thought.'

Rose suddenly wanted to laugh. If only Elizabeth knew! A nice man, indeed, puffed up with his own authority. But she lowered her head and murmured something non-committal.

'Well . . .' Elizabeth walked towards the door. 'Perhaps you could just see that Bean,' she gave Rose an amused smile, 'such an odd name! has the gig ready for me, and then I'll be on my way.'

'Certainly, Mrs Mount.'

Once she was doing things rather than allowing her thoughts to create anxiety and nervousness, Rose felt better. She found Bean and the gig outside the front door and helped Elizabeth climb the small step and seat herself.

'Goodbye.' Elizabeth gave a smile and a wave of her hand, then the horse was clicked into action and the gig went creaking down the gravel drive.

Rose stayed on the step, watching. From the brief sight of him, bowler-hatted, dark-coated, his unremarkable face amiably subservient, she thought Bean looked competent and biddable. And the renovated gig looked quite elegant with its glossy black wheels and chair-backed seat.

She closed the door, turned into the hall and felt her life branching out in a new direction. So Bean was one more inhabitant of the house, and no doubt a new girl had been taken on as scullery-maid. More mouths to feed, new servants to control and ensure that orders given to them were carried out. On returning to the drawing-room she found a tea tray waiting for her. Sitting in a chair by the open French windows, she stared into the autumnal garden and made a mental list of things to do. She must ask Mrs Briggs what she was preparing for dinner. Perhaps she should inspect the stable accommodation. Then she must find the bedroom Mrs Mount had spoken about. And then – and then?

She must be ready to meet Laurence. Her heart suddenly raced. He was somewhere in the house, she imagined. In the library, or even in his studio, pensively adding a brush stroke here or there to the portrait of her. Did he know she was here? Was he purposely avoiding her? Would it be uncomfortable, even unpleasant, living here if Laurence and his volatile moods were all around her?

A door in the hall opened and clicked shut. Footsteps sounded over the marble tiles, paused at the entrance to the drawing-room, and then entered. Laurence had found her. She tensed.

'Rose.' He coughed, cleared his throat. 'Thought I heard your voice. So you're here again – and for good, my beloved sister tells me. A helper, if you please! Well, I hope you enjoy her orders and whims and fancies. And, of course, you must share that wretched dog of hers.'

He was swaying slightly, standing in the doorway, his dark eyes gleaming, an almost predatory smile showing through moustache and curling beard.

Rose got up, uncertain what to do or say. This meeting was bound to be difficult, she told herself. And if he'd been drinking, as Mrs Mount had told her was his custom now – and it seemed he had – it would be best if she replied in a harmless way. Smiling stiffly, she stood quite still. 'Good afternoon, Laurence. I think I shall enjoy being your sister's helper. Of course, I still have my teaching position, so I shall only be here in the mornings and the evenings.'

'Sleeping here?'

She disliked his tone and frowned. Her voice was suddenly cold. 'Certainly. I could hardly be efficient in my new position if not.'

Laurence came across the floor, his smile broader now and his voice a little clearer. 'My dear Rose, how quickly you snap back at me. And I thought once that you were a sweet little country girl with no nasty ways. Was I so wrong, then?'

Ah, she thought, hope beginning to rise, *if we're back to teasing then things might be improving.* And suddenly it was easier to meet his eyes, return his smile and nod her head. 'I hope I have no nasty ways. Tell me about them and I will try and behave better. Now, would you care for a cup of tea? The pot is still hot.'

To her surprise he at once said, 'Thank you. Just what I need – tea and some words of sympathy from my golden girl. No milk and two sugars, please, Rose.' He sank heavily into the winged armchair opposite her.

And then she felt her worries vanish. They sat in the still warm sunlight that sifted through the bushes around the terrace outside, and drank their tea, and began talking as if her abrupt flight from the studio some days ago had never happened. 'The portrait, Laurence? Is it finished?'

'How could it be? I'm still waiting for a sight of your magnificent hair, dear Rose.' His smile was disarming and he passed his cup for refill.

'I'm afraid it's cold by now, shall I get Jessie to—'

Laurence leaned back in his chair. 'No, don't bother. I've probably had enough to drink anyway. Jessie. So that's the little charmer's name, is it? Frizzy hair and wicked eyes. Well, you never know, I might want to paint her, too.'

Rose laughed at the thought. 'She'd never sit still long enough. Jessie is a lively girl and I hope she'll settle down a bit now she's in service. Give her a chance, Laurence, and don't expect too much, too soon.'

He returned his empty cup to the tray. 'I'll keep my eye on her – just to please you, Rose, of course. Well, and how's school behaving? And what about that nice child, little Lucy Locket?'

'School is demanding, as ever – and Lucy is becoming a little more outgoing, I think.'

He sat there, looking at her, Rose thought, as if she were a problem to be solved. 'And I thought you were no more than a girl rowing her boat up to Abberton with nothing more on her mind than buying a few things at the market. Look at you, Rose: schoolmistress with a disciplined, caring mind, and now also taking on a job of running around after my darling sister and ordering all the servants about. I was wrong, wasn't I.'

She didn't know how to reply, feeling uncomfortable beneath his quizzing gaze.

But then the big smile broke out again. 'And I like what I see, Rose – like it more and more. You're going to fit in here, aren't you? You have the manners, the confidence, the knowledge. I wonder if you've found your true niche in life?' He nodded and she could only smile back.

Well.' Pulling himself slowly out of the chair, he stood, looking down at her. 'I think this indicates a celebratory drink. Shall we share one, Rose? Come now. Just a small glass to seal our restored friendship. Can't refuse, can you?'

How could she? 'Very well, Laurence, but really only a tiny one. I have duties to perform, you see . . .'

In the library she hung back, astounded at the untidiness and lack of fresh air. Empty bottles and stained glasses decorated tables and floor.

Laurence followed her gaze and laughed a little shamefacedly. 'Yes, I've been in a bad way since you left, Rose. And I apologize. Indeed, I can truly say that things will improve now that you're back. Yes, I promise.'

She walked across to the window, already planning that tomorrow Jessie and the new skivvy should clean the room through.

'What will you drink? Brandy? Madeira?'

Turning, she said coolly, 'Just a very small glass of Madeira please, Laurence, and then I must leave you. Your sister won't be out for very much longer, and I have to see about dinner.'

They touched glasses. Laurence drank with his eyes fixed on her face, while Rose looked down at the shabby carpet and thought of the million tasks awaiting her. Then, resolutely, but without hurry, she said, 'And now I must go. We'll meet again at dinner, Laurence.' She knew he watched her leave, but kept her back straight and closed the door without looking at him. Then, heading for the kitchen, she experienced a slow growth of contentment. She could fit in, here, in Sandiford House. Indeed, she was already enjoying her new life.

CHAPTER FIFTEEN

Even so, Rose felt nervous as Jessie's thumping of the dinner gong echoed through the house, and she came downstairs from the small, impersonal room in which she had unpacked her few possessions. She was worried about her manners, the unsuitability of her one and only best dress and the possibility of not being able to comprehend and keep up with Laurence and his sister's conversation.

But as Jessie slipped back into the kitchen, through the baize-covered door, a large grin beamed across the hall and then Rose was able to smile in return and tell herself: *stop worrying. Take everything as it comes. The worst that can happen is that you make a fool of yourself.*

Yet still the unease remained. Which fork to use? How did Laurence and Mrs Mount hold their knives? Should she refuse the offer of wine which Laurence was pouring into the elegant glass beside her plate? What if she spilled it across the starched white tablecloth?

Then: 'Rose, allow me to welcome you to our home, my dear. I do hope you'll be happy with us – and you must promise to tell me if anything upsets you – anything at all.' Elizabeth beamed a smile across the plates of mushroom soup which Jessie was serving from the large patterned china tureen.

Hearing those words, Rose felt all the stifled emotions of the day erupt and sweep through her: the pain of leaving Alice and Jack, then Thomas's unreasonable ultimatum and now this unexpected kindness from a woman she scarcely knew. She blinked, met Elizabeth's gaze and had to pause for control before answering in an unsteady voice, 'Thank you, Mrs Mount. I'm sure I shall enjoy being here. Thank you—'

Then Laurence's rich voice chipped in, returning normality to the moment. 'Just don't let Mrs Briggs dish up her usual vile porridge tomorrow, please, Rose. Tell her I'd prefer a kipper instead.' Across the table

160

she looked at him, saw warmth and a hint of mischief twinkling in his dark eyes, and knew, suddenly, that she could now dismiss her worries. She was among friends. It was a glorious thought, and she bent to her soup with a feeling of new self-confidence.

The small attic bedroom, with its sloping roof, had scarcely enough room to enclose bed, washstand, chair and small chest of drawers. The tiny window looked out on to the distant roofs of the village houses, and Rose felt it cold and impersonal, offering no welcome at all. It must have been one of the servants' rooms before the house was shut up. Was being here a reflection upon her lowly status? Yet, slowly, the thought became amusing rather than discouraging and she slept deeply.

She awoke early and at once washed and got dressed. The day was full of tasks and she knew this challenge must be met positively and with a clear mind.

So, down to the kitchen where Gracie Willmott, the new scullerymaid, was getting the fire to burn, heating up water for tea and for filling the copper jugs for the bedrooms. Nancy Briggs came in as Rose started opening cupboards and going into the larder.

'Well, you've made an early start, then, Miss Adams. Checking up, are you? Makin' sure I don't get through the food too quickly?'

Rose turned, saw the challenge in the sharp eyes staring at her so suspiciously, and knew that this hostility must be resolved immediately, once and for all. She smiled, shut the cupboard door, and went towards the big scrubbed table in the centre of the room. 'No, Nancy, not inspecting, as you might think, but simply finding out for myself what groceries you might need when I do the weekly order. Flour, I think, and am I right in imagining that you could do with some more beans for soup-making? We have to remember that winter is coming, and I know Mrs Mount enjoys your soup.' She saw the woman's face start to relax, and added, 'I shall be back for tea today so perhaps you could make a list, please, and give it me.' And then, mischievously, allowing herself a wry grin, she said, 'We must keep Walter Wheeler happy, mustn't we? A good grocer is every cook's friend, don't you think?'

Nancy Briggs melted slightly, cracked her face into a halfsmile and stretched up to the dresser for the brown teapot. 'Indeed he is, miss. Yes, I'll list all I need – and now will you have a cup of tea?' She turned to little Gracie, gap-toothed and wide-eyed and covered in a coarse apron far too big for her, standing with her mouth open. 'Go and tell that Jessie to finish setting the breakfast table and come here. Goodness knows where she gets to half the time . . .'

Breakfast was a solitary affair, with Laurence and Mrs Mount still in their rooms. Jessie served Rose's boiled egg and toast, poured her coffee, and said cheerily, 'I've got the evening off. Madam said as 'ow I could. Told her that my John's out with the fishing boats tomorrow, so we wants time together. Ever so nice, she was, says "yes, Jessie, enjoy yourself while you can", an' so we will.' With a broad wink, she whisked up Rose's empty plate, left the coffee pot on the table and vanished.

Thoughts ran around Rose's mind as she walked to school. The morning was dry, even hazy, with the promise of some sunshine later. But she hardly noticed. There was such a lot going on in her life now; how different from the old days before Laurence and Mrs Mount took on the tenancy of the house. For a moment she felt the pressure of extra responsibility but then pushed the thought away. How could she grumble, when her life was moving along the new path, the one she had been wanting for so long?

The usual routine awaited; Mr Toogood swept in at ten o'clock and prayed with the children, then heard their repetition of the week's collect. Then the classes separated and Rose shepherded her children into the small, rather airless room, where, under her inexpert fingers the harmonium wheezed out some familiar songs. 'The Ash Grove' was the children's favourite and they sang heartily, resulting in Thomas Devlin's opening the door and looking at Rose.

'They're in good voice,' he remarked, one eyebrow briefly rising to meet the blond hair, now growing longer and falling across his forehead, 'but I should appreciate some silence, if you please, Miss Adams. My class is reading aloud.' He nodded. And then Rose wondered what made him add: 'We're attempting a new book which they haven't seen before.'

They looked at each other over the children's heads and she thought she saw a certain embarrassment on his face. 'That sounds interesting, Mr Devlin,' she said politely. 'May I ask what its title is?'

'The biography of Isambard Kingdom Brunel.' He narrowed his eyes – not a frown, was it the start of a laugh? and she saw his mouth quirk upwards. 'I think it will be good for them to learn about his amazing work on the railways.'

'Indeed. Our railway in particular. Yes, he's a local hero.'

A moment's silence and then she smiled more broadly and dared to add, 'Why not take the children on a short journey on the railway? It might be interesting for them.'

This, as she feared, elicited no immediate response other than a more fiercely raised eyebrow. She sighed. 'Well, thank you for telling me, Mr Devlin. I'll make sure my children keep very quiet as your class reads.'

Another nod, a keen look and then he closed the door and she heard his footsteps in the next room.

As the children did their copy-writing, and then added and subtracted sums, their slate pencils squeaking on their slates, Rose felt a new warmth begin to spread through her and then fade away. She had been hoping that Thomas was seeing the potential in her new ideas; but now it seemed that the opposite was true. And then she thought: *perhaps he just needs to consider the railway journey*, and at once her mind grew more positive. After all, he had actually brought a new book into the classroom. Could it possibly be that he was slowly – far too slowly – deciding to update his teaching methods? And if so, was it because of what she had said to him yesterday?

Then Lucy's quiet, high little voice broke into her thoughts. 'Papa is going to let me go to tea with Stella one day soon, Miss Adams. She's my new friend.' And the child looked sideways at the older girl sitting beside her, who smiled and giggled before mouthing 'Thursday'. The two children nodded at each other, then returned to their sums.

Rose was delighted. Lucy, usually so shy and uncommunicative, was slowly coming out of her shell. And she was bright, starting to ask questions that brought new ideas and reactions from her classmates. *Will Thomas really let his little ewe lamb out of his sight long enough to let her visit her new friend?* wondered Rose, watching small fingers counting and slate pencils sticking in mouths. *I do hope so. It will do them both so much good.*

The morning passed uneventfully enough. Mid-morning the children rushed out into the playground, where they played skipping games and Lucy and Stella chatted companionably together as they sat under the birch trees beside the fence. At dinner time Rose ate her picnic lunch of bread and cheese and watched how the boys, both small and large, grouped into gangs and rushed around, playing rough games. Charlie Wheeler, she saw, was neater and less rowdy these days. She knew that he'd been made a monitor, dealing out books and even helping the younger children, which was obviously having a good effect. But Billy Netherton still hung about on his own, though at one point, when Charlie came too near, he adopted a boxing attitude and lashed out with pumping fists. Charlie laughed, poked the smaller boy in the ribs, but did no more.

So the boxing lessons were working, thought Rose. She wondered how Will Sharcombe was, and what he thought about her now living at Sandiford House. She hadn't seen him since May Bankes's benefit and that was several weeks ago. As the bell rang and she gathered the children back into the schoolhouse, she told herself – *Will Sharcombe – someone else to care about. As if I didn't have enough on my plate these days.* But the thought was more lighthearted than worrying and she smiled as she told the girls to get out their needlework while the boys studied the map of the world, pointing out the pink countries and learning about the Empire and the different cultures it contained.

Elizabeth poured the tea and watched Rose sitting back in her chair. 'You look tired,' she said. 'I do hope all this extra work isn't proving too much for you – a good rest on Saturday and Sunday is what you need, Rose. I shall ask Laurence to persuade you to sit down and do nothing. I think you pay more attention to his words than to mine.' But the smile was a warm, amused one and Rose said, 'Thank you, Mrs Mount. I'm not really tired, but perhaps a little overcome by my new life.'

She managed a wry smile which Elizabeth at once returned. 'As to that, dear child, you're fitting in extremely well. Which reminds me – the little attic bedroom that you have at the moment isn't at all what you deserve – it was simply the quickest to make ready. I shall tell Jessie and the new girl – I forget her name . . .'

'Gracie Willmott. She's young, but very willing.'

'Ah yes, Gracie. I shall tell them to open up that locked bedroom, the one I believe looks out over the marshes, and see if we can't make it nice enough for you to move into. Would you like that?'

Rose's weariness vanished. She sat up straighter. 'Thank you, it . . .' For a moment words disappeared and all she could think of was the old room, with its musty smell and crowding memories. She had panicked then – fled from it. So did she really want to live in it, sleep there? But the next minute she heard herself say warmly, 'Thank you, Mrs Mount. That sounds very pleasant. Yes, I'd like that.'

The teapot dipped for second cups, a fresh slice of cherry-cake landed on Elizabeth's plate, and she said graciously, 'Very well. I'll put it all in hand. There's a key somewhere – perhaps Laurence knows where it is. Now, Rose, do have one of those macaroons. I gave Mrs Briggs the recipe and she's done very well – they're extremely tasty.'

During the early evening Laurence persuaded Rose to climb the creaking stairs to the studio and she went with a feeling of uneasy expectancy. What would she see on his easel?

But his rich voice and unthinking friendliness was reassuring. 'Come over here, Rose.' He took her arm and led her across the room. 'Let me show you the portrait.'

They stood beside the easel and he whipped off the cloth covering it. 'Well, here it is. What d'you think?'

Expectantly Rose looked, prepared to admire and enjoy. She looked again and her smile vanished. Into the sudden silence fell around them, she said at last, 'It's a fine painting, Laurence. But . . . but it's not me . . .'

The portrait. Not your portrait . . .

Again she looked, scrutinizing every detail. Surely there was a faint likeness of Jessie in the full, pouting and over-reddened lips? Even a vague semblance of Lucy's far away stare in those pale eyes. But where was Rose Adams? And look at the hair – it wasn't hers. Yes, fiery, copper-gold, touched with blazing light as if it had a secret movement of its own, these painted tresses curled, snakelike over bare, sloping shoulders that slipped provocatively out of the old green dress. But there was no true semblance of her on that canvas.

Turning, she met Laurence's intense gaze. 'No,' she said. 'No.' Her voice broke into the silence, clear, strong and uncompromising as anger erupted. 'You've painted someone else; this isn't a portrait of me. You've cheated me, Laurence. You've taken all my time, all those days and hours, and this is what you've made of it.' Feelings soared, disappointment, humiliation and then outrage overflowed. Her voice rose. 'I'm sorry, but I don't want to see it again, not ever.'

How dare he? He'd made a fool of her. *How dare he!* She walked rapidly towards the door, but he was there before her.

His eyes were narrowed, his face suffused with what she recognized as passion. He barred her way. 'Of course you don't understand! How could you?' The words almost hissed out. 'A dreary servant from those squalid Canal Cottages down by the river – you know nothing of art, or how a painter creates from everything around him.' He came nearer, standing too close, his breath reaching her cheeks. 'What I've done, Rose Adams, is create a near-masterpiece which the old painters of the Pre-Raphaelite Brotherhood would admire. So how could a simple creature like you even hope to understand?'

She took a step back, appalled by his ferocity, shocked by the crudeness of his words and manner. He had ridiculed her and she was conscious of the deep, sharp hurt, but she was too angry to care any longer.

He stepped away from her and she saw him fighting with his passion. Slowly it faded. He sucked in a noisy breath, nodded at her, tried to smile, but she saw it only as a painful grimace. 'Go on, then, Rose, go down to your domestic duties and don't ever bother to come up here again. I don't need you any longer – no . . .' Suddenly the rictus smile shone through. 'I don't need you any more,' he shouted and stood back, clearly dismissing her.

Rose pushed past him, disturbed, but determined to keep her dignity. *A servant? No.* Down the creaking stairs, along the empty passage and down the elegant wide stairs sweeping into the hall. There, not hearing any following footsteps, she stood quite still and regained control of breath and feelings.

The oncoming evening darkened the house, the gas lighting not yet turned on. She found the half-light soothing and went slowly out of the front door on to the shadowy terrace, nerves still jangling, voices roaring in her ears. Early bats were flying around the eaves and she thought she heard a pigeon calling in the trees bordering the marshes.

Slowly she calmed herself. Laurence's portrait had been a shock, his attack an even greater one. She was unable to decide what she really thought, until it gradually came to her that this was one more strange and unhappy occurrence which, if she treated it sensibly, would have no effect on her present life.

But what would Mrs Mount think? Say? Rose foresaw a terrible chasm opening between them, if Laurence repeated his vile words to his sister. But surely Elizabeth wouldn't accept what he said – all that he thought of her companion? And then . . . would Elizabeth want to see the portrait? What would be her private thoughts? Fears sped onward, gathering more anxiety with each one. What would Mother think? Of course she would want to know about the portrait – but to see what Laurence had painted, even to imagine that that was how he saw her daughter. Rose shivered.

But, after a little while, she found the strength to try and push away all these unhappy and hurtful possibilities as, in the distance, she recognized the steady singing of the ever flowing river and, gradually a glimmer of new hope began to emerge.

The river had always been her friend. Now it was with her again. She thought of flotsam – branches, mud-coloured leaves, rubbish – gathering in convenient places along the banks, to be either swept out to sea, or deposited to rot away into the river-bank. Perhaps she could do the same with this business about the portrait. Go with it, or leave it behind. *She must make the decision. Her heart felt torn; but hope was growing.*

Positive thoughts began to form. She couldn't join Elizabeth in the drawing-room. What if Laurence was also there? But she must return. Duty called. Then, indoors once more, the quietness of the house persuaded her to go upstairs, and as she entered the little attic bedroom she felt easier. Slowly she prepared for bed. Sleep would help her escape her churning thoughts and, she hoped, heal her disturbed mind. But it took some time to come.

Gradually her tension resolved and decisions posed themselves. In future she would avoid Laurence as often as possible. Of course Mrs Mount must not hear about the portrait and Laurence's tirade. She couldn't believe that Laurence, passionate as he had been, would tell his sister how badly he had treated her. And then, just as sleep began sweeping away all those thoughts, one more jolted her awake, important and uneasy.

The locked bedroom which Mrs Mount had said she must move into was, in fact, no longer locked. When she had opened it with her hairpin, all those weeks ago, she had tried to relock it as she left, but without success: so the door, though closed, remained unlocked. Jessie and Gracie would be surprised tomorrow, when they went up there to clean it.

Next afternoon the woodwork class began even before Rose tidied away her school books and slates and put on her coat and hat. Curious, she paused by the door into Thomas's side of the partition and saw a heap of what looked like long poles lying on the floor. The boys were busy sorting them out, each lad taking his own and then looking at Thomas Devlin for guidance.

Not wanting to appear to be prying, Rose hesitated for a second, but something insisted that she stay longer. Thomas's voice was relaxed, his flat vowels more and more familiar to her these days. 'We shall need twigs,' he was saying, looking around his waiting class. 'Heather would be best, but we can't get that. But Mr Wheeler, who's kindly donated these broom handles, has come up with the good idea that hazel twigs will do. And he's promised a load of them from Farmer Sharcombe, who's been hedging this week and has several bundles to spare. So this evening we must prepare the binding. Listen carefully while I describe what I mean.'

He turned around suddenly and Rose had to move fast, letting the door close while she almost ran out of the schoolhouse. She couldn't face him – but why not? He wasn't Laurence – he wouldn't distress her. How did she know that? Walking back to Sandiford House in a rising wind that promised bad weather as the end of the month with its usual gales and storms approached, she found herself bewildered by feelings that were still too muddled to sort out.

It would take some time before she came to terms with the idea that the portrait was not of her; that Laurence had spent all his time painting someone else; perhaps a model he remembered from his life in London? Or perhaps just a fanciful form that filled his creative mind, as he had tried to explain to her. She could accept that, but it was too soon to forget his hateful words about her being just a servant. I am not, she told herself forcefully. *I have left the Canal Cottages behind. I now live here, in the house. I will never go back to that poor, sordid life, no matter what happens. I will go on, finding my way.*

By the time she was back in the house, preparing to go into the drawing-room for tea and trying to meet Laurence as if nothing had passed between them, she decided to clear all this confusion from her mind and concentrate on the next thing to do.

Perhaps she should go up to the unoccupied bedroom. Had the girls been told about the supposed ghost, she wondered, and smiled to herself. As she went up the first flight of stairs and along the passage she heard voices. Clearly the ghosts had disappeared. The bedroom door was half-open and inside Jessie and Gracie, instead of being down in the kitchen helping Mrs Briggs to prepare dinner, were clearly just amusing themselves by looking at all the old, strange things that lay about everywhere.

Rose halted at the door. Gracie had opened the wardrobe and was pulling out a skirt of black velvet encrusted with gleaming jet beads. Her childish face was full of amazement. 'Look,' she whispered, and turned to Jessie. 'I'd like to wear some'at like this.'

Jessie was standing at the dressing-table, opening drawers, bending down, examining what was there. She made no reply to Gracie's remark, and Rose thought she couldn't have heard – or else she was too busy looking at something which she had just picked up.

'Jessie?' Stepping into the room, just in time to see the girl swivel around, Rose noticed Jessie thrusting something into her apron pocket.

Her face was startled, her usual smile vanished and her dark eyes showed quick guilt.

'What are you doing?' Rose walked across the room, ignoring Gracie, who was still standing beside the open wardrobe. She had a bad feeling that Jessie was up to some of her old tricks. Surely not – not now that she had a respectable situation and was, seemingly, enjoying herself working here at Sandiford House?

The girl gaped and one hand clutched at the apron pocket. Rose's heart sank and her voice grew chilled. 'Give it me, Jessie – what ever you've taken . . .'

The object was small and circular. Rose turned it over and tried to work out where it could have come from. A bracelet, that was clear; it looked like a gold one with inset small stones of a dusty blue colour set in an intricate pattern; valuable, surely and one that belonged to the lady who lived here in this house, in this musty bedroom, so many years ago.

She raised her head, met Jessie's fierce stare, and at once knew the truth. Yes, this was a gold bracelet that Edwina Gray had once worn, and Jessie was trying to steal it.

CHAPTER SIXTEEN

Jessie's usual bright colour paled. 'Jest looking at it, that's all.'

Rose heard the note of aggression and kept calm. 'It was in your pocket. You were trying to steal it.'

Jessie stood firm, meeting Rose's eyes with an expression of growing defiance. 'Well, an' what if I was? 'Tis only an old thing; no one wants it now. I can sell it in the market, get good money for it.'

'Jessie, it's wrong to steal. And you're earning money now. Why must you run the risk of being found out and dismissed?'

A knowing smile softened the sulky face. 'I won't be sent off. Madam won't ever know. You wouldn't tell on me, Rose – would you?'

The truth was hard and Rose hesitated. No, she of course didn't want to tell Mrs Mount that Jessie was a thief because she knew what the outcome would be. Instant dismissal, and no character reference, which meant that Jessie would have a hard time trying to find a new position. So: 'no, I probably won't tell. But you must put it back where you found it – straight away.'

Jessie turned slowly to the dressing-table, and for a moment bowed her head. When she lifted it again the defiance was stronger than ever. 'Can't do that, Rose. Like I says, I needs the money.'

Rose frowned. 'But your wages—'

'Huh! Don't get 'em for ages, do I? An' I needs it now. *Now*, Rose.'

Uneasily Rose asked, 'Why, Jessie?'

The girl smiled, stood straighter, and put her red, workworn hands across her stomach. 'Cos I'm having a baby, that's why.'

Distress struck Rose – pity and then unexpected affection. Jessie, not yet sixteen, was going to bear a child. She would need money, but more than that, she would need great willpower and determination to face a society instantly condemning a baby born out of wedlock. And having a

170

baby meant being a mother, taking on the responsibility of another human being. Could Jessie do this at her age? Only if she had the support of a husband – and, as she had declared so blatantly – money.

'Are you and John getting married, Jessie?'

'O' course. We're goin' to do everything proper like – soon as we can manage it.'

Relief soared. 'I'm so glad. But that's no excuse for taking the bracelet.'

'I needs clothes for the baby. I don't jest want hand-me-downs. And there's the charge at the church – we don't have much, that's why I needs the bracelet.'

'No.'

They looked at each other and Rose guessed her face showed a harder expression than she felt. Jessie must realize that thieving wouldn't help and she had the awful feeling that if the girl took the bracelet, then she'd go on thieving. Forcefully, she said. 'Jessie, I'll promise to say nothing, but you have to leave that bracelet where you found it.'

The sulky face became hot and tight. Jessie's dark eyes spat defiance. 'I won't.'

'Then I shall go downstairs at once and inform Mrs Mount that I've caught you stealing.' It was little more than a threat, but would it work?

Jessie's breath was sucked in with a great gasp and impulsively she swung her hand across her body, slapping Rose on the cheek. 'You'm too big fer yer boots, Rose Adams!' Her rough voice filled the room. 'Madam's so-called helpmate, are you? No – jest a maid from Canal Cottages – like me, you are, no better. An' you think you can tell me what to do?'

Rose put trembling fingers on her smarting cheek, but refused to give way. 'Say what you like, Jessie. But unless I see that bracelet back in the drawer, and you on your way downstairs, I'll tell Mrs Mount.'

Across the quiet room she heard Gracie shifting restlessly. But she kept her eyes on Jessie, and at last saw the girl turn away, snatching the bracelet and push it into the drawer. Jessie shut it with a furious slam, then glanced back at Rose.

'All right, but you ain't my friend no longer. I won't never talk to you again. Here, let me pass.' Pushing Rose out of the way, Jessie stalked out of the room, followed by a silent, goggle-eyed Gracie. Their footsteps died away, going downstairs, and Rose heaved a deep sigh as she slowly went towards the bed, sat on it, and stared around her.

She felt the room was full of drama, its history pulling at her. Not just this hateful scene with Jessie, but other people, other happenings. It was as if the past refused to be forgotten. What was it about the house? Again, she soothed her hot face, but thoughts escalated. Why was she here, and what would happen next?

All the pictures that Laurence had painted for the school were packed into a large carpetbag, which he carried downstairs on his way out of the house. He walked fast, refusing to think about anything except giving all these rough studies – for object lessons, Rose had said – to the school. That would be one task done. Then he could get on with the next.

Thomas Devlin was in the playground, supervising the noisy children. Laurence didn't see Rose, and was thankful. He opened the gate, went in, avoided the groups of staring children and deposited his bag at the master's feet. 'These are for you. Pictures of things – sheep, boats, a chair, oh – and something else, what was it – a view of Sandiford House. I gather you use things like this for your object lessons.'

Thomas Devlin's eyes were narrowed, his voice was cool. 'Mr Vane?'

Laurence nodded impatiently. He had a lot to do, couldn't stay here talking.

But the quiet, steady voice continued. 'Miss Adams told me you'd painted some pictures for the children. Thank you, they'll be very useful.' A pause, an interrogation by the curiously bright grey eyes, and then: 'Would you care to look over the school? Miss Adams is inside, I expect she'll be glad to see you, to thank you for your work.'

'No.' Laurence had been avoiding her since that wretched scene in the studio when he'd lost his temper and said unforgivable things. He certainly didn't want to have to face her now. Quickly he turned, stumbled over a couple of small boys who had come up to watch what was happening, swore at them and made his way to the gate, out on to the path, and back towards the marshes. Didn't care for that schoolmaster fellow; too quiet, too obviously curious about everything. A sudden painful thought jumped out of that: too close to Rose; seeing her every day; working with her; getting to know her . . . *has she told him what I said? Blast his eyes, I don't care if she has.*

The path was wet through after a flurry of cold rain during the night and Laurence hurried through the clinging grasses, kicking at the piles of dead leaves, trying to avoid the pools of stagnant water. He slowed after a few paces, and looked about him. Something moving in the distance, below the trees bordering the the stream running through the marshes. A figure was moving in his direction, and at once his thoughts catapulted back to that oaf, Will Sharcombe, with his threats and sinister promises. What if Rose had told him about that business over the portrait? If so, the bloody turnip-head would probably be looking out for him again.

It wasn't difficult to build up hostility and anger, but not physical strength: his soft, indulgent life had said no to that, so he speeded up his steps. And then, as distance and safety claimed him once more, he became aware of the beauty around him. Self-pity filled him. In a different mood all this would have been material to remember and use. Wonderful shades of ochre, golden-brown and umber, the vivid scarlet and orange of spindle berries, dark, dead, mouldering blackberries, and over all a shaft of weak sun filtering through indigo clouds. What colours. . . .

Feeling calmer, he returned to reality. He must go home and carry out his plan. No time for thinking. And, thanks to that reminder of the oafish Sharcombe, he knew that action was everything.

School was a distraction to the memory of Laurence's hateful words and her hurt pride and Rose did her best to engage herself in the daily routine. She was still trying to forget the foolish, romantic dreams that had come in the night when she and Laurence had first met. Dreams that he, a gentleman, might helpfully ignore her humble roots, and even form an attachment to her. Getting to know him, she had thought he would be easy to befriend, to communicate with, easy to – had she really dreamed this? – to love. Now she knew better, but it was hard to eradicate those naïve, rosy hopes.

She had become aware lately that there was a growing need within her busy life for some sort of affection. Yes, she was fully employed and enjoyed all that she did, but . . . that small longing was slowly strengthening. Did all women feel this need for a man of their own? Again, Laurence's warmth, his physical attractiveness, raced through her mind. It was hard to banish those thoughts completely.

So Thomas Devlin, with his almost arrogantly straight back, stillness and flat northern vowels, was a good antidote. He needed somewhat acerbic treatment, she decided wryly, if she was to achieve her reforms in the running of the school. So she wrote out another idealistic timetable, emphasizing in black capitals the changes she envisaged, and once more left it on his desk when he was out of the room, just before school ended.

173

As she followed the children out of the gate she allowed herself a weak smile – something that had been hard to find these last few days – imagining how Thomas would react to the last item on her list.

A VISIT TO THE CLAYPITS. *The children should learn about their roots in this clay-rich district. Their parents nearly all work in the pits, and I want the children to be proud of the fact, not just ashamed to say 'a clay labourer' when asked the question, 'what does your father do?' I am hoping to arrange a visit.*

No, she hadn't added *should you approve*. Thomas Devlin, she decided, must learn to accept these new ideas.

Another day and rain was streaming across the marshes, trees were swaying and soughing, and over all the other noises of nature, the flooding river bellowed and slurped as it roared on down towards the sea. It was not a time for boats or men to be on those waters. After leaving the school Rose thought she must go home and comfort her mother on a dangerous day like this. Alice would be full of worries about her father.

She was halfway under the railway bridge when a large dark figure approached from the opposite side. 'Rose.' His huge smile lit up the sombre shadows.

'Will! What a dreadful day – I'm wet through already . . .' She smiled at him. Nice, simple Will, who would never behave as Laurence had done. What a relief to find someone of her own sort – someone who loved her for what she was. It crossed her mind to wonder whether he still did, but instead she said, 'I suppose you're on your way to your boxing lesson?'

'That's right. They little boys are comin' on well. Fightin' like men now. Even that scrap, Billy Netherton.' His grin was comforting and she felt she could go on talking, rain or not. But her life had its own timetable and she couldn't linger here if she was to go home and spend time with Mother. So: 'I must go, Will.' And then, turning away, she remembered the idea of the visit to the clay-pits. Swinging around, she said quickly, 'I want to bring the children to see you working in the pits. Shall I ask Mr Sanders to arrange it? Do you think he'll agree?'

Will took off his cap and scratched his head. He replaced it slowly. 'I'll ask, Rosie. I'll tell you what he says.' Then, the smile dying, 'I don't see you nowadays, do I? You'm too busy. Running the big house, so they tells me.'

She knew at once that gossip had spread rumours and was incensed. 'Yes,' she said sharply. 'I expect they did tell you that. And it's true. I have a very good position. I don't care what they say . . .' Laurence's contemptuous voice – *just a servant* – rang in her head and she instantly banished it.

Will looked at her silently, just nodding his head. She watched rain drip off his cap, and wrapped her coat closer round her neck.

'Goodbye, Will. Please let me know what Mr Sanders says.' She moved fast, left him watching her as she ran down the path, towards the cottages, the rain making a hazy curtain, enclosing her at last and leaving him quite alone.

Alice welcomed her with tears and smiles. 'My soul, you'm wet through. Come to the fire, maid, an' take off those soaking clothes. I was wondering when we'd see you – but there, you'm so busy these days. Good of you to come, love.'

Instant guilt struck Rose warmed herself and watched her mother spread the damp coat and hat on the back of the chair by the fire. 'Mother, this is still my home – of course I'm here and so glad to be back with you. How's your rheumatics?'

Alice held up knobbly fingers. 'As usual, but I manages.'

'And Father? How's he?'

'Coughin', coughin' all night long.' Alice's face was suddenly glum. 'Won't take notice of what I say, out in the weather in that old barge. And goodness, he'll be sodden today – not back till tonight with this late tide. Still,' and a small smile forced its way out, 'mebbe he'll rest up at the new shelter on the quay before he comes back up. They can get a cup o' tea there, even fry up some bacon. Jack says it's warm and comfortable, an' good to sit down by the fire. Your lady done it, so I hear – Mrs Mount, is it?'

Rose nodded and smiled. Something at least was going right. Elizabeth and Mrs Weston had spent so much time and energy – and money – on organizing the new lighterman's shelter and now Father was making use of it. Her smile broadened. 'It sounds good, Mother.' She pulled the cane chair nearer her stool. 'Come and sit down and tell me all the news. I've missed being with you.'

It was true. At home, in this draughty, damp little cottage, she felt warm and relaxed, with no duties awaiting her. Forgetting Sandiford House, she listened to tales of the latest Smith family squabbles, of May Bankes's boat repair which would cost so much money, and lastly of Jack saying that if his cough didn't get better soon – *oh, stop yer nagging – all right then*, he'd go and see the doctor.

But time sped on and she knew she must go. Mrs Mount would ask where she was. The kitchen staff would be waiting for her. And, she supposed, with a feeling of sudden unease, she must think of something ordinary and harmless to say to Laurence when he appeared at the dinner table.

'I must get back, Mother.' The coat was still damp, but Alice's arms were warm and her smile was radiant as she kissed her goodbye.

'Come again soon, maid.'

'I will. I will. Goodbye, Mother.'

The rain had stopped momentarily. The river still roared and surged, but the afternoon was a degree lighter and Rose's spirits soared as she headed for the path leading to Sandiford House. She walked past the well and under the railway bridge, out again into the marshes, now oozing and pulsating with floods. She paused by the big pool and peered around the wind-strewn bullrushes. Yes, the heron was there again – tall, motionless, beak down, waiting for its next victim.

She caught her breath. There was Thomas Devlin, too, standing not far away, a lump of wood under one arm. He hadn't seen her, was too busy watching the bird fishing for its tea. Rose stood still, wondering what to do, what to say. Had he felt her eyes on him? He was half-turning, at once smiling at her.

And within Rose a huge warmth ignited, a brilliant shaft of redeeming light. *He's pleased to see me. That smile is a real one. . . .* Laurence's vile words, Jessie's thieving, Mother's worries about Father – all these things suddenly filled her mind and before she knew it tears were pricking her eyes, tightening her throat, and all she could think of was *I'm so glad he's here though I know I'm making a fool of myself. But he won't mind. He'll understand.*

Thomas was at her side in four quick strides, the wood dropping to the ground. He put a hand on her shoulder, looked deeply into her swimming eyes. 'Rose, what's the matter? Can I help?'

'I'm – I don't know. I'm just feeling – very . . .' And the sobs burst out as he put his arms around her and drew her close. His coat was wet and her tears made it even wetter. But he was warm, strong, and holding her.

He said nothing, simply held her, let her cry. When at last the outburst calmed, he loosened his arms, looked into her reddened eyes and smiled. 'You'll feel better now. You're lucky to be able to let out your emotions.'

She sniffed, tried to find a handkerchief but had no luck. Thomas produced his own. 'Here, dry your eyes. I'll take you back to the house. You're wet through. I don't want my assistant to be absent because she's caught a cold.' That smile again, friendly and warm.

Rose took in several deep breaths and knew she felt better; much better. 'I'm sorry,' she whispered.

'Don't be. I'm glad.'

'Why?'

'Because I know you have a lot of responsibilities, Rose. I watch you, and I think you're working too hard. It's time you let me take over some of your duties at school.' Now he was firm and authoritative again, and she was saddened by the change. Yet he was here, in the rain, by the river, watching the heron. Alone.

Curiosity dared her. She said hesitantly, 'Why are you here, Thomas? And where is Lucy?'

For a moment he just looked at her and she guessed that such personal questions would be met with the usual blank politeness. But he said quietly, 'Lucy is having tea with her friend, Stella, and before I go and collect her, I thought I'd have a little time on my own.' He paused, then nodded at the lump of driftwood on the path. 'Collecting bits for my carving. I like to whittle away in the evenings.'

She thought he sounded embarrassed but she didn't care. At last he was opening up. 'In the rain?'

He smiled then, looking around at the shining wet marshes. 'Where I come from, they'd call this a mere drizzle. We Northerners are tough folk.'

'And we're soft in the south – is that what you think?' She was surprised, delighted, that he was talking so easily.

'Don't put words in my mouth, Rose.' Still he smiled and the arresting eyes seemed full of something new and pleasurable. 'Yes, I'd say you were all a soft lot. But delightful as well.'

Something had changed. His voice was quiet and low, but it had a vibrancy that she was unused to. And he had changed, too; talking to her as if she were a friend, not just an annoying school assistant who wanted to flout his ideas. She thought his face was less angular, his mouth softer, his expression happier. But it was still very odd, being out here, alone with him. She tried to return the conversation to more familiar channels. 'As for wanting to take over some of my duties at school, Thomas – well, I don't want you to.'

'I'm sure you don't.' He glanced sideways at her and she saw the amusement in his clear grey eyes. 'Clay-pit visit? What next? You'll be planning to take them on that railway journey if I don't stop you!'

Rose's mind cleared. They were back on the old footing, not exactly challenging one another, but sparking off ideas. She felt stimulated, and said firmly, 'I won't be stopped, Thomas. I shall keep on pestering you.'

Abruptly he met her surprised gaze, and said quietly, 'Please do. I should miss it if you didn't, Rose.' He paused, then whispered, 'Rose. . . ?' and in the pause that followed, while they looked at each other, slowly his hands moved upwards to cup her wet face.

She looked into intense, silvery eyes, heard again the note of what had sounded like hope in his low voice, and could find no answer. Emotions and dreams filled her. Instinctively, she lifted her head, put her lips on his for a second. His hands stroked her cheeks, and then he pulled away, even as she took a quick step away, instant shame overwhelming her. What had she done? Was her need so apparent? What must he think of her?

'I must go,' she called back over her shoulder, not looking at him. 'They'll wonder where I am. Thank you for rescuing me. Goodbye.'

She ran quickly, needing only escape and peace. But distant sobbing from the kitchen echoed through the house as she entered, and, meeting Mrs Mount coming downstairs, seeing her shocked expression, she knew that something awful had happened. So forget Thomas, forget Laurence and her hurt pride. She must do her duty as Elizabeth's helper and give what comfort and advice she could.

But, even as she took off her wet clothes, she knew that the day had provided something she would never forget. Thomas's hands on her wet face and the extraordinary pleasure of his mouth opening beneath hers.

Jessie was sitting at the kitchen table, head in her hands, crying, howling, her voice rising above the sound of the bubbling pots on the hearth. Nancy Briggs stood there, frowning at her, and Gracie leaned against the scullery door in her usual wide-eyed, gawping fashion.

'What'll I do? Now he's gone, what'll I do? I love him, I wants him back. Oh, John, John – what'll I do?'

Rose shut the kitchen door behind her, put her arms around Jessie's heaving shoulders and looked at Nancy Briggs. 'What's happened?'

'Boat went down in the storm. The boy gone and his ol' dad clinging to the wreckage when they found him.' She shook her head, turned to stir the boiling pot behind her. 'Bad business, but there, that's the sea for you.

Happens too often, it does.'

'Jessie . . .' Rose felt the woes of the world returning to enclose her. Somehow, though, she must be strong enough to help this poor child. 'Jessie, sit up and try and be brave. Look at me, here, take my handkerchief. Wipe your eyes.'

Reddened eyes turned and stared at her. Jessie straightened up, hiccuped and whispered, 'I loved him, my John. And now he's gone. An' . . .' A great gasp, another fit of sobbing; she looked down at her stomach, and her howls again filled the room.

Rose took her arm, half-lifted her from the chair, nodded at Gracie to come and help. 'We'll take her up to my bedroom,' she said. 'Up the back stairs. Take her arm, that's it. Come on, Jessie, you'll feel better out of here and we'll talk about it all.'

Upstairs, the girl fell on to Rose's bed and turned her face into the pillow. Rose sent Gracie down again. 'Tell Mrs Briggs I'll help lay the table – Jessie will be all right up here for an hour or so.'

For nearly an hour Rose stayed with Jessie, listening to the gulps and sobs, the distraught fears for the future, the anger with what had taken John from her. 'That awful ol' sea – he loved me – wanted the baby – well, what do I do now? My ma won't have me back at home when she knows I'm in trouble. And madam'll give me the sack. Oh, Lordie, what'll I do?'

'We'll think of something, Jessie. But now, come on, wash your face, try and be brave. At least you've still got your job.'

Rose watched her splashing cold water and towelling dry her despairing face, and thought hard. Mrs Mount musn't know about the baby – not yet, anyway. Nor must anyone downstairs; gossip would soon reach the Smith family if the other servants knew. So for the present, her secret safe, Jessie could continue working here. As for the future . . . well, perhaps something might be arranged but what, she couldn't even start to imagine. Quickly she put that extra worry away. At this moment Jessie must be persuaded to keep quiet and live as normal a life as she could manage.

As Jessie looked at her woeful reflection in the mirror Rose put her arms around the girl. 'You can come and talk to me whenever you like. I'll do my best to help you, but you must go home now, Jessie. I'll tell Mrs Mount I've given you the night off.'

'Thank you.' Jessie's voice was husky with grief, but she looked at Rose and gave her a watery smile. 'Sorry I said those things 'bout you, I wasn't thinkin' straight . . .'

'I understand. Now, do as I say, and go home. I'll help with dinner, and

I'll tell Mrs Briggs you'll be back tomorrow morning. All right, Jessie?'

The girl nodded, and together they went downstairs, Jessie into the scullery to collect her coat, and Rose into the drawing-room where Elizabeth sat, nursing Henny, and watching Laurence reading the evening paper.

'Rose!' Elizabeth looked up anxiously. 'Mrs Briggs has told me about the poor man being drowned. I didn't realize Jessie was planning to marry him. What a sad, terrible thing to happen. How is the girl?'

Rose nodded coldly at Laurence as he rose, then sank back into his chair and picked up the paper again; then she turned to Elizabeth. 'She feels her world has turned upside down,' she said simply. 'She loved John and they were to marry soon. I was going to tell you, but now this has happened everything has changed, of course.' She saw warmth and sympathy on Elizabeth's face and went on, 'I hope you don't mind, but I've sent Jessie home for the night. I'll help out in the kitchen. She'll be back tomorrow morning and I hope being with her family will have helped her to get over this awful shock.'

'Of course. What a blessing you are, Rose. You seem able to settle all the awkward moments. Thank goodness you're here.'

Rose smiled grimly. Would she be able, one day soon, to tell Mrs Mount the rest of Jessie's troubles? As Laurence looked over his paper and said something to his sister about a local happening, Rose had time to consider the problem. First of all she would have to tell Elizabeth the shocking news that the girl was pregnant. And then? Suppose she suggested that Jessie should come to live here, in the house, with her child? What would be the reaction? She sighed, imagining the upheaval, the remonstrances, the refusal to set aside old and traditional values. Elizabeth would take all this very hard, she was sure.

Laurence glanced at his watch, looked at her. Rocketed back to the remembrance of their last confrontation, Rose waited uneasily. Quietly he said, 'Nearly dinner-time, I think,' and she realized that the unspoken words held the implied thought that she should be in the kitchen, helping.

So he still thought of her as a servant! Angry pride rode through her like a galloping horse. She would give him no chance to further his rude thoughts. She, at least, knew how a lady should behave, even if his words and actions were beyond the pale. Rising, she ignored him, turned to Elizabeth, said politely, 'If you'll excuse me, Mrs Mount?' and receiving the approving nod, turned and left the room.

CHAPTER SEVENTEEN

The bedroom looked different after Gracie's and Jessie's cleaning. The floral curtains were lighter, having been taken out into the stable yard and given a good beating and the cleaned sash windows now revealed an amazing, stretching view.

From here Rose could see up river to the distant heights of the moor, across the water to the bosomy hills opposite, and closer, into the marshes, with their overgrown reeds, heavy trees and thick, windswept grasses. A frail autumn sun gave small patches of pale reflection as it discovered ponds and puddles and rivulets half-hidden in the wilderness and she stood there, admiring nature's impersonal beauty.

She turned and looked around the room. The dingy bed-curtains were gone, and the carved bedhead shone with fresh polish. She sniffed. No more mustiness or sickly air. Jessie had put some dried lavender in a pot on the dressing-table and Rose went towards it, wondering at the difference she saw about her. Her own small belongings took little space and she opened the wardrobe door, expecting to see the old dresses still hanging there. No, they'd gone. Had Jessie asked Mrs Mount what to do with them and been told to either give them to the poor or else store away somewhere? No matter, there was ample room now for her own few clothes: her coat, her best dress, summer shoes and two hats. Underwear was easily slipped into two drawers, and here she was, moving into the room that Edwina Grey had once occupied.

Laurence's words rang around her head. '. . . just a servant.' For a moment she felt the truth of it pulling at her strength. But then; *I am Mrs Mount's companion. And a school teacher. I am not just a servant any longer. He was wrong, so wrong. . . .*

She pulled open the small drawer on the top of the dressing-table and there was the gold bracelet. Remembering Jessie's covetousness, Rose took it out, admired the setting and the small blue stones and slipped it on to her wrist. But it felt wrong. Even if not a servant, she still wasn't gentry enough to wear such a rich and valuable ornament. Back it went into the drawer.

Slowly and deliberately, she took time to consider how she felt, now that she was here. Remembering her initial panic, she was able to smile at it; but there was still something she couldn't put her finger on. A sense of restlessness in the room which made her feel less than relaxed. Again – *history*, she thought. *Everybody who ever lived here is still around. And waiting – but what for? Is it this uneasy atmosphere that started the tale of the ghost?*

Suddenly, she wasn't sure that she could settle in this room, but that was ridiculous. She pushed away the negative thoughts. The room was clean and spacious, and offered a peaceful refuge where she could recover from all the responsibilities which her busy life seemed intent on crowding upon her. No point in giving in to fancies – she was far too sensible for that. Here she was and here she would stay.

School was as noisy as ever, and even the period of prayers with the Reverend Toogood didn't subdue the usual chatter and giggling once he had departed. Thomas Devlin nodded at her as she went into her own part of the classroom, but said nothing. With Lucy at her side Rose settled the children, repeating her method of teaching arithmetic, this time with a collection of horsechestnut conkers which she'd found beneath the big tree in the garden. She told the children that, if they worked hard, they could have the conkers to play with during the dinner-break. Small heads nodded and fingers began counting very hard.

At dinner-time Lucy stuck to her side like an insistent limpet. 'Miss Adams, will Mr Vane be giving us more pictures? I like him. He was nice to me.'

Rose looked into pale-blue eyes and wondered at how little we know of anyone's thoughts. Who would have imagined that Lucy would form an attachment to Laurence? Did Thomas know? And, if so, what did he think?

She said, 'Perhaps he will, Lucy. Shall I ask him?'

For a moment the child was silent. Then she said, very firmly, 'I'll ask him. May I come to tea again, Miss Adams?'

Rose smiled. 'Certainly. I'm sure Mrs Mount will be pleased to see you. But we must ask your father first.'

Lucy's chin pushed out. 'I don't have to ask Papa everything. I can go to tea with Stella, so why not with you and Mrs Mount?' Then she looked at Rose. Her voice was deliberate. 'And Mr Vane.'

'We'll see.' Rose decided this needed some subtle arranging. 'Now, Lucy, why don't you and Stella put your conkers on threads and do what the boys are doing? Only don't get into any fights!'

She watched Lucy eagerly moving away, conkers in her hand. Almost daily the child was showing more signs of independence and Rose wondered whether Thomas agreed with his daughter's need to make her own decisions. He would find it hard, she thought; as a father with no wife he must necessarily cling to his child as long as he could.

That brought her back to Jessie who, although still weepy and finding it hard to confront her lover's death, was working well and even being helpful to little Gracie. As for the baby – well, Rose returned to the schoolroom, knowing she must concentrate on other things than Jessie's problem. Life had to go on. Perhaps the Smith family might, after all, take both daughter and grandchild in when the time came, though she had little hope of it.

While the girls were sewing – making calico aprons, with very small stitches and trying not to get blood from pricked fingers all over them – Rose talked to the boys about the jobs their fathers did. Without exception, they were all labourers working in the nearby clay-pits. And what did they want to do, when they were old enough, she asked?

Billy Netherton's voice was loudest. 'I'm going to sea.'

'Dunno, miss . . '

They looked dumbly at her, and she decided that the proposed visit to the clay-pits was a necessity. Surely, once the boys saw how hard and filthy the work was, they might strive harder for an education that would enable them to move on to a better life? Crisply, she said, 'Very soon – perhaps next week – we're going to walk through the marshes and to the clay-pit where your fathers work. I know you go there sometimes, taking meals to them but on this visit you'll see exactly what sort of a place it is and what the work is like. Now, get out your reading-books.'

As the class ended the door opened and Charlie Wheeler came in, looking embarrassed, but striding down through the desks and benches to her table. He held something in his hand and grinned at her. 'Mr Devil . . .'' He broke into a smothered laugh, and the class joined in.

'Yes, Charlie?' said Rose with chilly calm. 'Mr Devlin, did you say?'

He straightened his face, nodded and held out his large hand. 'He said to give you this, miss. We've made the big 'uns, see, and my dad'll sell 'em in the shop, and he – Mr Devlin – said to tell you this is your new broom.'

Rose stared at the two-inches-tall miniature besom. Her heart suddenly leapt. A new broom. Hers. So was this Thomas's way of telling her that she could go along with her new ideas? *My new broom, sweeping clean. . . ?*

Removing the grin from her face, she looked back at the boy beside her. 'Please thank Mr Devlin very much. And tell him that I'm extremely glad to have it. Will you remember that, Charlie?'

'Yes, miss.' He wheeled about, marched to the door and she heard his voice repeating her words in the other room.

Rose put the small new broom on her table and smiled at it. Of course, it would have been so much nicer if Thomas himself had presented her with it – but she knew him well enough by now to realize that communication was a problem. And it didn't matter so much. For if his feelings allowed him to send her a message like this, it meant he was getting closer to an easier way of reaching her – should he want to. Abruptly she realized that she would like that, to talk to him, learn about his life before coming here, hear his aims and hopes and dreams. Give him time, she thought, and then wondered where such thoughts were leading. While the boys stumbled through their reading, her gaze returned to the broom. She was delighted to have it.

Later that afternoon Rose waited for Thomas Devlin to lock the school door. With Lucy beside him, he merely gave her a quick glance and looked intent on hurrying home.

Her voice stopped him. 'Thomas – thank you.'

His hand was on Lucy's shoulder as he turned. 'What?'

'The little besom. My new broom. Thank you. Did you make it?' And do you think I should be using it?'

His crooked smile was a mixture of embarrassment and rising amusement. 'Yes, I made it – a model for the boys to copy as they made the bigger ones, which they've done most successfully. Mr Wheeler has taken them into the shop to sell.'

'I know.' He was prevaricating, telling her unimportant details rather than acknowledging her thanks and seeing her pleasure in his gift. For a second she was angry, but pushed it aside and smiled. 'You said yourself it's a new broom – so are you thinking of allowing me a little more freedom with my timetable, Mr Devlin, sir? I need to know, because I want to plan the visit to the clay-pits very soon.'

Lucy chimed in excitedly. 'Papa, do say yes. I want to see the men working in the pits, it must be very hard work . . .'

Thomas looked down. Rose watched the expression on his face slide from uncertainty into resignation. He nodded, then looked back at Rose. One eyebrow rose quizzically. 'You have a fervent supporter here, so I suppose it's no good my refusing your request. Very well, Rose, go ahead and arrange it. But I shall expect some written work afterwards, with all the facts clearly understood and recorded.'

'Facts!' Rose wanted to laugh but thought better of it. No point in challenging those old ideas any further. 'Thank you, Thomas. It's very good of you to allow me this small outing.' She paused. 'But having given me a new broom, you must expect me to do some pretty interesting sweeping from now on.'

He was actually smiling back at her; his voice sounded lighter, the tone arrestingly warm. 'Well, what do you think I gave it to you for, Miss Adams?'

She was touched. Here at last, was the first sign of his slow acceptance of her reforms. Her pleasure was so overwhelming that she could easily have embraced him, but then, just in time, remembered Lucy's presence, and she also recalled how embarrassed she'd been that evening by the river, when she'd been forward enough to put her lips on his.

Suddenly it mattered very much that he should think well of her. She bowed, smiled at them both and said, 'I must be on my way home. Goodnight.' Then she turned and walked away.

Sandiford House was quiet as she went in, hung up her coat and hat and then walked towards the drawing-room. Elizabeth stood by the French window, Henny at her feet. The dog looked back as Rose entered, wagged her tail and then whined up at her mistress.

Slowly, Elizabeth turned around. 'Rose.' Her face was paler than usual, the dark eyes more deeply set. Her voice, thought Rose, suddenly uneasy, sounded weaker, not so dominant and she realized that Elizabeth was extremely disturbed.

'Yes, Mrs Mount? I'm here. Can I do anything for you?'

'No. Thank you. Let us sit down. I have something to tell you, Rose.' She walked heavily towards her winged armchair beside the fireplace where a fire crackled and glowed, at the same time gesturing Rose to sit on the chesterfield opposite.

Rose watched anxiously. Elizabeth was breathing very fast and seemed unable to stop her hands trembling. On the floor by her chair a parcel stood, propped against the fender, but she ignored it. She looked across at

Rose, managed a sort of smile and then said slowly, 'Laurence has gone. Left us. Apparently Bean drove him to Abberton station very early this morning before any of us were awake. Henny didn't bark. 'Unconsciously, she stooped and petted the dog at her feet. 'He just . . . went. I – I cannot quite believe he could do such a thing without telling me.'

Rose heard the break in the strong voice and looked away. To see Elizabeth in tears would be embarrassing for them both. Quietly, she said, 'I'm so sorry, Mrs Mount. You must be terribly upset. Did he give any reason for leaving?'

Elizabeth straightened her shoulders, tightened her lips and met Rose's concerned gaze. 'Yes,' she said, turning to the small table beside the chair and picking up a letter. 'He says that coming here to Sandiford hasn't been at all fulfilling for his creative work. He has returned to London – will be staying with a friend, apparently – and wants me to send him money.'

She looked at Rose with a look that expressed all the emotions inside. Growing anger, pain at being discarded so easily, dismay at the potential of her brother's future back in the maelstrom of bohemian London. 'Money!' she said bitterly. Her smile was grim. 'Of course he wants money. He has none. I presume he will now go back to his old studio if it's still vacant and pick up where he left off before we moved down here. More bills, more scandals – back to painting red-haired girls in green dresses. Oh yes, I saw your so-called portrait yesterday. Now, of course it's gone with him. I wish him well, but I foresee only more trouble.' She found a handkerchief and wiped her eyes, sitting very upright and, Rose thought, daring Laurence to ever communicate with her again.

Sitting in silence, Rose wished with all her heart that she could find words to console Elizabeth, but none came. After a few seconds she dared to reach across, to touch the trembling hands locked on Elizabeth's lap. 'Perhaps it's for the best, Mrs Mount,' she said hesitantly. 'Laurence – Mr Vane – wasn't really painting what he wanted. My portrait . . .' Suddenly the words choked in her throat and Elizabeth stared. Rose went on: 'It wasn't a success. Like you said, he had painted a girl in a green dress, and it was only my red hair that he wanted to copy. It wasn't me at all.' She swallowed the lump in her throat.

'My dear girl.' Elizabeth's hands clasped hers. 'I didn't know – didn't realize he had been so unkind, so unfeeling . . . and all the time, as I watched you together, I was hoping that something was changing in him – that, given time, there might be a chance of well . . .' Her mouth tightened, she withdrew her hands, sat back and held herself very straight in the chair. They looked at each other and then Elizabeth bent, picked up the parcel by her chair and handed it to Rose. 'He left this for you.'

By now Rose was in control of her own searing emotions, and was able to take the parcel and carefully remove the string. She unfolded the brown paper, found a note with her name written on it, and took a huge gasp of breath.

Laurence's writing was black and large. He said simply, *With my love, dear Rose. Please forgive me.*

Elizabeth said sharply, 'What is it? Let me see . . .'

Rose put the note into her pocket and held out the small picture. It was an unframed canvas worked in charcoal and was a true likeness of her, looking away from the painter, but with a serene expression on her face. Her hair was coiled at the nape of her neck, and she knew that this was surely Laurence's apology for the hurt he had caused her.

Elizabeth said slowly, 'He's caught you, hasn't he? It's extremely good.'

Rose sat with the picture on her lap not knowing what to think. Yes, Laurence had in the end created a good portrait of her, but she felt that in no way did it make up for his cruel words. She sat, looking at the picture for some time, and then, sighing, put it aside.

The next morning Billy knew he was needed on Mr Adams's barge. Today the weather was bad, and the gales that always came at the end of September were already blowing downriver and making white-topped waves that crashed wildly against the banks. He knew he'd be in trouble with the Old Devil – Charlie Wheeler's name had stuck – when he went back to school, but Mr Adams wasn't well and didn't seem able to manage the poling like he used to.

'What you doing here, then, Billy?' Cough, cough, went Mr Adams, sweating over the shovel as he dug clay and loaded it into a barrow.

'Helpin'. I can load that barrow when it's full.'

'Huh. You got sparrow's muscles, boy, you can't manage that.' But Jack leant on his shovel for a long moment and spat into the open pit beside him.

Billy heaved and shoved and managed. He'd show Mr Adams how strong he was, what with the boxing lessons and suddenly growing a few more inches all round. 'I'll come with you on the barge. Help off load.'

Jack stared, frowned, sucked in a breath and shook his head. 'No, you don't. Get into trouble that way, boy.'

'I don't care. I'm comin'.'

They looked at each other in silence for a moment. Then Billy said bravely, 'You'm not as strong as you were, Mr Adams. You need help.'

Jack shouted to Joe, who was loading the second barge. 'Boy reckons I needs help. You hear that, Joe? Crap, I say.'

Joe, short, swarthy and with greasy grey hair under a dirty cap shouted back, 'Take what's given, I reckon. You'm coughin' too much, lose lots of time. An' anyway, said you was goin' to see doctor. Bin, have 'ee?'

A scowl and another burst of coughing was the answer. Joe returned to his shovelling and Billy knew he was right to be here.

It was a crowd with him on the barge as well as Jack, and he had to hide himself in case Mr Sanders, the clay-pit manager, saw him. The ungainly boat swayed and drifted at its mooring as the waves slapped at it, then the wind took them into the current and the long poles were badly needed. Jack, and Joe on the following barge, were having trouble controlling the momentum of their overloaded craft.

In his element, Billy strove to help. 'Give us a go, Mr Adams?' he pleaded as Jack, bent almost in half, heaved at the long pole.

'Get out of it, boy. You couldn't manage to pole a twig, let alone this old boat.' Jack felt weak and was furious with his body for letting him down. All his working life he'd been strong and able. Now, with the cough sapping his energy, and the storm brewing, he was ready to lash out at anyone offering help or sympathy. The boy was a proper nuisance; who did he think he was, by God? Back to school with him tomorrow, or else.

But as the hours passed and the barges neared the harbour in the estuary ahead, Jack was grateful – though he couldn't say so – for Billy's hands and his willing strength, however small it was, for the wind tunnelling up the river from the open sea was getting increasingly rough and the result was a confusion of heaving waters and the increasingly uncontrolled billowing-passage of the barges.

But in the end, with much shouting and thumping and heaving of ropes, the boats moored at the harbour, and the off-loading began. Cranes dipped and creaked as the clay was swung into the waiting ship's hold and the men on the quay fought the rising wind as they worked. The job was long, heavy and backbreaking. Both Jack and Joe were thankful for any help; even the boy's small efforts were making a difference.

At last it was done. Now they could rest before taking the empty barges back to the Sandiford quay upriver. Jack stood on the quay, back to the wind, bent double as the cough attacked again. He needed rest, a drink, warmth – his scowling gaze fell on the newly established building opposite – LIGHTERMAN'S SHELTER, said the big painted board above the door. He'd laughed when it first appeared. Who were these posh, expensive ladies, going on about stopping drinking, but now it seemed an answer to his increasingly weary body. Pulling his jacket closer around his throat, jamming his cap more securely on his head he marched up to it, opened the door and went in.

A stout lady stood at the end of the small hut, looking expectantly at him. She wore a big hat with a dead bird of some sort on it. Jack cleared his throat. 'Got a drink?' he asked hoarsely, wondering what sort of answer he'd get.

'The tea urn is hot. Jennie will pour you a cup.'

The girl standing beside her nodded and turned to the large urn on the table that filled the space in the far wall.

Coughing again, Jack watched her pick up a mug and put it beneath the tap. As she approached with the steaming drink she smiled shyly and he mumbled his thanks.

The lady was looking at him almost severely. 'You're not well. What a terrible cough, Mr . . . Mr. . . ?'

He sat down suddenly on the nearest chair and slurped the tea, glad of its warmth. 'Adams,' he muttered.

'Adams?' The plummy voice rose, and its owner came nearer, hovering over him. Jack was suddenly too weary to care about anything. He drank again and wished the woman would leave him in peace. God damn all do-gooders, he thought malevolently.

But no. She was going on. 'Then you must be Rose's father – well, fancy that! I'm Mrs Mount, and your Rose is my trusty helpmate. A dear, good girl, so helpful and willing.'

He looked up, met the dominating smile, and realized he'd met his match. He nodded his head and held the empty mug out for a refill. Talking about Rose Victoria, was she? Helpful and willing? But he didn't have the energy to laugh. Instead, 'Yes,' he said weakly, 'Rose Victoria, she'm my daughter. More tea, if you please, ma'am.'

The hot tea was bliss, even though a nip of something else would be better. Warmth spread through him and his aching body felt stronger minute by minute. Thank God the woman didn't say any more because Joe and Billy came in demanding tea as well, and that took her attention away from him. But it seemed no time at all before Joe came over to him, frowned and said, 'We've gotta get on, Jack. Wind's whipping up even worse, it'll be a bad trip back. No good hanging about. Ready, are you?'

Jack heaved a huge breath, forced himself up and nodded, but had no breath with which to answer. Joe looked back at Mrs Mount, who was clearly about to leave the shelter, rearranging her clothing and giving last instructions to the girl, and said roughly, 'Thankee, lady.' Then he opened the door and led the way to the moored barges.

The wind was now blowing in enormous gusts that had men on the quay bending into it, their hats blowing away, trying to avoid the waves slapping up over the harbour walls. With difficulty Jack made his way to the first barge, nodded to Billy to slip the rope, and then somehow found the strength to force his pole into the turbulent waters, hoping to control the boat into a straight path out of the harbour, under the bridge and so on into calmer waters and home. The rope between the barges rose and sank as the billowing waves attacked it, but eventually they were on their way.

Billy crouched down, pulling a tarpaulin over his already soaked body. 'Will us get home safe, Mr Adams?' His shrill voice rose over the noisy wind and he cowered as a wave sluiced over him.

Jack coughed, spat, tried to anchor his feet more steadily in the rocking boat. ' 'Course us will. Keep down, boy, an' don't get in me way. This here's hard work.'

Once out of the harbour they saw the bridge just ahead of them. Jack's barge, poled with almost fanatical strength from weakening arms and torso, moved forward and seemed safe on course, but then, on the ebbing tide a huge wave came rolling in from the other side of the bridge, and suddenly both barges were floundering. Jack heaved at the pole. Suddenly danger was too close. He looked back at Joe, saw his boat swaying uncertainly in the rolling force of the waves, and let out a great shout of warning as the second barge slipped sideways, around the far side of the bridge pier.

'Cut the rope,' he yelled, but the wind took the words.

Billy was up, staring at Joe who poled madly, trying to bring his barge back again. 'He didn't hear you – what'll us do, Mr Adams?'

Jack didn't hear, either. But he felt the huge tug that suddenly and shockingly pulled his barge towards the stone pier, and knew that the fouled rope was entangled around it. He shouted to Billy – 'get down, hold on' – and then felt himself flung over the side into the churning water.

Difficult to breathe, coldness engulfing him, the weight of sodden clothes dragging him down, down. 'I'm done fer,' Jack told himself, almost with relief, and then, as his half-filled lungs threatened to deny him another gasp of breath, wondered briefly what Alice would do without him.

CHAPTER EIGHTEEN

Billy had run the mile and a quarter from Culmouth down the river path to Sandiford Quay. Pausing, he leaned on the jetty and snatched a laboured breath. Which way to go now? No, he didn't want to be the one to tell Mrs Adams the news, but he reckoned Miss Adams would still be at school and she'd know what to do. He turned right, down the lane and arrived in Rose's classroom just as she was collecting up books and getting ready to leave.

Puffing, sweating, a drowned rat with wild eyes and a voice that could hardly speak the words thumping in his head, he gasped out, 'Mr Adams – overboard – we pulled 'un out and he bin took back 'ome.'

Rose was at his side, gripping his wet shoulders, eyes fierce with anxiety. 'Is he all right? How bad is he?'

Billy shook his head and subsided on to the nearest bench seat. 'Dunno. Jest come to tell you.'

Even in her distress, Rose thought of the boy's condition and weariness. 'Go home, Billy, go and get dried out. And thank you.'

The door opened and Thomas Devlin came in. His face tightened. 'What's going on in here?' A frown. 'Why are you not in school today, Netherton?' And then, realizing that the boy was too exhausted to answer, he looked at Rose and at once his expression changed. 'Bad news? Tell me.'

Pushing clumsy arms into her coat she swung round and faced him. 'My father.' Her voice shook. 'An accident with the barges. I must get home – my mother needs me . . .'

Thomas stepped closer. 'Of course,' he said. 'I'll send someone with you.'

'No, I can manage—'

'Nonsense. I won't allow it. I'll send Lucy home with Stella and then

I'll call on Mrs Mount. I'm sure she'll allow the gig to collect you – do anything that needs to be done. Just wait a few minutes.' He turned, looked at Billy. 'Netherton, if, as I imagine, you've been helpful to Miss Adams, I'll forget about today's truancy. Go home now, and be here on Monday morning. Understand me?'

'Yes, sir.' Billy's voice was weak; he swayed as he stood up and Rose saw Thomas's arm reach out to support him. The boy grinned, regained his balance and then stumped to the door. 'Thank 'ee, sir.' He disappeared and Rose met Thomas's eyes. 'Truly, I can manage by myself.'

'Rose, please allow me to organize things. This is a terrible blow – I don't suppose you're able to think straight.' His voice was authoritative, but his eyes crinkled and that half-smile flashed out. 'Now – Wheeler, I think . . .' At the door he hailed the tall boy walking across the playground. 'Wheeler, Miss Adams needs to be accompanied to her home. Please go with her, make sure she doesn't slip or fall in the marshes, and then wait at her home in case she needs anything. Is that clear?'

Rose saw Charlie Wheeler blink but instantly agree. She was surprised at Thomas's choice of escort but too confused to argue. And once outside, with the wind threatening to blow her off balance, she appreciated the offer of Charlie's strong right arm to help her reach home safely.

She rushed up the creaking cottage stairs, and stopped in the bedroom doorway. Alice sat beside the bed, her eyes fixed on Jack's body beneath the faded quilt. There was a smell of wintergreen and the steamy heat of a newly boiled kettle. Jack's noisy breathing filled the room and at once she understood. Thank God he was alive, but his chest, although clear now of river water, was still filled with the residue of the cough that had plagued him for so long.

Alice looked across the bed. 'Got him out of the water, they did, young Billy and Joe, and then carted him off to the hospital. The pneumonia, the doctor said, and he should stay there, but you know your father, gotta come home. So the carter brought him back.'

Rose kneeled by her mother's side and put her arms around her. Alice tried to smile through her tears. 'Someone told you, then, maid?'

'Billy did and Mr Devlin sent Charlie with me while he went to ask Mrs Mount for the gig. Mother, surely we should get Father back to hospital? I mean, he's very ill and the doctor said—'

'He won't go. Said no just now. But his breathing's worse . . . oh maid . . .' Alice's face suddenly collapsed and she bent her head, one hand to her mouth, the other clutching Jack's, so still, calloused and dirty on the white coverlet. 'He won't die, will he? Not my Jack.'

Rose sucked in a trembling breath. She must be strong. Reassuring. 'Of course he won't, Mother. Not Father, with all his strength and willpower. He'll be up and about again before you know it . . .' And then she stopped.

Jack was gasping, his eyes suddenly wide, staring at her, his mouth opening and shutting like a winded fish. Harsh, rattling sounds came out, then words they couldn't hear. She and Alice bent nearer, listening, trying to make sense of his wild ravings. Cough, cough, and then his voice became just a whispering, slow babble, thick and indistinct, but every word sank into Rose's disbelieving consciousness.

'You'm not my girl. You'm the baby given to Alice. Said as I'd take you on – my little maid, and not tell. But you'm not my girl – Rose Victoria – not my . . .'

Then the whispering stopped. Jack closed his eyes, breathed a rattling, long sigh, and the room was suddenly, shockingly, silent.

With Alice in her arms Rose wasn't at first able to think logically. Father was dead. He had said she wasn't his daughter, but a baby given to Mother. Confusion mingled with a terrible sadness, a sensation of utter emptiness. All she could do was to try and comfort Alice. Instinctively she knew it wasn't the time to ask the questions spinning through her mind. Later, when Father had gone, when Mother had had time to think about it, she would speak.

After a little while a sense of the quietness of the cottage infiltrated her churning thoughts, and she knew there were things to be done. Leaving Alice by the bed, she found Charlie Wheeler standing downstairs, look-ing awkward. Her heart warmed towards him; she smiled and said halt-ingly, 'Thank you for coming with me, Charlie. And now – would do you one last errand before you go? Run next door and ask Mrs Smith to come round. My poor mother needs company and I can't stay.'

Duties, responsibilities, so much to do, so many people to care for – how could she possibly manage? But she would – somehow. She saw Charlie go down the path to the Smith home, then she went back into the cottage, pushed sticks into the fire and put the kettle closer to the flames. Tea was a panacea and would help them both to return to mundane things, but in spite of her actions, all she could think of was Mother, who was not her real mother, with Father, upstairs, alone.

And then – *Oh God, I don't know who I am.* The thought hit her like a strike of lightning, searing, destroying. She stood by the fire, staring into the flames as they licked the dry sticks, and felt as if her whole body was being crushed beneath a gigantic, impersonal yet brutal force.

But slowly strength came out of nowhere. Resolutely she made tea, took a mug to Alice who was still sitting by the bed, and waited until she saw her slowly sipping, her haunted face a picture of despair and memory. Then Susan Smith arrived and promised to stay for an hour or so. 'You bin good to us, maid, I'll do what I can fer your poor mother in return. 'Course, you got things to do – the doctor – the coffin – the vicar . . .' She went upstairs and Rose heard her comforting Alice.

There came a knock at the door. Thomas Devlin stood there. 'Rose?' His head was bent beneath the height of the doorway, his lean face anxious and she felt weakness return. He was strong, he could help her bear this terrible burden that seemed to be crushing her very soul. He would enable her to deal with this extraordinary news that was turning her life upside down.

She had no words, could only shake her head and put her damp handkerchief to her eyes but he understood. Opening his arms, he took her into them, kicking the door closed behind him. 'My poor Rose. Let me help.'

She heard the quiet, low, compassionate words. felt them slowly beginning to soothe the unruly fears and shocks that still fought inside her. When the tears had run their course he sat her in the cane chair by the hearth and knelt beside her. 'You're shocked,' he said slowly, watching her. 'Can I help?'

And suddenly she needed to tell him. Lifting her head she grasped his hand and held it tightly while the words rushed out. 'Before Father died he said I wasn't his daughter. Just a baby, given to Mother.' She caught her breath. and then said vehemently, 'Oh God, I don't know who I am . . .'

'Yes, you do.' His voice was firm. He smiled into her frightened eyes.

'You're Rose Adams. You're strong and capable. Who ever your mother is, she would have been proud of you.' With both of her hands in his, he drew her close, bringing her wet cheek against the rough tweed of his jacket. She felt his heartbeat, slow and steady, smelt the faint scent of soap and at last her thoughts began to drift back from fear and despair.

For a long moment they stayed there as Rose tried to control her breathing. Then, slowly, Thomas got to his feet, gently pulled her up and with his own handkerchief wiped her tear-stained cheeks. 'Will Mrs Adams be all right here for a while? I'll take you back to Sandiford House and then call on the vicar. I'll do what's got to be done, you needn't worry about anything.'

She looked into his eyes. 'How kind you are.'

'No, just that I'm experienced in this sort of thing. Remember, I know about death.' For a second his face tightened.

Of course – his wife. Somehow she found a smile. 'Thank you, Thomas.'

'Tom.' He was watching her very carefully.

'Tom.' A good, plain name for a strong and kindly man. 'Thank you,' she said again, her voice tremulous. But then things began to fall into place as today took the place of the haunted and mysterious past and she felt duty calling her.

She must tell Mrs Mount what had happened and leave Alice to Susan Smith's neighbourly company. Once Father had gone from the cottage there would be other things to think about – where Alice would live, truths to discover, the business about the baby . . . but she could only take one thing at a time.

So, 'I must see Mrs Mount,' she said very firmly.

'The gig is waiting by the inn. Bean will take you to the house and bring you back if that's what you want. I'll do all that's necessary for your father. And perhaps a neighbour. . . ?'

'Susan Smith, she's upstairs.'

'Very well. I'll ask her to stay the night with your mother. And, Rose . . .'

She heard the concern in his quiet voice. 'Yes, Tom?'

'Try not to worry. Everything will be all right.'

She had to smile. 'How do you know?'

He just nodded, lifted her hand, turned it and kissed the palm. 'Trust me, Rose.'

'I do. Oh yes – I do . . .' His faith and kindness went with her as she found the gig and was driven to Sandiford House.

Elizabeth was deeply shocked to hear of Jack Adam's accident and subsequent death. 'Your poor mother. I saw him yesterday, at the shelter. That cough . . . what a terrible thing to happen – what can I do to help her, Rose? Is anyone with her? Will she need assistance of any sort?'

'I don't know, Mrs Mount. It's too early to make plans, but thank you for your offer.' Rose's voice was clipped and unsteady. She couldn't – not yet – tell Elizabeth the truth about the baby being given to Alice. How could she? She didn't know the truth herself. It must wait until Alice was ready to talk.

She made an excuse to go to the kitchen and supervise the dinner. It was good to have something real to do. Nancy Briggs, Jessie and Grace had, of course, heard about Jack's death.

'Sorry 'bout your pa, Miss Adams. Will Sharcombe called in, said he had a message for you, but guessed you weren't here. He'd heard, you see . . .' For once Nancy's manner was gentle.

Jessie put an arm around Rose and hugged her. 'Sorry, so sorry – first my John and now your dad . . . that demmed ol' river.'

Rose looked into the dark, woeful eyes and said quietly, 'Thank you, Jessie. We'll just have to get over it, won't we? Keep going.'

The girl nodded, touched her stomach and lifted her head defiantly. 'That's it. Keep going.'

The night was a long one. Rose was driven back to the inn, and then accompanied by Bean along the path to the cottage. At some point the curate called, said prayers over Jack's body, comforted Alice, had a cup of tea and departed. The carpenter came to take measurements. More tea and a few heartfelt words – he'd been one of Jack's drinking mates. Susan Smith went back to her own home. Alice came downstairs and suddenly she and Rose were alone.

Sitting each side of the humming fire, they looked at each other.

Alice sighed. 'You wants to know – o' course you do.' Painfully she eased into her cane chair and looked at Rose with eyes already retreating into memory. 'I'll tell 'ee, maid.'

It was all so long ago, Rose realized, listening intently, more than twenty years, when Edwina Grey – 'Miss Grey', Alice called her reverently – met a man far below her class and fell in love with him.

'Some sort o' music teacher he were, and she thought the world of him. 'Course, her family wouldn't have it. But Miss Grey, why, she were a lady with lots of fire in her, she went after him.' Alice paused, nodded, looked at Rose and smiled sadly. 'They loved each other. And then he got her with child. You.'

Rose waited. She watched Alice's face. A music master. A lady from a gentrified family. *She was their baby* . . . 'Yes? Go on, Mother.'

The word hung between them and there was a moment of awkwardness. But Alice just sighed and went on with the story. 'She wanted to have the child but her family threatened to send her away until it were born, then have it adopted; no one must know, you see, that would be terrible. She refused. Said she'd have the baby here in her home, keep it – but they went on and on till in the end . . .'

Tears trickled down her face. 'One night Miss Grey called me into her room and I helped her get the baby born. No noise, just her determined to have her child. But oh my, how she bled. I wanted to get help but she said no. And then, before dawn – I remember it, the pale light through the curtains – she said I was to take the baby. Keep it as my own. She'd help with the money, she said.'

Alice blinked away the tears, stirred and glanced at the *Old Moore's Almanack* hanging on the wall beside her. 'Nearly twenty-one years, as I remember. Your birthday, maid – soon, isn't it? – why, you'll be twenty-one.' She paused. 'I dunno where all them years went . . .'

Rose had no words; her eyes were fixed on Alice's face. Her mind was filled with images, voices, pain and desperation.

'And then – well, I didn't know, did I?' Alice's voice rose, full of regret. 'I jest thought this was Miss Grey's funny way of hiding the baby and not upsetting the family any more. How did I know what she was going to do?'

'What . . . did she do?' Rose leaned forward, impatient, expectant, frightened.

'She said as she was all right. I must clear up the mess and take the baby home and she'd explain to Madam and Master. But she didn't – she must have known that the bleeding was too much – so she dragged herself up and went out, over the marshes. So as not to give trouble to the family, you see. Well, that's how it was.'

'But, Mother, what happened then? Where did she go? Did they find her?'

Rose tensed. This was a cruel tale, and the woman who had loved so deeply and given birth in secret was becoming a real person. She hoped – almost prayed – for a happier ending. Recovery, perhaps reunion with her family – but always without her baby.

Slowly Alice said, 'No, never found her. Police looked and there were stories in the newspapers, but they never knew where she'd gone. Gone, just gone.' She breathed deeply, wiped her face and looked at Rose. 'And I had you. The family moved away and no one knew about you. Until I met Jack and I told him and he promised never to say a word. We was married and he knew he must keep quiet or I'd be off. So he kept our secret. Until now . . .'

Until now. Rose stirred in her chair, leaned to the dying fire and poked the embers. Looking across at Alice, she wondered what to say, what to do. No longer Alice's child, the fact hit her with an almost physical blow as she realized she belonged to a higher class. Her troubled mind slowly allowed certain things to become clear. No wonder that bedroom – her real mother's room – was so full of memories and atmospheres. It had all happened there; the first thrill of love, the trouble with the well-meaning but autocratic family, the sudden knowledge of pregnancy, and the growing despair about the future.

Edwina Grey, she knew now, had been a strong, wilful young woman who had seen only one path for herself and taken it without shirking. So she, daughter of that woman, must copy that strength and resolution. It was a positive thought, giving her enough willpower to get up, smile down at Alice and say quietly, 'Thank you, Mother, for telling me. And for loving me all these years.'

They looked at each other through the shadows made by the oil lamp on the table. Rose knew herself to be on the edge of a painful decision. Sandiford House was where she belonged, yet her real home was still here in the cottage. Then pushing aside the self-pity, all she knew was that she just had to go on. Bending, she kissed Alice's cheek and asked tenderly, 'Will you be all right here, alone? You see, I must go back to the house.'

' 'Course you must. 'Tis your proper home. Yes, I'll be all right. An' I'm not alone, maid – Jack's still upstairs.'

Alice's loving courage gave Rose a good feeling and she went out into the dark, windswept night to find Bean waiting. They walked along the path in silence, and Rose felt at one with the surging river. It flowed on beside her, quiet and determined and with it came new hope. She realized that both their journeys had become urgent now, and increasingly fast-flowing.

Time seemed to become one long day, no end to it, no end to the events filling it. Elizabeth Mount received Rose's extraordinary news in silence, before slowly recovering, holding out her hand and saying unsteadily, 'Whatever you decide to do, Rose, please allow me to help – if I can. Of course you must continue living here – we all depend on you so much. But – the school . . .' She shook her head. 'Why not give it up? As the late Miss Grey's daughter you are going to have a new position in the community.' Delicately, she added, 'No one will expect you to still be a schoolmistress.'

This was a new thought, but Rose realized there was truth in

Elizabeth's words, and wished she could talk to Tom Devlin about it. He was always so sensible – so strong. He would know the right thing to do. But if she wanted to see him, she must go to the schoolhouse, and she wasn't ready to appear in public yet; not until the news – already, doubtless, the gossip of the whole village – had died down.

'And then there's the question of mourning, my dear,' Elizabeth said quietly. 'I suggest we might drive into Abberton and look at the local black shop. I mean, I don't suppose you have anything suitable . . .' her voice drifted away in embarrassment.

No. Rose agreed that her small wardrobe contained not a single black garment. Yes, she must acquire some mourning and so must Alice. And where would Alice live now? And then there was the funeral. She looked at Elizabeth, a sudden, terrible feeling of desperation hanging over her like a black cloud.

'I don't know who I am,' she whispered. 'I don't know how to do it all . . .'

Shutting her eyes, she felt emotion swamp her, underpinning all the old capability, the pride, the certainty of knowing where she was going with her life. Alone now, suddenly expected to live like a lady, with many other people depending on her. *What am I to do?* Tears came then and she hunched in her chair, careless that Mrs Mount might be upset, or even irritated by such lack of self-control.

But Elizabeth's own eyes were pricking and she felt again the surge of painful emotion that she had been repressing since Laurence's departure. Now she wiped away the tears, forced a smile and determinedly strengthened her voice. Getting out of her chair she went to Rose, taking her hands and drawing her to her feet. She smiled and said, a little unsteadily, 'Why, what a couple we are, Rose! Both of us weeping when we know that'll get us nowhere. Now, my dear, I suggest we have an early luncheon and then we'll go shopping. And I'll send Bean to invite the vicar to tea so that you can discuss the arrangements for your poor father's funeral. And I suggest you think seriously about informing Mr Devlin that you will be absent for at least a few days. That will give him time to make other arrangements.'

A tap sounded at the door. Rose wiped her eyes and was thankful that she had at least one good friend who would help. Jessie appeared. 'Please, madam, young Charlie Wheeler's in the kitchen. Said Mr Devlin sent him with a message for Rose – I means Miss Adams. Can I show him in?'

'Of course.' Elizabeth smiled at Rose, lifted one eyebrow in surprise and told Henny not to bark as Charlie came into the room.

Clearly embarrassed, he held his cap in both hands and stood very straight, his adolescent voice cracking a bit as he said, 'Morning, ma'am. Mr Devlin, he said to come and tell Miss Adams that he and Will Sharcombe have arranged a trip to the clay-pits, just like Miss Adams wanted. But he said for her not to bother, with all her troubles, and that. Said he'd take the whole school and they'd write it up for her when she comes back. Facts, he said. Well . . . that's all, ma'am.'

Rose caught Elizabeth's amused smile and felt cheered. Not one friend, then, but definitely two – fancy Tom doing this for her. She looked again at Charlie, saw how much tidier he was these days, how much shorter his hair and thought she glimpsed a refreshing look of humility on that once arrogant face. And it dawned on her, yet again, that Tom Devlin, however deeply his ideas about education might oppose her own, had an authority and a vision that were achieving surprising results.

Elizabeth, watching, interrupted Rose's silence. 'Thank you, Charlie. The message is quite clear. And I'm sure Miss Adams will want to send one back to Mr Devlin. Go into the kitchen and ask cook for a drink and a little something to eat while Miss Adams writes her answer.' She nodded at the boy, then looked back at Rose. 'Sit down, my dear, and take your time. I'm sure that young man won't mind being indulged by Jessie and Gracie.'

She picked up Henny and, with the dog under her arm, walked to the door. 'Use my writing desk, by all means. Give your note to the boy and that'll be one thing out of the way. I shall give Henny a little run in the garden – and by then it will be time for luncheon.'

Alone, Rose found notepaper and pen and ink. She sat at the desk in deep thought, wondering how to put into words all that she felt, and then decided it was an impossible task. She needed to see Tom, to talk to him in person. But how? And where? The new lady living in the big house could hardly meet her schoolmaster friend down by the river – what would the village say?

Slowly then she began to understand what this vast change in lifestyle would mean. Everyone would expect her to be different. She must dress in a more worldly and expensive style; her voice should become more ladylike; and she must bide by the manners and mores of the gentrified estate into which she had been born. And she must start now.

So, *Dear Tom*, she wrote. *Thank you for the message delivered by Charlie Wheeler. I'm glad you're taking everyone to visit the clay-pits and I look forward so much to hearing the facts*, heavily underlined, *about it afterwards. In the meantime—* Here she paused, bit the end of the pen and thought hard, and then, feeling rebellion rise in her, added a few more words. *I don't intend to give up my position as certificated pupil, or assistant teacher but feel I should absent myself from school for a few days as there is so much to see to. Perhaps Miss Hodge might offer her services, or even know of someone who could fill in for me.*

Another pause. How did gentry end their letters? What a lot she had to learn. Boldly, she wrote, *Yours sincerely, Rose* and hoped he would understand the feelings behind the bald words.

She sealed the envelope, looked at it, then went into the kitchen where Charlie was grinning at Gracie and Jessie and telling them some astounding tale, no doubt based on his own cleverness.

'Please give this to Mr Devlin, Charlie.' The boy nodded, snatched a last biscuit from the plate on the table, grinned at the girls and launched himself out of the back door.

'Gettin' proper handsome, that boy,' said Jessie, and then, giggling, joined Gracie in the scullery.

Rose smiled. So Jessie's spirits were rising again. That was a blessing. Elizabeth had become a friend, no longer an employer, and Tom had accepted one of her exciting plans for the schoolchildren. The black shadow shifted slightly from her shoulders, and she went upstairs to her mother's bedroom with new strength.

But then, as she entered, she felt the chill of past experiences here, for Edwina's unhappiness and despair had left an atmosphere of sadness which would be hard to overcome. Rose closed the door behind her, walked to the window and saw the glint of weak sun on the racing river, in itself a moment of hope and optimism. Then she turned to the dressing-table, opened the small drawer beside the mirror and took out the gold bracelet. Again, the symbols ornamenting it made her look more keenly. Minute flower-heads linked by thin tendrils stretched around the bracelet and she saw shining, tiny blue gemstones in the centre of each flower. It was without doubt a costly piece of jewellery.

She fastened it around her wrist and, turning her hand one way and then the other, saw the gold shine, the gemstones flash as if suddenly new life had surged through them.

My mother – Edwina – wore this so I shall, too. I hope she would be pleased – yes, I think she would. The thought was a positive one, and she managed to smile as she began looking through the wardrobe for something suitable to wear to the shops later in the afternoon.

201

CHAPTER NINETEEN

The funeral took place on a damp, cold day with a threatening wind tossing the trees about over the marshes. Rose, in her black bombazine dress and small veiled bonnet discreetly concealing her flamboyant hair, had walked beside Alice, frail and lame, also in black, as the coffin was taken by cart to the village church.

The service had been quiet, with few mourners, but once beside the open grave, with Alice's thrown handful of clay signalling the end of the ceremony, Rose, looking around had realized, with surprise, that not only were the Canal Cottagers there – the Smiths, the landlord from the inn, the Nethertons and the rest of them, but some of the Cullington villagers mingled with the small black-clad groups, now dispersing and going their own ways.

She felt unstable and tears came easily, but a new thought helped disperse them; was this the unexpected reconciliation of villagers and cottagers that she had once thought impossible to achieve? If so, then at least one good thing had come from Jack's death.

And now it was over. With Alice's hand in the crook of her arm, Rose walked carefully back across the wet, oozing marshes, inwardly striving towards the knowledge that life always went on. What ever the tragedy, or the happiness, nothing would stop time continuing. So she was calm and friendly to the few mourners who came back to the cottage, who drank tea and ate Alice's cold cooked ham, and told each other that Jack, despite his drinking and volatile temper, had been one of them – a man who lived hard and made the most of his well-deserved time away from the barges. After all, they murmured, he was just one of a community; what had come to him might well happen to any of them, any time.

Susan Smith took Rose aside. 'Our Jessie,' she whispered, face tight, eyes glancing aside to see that no one heard, 'in trouble, she is. I wants her home but her pa says no. What'll us do, Rose?'

'She's staying at Sandiford House, Mrs Smith. I shall try and look after her.'

'What? An' the baby?'

Rose took a deep breath. Her family. Her friends. Her dependants. 'Yes, and the baby, when it comes. And then we must hope she'll find a good man who'll marry her and take on the child.'

Susan stared 'Well, I never did. Sure, are you, Rose?'

'I'm sure.'

Another long stare. And then, with a shake of the head, Susan, turned away, muttering, 'I'll believe it – if it happens. But thanks, maid – us'll jest have to see, I s'pose.'

See what happens. Yes, Rose thought, as she embraced Alice and walked back towards Sandiford House. It seemed the most sensible – in fact, the only – thing to do. As she walked her mind sorted out the numerous problems which continuously circled. Alice had said she wished to go on living in the cottage. She was happy there, with her memories. But Rose knew the rent had to be paid, and that her mother must be fed and kept warm. Money – where was it to come from? She had a little left from her meagre savings, but after buying mourning for them both and financing the funeral tea, there were few sovereigns left.

She must keep working. Yes, she had told Tom she would be away from school, thinking secretly that she would not return at all because Elizabeth had said it was the wrong thing for a lady to do. But – money? Rose stopped beside a large puddle and watched the water soaking her boots, her mind too busy to care.

She would find a new position. Perhaps an advertisement in *The Lady*? Words ran around her busy mind. *Qualified lady teacher desires position and accommodation.* Would that find her something suitable? She skirted the puddle, frowning, and walked on, still wondering. But, at a new school, she might dislike her fellow teachers, or not fit in. Or it might well be a post away from here so what about Alice? And she'd told Susan Smith she would look after Jessie and the baby. How could she do that, teaching in a strange school, probably in a strange part of the country?

As Sandiford House came into view through the damp mist, a new decision suddenly sprang into her mind. *I shan't leave here. I'll go back to school. I must earn enough money to pay the rent for Mother, and for us at the house. I can't expect Elizabeth to continuing paying any longer. Yes, I shall keep teaching. And I shall start tomorrow. Tom will be surprised, and of course everyone will be shocked. . . .'*

Lifting her head she put a hand to the hat that the wind threatened to whip away, and smiled into the darkening afternoon. *I don't care what people will say. My mother was a strong woman with a mind of her own, and I am going to be the same. I – don't – care.*

She arrived back at the House glowing and optimistic, sure she'd made the right decision. Then she heard Elizabeth calling her into the drawing-room and she went in, removing her gloves and bonnet, and smiling.

'It all went very well, Mrs Mount. And my mother was so brave.'

Elizabeth was sitting by the fire with Lucy Devlin on a footstool at her side.

They had been playing patience, Rose saw. Now the child got up and ran to her.

'Miss Adams – I had tea with Mrs Mount. We had jam tarts. Mrs Mount says I may come again. I'm so glad. I love being here.'

As she sat on the chesterfield, Rose thought how different this Lucy was from the little silent girl whom she had first met at tea with Miss Hodge. Now Lucy was taller, plumper, walked with less of a limp, and had a lot more to say for herself. Rose watched Elizabeth smiling at the vivacious little face, and realized that Lucy's affection and constant presence – here so often, nowadays, it seemed – perhaps, in some strange way offered comfort, even replacing the sisterly love Laurence had ignored. She saw Elizabeth relaxing, stroking Henny with one hand and then pulling Lucy an inch or two nearer her as she again dealt out the playing-cards.

The room became quiet. The fire crackled. Rose leaned back against the chesterfield and thought about returning to school. Until Tom Devlin arrived on the stroke of six o'clock, his presence abruptly filling her with new doubts about her decision. But one look at his slightly rusty black overcoat, at the sight of his large ungloved hands, his slightly hesitant smile as he entered the drawing-room, and she felt the old warmth rise within her. His bright hair had grown even longer and he was almost handsome. Not as Laurence had been, of course, but in a different way. Her heart leapt and a foolish thought flew into her mind. More exciting.

His voice brought her back to reality. After answering his hopes that the funeral had gone without too much sadness, and accepting his condolences, she broached the subject of school with a new determination.

'I've decided to return to school, Tom. I shall be there tomorrow morning.' She heard Elizabeth catch her breath but avoided her disapproving gaze. 'I hope you agree with this?'

For a moment he was silent. She watched thoughts come and go on his frowning, lean face and found she was breathing faster. How foolish – he had no power over her. She was a certified pupil teacher in her own right, and, despite some critical comments from certain people, had no reason to resign from her position. The silence went on too long and she said unsteadily, 'Just because I've discovered who I am, surely there's no reason why—'

The frown faded, but his voice was clipped, quick, unhesitating words cutting into hers. 'If you're willing to put up with the criticism such an action is bound to arouse, then of course, I shall welcome you back to the schooL But please consider the effects very carefully.'

They looked at each other and she saw feelings only half-concealed. Then his voice softened, the mouth stretched and she guessed that, like her, he might find all the expected criticism amusing rather than painful. 'Tomorrow,' he went on more easily, 'I've planned – with Will Sharcombe's help – to take the children to the clay-pits. Mr Sanders, the manager, is allowing him to show us around. It should be extremely interesting. Of course, you won't—'

'Certainly I will!' Her turn to interrupt, her voice high and warm. 'You know it was my idea in the first place – so how can I possibly not come? What time do you intend to leave? Shall I come to school first, or join you by the lock?'

Now he was definitely almost laughing, his eyes gleaming, flashing her that brief smile she always enjoyed. 'Nine o'clock at school, please, Rose. And wear your strongest boots – I understand the pits are very muddy. And now . . .' He looked at Lucy, still sitting at Elizabeth's side. 'We must go home, Lucy and I.'

'I don't want to.' Into the quiet, warm atmosphere of the room, Lucy's little voice spoke out shockingly strong and firm. She looked up at her father and lifted her small, determined chin. 'I don't like Mrs Benthall, she's horrid. I don't like living in her house. I like being here.'

Again, silence. This time Elizabeth looked at Rose, who opened her eyes wide and then turned to look at Tom. His smile had gone, the expression on his face now thoughtful and concerned. He put out a hand and stroked his daughter's shining hair. 'We can't avoid not liking some things in life, Lucy. We just have to put up with them. Mrs Benthall does her best for us, you know, so perhaps we should try and be nicer to her. So come along, my love, say goodbye to Mrs Mount and Miss Adams, and thank them for having you to tea.'

'I'm not coming.' Lucy stood up and grabbed Elizabeth's hand, her voice shrill and tearful. 'I want to stay here. Please, Papa, please—'

'No. We're going home.'

Such authority, thought Rose, half admiring as she watched the painful clash of wills and realized Tom's inner and often concealed strength. He would always do his duty, even to the extent of hurting Lucy's impressionable feelings.

Lucy burst into tears, buried her head in Elizabeth's lap and sobbed loudly but Tom carefully gathered her up, took her in his arms, her head against his breast, and whispered in her ear.

Rose and Elizabeth looked at each other but neither moved. This was a family matter and Tom was clearly well qualified to deal with it. No interference was necessary. But, in Rose's mind, another unexpected idea arrived. If she was to remain at Sandiford House – and of course the future was very uncertain – but suppose, just suppose she did, how good it would be to have a child in the house. *Children make a home* was her instinctive thought. And then, a minute later, another of those weird, instinctive certainties, whispering in her mind. *And this house would love to have children in it again. A proper home once more.* Closing her eyes, she struggled to keep calm.

The awkward incident was over. Lucy obediently put on her coat, dried her red eyes, curtseyed her thanks to Elizabeth and Rose, and went out of the house in front of Tom, who apologized for her behaviour, shook Elizabeth's hand and then nodded politely at Rose. 'If you're quite sure of what you're doing, then nine o'clock tomorrow,' he said shortly and followed Lucy down the path.

They didn't discuss the matter; Elizabeth returned to her perusal of the local paper and Rose excused herself to go up to her bedroom to let things run around her mind and to decide how to dress for the trip tomorrow to the clay-pits.

The morning was cold and drizzly. Excited voices rose above the river's flowing song as the children filed across the marshes, Tom leading them and Rose at the end of the column. Once she had reached the school Rose had forgotten her uneasiness at being seen in mourning on the day after her father's funeral, actually returning to work. *Let them think what they like, say whatever they want*, had been her resolution as she left Sandiford House, but now she was simply enjoying being here, whisking up the skirt of her coat to avoid puddles and overgrown grass, pulling her hat on more firmly to keep her hair dry, and hoping Will Sharcombe would fulfil his promise to enable the children to see exactly what happened at the pits where most of their fathers and brothers worked so hard.

Passing the lock they reached the basin where the first of the clay-cellars lined the path; ugly grey buildings with strong buttresses sloping out on to the path. The children picked their way across the muddy ground, already wet and clingy as the clay loadings spilled from buckets and barrows and carts. Water slapped at their feet as the barges awaiting loading rolled and swayed in their moorings and the drizzle became rain.

Billy was informative, his voice rising high about the chatter and noise of the quay. 'I used to help Mr Adams do this – muddy ol' work, hard, too, but I liked it.' Other children joined in. 'I come 'ere to bring my dad his breakfast sometimes.' And then another small voice piped up, 'I come with his baccy which he left at home one day.'

Rose knew such things happened. It was a familiar and irritating fact that children were often absent from school because they were needed for family purposes. Her resolution grew. Surely, if they understood these harsh conditions of the clay industry, they would work hard to achieve better lives?

Over their heads Rose met Tom's quizzical grin and nodded. She felt there was new hope of reforming old educational ideas in this visit – and she was responsible for it. How could she possibly give up teaching, in that case? Smiling, she greeted Will Sharcombe when he appeared around the corner of the clay-cellar.

'Good morning, Will. It's good of you to offer to take us over the pits.'

To her surprise he merely nodded. No smile of pleasure at seeing her. No warm words just for her, but instead a barely polite reply. 'That's all right, Miss Adams. Bring them along here, will you?'

He led them around the end of the cellar, out of the danger of the overspilling loads of clay, and over rough ground towards the nearest pit. The children sounded excited now, and Rose gathered her small group together, saying, 'Stay together – don't get too near the edge. Charlie, make sure everyone is safe, please.'

Tom and Charlie, now a reliable monitor, were ahead of them, the bigger children pushing forward to get the best view as they approached the working pit. Rose, concerned for the safety of the smaller children, hardly had time to look into the ugly, huge hole that opened up in front of them until she was sure there was no real danger.

There were cranes and derricks, swaying and clanking as they received the wet lumps of clay being hauled up from the interior of the pit. Down there Rose saw, as she carefully peered over the edge, were moving figures, wet clothes the same colour as the clay, digging away with strange tools.

She knew these tools, all had played a part in Jack's grumbles during her life.

'Demmed thirting irons, weigh nearly a stone, they do, and they lumpers, even heavier. Man gotta have strong muscles to use 'em.' Yes, Father had had a hard life, and now she had kinder memories of him.

She saw the timber bracing the edges of the pit, watched the men heaving at their tools down there, heard the grab crane overhead, watched it swooping to pick up the dug out square lumps, and realized yet again that this was a dangerous life. God help any child who would join the clay labourers when he left school at twelve. And again, her determination to educate them to better things soared through her mind.

Will Sharcombe came from behind, standing at her side. 'Hard work, eh, Rose?'

He sounded more friendly, and she turned, smiled at him. 'You should know, Will. It's your daily occupation.'

He nodded. 'Proper hard, but someone's gotta do it. That clay has to go up north to help with the potteries.'

Together they continued watching the digging and heaving in the pit. 'Sometimes find strange things down there,' Will said casually. 'Found a body not long ago, not in the pit, but near the edge where the old ditch used to be. Had a pendant round its neck, pretty thing, gold I'd say, with little stones in it. Told the police, and they'm trying to work out who it was.'

Inside Rose something cold jerked and knotted hard. She stared at him. 'A body? A man or a woman?'

He took off his cap, scratched his thatch of hair. 'Woman, I think. Why?'

Rose could hardly breathe. 'Tell me about the pendant, Will. Did you see it?'

'Yes – like I said, gold, with patterns of flowers on it and those little blue stones. Manager's still got it in his office, don't know what to do with it, see.'

In her bewildered mind she saw the patterns and the blue stones. The pendant sounded like a match for Edwina's bracelet. Momentarily she swayed and Will caught her arm.

'What's up? You ill, Rose?'

She clutched at him, trying to smile. 'No. Just – a bit – well, surprised by what you told me. Will, do you think I could see it – the pendant?'

He frowned, pursed his lips, then nodded. 'Dunno. I'll go and talk to Mr Sanders. Come to the office on your way home and maybe he'll let you see it.'

'Thank you.' She took in deep breaths, knew she must be strong and said again, 'Thank you, Will.'

For a second he stayed at her side. His expression changed and she saw embarrassment cloud his usually cheerful face. 'Rose, sorry I said what I did, when you came. Just that – well, you'm a lady now, and I'm only – what I am. So we can't be friends like we was.'

Regret hit her hard. 'Why not, Will? I haven't changed, I'm still your friend.'

'But not my sweetheart no longer – nor ever will be.'

The children were chattering and pointing, caught in the thrill of seeing great lumps of clay come out of the pit at their feet. As she turned to make sure they were safe Rose heard the chill in Will's low voice and wished with all her heart that learning about her strange background didn't necessarily have to result in changing so many things.

She looked back at him. Only the truth would do for such an honest friend. 'No, Will, not any longer,' she said gently. 'I have to live a different life now – but I hope we'll always be friends.'

He nodded, then turned away and left her alone with the noisy children and the knowledge that something enormous and confusing had happened and that, somehow, she must come to terms with it.

When Tom Devlin made his way towards her through the now heavy rain and the thronging children she was once again in control of herself. 'Interesting and exciting, Rose,' he said with his crooked smile. 'You were right, of course – it's high time the children learned about this sort of thing. I shall make sure they write about the visit.' The smile flashed again. 'With plenty of facts, of course.'

Then his smile died. 'Are you all right, Rose? You look pale – perhaps you shouldn't have come. Let me take you to the manager's office where you can rest and have a drink of water.' He put his hand on her arm and she pulled back. He mustn't touch her; not now, when her whole being was swamped with emotion. She couldn't trust herself, remembering the times when she had given way and sought rescue in his arms. But not today. Not with the children to look after. Not with this extraordinary news about Edwina filling her mind.

So, 'I'm quite all right, thank you, Tom. But if you could be so good as to ask Charlie to look after my children for a few minutes I'd be grateful. You see, I told Will Sharcombe I would see him before we go back. I'll go to the office, he'll be waiting for me there.' Her voice was almost normal and she walked steadily away from him, but inside the hard knot grew ever more painful and burdensome.

Mr Sanders fished around in one of his untidy drawers until he drew out the dirty, coiled up piece of jewellery. 'Want to see it, do you, Miss Adams? Don't know what to do with it – police said jest hang on to it till they identify the body. But that was weeks ago.'

Rose took the pendant, her eyes boring into its clay-clogged details. Yes, the flower patterns were the same. The tiny decorative stones would be a strong blue once they were cleaned. There was no doubt in her mind now that this was a matching piece to Edwina's bracelet. She raised her head, saw Mr Sander's curious eyes fixed on hers, and said coolly, 'I wonder if I might borrow it, for a while? Until the police have come to a conclusion, that is. You see – I know someone who has a rather similar-looking bracelet. Perhaps a sight of this might help clear up the mystery.'

Mr Sanders sniffed hard, frowned, swung on his heels, and considered, but nodded at last. 'All right, Miss Adams. But I wants a receipt for it. Jest in case the police get funny with me, letting it go.'

She signed her name – Rose Victoria Grey – and watched his face register the unexpected signature. But he merely nodded again, and she had to accept wryly that of course the gossip about her true birth had flowed like water throughout the whole district.

'Thank you, Mr Sanders. And thank you for letting us bring the children here; they've enjoyed themselves and learned a lot.'

Another sniff, and a sly smile. 'Get 'em used to what'll be expected of 'em once they come to work, eh, Miss Grey?'

She didn't answer, merely nodded at him and walked to the door where Will waited. Together they stood sheltering from the rain in silence, Rose's mind overflowing with the new, extraordinary knowledge, until the children returned from the pit, wet through, but with excited faces and whispers of forbidden chatter.

They trudged back over the marshes through rain that grew increasingly heavy, and she was thankful to reach the school where the wet clothes were hung around the fire. It was wonderful to have to concentrate on arithmetic and writing and then to discuss the clay-pits, instead of worrying about who she was, whose the body was and what she must do next.

At home, in her room, she found that the pendant was an exact match to the bracelet. Same patterns, same blue stones, once she'd washed off the clay. She sat on the edge of the bed and looked at the painting of herself that had been Laurence's parting gift; Rose Victoria Grey, daughter of Edwina, who gave her baby to Alice Adams and then, dying, wandered through the marshes, finally falling into a ditch where she had lain for almost twenty-one years. Edwina, who had loved deeply and foolishly, but whose memory was now, amazingly, bringing new life to the daughter she had abandoned.

Walking to the window, Rose heard the rain pounding, saw the sky grow steadily heavier and darker, while her mind reworked memories, fancies, regrets, and lost love. And then, turning away, she knew exactly what she had to do.

Tomorrow, send a note of absence to Tom, ask Elizabeth for the use of the gig, and then drive into Abberton. To the police station.

CHAPTER TWENTY

Teatime already. Where had the day gone? Wearily, Rose sank into her usual seat, watching Elizabeth pour tea. Her mind still whirled, but she knew she owed it to Elizabeth to tell her all that had happened. Slowly, she found words.

'Sergeant Dunn was very nice. He said he knew about . . .' She faltered, saw anxiety spark in Elizabeth's watchful eyes, took a deep breath and went on, 'about the body being found and then I showed him both pieces of jewellery. He agreed they were the same pattern, probably a set, and said it was likely that it was Edwina's body . . .' She swallowed hard. 'He said he would have to inform the solicitors acting for the Sandiford estate – and that I would be hearing from them.'

She couldn't talk any more. It was an effort, feeling blunt words dig deep into the feelings that filled her. The events of the whole day: the note to Tom, saying she had important business to do, which of course would mean he had to cope with the entire school in her absence, the interview at the police station and the difficulty of trying to keep calm while telling the large, silent man watching her across the desk the story of her dead mother and the urgent need to identify the skeleton found in the clay pit as her, had been one of emotional agony.

Elizabeth stirred sugar into her cup. 'So you just wait to hear.' Her smile was warm. 'Dear Rose, I am so sorry for what you are going through. And I can do little to help.'

Rose decided self-pity would get her nowhere. 'You do help, Mrs Mount,' she said more firmly. 'By listening to me. By letting me talk. By understanding – and not judging.'

'Very difficult not to,' Elizabeth said wryly. 'But as a childless woman, I can only imagine what your poor mother went through.'

'Yes.'

Images, visions, voices. Would they haunt her for ever? Rose tried to drink her tea and change the subject. 'Is it still raining, I wonder? The river looked very full when we drove past it this morning.' More imaginings brought new shock. 'I do hope it won't flood. If it does Canal Cottages will be filled with water . . .' Her voice rose. 'My mother must be worrying.' She jumped up, almost knocking over the small table at her side. 'I must go and see if Alice is all right. I'd forgotten about her – oh, God, what else is going to happen?'

Quickly Elizabeth was there, her arm on Rose's shoulders. 'I think – I hope – you're worrying unduly, Rose. But, as you say, the rain is extremely heavy and the marshes already look full of water. I will send Bean along to the inn and if anyone needs rescuing he'll bring them back here. Sit down, my dear, drink your tea. I'll ring for Jessie and she can tell Bean what to do.'

But Rose pulled away. She was the one who must go and find Alice. 'No, don't bother, I'll get my coat and find Bean. I'll go with him.'

'No, Rose, you mustn't do that.' Elizabeth's voice was authoritative but Rose didn't care. She was out of the door, pulling on her coat, jamming her hat on her head, running through the kitchen into the stable yard. 'Bean, please harness the gig – quickly.'

Jessie shouted after her as she approached the stable. 'It's high tide tonight, Miss Adams. Is the river going to flood? Oh, lor', what about my ma an' pa an' the boys. . . ?'

But Rose had no time to answer. Sitting beside Bean she held on tightly as they drove through rain that came down in straight, stinging whiplashes, making them lower their heads. Through the village, down the lane, reining in the cob outside the inn.

There were crowds of people moving around the dark quay. She saw Billy there, Joe beside him and several other lightermen, all desperately trying to moor their boats out of the swirling torrent of the raging incoming tidal waters. But it wasn't just the boats they were trying to rescue – Rose watched in horror as a small straggle of people came out of the darkness, struggling unsteadily down the flooded path from the cottages. As they approached the quay, lit by lanterns, she made out faces. Susan Smith was pushing a perambulator filled with cooking things, food, bedding, children's toys. Billy's father was holding the new baby, constantly turning his head to cheer on his following wife. And Alice slowly, painfully, limping behind, something brown in her hand. . . .

Out of the gig in one huge jump, Rose dashed towards her. 'Mother!'

213

she shouted. 'Mother!' Water filled her boots, soaked her skirt, the wind wrenched at her hat and blew hair all over her face, but nothing mattered. She was at Alice's side, arms around her, almost pulling her along. 'Thank goodness you're safe. Oh, Mother.'

Alice was like a drowned bird in her arms, clutching Jack's cap tightly in one cold hand, but smiling as she murmured, her thin voice hardly audible over the sound of the raging river, 'Maid, you shouldn't be here – oh, but I be glad you are.'

Rose pushed her way through the troubled groups until she found Bean, close to the gig and looking around him. 'Bean,' this was no time for formality, 'I can't keep calling you that, what's your Christian name?'

'Nicholas, ma'am.' He touched his hat and she thought what a pleasant smile he had.

`Nicholas, please help my mother into the gig with her few belongings, and then drive her to Sandiford House. And give Mrs Mount a message from me: ask her to look after my mother until I return. Oh.' Suddenly she remembered Susan Smith and the pram. 'And tell Jessie that her family is safe. Will you do that?'

'Yes, ma'am. And,' he was looking around him, 'Would you allow me to take a few others as well? I mean, to take them to the schoolhouse, on the way . . .'

'Of course. A good idea.'

The schoolhouse? Relief flashed through her mind as she helped Alice climb into the gig. So the flooded-out people from the cottages were going to the schoolhouse where they could be dry and warm, and perhaps someone would find food for them. Surely only one person could have suggested this refuge?

Then she saw him: Tom Devlin, his fair hair a wet slick down his forehead, the long black overcoat already heavy with rain. He was too occupied to see her, but Rose smiled thankfully as she saw him helping the survivors from the cottages into a couple of horse-and-carts waiting in the lane at the end of the quay. Family by family, they pushed their few bits ahead of them, then scrambled up onto the heaped piles of clothes and bedding and household goods that they had managed to save from the flood. And then, slowly, the long drive began into the safety of the village until once again the lane was empty.

She watched Nicholas Bean collect another family of survivors, crowding them into the gig, and then, carefully, following the trail down the lane. She found Tom, standing in the middle of a group of downcast cottagers, listening, giving advice, then telling them to wait for the return of an empty cart. 'You'll be safe enough,' he said, reassuringly. 'The schoolhouse has a fire and we'll find bedding somewhere. And you'll have a meal. Mr Wheeler, from the shop, is arranging for food to be brought round for you. Now, just wait under the trees for the carts to return. It's shelter of a kind.'

He turned and saw her. 'Rose!' She saw a gleam of surprise, relief – was it pleasure? – in the grey eyes and instinctively put her hand on his sleeve.

'You're wet through, Tom.' She smiled weakly. 'And so am I, and so is everyone – but you're saving them.'

'With the help of the rest of the village,' he chided gently. 'Charlie Wheeler got his father to agree to feed them, the coalman brought a load of coal in his handcart, and the draper promised to find some sale blankets for the night. But Rose, why are you here?'

'My mother.' Her smile died. 'I mean Alice. I've sent her back to Sandiford House. Mrs Mount will look after her.'

Tom looked quizzical. 'Lucy's there, too. She set up such a clamour when I said she must stay alone with Mrs Benthall that I had no option but to take her to Saniford House and ask Mrs Mount for sanctuary for the night.'

'Elizabeth will be pleased!' But even as she tried to laugh, Rose's eyes were suddenly hazy with tears. He had thought of everything. And more than that: she realized suddenly that it was almost entirely due to him that the villagers were now helping their old enemies from Canal Cottages to survive and find comfort.

Weakness struck her then as she again looked around, through the rain, towards the river, where the swirling current rocked the moored boats and brought the branches swaying down to the water. Noise filled the air as the river roared and trees complained. 'It's all so awful . . . I don't know what to say.' She swayed and at once his arms were there, catching her, holding her safe.

'Don't say anything. Go into the inn. I'll come and collect you and take you home when the gig comes back. Do as I say, Rose – don't argue.'

The schoolmaster voice. Strong arms half-carried her towards the door of the inn. She could do nothing but obey him. In the candlelit room she sat down, drank the shot of brandy the landlord produced, smiled vaguely, and wondered what else life might be about to throw at her.

Perhaps she slept – until Tom's voice opened her eyes. It seemed quieter. The river no longer filled the world with raging noise. He stood beside her, wet through, wiping the hair falling over his eyes. His hand reached for hers and she felt, instantly, a surge of new strength. 'It's stopped raining,' he told her. 'And the tide's turned. Everyone is safe; Mr Toogood took the few people who couldn't crowd into the schoolhouse to the vicarage. And now I'm going to take you home.'

She stared up at him, and knew, true and certain, that he was a fine man. No matter that he was powerful and authoritative, sometimes even dictatorial; the gentleness and compassion, the wisdom was there beneath those outer attributes. 'Tom,' she whispered, 'I have to do one more thing. Go home and find Alice's old box of treasures. She mustn't lose them. It's only a step, I shall be all right.'

'I'll come with you.' He drew her up, frowning, eyes watching anxiously as slowly she secured her hat, fastened her coat.

They walked together, his hand at her elbow, along the flooded path. He held a lantern and there was just enough light to see through the shadows, the puddles and the waving grasses and bushes that lined the river. Rose said nothing. She could only think of two people – Alice, and Edwina. Alice was safe, but Edwina still had to be identified and buried. She stumbled as they reached number two, and Tom put his arms around her. 'Tell me where to look. I'll go in.'

'No, you don't know the way.' Somehow she found strength to enter the dark doorway while behind her he held the lantern high. Feeling her way upstairs, with the dampness rising through her already wet boots into her bones, she knew where the box was. All Alice's memories were in that old box. It was vital to her happiness.

Pushing it into her pocket she turned and found herself directly facing Tom as he stood at the top of the stairs. Swaying, she stumbled, would have fallen but for his body blocking the way. His arms enclosing her. Again, that miraculous comfort. His low, passionate voice whispering into her ear, 'Rose, Rose, if anything happened to you, I should be lost.' The words died and in the silence she rested against him. This was the place she needed to be. 'Oh, Tom,' she said weakly and then lifted her head.

His mouth found hers and she tasted the sweetness of his kiss. The lantern on the floor beside them flickered, and outside the river rolled and surged, but nothing in the world mattered to Rose except this one, magical moment. She longed to stay there. He was wet, but his body radiated warmth. For several seconds it seemed that time had stopped. They kissed again, but slowly memory began to intrude into Rose's sense of contentment. So many things to do, people to care for, duties to answer. And she must, somehow, tell him about Edwina.

She drew back. 'At the clay-pit,' she murmured, 'they found a body. I think it was my mother.' And then, because she had no more strength to explain, 'Oh, Tom . . .'

His arms found her again. His heart beat was steady, his breath warm on her wet face. She expected more kisses, but then, slowly, he stepped away, looked down into her pleading eyes and said in a firm, unsentimental voice, 'My poor darling. Come, I'll take you home. You've had a terrible day.' Holding her arm, he turned and led her down the staircase, holding the lantern again high above her head.

Outside they walked in silence beside the brown, churning river, her thoughts dismayed and herself almost too weary to deal with them, his brisk steps showing her just how foolish had been her hopes there, in the cottage darkness, at the top of the staircase. Perhaps she had just imagined his low words, his strong, sweet kisses. Closing her eyes, she leaned on his arm and focused on keeping safe on the muddy path.

Nicholas Bean waited with the gig and they climbed in, still without speaking. In Church Street the gig stopped while Tom got out, looked up at Rose, and smiled, an almost impersonal expression on his taut face. 'Sleep well,' he said, 'and I hope to see you in the morning. Goodnight, Rose.'

She caught her breath, then let it out in a huge sigh. Wearily she nodded at the watching groom. 'Home, Nicholas, please,' she said.

The next few days were too busy for her to think about anything except for joining Tom and several villagers in the schoolhouse, helping the cottagers to collect themselves and make the best of things until their homes had dried out. She taught the children in the small classroom, thankful to concentrate on sums and words and needlework, and drill outside in the playground when at last the rain stopped for good and a weak sun began drying things up.

At home she continued to run the household; to give Elizabeth time to drive to Culmouth and oversee the running of her precious Lighterman's Shelter; to watch Alice slowly recover from her ordeal and begin talking to the girls in the kitchen.

'I shall be all right here, maid. I'm used to being below stairs, see. You an' Mrs Mount must be upstairs, but I'll stay here.' Alice, still carrying

217

Jack's cap with her, sat by the fire while Nancy Briggs cooked, and showed her the precious baubles in the box of treasures. Rose thought she looked content, and felt that one problem was resolving itself.

The others remained, uneasy and disturbing: Tom's sudden withdrawal from their embrace; the awful waiting to hear about Edwina's body and the knowledge that eventually it must be buried. All these things took up her time and her energy, and it was only some three days later when she suddenly realized the date was 30 September – her birthday.

Before Jessie appeared with the morning tea, Rose lay in the big four poster, thinking about Edwina and her birth, probably in this very bed. And today, instead of clouded, worried thoughts, she was unexpectedly filled with hope as Jessie bustled into the room, putting the tea tray beside the bed.

'Happy birthday, Miss Adams.'

Rose sat up. 'How do you know?'

'Your ma – I mean Mrs Adams – told us. Oh yes, it's gonna be a proper birthday all right.'

'What do you mean?'

'Never mind, miss,' Jessie's eyes gleamed. 'Jest get up and come downstairs.' She flitted from the room, still grinning.

Breakfast was laid in the morning room and Rose was amazed to see all the servants standing just inside the doorway as she entered. Nancy Briggs, Gracie, Jessie, now a somewhat plumper figure, Alice and even Nicholas Bean, all smiling at her. And there, at the other side of the table Elizabeth Mount and Lucy. Such smiles. Such obviously happy anticipation.

Rose blinked. 'What ever. . . ?'

Lucy presented a card, one she had made herself with Elizabeth's help. Flowers, fairies and golden hearts decorated it and the words were simple. *Happy Birthday, dear Miss Adams. With love from Lucy.*

Suddenly overwhelmed with emotion, Rose realized that, even though she'd forgotten until this morning what the day was, her friends in the house had gone to the trouble of reminding her, helping her celebrate it.

There was a big wrapped gift from Elizabeth, some flowers from the girls in the kitchen and Nicholas, and a large, official-looking letter which Rose put aside until all the thanks were given, the gifts admired, Alice's kiss returned, and, at last, breakfast was brought in.

She ate little because happiness filled her. Lucy chattered on and

Elizabeth replied, and then, when the meal was over, Rose turned to the letter and opened it, not knowing what to expect – unless the police had written to her about their enquiries.

Thick, expensive writing paper unfolded. She saw the heading: THE SANDIFORD ESTATE TRUST, and yesterday's date. Sitting very still, she read on.

Dear Miss Grey
As the solicitor acting for the Trust, I have received a communication from the local police informing me that a body found recently in the Howarth Clay-Pits has been identified as that of your late mother, Miss Edwina Grey.

The Trust wishes to carry out its instructions given by your late mother before she disappeared. She left the House and the Estate, together with a fund of money, to you, her heiress, if you could be located when you came of age. I understand from her will that the thirtieth of September is your twenty-first birthday and so I am informing you of this legacy. If you have any queries or problems, please communicate with me. I shall be happy to help in any way I can.

Yours sincerely,
J.P. Crowther.
Senior Partner, Crowther & King, Solicitors.

'What is it?' Elizabeth's keen eyes had missed nothing, seeing Rose's colour come and go, watching her staring into space, the letter falling from her hand.

Rose returned to reality. She looked at Lucy, at Elizabeth, thought of Alice breakfasting in the kitchen, and said shakily, 'I'm an heiress. Everything belongs to me – the house, the estate. And the money . . .' Suddenly she collapsed, face in her hands, body slumping in the chair. Tears streamed down her face and sobs racked her as emotions became too vast and painful to control.

'My dear Rose!' Elizabeth's arms slipped around her. Lucy came to her side, whispering, 'Miss Adams, don't cry,' and slowly Rose realized that she was weeping with relief because the problems were solved. The past had caught up with her at last and a new image of life ahead was vanquishing the painful memories.

*

The birthday party, after school that afternoon, was a great success. Not too noisy because, after all, the house was in mourning, but still providing happiness and satisfaction to everyone. Guests had been invited: Mr Toogood the vicar, the other school trustees, Charlie Wheeler and Billy Nethercott, Miss Hodge, and Tom Devlin.

There were further gifts; a flurry of flowers, some sweets from the Wheeler shop, a pretty pebble Billy had found on the beach, a religious tract from Mr Toogood, and initialled linen handkerchiefs from Miss Hodge. Rose moved from one little group of well-wishers to the next, smiling, thanking them, asking for news of the homeless cottagers and eventually ending up beside Lucy and Tom.

'My very best wishes, Rose,' said Tom in his clear, schoolmaster voice, but Lucy clutched at his arm. 'Papa,' she whispered loudly, 'give Miss Adams your present.'

Rose watched Tom's face soften. She thought he looked uncertain, so tactfully she suggested they took a turn on the terrace now that the garden had dried up so well. 'Come and see the winter jessamine,' she invited, and saw his mouth quirk upwards with amusement as he nodded and followed her out through the French windows.

Turning, they faced each other. Shadows were deepening between shrubs and trees and only the light from the drawing-room windows lit the stones they stood on. Rose waited. Perhaps he would say the things she had expected on that tragic night when he had held her, kissed her, seemed to be about to speak, but then had turned away.

But no. Taking something out of his pocket, he looked down at her, his eyes searching her face.

Faint hope still lived. 'What is it, Tom?'

'I have something to give you.' He held out a small piece of wood that covered his palm. 'I hope you like it . . .'

She took it, examined it carefully. The tall, elegant figure of a heron, carved out of driftwood, instantly reminded her of their strange and unexpected embrace by the river all those weeks ago. So he hadn't forgotten. If only he would tell her so. Somehow she pushed aside the disappointment and smiled up at him, deeply touched by his gift. 'It's beautiful, Tom – thank you so much. What exquisite work.'

'Rose.' He drew back into the deeper shadows, taking her hand, pulling her with him. She went willingly, wondering, hoping. 'You know I can't say the things inside me. It's a terrible fault and one I haven't yet overcome. But carving – making the heron for you released so much that has been filling me ever since we first met. I want you to have this to remember me by – that is, of course, if you care to do so.'

The new happiness began to chill. 'To remember you by, Tom? Why should I do that? Are you going somewhere?'

He shook his head, tightened his mouth, firmed his voice. 'No. I hope to stay here in the village until it's time to retire from the post I hold in the school. It's just that – well, Rose, I have to say this; you're now a lady of genteel birth and I would never presume to bother you with my affections. I mean – I'm just a schoolmaster, with a crippled daughter . . .'

Her world crumbled, but she refused to give way. What nonsense! Staring at him, looking directly into those intent eyes, seeing his face taut and disciplined, slowly it came to her that she would never change his mind. He had said his piece and it turned out to be nothing that she had hoped for – yes, if she were true, had longed for.

Pride came to her aid. 'Very well, Tom,' she said in her most educated accent. 'If that's how you feel, then there's no more to be said, is there? Thank you for your kindly words and your loving feelings, which I return as well as I am allowed to . . .' Anger began to replace the pain and she welcomed it.

They were staring at each other and the moment stretched on until Lucy's voice called from the open French doors. 'Papa? Miss Adams? Aren't you cold out there? Will you come in? We're going to play charades.'

As she watched her laughing, happy party friends continue to celebrate her birthday, Rose told herself it was a day she would never ever forget.

CHAPTER TWENTY-ONE

Next morning, as she walked downstairs, prepared to call on Mr Crowther and learn more about her legacy, Rose had a vision.

It came swift and vivid, sweeping into her mind as she walked beneath the eyes of the Grey portraits on the walls of the staircase. A vision of the old, lonely house now regenerated and vibrant, full of life and energy. It stayed for a few seemingly endless seconds and she stood quite still, halfway down, relishing it.

Nancy Briggs, Jessie and her baby to be, Gracie and Nicholas Bean, whom she had watched smiling attentively at Jessie only yesterday, all living happily beyond the baize door; Alice, persuaded to leave the kitchen, Elizabeth and Lucy busily chatting in the drawing-room or making domestic plans in the morning-room, perhaps admiring Henny on the terrace in the garden.

And herself, Rose Victoria Grey, who had just come down from the bedroom where she had been born, understanding that she had done all she could to help the house back to loving life, to become, yet again, a real home, full of energy, strength and promised happiness.

Now, at last, the whispering voices that had taunted her, troubled her, ever since her first visit here, were stilled. Then, as rapidly as it had come, the vision vanished, but the reality of it filled her. She had been born again, she was where she belonged. And then undiluted joy came, warm, unbelievable and full of rightness.

I am happy.

She went on downstairs, and then, looking around the empty, spacious hall, one jarring and painful fact centred in her mind. Yes, here she was at home, with money to keep it running and looking beautiful. She had her friends and loved ones around her. And yet. . . .

Someone was missing. Somebody who would love her in return; somebody she could give herself to with all the joy in her newly released soul. She needed a man to share the rest of her life. Who was it to be?

Into her mind flashed memories of Laurence. His warmth, his volatile personality. Should she write and tell him of her birthright? Invite him to come down to Sandiford House on a visit? Then she thought of the portrait and the girls with red hair and green dresses, and her smile faded. Instead a different face filled her mind and she quickened her steps.

Tom Devlin was just locking up the schoolhouse. All the survivors of the flooded cottages were back in their homes, and Lucy had, yet again, gone to the house for one more night. He heard a voice calling him and he turned quickly, frowning into the gathering darkness.

It was Rose, black-clothed and lovely, radiant hair showing just a few curls beneath her hat. Her voice was as firm and clear as usual, but her expression was unfamiliar. 'Tom, I need to talk to you. Please unlock the door again so that we can be in the warm for a few minutes.'

'What is it?' His own voice was sharp.

She smiled and he thought he saw amusement in her expression. 'Please do as I ask, Tom.'

Unsettled, he did so, ushered her into the warm classroom, then looked at her. 'Is something wrong?'

Now her smile blazed. Those green eyes were lustrous and soft, full of warmth and strength; full lips lifted into an expression that made his heart suddenly race. 'Nothing wrong, Tom. Just that I want to ask you to marry me.'

His breath caught in a gasp and he was baffled; completely undone, at a loss how to reply. But, at last, slowly and joyfully, something opened within him and he knew feelings were ready to flood out. He smiled. His adored Rose. The woman who had irritated, charmed, worried him, and yet who had always been his love.

Her hands reached out for his, her dear face came close to him, looking up and smiling, full of all the promises and thoughts within. How could he stop himself?

He didn't. Drawing her close, he inhaled the scent of her hair, put his lips to the softness of her cheeks, and whispered, 'Of course I'll marry you. But, Rose . . .' Disturbingly the old ties bound him again. 'You're a lady . . .'

She laughed, lifting her head so that he could kiss her throat. 'A lady. Yes, I know. You told me so the other day.'

223

'And I'm . . .'

'Just a schoolmaster. Stop repeating yourself, Tom. I don't care what you are, I love you. I need you.' She paused. Her voice lowered. 'I want you. It's as simple as that. So . . .'

For a second she slipped back from his arms, looked at him, then stepped into them again. 'Say you love me. Go on, find those dangerous words – please . . .'

Now they came without any thought, any fear, any revulsion. 'Rose Victoria Grey, I love you.' Laughter bubbled through the wonder of the moment, and he kissed her with the passion for so long buried inside him. Yes, his happiness told him, it was as simple as that.

Later, they walked across the drying marshes to the river path, still muddy and slippery after the flood. They kissed again beneath the railway bridge. She put her hand in his. No need to talk. All had been said and agreed. Now was the time simply to accept their love.

Rose looked at the river, saw it flowing past her, the brown of the disturbed clay still evident, but as beautiful as ever in its easy flow and changing colours. Happiness persuaded her to think that the gleam of frail sun on the moving water was a friendly wink, that the river smiled at her as it continued, singing, on its everlasting journey.

Soberly, she knew that her own journey had come to a place where the new life stretched invitingly ahead. Of course it wouldn't all be happiness and content, but now, with Tom beside her, she was ready for anything.

Swinging their hands, looking at each other, smiling, saying foolish, loving words, Rose began planning their future. 'So much to do, Tom. Edwina's funeral, a year of mourning, and somewhere in between, our wedding . . . and do you know, I think I shall rename the old house. The river has been such a part of my life – yes, I shall call it River's Reach . . . what do you think?'

She said no more because his arms were around her, his mouth silencing hers and all that mattered was the moment.